AFTER THE WAR

A decade ago the terrible demigod, the
Kinslayer, returned from his long exile in
darkness, leading an army of monsters and
laying waste everything in his path.

The nations of the world rallied, formed
hasty alliances, fought back the tide.
A small band of heroes, guided by the
enigmatic Wanderer, broke into the
Kinslayer's palace and killed him.

But what happens when the fighting's done?
When the old rivalries are remembered,
when those who are hungry and broken turn
to their neighbours in need?

After the War is a story of consequences.

First published 2018 by Solaris
an imprint of Rebellion Publishing Ltd,
Riverside House, Osney Mead,
Oxford, OX2 0ES, UK

www.solarisbooks.com

ISBN: 978 1 78108 579 0

10 9 8 7 6 5 4 3 2 1

A CIP catalogue record for this book is available
from the British Library.

Designed & typeset by Rebellion Publishing

Printed in Denmark

REDEMPTION'S
BLADE

ADRIAN TCHAIKOVSKY

SOLARIS

CHAPTER ONE

THE BATTLE OF Bladno was supposed to be a turning point in the war. The army of the Grand Alliance had fully mustered, meaning that the neighbouring kingdoms of Cherivell and Forinth had finally stopped fighting each other and united against the Kinslayer, together with a handful of expatriates and a penal legion from Tzarkand. The Kinslayer, for his part, had finally grown the dragon Vermarod the Invincible to full size and was cackling with glee, ready to unleash the beast. Bladno—formerly a prosperous town, but now known just as a battlefield—had been seen by everyone as the make-or-break of the war.

Which same war had then rumbled on for another six years.

From the Kinslayer's perspective, the Grand Alliance lost decisively and the armies of Cherivell and Forinth had effectively been stripped of any ability to stop him swanning over the borders as easily as he pleased. From the free world's perspective, Vermarod the Invincible was spectacularly dispatched by Celestaine, the Champion of Forinth, and the Dark One had sunk so much of his power into the enormous dragon that even he was forced to sit back and take stock. For the next three months neither side had known what to do; there had been so little fighting it had almost felt like peace.

Celestaine remembered. Everyone had been trying to go for the eyes, as the absurd reptile had blundered through the battlefield, trampling soldiers of both sides by the hundred. Vermarod had been bred to relish human flesh, armed with acid spit and withering breath, but once the battle got underway the beast had spooked and floundered about, bringing ruin to just about everyone. "The eyes, the eyes!" the generals had shouted, and countless archers had met their end under the corrosive spray of the frantic monster's wheezing as they tried for a shot. Then Celestaine had clambered up a leg—for reasons of His own the Kinslayer had built the thing low, like a lizard—and run up until she stood on the plateau of its head. There, she had driven her sword to the quillons into its skull and ended the miserable monster's rampage. But then, one benefit of a Guardian giving you a sword that cuts through anything is that it will actually cut through anything, dragonbone included.

She had told herself, *I remember,* all the way down the road back to Bladno, but when she got within sight of the place, she didn't need to remember it after all, because Vermarod was still there. The bones of the Kinslayer's great war-beast dominated the landscape, its spine curved in a great half-circle, its ribs arching into the sky like curved towers. There was no hide left on it, which was a shame for personal reasons, but someone no doubt still had some as a souvenir. After all, the stuff was impossible to sew, flame-proof and immune to decay, so what would anyone have *done* with all of it, exactly?

For there were people at Bladno. There were quite a lot of people, in fact. All the final armies of the free world had come this way, when the tide of battle turned and the Kinslayer met them for one final fight at the gates of Nydarrow, his greatest fortress. Most of the survivors had come back this way and got no further. Many had no homes to return to, nor purpose, now their task was done. Celestaine knew the baggage trains that armies accumulated, and the new community at Bladno looked like the baggage train of the gods themselves, a thousand tents, a hundred slanting shacks built up against the bones, a handful of real buildings already emerging from the human wreckage. She saw a smithy and the great covered square of an Oerni-style market, while a well-known taverner with pretensions of grandeur had set up in Vermarod's skull and festooned it with flags and banners. Celestaine felt an unwanted stab of pity for the fallen beast. *At least it looks like he's having a good time at last.*

"Did you see the thing when it was alive?" she asked the companions who loomed at her shoulders.

Nedlam hadn't and didn't seem interested. Heno tugged on the silver of his beard. "Not this one. I saw some of the smaller ones bred." The deep rumble of his voice buzzed under Celestaine's chestbone and she twitched her shoulders. "Your man is here, this pity-creature of yours?"

"Don't call him that," she snapped at him immediately, and heard his impatient hiss of breath. Heno wasn't good at empathy. It was something she was trying desperately to teach him, something she was hoping he could actually learn. She had made quite a bet with the world on that score. "But here, yes. There's a community of his people nearby, on the Forinth side of the border. This is the biggest landmark for miles around. Everyone can find their way to Bladno these days, and once you're in Bladno, everyone can find their way to the Skull Cup."

Nedlam, who hadn't heard the name of the place before, found it hilarious, but then it was probably pitched at about her level. Celestaine signed and slowed her horse, putting a little pressure on the reins until the animal consented to turn a little to let her look at her friends.

Friends? Do I call them that in open conversation? What, then? Don't know. People I can't in all conscience get rid of?

Celestaine was, according to the bards, a 'silver beauty': skin like milk, blue eyes, hair so pale as to be white. The bards, most of them, had never actually seen her out of her armour, despite several offers from the more incautious rhymers. But yes, she was fair and pale, though her hair had been hacked short to go under her helm, and was now growing out into an uneven mullet and getting in her eyes. Her face was long and, when not animated by any particular emotion, tended to settle into an expression of narrow-eyed disdain that some men took as a challenge. Though in her experience only the most tiresome of them, which was a shame. She *was* tall, though: long-limbed and broad-shouldered, and there was a lot of the war left in the way she held herself or sat on a horse. On the road, a quite large band of brigands had erupted out of the undergrowth around her and her companions and then immediately thought better of it and gone peaceably about their business. One of them had even muttered an apology. But perhaps that hadn't been her; probably it had been the others.

They had shrouded up, this close to Bladno. Once they'd started getting the expected looks from the other traffic on the road, both of them had put on their cloaks and hoisted up their scarves until only their small hostile-looking eyes could be seen in a little strip of blue-grey skin between nose and brow. It was not a disguise. There really was no disguising what they were.

"You're doing it again," Nedlam pointed out, tapping her own head through the hood. "Thinking. Always leads to ruin."

"Someone's got to," Celestaine pointed out. "Look, we'd better get off the road and make a plan."

"Plans, plans, plans." Nedlam shrugged. "You want fire? I'll go get trees."

"Wood," Celestaine corrected. "We'll camp out of sight until it's getting dark, then I'll go in and test the waters. Bladno's going to be crawling with veterans. Who knows how they'll take to a couple of Y... you."

Nedlam ambled off to break branches. Celestaine winced when Heno's sardonic voice put in, "'Yoggs.'"

"I said 'you.'"

He chuckled darkly. "Celest, of all the monsters in creation, you don't need to tell *me* about the power of old habits."

THEY WOULD NOT stay still for long, she knew. Best to get in and out before Nedlam got bored and came looking for her. *And aren't they supposed to be good at doing what they're told?* But she was generalising, of course. She always fought it; she always did it. Everyone did. And probably doing what they were told had never been Nedlam or Heno's strong points, even back in the day.

The road into Bladno—or at least into the splayed architecture of Vermarod the Invincible—was quiet by the time she took it. People didn't travel at night so much these days, not with all the memories of what the dark could bring. She passed through a gate under the arch of the dragon's pelvis, half-buried in the dirt. A couple of leather-jerkined malcontents watched her pass, and possibly they were employed for that purpose by someone who claimed authority over the camp-town, or maybe they were just freelance starers. From there, her increasingly ill-tempered horse trod the winding path up towards the Skull Cup, surrounded by the sounds and smells of humanity and its allies doing their best to put the war behind them. Her ears told her of at least a dozen impromptu drinking dens, as many brothels in raucous, full-throated business, and at least one murder over a suspiciously lucky hand of cards. That last made her tug on the reins, hearing the shouting and the screaming. That old tyrant, Duty, twitched in her, but she told herself, *You can't save everyone.* And anyone gambling in Bladno, let alone cheating, probably knew what they were getting into ahead of time. *No innocents on a battlefield, remember? And no innocents walk off one afterwards.*

The great skull of Vermarod wasn't really big enough to fit a whole tavern in, but the enterprising proprietor had dug down under the jaw so that the bony edifice made a roof over a half-subterranean taproom, and cellars dug deeper still. The sight made her wince, because the man she'd come to meet would have bad memories of enclosed spaces, and she hadn't thought that through. *What if he bolts? What if he takes it as an insult?* The Aethani had been proud once, so everyone said. Proud, before the Kinslayer had humbled them. And this one probably proudest of all.

But she'd sent the message. She could hardly reach back through time to change the details. *Why don't we take tea on a rooftop somewhere nice instead. Nice and airy, remind you of everything you've lost.*

"Sir, will you be stabling your horse now, sir?" A boy was abruptly beside her and she twitched, fighting reflexes flaring up and being pushed back down before she could kick him in his conveniently-placed head. She gave him a narrow look, because stableboys and young horse thieves looked remarkably similar in a bad light, and both could be found lurking near stables. In the end, though, she was just so sick of being *on edge* about everyone.

"Feed him, groom him." She gave the boy a coin, which almost slipped through his fingers as he stared at her.

"What?"

"Forgive me, Great Lady." He actually dropped to his knees. "I didn't know you."

"I don't want you to know me." She swatted at him when he tried to return the coin. "Look, just deal with the horse, please."

"You're Celestaine the Fair," he choked out.

"I'm Celestaine the *what?*" she practically spat, because that was a new one.

"I saw you when you rode out," he breathed reverently.

"You couldn't have been with the army."

"I was with the baggage train!" He looked utterly distraught that she doubted him. "You killed the Kinslayer!"

"I... helped. There were a lot of us." *The Slayers. Because 'Kinslayer-slayers' just sounds stupid.* "Some of us didn't come back. Remember them, not me." But his eyes were wide as an owl's and she knew she didn't have the words to talk him out of whatever glorious picture he had in his head. "Just... do the horse, sort him out, would you? Do it for me, hey?"

The way he nodded, she wouldn't have been surprised to come back and find her horse painted gold or something. *And I thought bringing the other two would kick up a fuss.* She would have killed for a decently sinister cowl right then, but her cloak was that uniquely Forinthi garment worn over one shoulder and then about the waist like a sash, dyed a dark burgundy that vaguely approximated her family colours. It didn't have a hood because her kin preferred wide-brimmed hats when it rained, an accessory she had unaccountably mislaid. Steeling herself, she ducked under the denuded sockets of Vermarod's jaw and stepped down into the Skull Cup.

A minstrel struck up just as she stood in the doorway and, though all everyone sung these days was rousing songs about won battles and defeated enemies, this was a song of home, an old Forinthi ballad. *Come away, come away, love of my eyes.* It struck her motionless, a shard of the past suddenly jammed into her from ambush. She remembered Ralas singing it, years ago during the war when everyone had wanted very much to be reminded of hearth and home. Ralas had known everyone's home songs, all the half-secret, half-forgotten childhood songs that gave you strength and brought on the kind of tears that healed you. He could charm the birds out of the trees and the autumn leaves back into them, could Ralas. She'd never known a singer like him.

Dead, dead these three years now. The thought clutched at her heart and her throat. Dead in some torture chamber, after the Kinslayer heard some lampoon of his and promised to make him *really* sing.

Then the minstrel spotted her, standing there like her own ghost, and the old Forinthi ballad died a death and he was straight into 'The Blade of Castle Mourn,' which was at the top of a fair-sized list of *Songs that mention me that I don't like* and everyone was turning to look at her.

She wanted to go, then, but she'd told Amkulyah to meet her here, without really thinking it through, and so she was bound by the tyrant Duty once again. She strode in, trying not to scowl too much or knock her sword against people, because the scabbard was decidedly worn now and she didn't want to accidentally dismember one of the patrons.

That thought, and the follow-on that maybe she could rescabbard the damned thing while she was here, got her to beneath the bone dome that was Vermarod's brain case without drowning under the offered drinks and congratulations from all sides, and by then she'd spotted her man. The Skull Cup was crowded, but he was sitting at a balcony table with a lot of clear space around him. The sight of him turned her stomach. She'd thought he'd be bundled up like Nedlam and Heno— though not for the same reasons. Instead, he wore his injuries like banners. His eyes, huge and round, always the dominating feature of any Aethani face, were fixed on her.

She strode up the rickety stairs and made sure she kept her eyes on him, no matter how painful the sight. This was the *point*. This was a wrong she could try to right. This was Celestaine *helping* rather than filling her boots or drinking herself into oblivion like every other great war hero seemed to be doing.

There were other winged people in the north, she'd heard, casting shadows over the ice, but wings meant the Aethani to most people. Their kingdom was west of Forinth, where the land started creasing into mountains. She'd been there once when she was young, some scheme of her mother's that hadn't come off. She remembered lots of trees, and the dwellings of the Aethani built above them, impossible for any foreigner to even reach without a ladder. She remembered the locals flurrying back and forth or soaring overhead, effortless and elegant. The sight had stayed with her all through childhood. The Kinslayer's assault on Aethan, his lightning-fast destruction of their towns and temples, had lit a fire in her, sent her to argue with the clan chiefs and the Queen's Council to get Forinth in arms and fighting.

Aethan wasn't green any more, they said, but that was nothing to what the Kinslayer had done to its people.

There were many things the Kinslayer had done that were simply cruel for the sake of being cruel. He had taken joy in torture, of both the body—with whips and blades and hot irons—and the mind. He had revelled in the egregious exercise of his powers. People still talked about Hathel Vale, that might yet burn forever, unconsumed but leaping with flames. There had been a clan of Draedyn—wood spirits— bound to those trees, and if you went near Hathel you could hear them screaming as they ran mad with a pain that would never end. There were the Vathesk, too—the great crab monsters the Kinslayer had conjured from some otherworld to be his suicidal shock troops. Scores of the creatures were left over from the war, big and sad and without any malice in them now their chains had been broken. Except there was nothing in this world they could eat, and nobody who could repatriate them, and so they starved, day to day, and yet never died.

So many wrongs, so little time. And of them all, Celestaine had looked at the Aethani of childhood memory and said, *That is where the true spite is. That is something I will fix.*

When humans depicted Aethani in books and tapestries they tended to show them with great feathered wings like birds, because flying meant birds for most people. Amkulyah was a very pointed lesson on why the Aethani weren't like birds. Sitting, watching her, he seemed hunched, his narrow manlike shoulders in the shadow of the two other pairs of limbs that folded behind them, and all the heavy musculature that powered them. She remembered the translucent vanes of skin that stretched between those four wing-limbs from her long-ago visit—unfurled, they'd have touched the walls at either end of the Skull Cup without difficulty, bright with patterns of clan, ancestry and personal history. But there was no danger of Amkulyah throwing those wings wide to upset people's drinks. The limbs were still there, like ragged insect legs jutting from his back, still bedded in that slowly atrophying muscle. They ended in gnarled stubs where the last long joints had been hacked away, and the delicate vanes themselves had been carved close to the bone. They twitched, those crooked stumps, trembling and reaching as though clutching for the sky that had been taken from them.

Amkulyah's face was gaunt, the skin tight on the delicate bones of his skull. Everything about him was slender, fragile-seeming, yet he would be deceptively strong beneath the surface, built to balance all the competing tensions of flight. His eyes were huge, the nose and slash of a mouth almost an afterthought, a thumbprint-looking tattoo on his chin standing in for the beard he couldn't yet grow. He wore a backless shift, tied at the neck and loose on his thin frame. Only a leather circlet with a gold disc at his brow marked him out as anything more than another Aethani refugee.

"Your Highness," Celestaine started, but he waved the title away, staring at her.

"You're right. Obviously we should meet here to avoid untoward attention." His deadpan gaze took in the taproom, half of which was still staring at her, most especially the furiously twanging minstrel.

A very few of the Aethani lit out the moment the Kinslayer's armies appeared at the border, but the war had been young, then. Nobody had realised who the Kinslayer was, and Aethan had been wealthy, layered with centuries of tradition. The winged people had been weighed down by all that they didn't want to leave behind. And probably they had told each other, *It can't be that bad*, like so many others back then. They had gone to the Kinslayer and he had chained them, and he had cut off their wings, each and every one. He had evacuated the entire nation of them, men, women and children, from their beautiful lofty towns. He burned everything they had ever built or made and he had put them—a people of the sky with a horror of close spaces—into the Dorhambri mine. The Aethani still existed, those that had survived the years of claustrophobia and backbreaking work, but only in camps. They had lost their culture and they had lost the sky.

Celestaine had heard a very learned man claim that using the Aethani as slave miners had set back the Kinslayer's invasion plans by six months, because they were so very poorly suited to it. That was what had set her on this course, to somehow restore what had been taken from them. The scourging of Aethan had not been for power or for pragmatism, but pure spite.

Meeting Amkulyah's doubting gaze, she shrugged off all the attention from below. "I pledged my help, and you have it. What can be done will be done, Your Highness."

Somewhere within his huge round eyes he flinched. *Highness of what, exactly?* She saw just how unimpressed he was by 'What can be done…' too. *Still, he's here. He came.* Her next words were cut short as a hollering started up outside, which she took for the usual sort of brawling a place like this new Bladno must breed. A moment later, though, a harsh ululating call went up, setting everyone on their feet and most of them with weapons to hand. Amkulyah's scarred flight limbs clenched as though he had a dying spider grafted to his back. Everyone knew that call, the battle-hymn of the Kinslayer's most feared vanguard. For a moment, the war was still on and they were still losing it.

Except Celestaine knew exactly what must be going on, and was vaulting down the stairs, elbowing gawkers out of the way. She had been too long. Her friends of the road had got bored.

CHAPTER TWO

NEDLAM AND HENO, then, out in the dirt streets of the Bladno camp beneath the arching ribs of Vermarod. They had their hoods and scarves down, not that the garments served to hide what they were. A crowd was already gathering: swords, clubs, spears, bows. Neither of them looked daunted. Nedlam was even looking forward to it, from her expression. Celestaine was already shouting, though, hoping her fame would suffice to stop the arrows flying. She fought through the crowd, and when they saw who she was they let her pass, thinking she was going to rid them of this new menace. Right as she stumbled into the open, Heno thrust a hand up and conjured a ball of cold white fire. The crowd rippled back, leaving Celestaine facing the pair of them, because everyone there had seen what *that* fire did when it burned.

For a second, she was looking at the two just like the others, because she had fought a war for ten long years and, for most of it, she had been looking into faces just like these.

They were Yorughan, both of them. The Kinslayer had a lot of minions, whole twisted races he had bred beneath the earth while he plotted his timely revenge. Every soldier of the free world was well acquainted with them: the creepy, sneaky ones; the clever trap-makers; the great monsters. But the Yorughan were the ones to fear, the battlefield elites, stronger even than the Oerni or the Frostclaw Clans, and with all the initiative and cunning of humanity. They were the line-breakers, the wall-takers, unstoppable warriors and battle magi, and there were two of them standing right there as though all the Kinslayer's armies were at their back.

It was an effort to do the right thing then. The hatred of every other human and Oerni and everyone else was stinking in the air, her hand was on her sword hilt, and she could have taken the path of least resistance. But if there was one thing Celestaine never did, it was make it easy on herself.

"They're mine!" she shouted into that expectant hush—a hush that expected nothing from her except heroic butchery. And then, because she didn't like the connotations, and because she was infinitely pedantic when it came to herself, "With me. They're with me." She took a deep breath, ordering her words. "They came here with me. They're not enemies. The war's over."

She looked from face to face. Nobody there believed the war was over, not in the heat of the moment, with two Yorughan in front of them. Looking at her companions of the road, Celestaine could see the problem.

Hard to look at either of them without their first meeting coming to mind. She'd been on that final desperate mission with the others—all the Slayers, whose names were in everyone's songs now. The armies of the free world had been outside the walls of Nydarrow and dying like flies to hold the Kinslayer's notice—because if he loved any one thing, it was seeing the mortal races fall before his hordes. They had fought and died, and died more than they fought, mostly, and she and the others had been inside the walls of his fortress trying to get to him. It had taken a demigod to get them in, and it had used the last of their luck as well: Celestaine and Lathenry had been cut off from the others and caught, and that had been it.

Except, while she had been manacled to the slab and awaiting the Kinslayer's personal pleasure, in had come a couple of monstrous figures. She'd thought they were her torturers, but then they'd started talking like reasonable people. Or at least Heno had done the talking; Nedlam had just taken up half the room and picked her teeth.

They'd not looked like reasonable people. In the torture chamber, they had looked the most ferocious monsters Celestaine had ever seen—she who had slain Vermarod the Invincible. Their faces had been painted with human blood, Heno's in delicate spiralling patterns and Nedlam's just splashed all over. The spatter-patterns across Ned's heavy iron pauldrons had stuck indelibly in Celestaine's mind, up to and including the tiny hand-print smeared down her breastplate, because when the Yorughan painted themselves up for war, they took the blood hot and fresh from the source.

The Kinslayer's minions had been slaves to his will, everyone knew it. Let any of them fail him and he could crush them, drive them berserk, force them to fight to the last scrap of flesh. And most of all, he denied them the chance to look in the mirror and see that they were slaves. Except Heno had, and he hadn't liked it. He was ready to stick the knife in his master's divine arse, and he was offering a deal. And so Celestaine and her companion had gone free, rejoined their comrades and been led to where they had needed to go, to earn their place in all those tedious drinking songs. Treachery had brought down the Kinslayer, and that was a truly poetic thing. Shame the songs never got round to mentioning it.

Nedlam was the bigger of the two. At a few inches over eight feet, she might even be the bigg*est*. She wore some of her old kit—a sleeveless hauberk of scaled red hide that fell to her knees was the most obvious piece of Kinslayer uniform she'd held on to—along with various odd pieces of human-sized plate strapped wherever they would fit about her huge frame. Her skin was blue-grey, veined with pale streaks like slate, and her dark, spiky hair always ended up in a lopsided coxcomb no matter what she did with it. Her tusks, twin curves of sharp ivory jutting from the corners of her mouth, were capped with silver. Sloped over her shoulder was an iron-studded club that weighed as much as a man.

Ned was one thing—there had been plenty like her in the Kinslayer's vanguard, even if most hadn't been so big. Heno was the one everyone was goggling at; he wasn't your regular Kinslayer elite. His hair was silver white, worn long to the shoulders. He had a beard he trimmed to a point and long moustaches—before she saw him, she hadn't realised Yorughan even had facial hair, beyond a sandpaper stubble. He was a foot shorter than Nedlam, but his tusks were longer, curved upwards like a boar's, one of them scrimshawed with intricate arabesques. He still wore the white-edged long coat of leathery hide that marked him as a Heart Taker blood magus, most feared of all the Yorughan. His order had been the slaughterers of the innocent, the salters of the earth, the conduits for the Kinslayer's terrible power.

"The war's over," Celestaine shouted at the crowd, waiting for that one arrow, that one veteran's past that was too scarred to hold back. It would almost be a relief to discover her sainted name wasn't actually a talisman of strength to the world. She would feel less *responsible* for everything.

But the minstrel was there, of course, and the stableboy and plenty of others who knew her face—this was the Forinthi Marches, after all. She was the local girl done good. She saw them scowl and frown and mutter, but the weapons were grudgingly lowered.

"Put that away," she snarled at Heno from the corner of her mouth. He eyed her sidelong—that look of his that spoke of a desire to cause chaos just to see what came of it—but a flick of his fingers sent the orb of pale fire boiling into nothing.

"They're with me," she told them all again. "They're helping." *Not right at the moment they're not. Helping would be staying out of sight.* But what then? Would she keep them in a sack as she traipsed around the world? The whole point was that the Kinslayer was dead. It wasn't as though all of his minions had just gone up in smoke.

Some of them had, but not all of them. She felt her attention dragged up, and saw Amkulyah perched in the eyesocket window of the Skull Cup. Celestaine could practically see the Aethani prince's faith in her waning.

"Come on inside, then, since you're here," she growled at her companions, leading the way through the crowd. Not too effectively, it was true, as Heno was half again as broad as she was, and Nedlam broader still, but at least she was *doing* something.

'Sceptical' didn't do Amkulyah's expression justice, but he didn't just bolt the moment the two Yorughan sat down at his table. Celestaine would put money on him having a knife out where they couldn't see it, but he stared down the hulking pair with something approaching regal disdain. Celestaine had to look really close to see the fear behind it.

"When you sent your message, you neglected to mention the sort of help you were hiring."

"I didn't hire them," Celestaine started. Simultaneously, Nedlam said, "We get *paid* now?" Her ferocious expression suggested she was about to murder a baby, and Amkulyah probably didn't parse it as an easy-going smile. The Kinslayer had bred them well: there wasn't much that showed on the average Yorughan's face that wasn't terrifying.

Heno cleared his throat and splayed a hand over his chest, the universal indicator of slightly fake humility. "The noble Celestaine saved us from death in the fortress of the Kinslayer. We are bound by our warrior honour to serve and aid her in her quest." He spoke well for a Yorughan. They'd both learned several of the free folk languages during the war, because most of the fortress garrison got interrogation duty every so often. Nedlam's tusks made her sound jovially drunk, which must have enlightened the beatings she was expected to dole out. Heno talked round his precisely, the consonants clicking cleanly over the burr of his deep, rich voice.

And Celestaine knew it was rubbish. The Yorughan didn't have warrior honour. They weren't like the Frostclaw, with a generations-long heritage of clan war. They had been bred efficiently to be war-monsters by the Kinslayer's brutal hand. That such treatment had turned out creatures—*people*—like Heno and Nedlam was a testament to the limits to even His power.

Amkulyah stared at them thoughtfully. Yorughan faces were long, with heavy jaws and buttressed brows. Their eyes were small and deep-set, their noses far too slight for their famous sense of smell, their mouths thin-lipped and dominated by the curving tines of their bestial tusks. Here were faces twisted by a divine hand to be incapable of fine expression, intended as masks for monsters equally incapable of finer feeling.

Heno smiled. He had worked hard on that smile, practising it in mirrors and still water until it was almost urbane. Even so, Amkulyah would have been pitifully frail for a human, and any human was small before a Yorughan.

But at last, Amkulyah said, "You said you could help."

"Help your people," Celestaine agreed. "I said I wanted to try." *Did I say I actually* could? *Maybe I did. That was unwise.* "I want to help. If I can bring some sort of succour to the Aethani, then I will. My sword is at your disposal." She glanced down at it as she said it and swore, because the scabbard of reversed hide had finally given way, the impossibly keen edge naked to the air. She must have come perilously close to cutting someone's leg off on the way back to him.

"How?" Amkulyah asked, and then again, "*How?*" when he

saw her distracted. "I thought you had some magic plan. You know wizards. You know Guardians."

Celestaine put her hands up defensively. "I do, and I'll try all of them." *Those who're still alive. Those who haven't gone to ground where I'll never find them.* "And more. There's all sorts of magic turning up, now the Kinslayer's coffers got opened up." *And looted and scattered, but we'll deal with that when we get to it.* "There are holy relics, great artefacts, potions, grimoires—there's a whole *market* in high-powered war surplus right now. Something will be able to help, Prince Amkulyah." She almost said *please*, almost begged to be able to help. The sight of his butchered, spiky flight-limbs was like an awl jabbing into her.

"Some of my people think we should just get on with it," the Aethani said quietly, and at last his calm mask slipped and she saw how very young he was, how he too was crippled, not just by the lost wings but by a responsibility he could not discharge. "They say, nobody else has wings, or almost nobody. They say, we can do other things. And our children might learn to fly on their own, without us to teach them." He paused, eyes on something they couldn't see. "Or we'll cut them too, to make them like us, because we can't bear to see them drag those useless sheets of skin around behind them, and we can't bear to see them do what we've lost."

"No..." Celestaine breathed.

"I hear it. It's like a cult, growing amongst them. Some of them say, the gods can't have meant for us to fly. They say the Kinslayer's hand was the gods' will. It's easier, that way, to think that it was all *meant*."

"But you don't believe that," she told him desperately.

"I? No, not most of the time. But there are days..." He brought his hands up, and yes, there was the knife he had been holding as inadequate insurance against Yorughan treachery. Neither Heno nor Nedlam spared it a glance. "You want to help, Hero-Champion of the Forinthi, Slayer of the Slayer. I will go with you. I will do what I can to help you help my people. And if there is no help, then…" He made an odd gesture, the last fingers of each hand flicking up and away. *Dust on the wind*. The nightmarish clutch of his back echoed it. "No more 'prince,' though. We are brought low, so what use is 'highness' to us?" And to her horror he meant it, the play on words: the worst, most bitter joke she ever heard. "Amkulyah. Kul, if that is too much."

Then a girl was at the table, almost at Amkulyah's ravaged shoulders to keep away from the Yorughan, but putting mugs down anyway. "From a friend," she whispered, jabbing a finger down into the lower taproom.

Celestaine followed the digit, wondering if someone was about to try poisoning her companions; something more easily tried than succeeded at, in her experience. Their benefactor, or possibly murderer, was a hooded figure sitting alone at a shadowy table, a long white beard taking up most of what could be seen of his face and a long-stemmed pipe in his hand. The hair on the back of her neck prickled.

Am I really going to say it? But she was already saying it as she stood. "Stay here. Look after him if anything happens."

Nedlam grimaced ferociously at her in what Celestaine knew to be mild exasperation. Heno tapped her arm.

"Better to leave that here. We'll watch it." He nodded at her sword.

"Good idea," she admitted, and gingerly freed it from the unseamed wreck of the scabbard. Even placing it on the table with utmost care she shaved a slice off the wood. The Guardian named Wanderer had given her that blade. It would cut through metal and magic and anything else she had tried without slowing much. Certainly there was a slot somewhere above them in Vermarod's brainpan to demonstrate just how potent it was. Which meant actually carrying it anywhere was a logistical challenge.

"There's probably more of the hide somewhere around here," she said, at the head of the steps. "Someone's curtains, or shoved in a trunk. Maybe we can buy some." The invincible dragon's scales had been the only scabbard lining to last more than a month.

The crowd parted as she strode over to the stranger's table, but she felt this time it wasn't her name and reputation, but some other influence gently nudging them out of her path. She saw the old man's lips curl into a slight smile. His eyes glinted within his hood.

"Well met, proud Celestaine, Champion of Forinth." His voice was warm and avuncular. "Will you not join me, and perhaps learn something to your advantage?"

She glanced around the taproom in case it was an ambush, rather than what she suspected. She'd have preferred the ambush, probably. For a room full of war veterans, walking wounded and those who'd been forced to make hard choices, everyone seemed to be intent on innocent amusement. She sat.

"A strange chance brings the Slayer of Slayers across my path this night," the old man started, and she jabbed a finger at his face, almost poking him in the twinkling eye.

"Enough," she told him. "You think I don't recognise you?"

For a moment his look of wounded bafflement was so good she almost fell for it. Maybe this was just some mysterious old man hanging out in an inn, waiting for a questing hero to come by. But she looked past the unfamiliar face and saw something buried behind that grandfatherly gaze that she knew. She thought she'd lost him, but she just wasn't that lucky.

"Come clean," she warned him, "or I spill the beans right here and now."

"All right, all right." The face didn't change, but the way he held it did, and all that warm beardy cheer just evaporated, leaving something entirely more shifty and furtive. Which was still an expression ill-suited to the face of a demigod.

"Deffo," she told him, "what precisely is going to get you to leave me alone?"

A thousand years ago, so the songs and stories told, the gods sent into the world their immortal messengers and servants, to guide and protect the fledgling mortal races and teach them the gods' ways. Guardians, they were called, and in those early days they travelled from place to place, facing off against the primordial monsters that had grown in the earth, banishing giants, teaching and living up to their name. They were never many, and most grew to love and value the fragile races placed in their care. And if there were not quite enough to go round, well, who would guess that certain untended races might go astray later? And if one of them was less than delighted at an eternity of service to lesser beings, that also went unremarked, even by their more compliant peers.

Most of them gravitated to one or other of the emergent cults that would eventually become temples and priesthoods, taking second-hand veneration where they could. Those shrines and churches that the Kinslayer had left standing still celebrated their great deeds with statues and friezes and songs. They spoke of such as Wall and Wanderer, Fury and Diviner, Lightbearer and the Undefeated.

Celestaine stared across the table at the Undefeated, or at least the mild old man's face he wore, and reminded herself that he had kept the truth of his name by running as fast as his semidivine legs would carry him and lifting not one finger to help the free folk in the war. He had not believed the Kinslayer could be beaten, and had gone to find a hole to hide in. The Kinslayer had earned his name by killing other Guardians, and several of Deffo's kin had met their end, whether gloriously or ignominiously, during the war; the Undefeated had not intended to be one of them. Which made his position rather awkward, now the Kinslayer was dead and they were singing songs about the winners.

"Look," said the Guardian, cringing a little when she fixed him with her gaze. "I'm just saying, think about it. I've got power, still. Don't look at me like that. Just because I... doesn't mean the gods didn't send me, in the start."

"They've said you're back in their good books, have they?" Celestaine asked with arched eyebrow. Because, barring very recent developments, the gods were talking to precisely nobody. The Kinslayer had severed Them from Their adherents at the start of the war, and neither priest nor Guardian had felt Their touch since.

"I don't need the gods," the Undefeated hissed, hunching close. "You're right, they're gone, probably not coming back. Probably they lost interest in all of this long before the war, right? But you, Celest—" He stopped at her sharp gesture. "Celestaine, then."

"You know who gets to call me Celest? Other Slayers, two Yorughan and the Wanderer, if he ever comes back. Not you."

"Yes, yes." He waved down her objections, eyes swivelling about as he tried mug an air of intimacy between them. "Just a word, Celestaine. Just a kind word is all I need. From you, it'll count. You killed the Kinslayer."

"With help, not from you."

"But who knows, eh?" His ingratiating grin made her shudder. "Just drop a word to that minstrel over there. Tell him the Undefeated had your back. Tell him I held the door, gave you secrets, killed some Vathesk or an Umberwyrm so you could get to where you needed. It doesn't have to be anything big, just say I *helped*."

"But that would be a lie."

"They wouldn't *know*."

"You know who helped? The Wanderer helped. Of all of you bastards, he actually helped where help was needed. He didn't go off half-arsed and get people killed, he didn't just turtle somewhere the war never reached, he didn't turn himself into a weasel and hide in a rabbit-hole."

"It was," he hissed through gritted teeth, "a *badger*. And where's your precious Wanderer now, eh? You think you don't *need* us Guardians? Who else have you got?"

She cut him off. "Right, listen. I am going to restore the Aethani. Give them their wings back. Can you do that for me, Deffo?"

The Undefeated stared at her.

"Or do you know *how* I could do it?" she prompted.

"That's... impossible... The sheer power." He shook his head. "Why are you even bothering? They're a dead people, a lost cause. You need to rebuild." His face lit up with the sort of craftiness a seven-year-old indulges when they have a plan to get more sweets. "Go to the Forinthi council. They're still looking for scions of the Royal line, aren't they? I could tell them you're the heir. I'm a Guardian. I'll say the gods revealed it to me before the war. After all, they're not going to say any different now, are they? You can be Queen, and you can say that I..."

She stood, abruptly glad Heno had her sword. "Just leave me alone. You won't get your validation from me." She could feel his desperate, cringing gaze on her back all the way up the steps to rejoin Amkulyah.

CHAPTER THREE

So SHE MADE do without divine assistance. At the end of the day there was only one Guardian she would trust as far as she could throw him and, like the Undefeated had said, *he* had gone.

Magic was what she needed, but magic of an order of magnitude beyond anything even the strongest wizards could throw around. Magic from the early days, when the gods were closer to the world, when the Guardians were stronger, when the world was wilder. Back then, back when even the Kinslayer had a different name and a very different reputation, there had been things of power in abundance, according to the stories. The world had been made in a whirl of fierce magic and the gods had been many, tugging in different directions, or so Celestaine imagined. Not all their strength had gone where it was supposed to. The early world had been a place of chimaeras and prodigies. There had been great monsters as cunning as men and gifted with elemental powers: phoenixes and salamanders, basilisks and thunder dragons, cattle of gold and serpents of gems. Life in those days had been hard for poor mortals: hence the need for the Guardians. And some of those fabulous monsters had been slain and some had diminished or been replaced by their lesser spawn, but now and again one found a tooth, a claw, a preserved eye in which the flames still glittered.

One found gems cut by elder craftsmen who were more than mortal, cloth woven from the wind and the sea, swords that could cut through anything...

Her sword had only one power. It wouldn't be healing wounds or mending wings any time soon. The war had turned up a scattering of these artefacts though, either employed against the Kinslayer or uncovered by him, for he had always been greedy for more power. A century ago he had drunk the blood of one of his brothers, earning his new name and revealing his true nature. The other Guardians had driven him into the earth then, howling for vengeance but unable to destroy him. When he had resurfaced a decade ago to start the war, he had seized every relic and scrap of power he could find, and with it he had challenged and broken all the armies of the free folk and killed a half-dozen other Guardians as well.

And we killed him. The memory was not one of triumph so much as chaos and panic. They had seized their moment knowing it would only *be* a moment. Lathenry and Spinaros and the rest, everyone just bundling in and unleashing magic, arrows, blades. Thanks to Heno and Nedlam, they had come to the Kinslayer while he was resting, engrossed in the battle outside his fortress's walls.

She remembered his hand thrusting out to tear Lathenry's heart from his chest, peeling the old man's armour back like orange rind. And she had cut it off, that hand. The blade that cut through anything had not slowed for the Kinslayer's wrist. That was when she had realised he could be beaten. Semi-divine, engorged on power, and yet his hand was twitching on the ground like a dying spider.

And I should have gone straight to his vaults and robbed the place blind for relics. But she hadn't been thinking, back then. The Kinslayer's fortress had been comprehensively sacked by a hundred hands, both free folk and the more independent of his former minions. Everything had gone everywhere, and she had no idea where to start or even what to look for. She had given Amkulyah hope, but she didn't actually know how to restore his people; she just wanted desperately to do it, to make the world better one wrong at a time.

She had left Heno, Nedlam and the Aethani prince in the Skull Cap, desperately hoping that her writ would stop anyone doing anything to them, and that Heno would stop Nedlam doing anything to anyone else. The sense of sands rushing in the hourglass was strong on her as she pushed her way through the covered market, as though she would find a miracle for sale for copper scits on some Oerni trader's table.

There were a lot of Oerni there, almost as tall as a Yorughan though not as broad. Oerni lived in enclaves throughout all the kingdoms of the free folk, another race the Kinslayer had delighted in enslaving. He valued only their brute strength, caring not at all for their craftsmanship or their long histories. Ralas the bard had known a dozen Oerni family sagas, each one meticulously crafted, passed down perfectly from generation to generation. Hundreds of such stories had been lost, when the Kinslayer had worked whole families to death.

But, scattered as they were, the Kinslayer never dealt a deathblow to the Oerni culture. They had always been ready to up sticks and go elsewhere when the mood took them, and they were self-sufficient and tough. And they fought: no warriors by nature, but they had been engineers and smiths for the armies of the free, and in the worst pinch they had held the line with sheer force and heavy armour. And now the war was done, they were the quickest to get back on their feet, as evidenced by two out of every three traders at this market, towering head and shoulders over Celestaine.

Much of what was being sold there was nothing special, or wouldn't have been before the war. Right now there was a lack of decent pots and pans, furniture, tools, and most especially food, after too many harvests had rotted or burned. All around

Celestaine people were rebuilding their lives, and the Oerni were helping. Yes, they were charging copper scits and silver pollys, but the prices were far lower than she'd expected. All around her the big-hearted big folk were industriously working at their lathes and anvils and looms to make the world better for everyone.

Celestaine searched her heart and found that she was jealous. *I would rather be a mason or a carpenter than a warrior now. What good are my skills, and what use has the world for them?* She had killed the Kinslayer, but the world would be rebuilt by others. *But maybe, just maybe, I can save the Aethani.*

She pressed on past the bustle of mundane tradesmen, looking for stranger goods. Towards the far end of the market there were fewer Oerni, and a more diverse rabble of suspicious-looking characters took their place. She saw several Cheriveni from across the border, always opportunistic, selling books and scribes' services, potions, unguents and magical trinkets—the sort of thing that might stop working a day after you bought it, unlike a chair or a hammer. There was a Tzarkoman working as a tattoo artist, imbuing the ink with blessings as she needled them into an Oerni's mottled skin. Celestaine pushed on, looking left and right and keeping a hand near her purse just in case. Above and beyond the Cheriveni toys and minor enchantments, she had a sense of greater power. Travel with wizards enough, fight enough Heart Takers and death cults, and you got to know the sniff of it. Surely nothing that would turn the world upside down—not here, not sold openly—but she was after information, and the trade knew the trade.

The place she found was shrouded with hangings and tapestries, arranged to make an irregular, rambling tent under the cloth ceiling of the covered market. Makeshift tables held tottering piles of all manner of junk, some of which was presumably of value to someone. She ducked inside, ready for an attack; clamouring warnings from a part of her mind she hadn't been able to turn off since the war. Perhaps she'd smelled something of the enemy, because the first living thing that met her gaze was Grennish, a skinny little long-limbed thing that would have looked frail next to Amkulyah. It was propped on a high stool, a set of Cheriveni lenses perched on its forehead, caught midway through examining a partially dissected brass head she recognised as belonging to the famed—and, when it came to the war, mostly useless—mechanical army of Duke Timoran. Some minion of the Kinslayer had plainly taken an axe to the head, but the Grennishman was apparently not giving up hope. Of all the Kinslayer's slaves the Grennish had taken to free life most readily. They were small enough not to be threatening, they had a lot of useful skills and they'd been bred to think and solve problems, meaning they'd always been less under the enemy's thumb than the rest. This one had plainly not escaped the sharp end of the fighting, though, with one leg ending in a brass-capped stump. When it looked at her, she saw six eyes in columns up its forehead, blinking lazily out of sync with each other. The Grennish varied a lot.

"Chief's round the back," it told her, somehow making the simple utterance sound like an insalubrious invitation. Its tusks had been filed to stubs.

She shrugged. "You have anything for healing?"

One of its main eyes, magnified behind the lenses, drooped shut and then sprang open. "Paper cuts, broken hearts, bad dreams, lost limbs…?"

"Lost limbs." She didn't want to know what a Grennishman thought a broken heart meant.

It sucked its breath in between its teeth in such a Cheriveni 'you'll-be-lucky-more'n-my-job's-worth' way that she laughed, and it grinned back at her, all those sharp little fish teeth. "Not here, lady. Thing like that comes in, gone in a blink. Collectors always about this town like corpse-flies, every time something comes in from the west." Meaning *from the Kinslayer's lands.*

Of course this had all been Kinslayer lands not that long ago, but the west was where the enemy had amassed his forces and his treasure.

"I'll pay for some names. People who buy, preferably who don't just sell on, but I'll take what I can."

The Grennishman rolled an eye like a greenish marble towards the back of the tent, obviously hoping this was a bonus it wouldn't have to share with its 'chief.' "Yesyes, but let's see some coin, shall we? Fast learner, me." She'd heard some of the Grennish were amassing small fortunes as smugglers for years during the war, undercutting their dark master and selling weapons and magic and even people to the free folk. They'd picked up a money economy quickly.

She showed it a single gold sun. "One solly for your best lead." *And if that doesn't work out, I can get more leads when I'm there.*

"Lovely, lovely." It hunched forwards, brass head forgotten. "You know Cinquetann Riverport?"

She did: just across the Cherivell border. Not so very far.

"Our best buyer. Doctor Catt. Takes in all sorts so long as it's got some blood left in it." Meaning, she hoped, magical power. "His men come through every few days and pay good gold. On the road of the Gracious One Hospice, or what's left of it."

She flipped the coin and the Grennishman snapped the solly out of the air with unnerving speed.

"You didn't hear from me, right? Don't want to upset our best customer."

"Your honour's safe." She ducked out of the tent, wondering if that was something Grennishmen cared about or understood.

After the cloaked gloom of the tent, the rest of the market seemed too loud, too bustling, full of people who were looking far more than they were buying because money was scarce now. Scarce, except for this Doctor Catt and his fellow vultures, anyway. *And I'm not exactly starving.* She still had a little of the clan coffers to fall back on, if the others left under the Fiddlehead banner hadn't spent it. But her clan had been rich in name and poor in actual money since before the war. The Kinslayer wasn't responsible for everything.

Godsdamned Cherivell, though. Better get ready to be looked down on. Better get ready for everything in triplicate. The Forinthi and the Cheriveni had never got on, to the extent that the war had been four years in before they had managed to bury their collective hatchets. And the thing about burying things was that you could always dig them up again, if you remembered where you'd put them.

With that jolly thought, she went back to the others. Nedlam had not destroyed the Skull Cup in her absence, and in fact she and Amkulyah were in quiet conversation when she arrived, the Aethani sitting beside her, almost small enough to go into the Yorughan's pocket.

But if not Nedlam, then…

"Where's Heno?" she asked, stomach sinking. Nedlam got into trouble because she didn't think. Heno got into trouble because he *did.* Or got everyone else into trouble, more often than not.

Nedlam shrugged and stretched, showing her brutal teeth in a great yawn. "Don't know. We on the way out of here any time soon? All too quiet and nice-like for me."

Celestaine's stomach sank further, because if Bladno's brawling nest of veterans and camp followers was too quiet, then Cinquetann was going to be a problem. *But I knew how it would go when I agreed to bring them with me.*

"Well, then…" she started, before spotting Heno elbowing his way through the crowd, grinning through his tusks as they eddied back from him. Lots of disapproving looks came Celestaine's way, for making it impossible to drink to forget, but somehow nobody had got nostalgic enough for the war to throw a bottle at either of them. The thought gave her a little spark of hope.

Heno arrived and laid Celestaine's sword on the table with a magician's precise care. His hands were remarkably deft despite their size and claws. Beside the blade he laid a roll of hide. Celestaine stared at it, seeing the delicate scales there, a little dulled with time but still strong. They were small enough that they must have come from Vermarod's throat, or the fine skin of its joints. Even there, they would be strong enough to ward off blade or bow or siege artillery. She could make a scabbard from them to last the next few moons at least.

Heno grinned, cocking one silver eyebrow. "You need?"

"I need," she agreed. "Thank you." A display of affection out here in the open was a bit much for her Forinthi propriety, but she put a hand on his coat-sleeve's cuff, feeling him twitch at her touch like a dog.

"That's good. Do you have what you came for? We should be leaving now." He cast a bright gaze across the taproom, looking for threats.

"Why...?"

"Because there's some very rich man who probably runs this camp who has a big square hole in his curtains, and he will have questions." Heno had worked on that grin, such a non-Yorughan expression.

Celestaine was aware of Amkulyah's judging gaze on her.

"Well it's about time we hit the road anyway," she decided grandly. "Middle of the night. Best time for travelling. Who wants all the heat and the dust, eh?"

"What have you found?" the Aethani asked quietly.

"A lead. The name of a man who might have something, or know of something, that can help you. How much do you travel with?" For a moment she thought that all the *Your Highness* would come back and he'd have four wagons and a retinue, but the Aethani's reliance on material wealth had been lost along with the wealth itself.

"Nothing I can't carry." He stood, still not coming to the seated Nedlam's shoulder. "One moment to settle my account."

They watched him go. Celestaine waited for some snide remark from Heno, but the magus was silent, his face a mask.

Nedlam chuckled. "I like him," she said.

THEY ONLY HAD the one horse and Amkulyah had never learned to ride. Why would he? Before the Kinslayer came he could have flown from Bladno to Cinquetann in less than a day. Now he walked, and probably he would have been a drag on their progress every step if he hadn't been kept as a mine-slave for years. The work hadn't bulked out his slender Aethani frame much, but it had given him a plodding endurance Celestaine could only envy. His possessions amounted only to a sling bag, a quiver and a holstered bow.

Nedlam grunted in approval. "Remember that bow I had once?" she asked Heno. "Shoot to the horizon, I could."

"Whether you needed to or not," the magus noted. "That's why they took it off you."

Celestaine had seen a few Aethani fight—mostly those few who'd got out with their wings. They had the eyes of a creature that needs to spot small details from way up high, but probably their prince hadn't needed to spend his time practising at the butts much. She hoped they wouldn't need to find out. *After all, the war's over. Nobody needs to fight any more.*

She clung to that thought the next day because the Cheriveni already had people at the border crossing, where the silver course of the Bladen formed one of the few historically stable boundaries between their nation and Forinth. There were only two soldiers and a bureaucrat huddling from the rain under a lean-to, and at least nobody mentioned trade tariffs on dyes, which for complex geopolitical reasons had caused more fights than any number of spies or assassins over the years. Still, they looked at Nedlam and Heno very narrowly, and then at Celestaine herself, getting her to spell her name three times and casting sidelong looks at her clan colours. Of course, she hadn't helped matters by getting out her embroidered tunic with its fiddlehead fern device and looking every inch the Forinthi warrior, but that was what you *did* when you visited the neighbours: you damn well reminded them who you were.

They obviously wanted to make some sort of petty trouble for her, to remind *her* who *they* were, but Amkulyah defused the situation in the end. It wasn't anything he said, it was just their realising what he was. At first probably they'd seen just a skinny little man with big eyes and some sort of pack on under his cloak. As they'd kicked their heels and the Cheriveni had shuffled their papers, though, he had become more agitated at the delay. Celestaine had watched his cloak twitch and shudder as his stunted wing-limbs tensed and clutched. The bureaucrat had seen it too, and the realisation had hit him almost visibly. Empathy sat awkwardly on the man's lean face, but to his credit he waved them through immediately, Forinthi clan pride and Yorughan barbarity notwithstanding. Then they were in Cherivell, passing fields being reclaimed from the ashes, villages still half-standing, the scaffolds of fresh building work, and around all of that, the tents and shacks and scattered pieces of all those people the war had unshelled from their homes.

CHAPTER FOUR

CINQUETANN HAD SURVIVED the war with most of its buildings intact; a lot of the Cheriveni townships had. By the time he had regrouped his forces after the Battle of Bladno, the Kinslayer was feeling the bite of supply lines and logistics. He occupied Cherivell one community at a time, held a round of public executions as a show of force, and put the rest to work greasing the wheels of his increasingly unwieldy and scattered host. The Forinthi jeered and called them collaborators, but in truth the Cheriveni had run all sorts of resistance operations under the Kinslayer's boot, aiding the spies of other powers, freeing slaves and evacuating those under sentence of death. They had fought on the battlefield too, at Bladno and with expatriate units on every field after that. The Forinthi wouldn't call it fighting—in Forinth a fight was swift and wild, lighting attacks and feints by a people who prided themselves on their... well, they'd have said their warrior spirit, but Celestaine thought what they prided themselves on was pride itself, most of the time. When the Cheriveni took the field it was not as warriors but as tradesmen and farmers in the best steel armour they could get, fighting in tight blocks of pike and crossbow with parade-ground discipline.

But the best armour in the world didn't help against someone like Nedlam with a hundred and twenty pounds of metal-studded flintwood, because even when the steel held, the flesh beneath was pulverised by the shock. It didn't help against the cold fire of the Heart Takers or the ever-hungry mandibles of the Vathesk, or a score of other monsters the enemy could put on the field. The Forinthi, striking fast and loose-knit, had been far more suited to the Kinslayer's war than the pedestrian Cheriveni, and Celestaine hated it. She despised the kneejerk nationalism of the clans, even as she played to it by getting herself up in full Fiddlehead livery to cross the border. The Cheriveni's training and forethought ought to have ruled the field, instead of which they had been butchered, losing far more than their warlike neighbours.

A district on Cinquetann's outskirts had been razed, probably in retaliation for some act of defiance against the occupation. There was plenty of scaffolding up, and the bustling Cheriveni were working with counterweighted cranes to stack it higher. They stopped when Celestaine and her companions came into view, though. Every set of eyes watched Nedlam and Heno: she could almost smell the fear. There would be Grennish all through Cherivell—she'd heard that half the administrators the Kinslayer had set over them had turned coat the moment the war ended, if not before—but there wouldn't be Yorughan. The elite warriors had been called back to the Kinslayer's inner fortresses for the last stand, in those parts still referred to as the Unredeemed Lands. They would remain a symbol of terror and loss. Nedlam and Heno hadn't even been all that welcome in Bladno, after all; and this was Cherivell, this was civilization.

"So now you tell them all, 'I am Celestaine the Slayer,'" noted Heno, *sotto voce*. "You tell them how we're all friends, right?"

She looked at the Cheriveni, standing and watching with hammers and crowbars in their hands. Probably some of them had been soldiers and would remember the Slayers, but she was Forinthi, and even fighting side by side there had been little love lost.

"We just go on," she told them, the same words she had said to herself every morning since the war started, and hadn't stopped saying since it stopped.

Soon after, they were in Cinquetann proper, where the buildings—though scarred and smoke-blackened, here and there—had survived the war intact. Celestaine could spot exactly where the Kinslayer's additions to the town's décor had been torn down: the Cheriveni, left to their own devices, had little use for gibbets, and preferred builders' scaffolds to those of the hangman. One metal cage remained, turned into a planter for flowers that were just starting to bloom. She liked that.

There were plenty of locals about, the town still playing host to refugees from communities that had met with the Kinslayer's displeasure. The Yorughan attracted more and more attention, but Celestaine and Amkulyah got their share of stares. In the past any Cheriveni town would be a melting pot of visitors, who they'd greet with open arms; who else were all those regulations and tithes for? These days even someone in Forinthi dress was getting hard looks from people who didn't have much left and were worried someone might take even that. The fear never quite changed into anger, but the place was the ghost of the busy, mouthy Cherivell that Celestaine remembered not liking before the war.

"I count a lot of guards," Nedlam noted. "Not so many legs and arms, though."

There were indeed plenty there in the powder blue and black of the Cheriveni army, sitting outside buildings or standing on street corners. The number of missing limbs was surprising unless you considered how many of the Kinslayer's monstrous legions could smash or shear away a leg with appalling ease. Cinquetann had a lot of veterans who'd only *mostly* come home, and Celestaine appreciated that they were finding a place for every one of them. Extra uniforms on the streets probably helped everyone else's peace of mind, too.

Before they were halfway to the Street of the Gracious One Hospice, they were finally bearded by someone in authority, with half a dozen more or less complete soldiers at his back. She recognised him as a housegrave, though what that meant in the hundred strata of Cheriveni officialdom Celestaine had never worked out. He wore one of their magisterial gowns in black velvet, high-collared and split down the front from the waist to reveal a white under-robe with entwined gold floral motifs beneath. He had a rod that was too short for a walking stick and so presumably served as a badge of office. Like most Cheriveni he was small, his ears slightly pointed. Like most of them past a certain age, his face was creased and pouchy. Celestaine drew herself up, waiting to see what sort of trouble they were in. Every Forinthi learned at her mother's knee that the Cheriveni were paper vampires, draining the life of others with their writs and laws.

Her heart almost broke when the self-important-looking little man crept close and whispered, "Please don't cause any trouble." She felt like demanding of the whole town just what the Cheriveni spirit had come to, insisting that they imprison her because of a spelling error on some scroll or other.

"It's just, well, we welcome foreign custom, y'understand," he muttered, eyes flicking to Nedlam, who had chosen to loom like an oak tree at Celestaine's back. "I mean, there's even a Yogg work crew helping rebuild the paper mill. But…"

Heno chose that moment to snicker, a deep sound like liquid murder. The housegrave flinched.

"I mean, y'see, welcome to our town, please, sample our wares, try the food," *spend your money*, "but no trouble, please."

He was terrified. Not of her, not even of Nedlam and Heno in particular, but of the thought of more fighting, more blood spilled. Celestaine suddenly felt that all the scaffolding, all the town's life and bustle was just straw. A strong breeze would have scattered it.

"We'll be gone before you know it," she said. She wanted to sit the petty bureaucrat down and buy him a drink and tell him it was all going to be all right, that the war was done and life would be better hereafter. She wondered how he had weathered the occupation, and decided he had probably fought paper-and-ink battles to cripple the Kinslayer's resupply efforts, and possibly seen a relative hung or beheaded for more direct action. *Everyone's got a story.* "No trouble, I promise you." And she cast a warning eye at the two Yorughan.

Heno gave everyone his best sweet human-style smile.

She agonised over the decision for a while, but decided that the Housegrave's polite warning would probably be reiterated with considerably more punch in the nicer parts of town where Catt had his corner. Trouble enough being Forinthi and armed; she didn't fancy her chances getting some wealthy Cheriveni collector to give her the time of day with a pair of Yorughan at her back. With that in mind she found an inn that still had most of its windows and overpaid for an upstairs room and a general lack of questions. The woman behind the bar was plainly glad to see the coin.

"This is a bad idea," was Heno's take. "Give them two hours to build their courage and they'll come and kill us."

Celestaine shook her head. "I don't think so. Tax you, possibly." But fear made people do strange things. Better find this Doctor Catt quickly.

THE AREA AROUND the Gracious One Hospice was still the better part of town. Celestaine saw fewer of the dispossessed, more people in livery, the houses larger and the war damage already patched. In contrast, the Hospice itself was a wreck no amount of spot repairs would fix. The Kinslayer had had a personal grudge against the gods that had set him and the other Guardians as servants to the mortal races. After silencing the gods' voices—however he'd done that—he'd razed temples wherever he could, and most especially those devoted to healing and peace. Celestaine had always been puzzled that war temples actively resisting the enemy had not attracted quite the same unrelenting oblivion, but Lathenry had the answer: cults and temples that preached war and reprisal were the Kinslayer's mirror, espousing his own philosophy even as they opposed him. What he could not abide were those who said there was a way of life where nobody had to fight.

Certainly the Hospice was just a jagged shell, the surviving stonework coated with a silvery patina that showed the fury of the magical fire that had gutted the place. Nobody had started rebuilding or replacing it yet, and she'd heard that the entire order of healer-priests had been put to the sword.

The street she walked was lined with shops, most of which were shuttered up. A few still did business: a diviner had her daily tables out front to entice those about to make momentous decisions. The next door building was shared by a bookmaker, an armourer and a weather magician, which must make for some interesting conversations at lock-up time. After a handful of vacant shopfronts, she came to a neat little building whose sign read, *Catt & Fisher, apothecaries, physicians, notaries of law, lawyers of note, dealers in the unusual.*

She pushed at the door a little to give the bell inside the chance to ring, and then stepped in.

The air inside the shop smelled of cloves and preservative and faintly of decaying taxidermy. To Celestaine's left was a forest of herbs, hanging in ragged bunches from the beams. To her right was a little desk set with inkwell and coarse paper. Shelves on the back wall held a variety of what was best described as arcane tat: leaded flasks, brass brooches, clay Tzarkand death masks, antique scrolls that looked as though the ink was still wet. Standing between her and the tat was a glass counter showcasing slightly better tat and a tall, long-faced old man, his jowls and chin blue with stubble. He wore a woollen gown that had seen better days, as he himself surely had.

"Catt!" he snapped. There was a pause in which he stared at Celestaine without quite acknowledging her existence. Then: "Catt! Catty! Customer."

"You see them, I'm busy," came a sharper voice from the back.

"I'm on lunch." The long-faced man held Celestaine's gaze as though daring her to point out the utter lack of anything edible to be seen.

A few expostulations came from the back, but at last another man bustled up, of an age with the first but looking as though he'd got all of the sunshine in their collective lives. His head seemed to be mostly forehead and beaming smile, with a pair of genial eyes balanced between them. A band about his brow held a set of lenses—at least seven of various magnifications, and perhaps enchantments—and he was just struggling into an over-robe of deep blue and silver, gesturing for his fellow to help him.

"Now, my dear lady of Forinth, what meagre service might such a plenipotentiary be seeking in our humble establishment?" he trilled. "Doubtless your enthusiasm for the bounty of our municipality has led you to an infringement of some inconvenient local ordnance and you require a modicum of clerking to extricate yourself?" Without any obvious transition he was seated at the little desk, dipping a pen in the inkwell. "Perhaps a warrant of good character, or an affidavit of payment for your creditors?"

"No—" Celestaine started.

"Of course, and forgive me for suggesting that a Forinthi might find our rather procedural society unintuitive, most noncosmopolitan of me. I understand your hesitancy, of course, but you have doubtless come to Cinquetann's pre-eminent chirurgeons because of some discomfort, perhaps as the dolorous consequence of a moment's abandon?"

Celestaine, her words swept away in the flood, just goggled at him, until the long-faced man clarified, "Got the clap, or up the duff."

The loquacious Cheriveni rolled his eyes. "I generally find a little circuity of language allows me to anticipate a multitude of needs on the part of my client."

"Nothing like that," Celestaine snapped, because surely this wasn't the man she was here to see. "I'm looking for Doctor Catt."

"Serendipitously, you have located him, and he is entirely devoted to your service. The sour fellow pointedly not eating his lunch is my perspicacious colleague Doctor Fisher."

Doctor Fisher grunted and made a big rattling show of tidying shelves.

"I understand you're a collector," Celestaine said.

The difference in Doctor Catt's manner was remarkable. His hands, which had been clasped piously before him, now settled on the countertop, fingers twitching as though he was already imagining holding some new acquisition. Some of the bonhomie fell away, although the man was still patently very pleased with himself. "Selling, I take it? And you've come straight to the source rather than traffic with my agents. High commendable. Something of the enemy's, perhaps? On your person, or…?" He flicked one of the lenses down. "Or perhaps a certain caution conspires to your leaving this treasure somewhere safe until a transaction has been formulated…?"

"Catty," Fisher said, in a terrible stage whisper, "the *sword*."

Catt's attention slid down to Celestaine's waist and the roughly-bundled weapon belted there. His magnified gaze widened and he said, "Huff," rather than the polysyllabic utterance he'd no doubt intended. "Well I suppose we'd better remove to the back room to engage in some civilized negotiation."

* * *

"First off," Celestaine said, "I'm not selling, not exactly, but possibly I'm buying, depending."

There was hardly any more space in the back than the front, but there was a lot less cheap tat. This was plainly where Doctor Catt preferred to spend his time, and he had ensconced himself in a high upholstered armchair, the feet of which were carved into bird claws that occasionally flexed their wooden talons and rucked up the rug. Around them was an esoteric collection of artefacts on shelves and little tables: some of gold and gems, others just pots and bones and bits of wood, but everything obviously of value to the proprietors of Catt & Fisher.

"You set out your armies with a very broad front," their host observed. "And I'd venture to suggest you're no quotidian veteran looking for a post-martial nest egg."

"She's Celestaine of Fernreame. She's a Slayer," came Fisher's gravelly voice from the shopfront. "Who else'd have that blade? Close the deal, Catt."

"I'm not selling my sword," she started, but then blinked. "I will *trade* my sword—this sword, that killed the Kinslayer—in return for something that can do what I need." She waited for the rush of avarice, but Catt just leant forwards in his big old chair, all keen interest.

So she told him: the Aethani, everything. Saying it here, in this cluttered Cheriveni back room, she felt the weight of the task on her. To restore a whole race! Surely just to give Amkulyah back his wings would require the benevolence of the vanished gods. *All* the Aethani? Catt would laugh her out of his shop.

And yet he didn't laugh, though that smile hadn't gone anywhere. He took the lenses off and fiddled with them, his gaze far away for a moment. "Entirely creditable charity," he said at last. "Noble intent. Such benevolence."

"Have you anything that will do it? Or even help?" She glanced about the room. What she needed could be right *here*, catalogued on some shelf or other, lying idle in the hands of this collector. "This is the sword that took the Kinslayer's hand. Wanderer himself gave it to me. If you can do what I ask, it's yours. And more—if being owned by me has any virtue, you can have all that's mine." She knew she was going too far, but he *hadn't* just laughed her ambition to scorn. His expression admitted that she could actually achieve what she had set her sights on.

"Alas, alas, my little collection here lacks artefacts of such puissance," he said at last. "For pure healing—well—perhaps the Orb of Nine Blessings from the Sanctuary of Imrath, except the Kinslayer destroyed the latter, and the former was lost long before. Or there was the Head of Lucanfre, that knew how to cure any ailment or injury, but the Gracious One spoke through it, they say. It was mute when we lost the gods, and then the enemy flensed it and turned the skull into a goblet. And it's not as though *he* made any healing regalia. You know how he was."

Celestaine nodded bitterly.

"You're sure I couldn't persuade you to part with that most potent sword?" Catt pressed hopefully.

She shook her head. "I can give you a... glove or something, if you want the provenance."

He shook his head mildly. "Potence only, not provenance."

"We like things that *do* stuff," Fisher put in from the doorway. "What about artefacts of making and unmaking?"

Catt raised an eyebrow. "Oh, now, that's a notion worthy of consideration." At Celestaine's slightly frustrated look, he shrugged. "Much of what the Kinslayer did—the big things, breeding his monsters or opening doors to otherworlds, or for that matter twisting and shaping whole races, in his years beneath the earth before the war started—most of what he achieved was by his own innate power; but he had an eye for trinkets and toys that would let him gain more purchase to corrupt and remake the world. Some things he found, others he made during the war. Believe me, there are all sorts of indications that what he had in mind for the world *after* the war would make the war itself look like a good-natured scrap between adolescents. The Aethani are unfortunate casualties, of course, but I rather think we'd all have gone the same way in the end. So, you know, well done you."

"Artefacts of making," Celestaine prompted.

"What do you think, Fishy?" Catt looked past her to his associate. "Is there anything still out there? So much was lost in the war, destroyed by one side to keep it from the other or some such foolishness. If only people would have a care for the future. My dear Forinthi lady, did you ever see the Rosen Diadem?"

"Of course." It had been the crown of Forinth. "The Kinslayer destroyed it."

"The diadem, but not the Rose-Stone it contained; that, he kept." Catt's voice turned dreamy. "The Queens of Forinth could cure nineteen different ailments purely by touch—fair fit to put us out of business, hm, Fishy? *There* was a stone of power. And then there was the Merit-Knife, made of a single razor-edged sapphire." His hands described a narrow shape in the air. "Lost when the Warden of the Frostclaw Clans fell at Touremal. The hilt I actually have over there, but it has little magic left in it. The blade passed into the hands of the enemy. And there was the Verdigris Agate, that the Kinslayer's people unearthed from the mounds at Blaze Howe. I could go on."

Celestaine had no doubt he could. "How does this help?"

"Because all these things were puissant in their way, but not enough to truly reshape the world the way you want. But what is less well known is that, towards the end of the war, the Kinslayer mastered them, bent the power within them to his will, and had them set into his crown. It was to be the world-crown, the symbol of his dominion over all the lands, all the people. He never got the chance to wear it; you saw to that, thank all the absent gods. But what rumour we've been able to parse says it was fashioned, or that its manufacture was almost complete. And though all the ancient relics of making and unmaking may be lost beyond trace or trail, if anything in this latter age has the power to work what you need, then perhaps the Kinslayer's crown is it."

Celestaine considered this for a few heartbeats. "Forgive me for saying so, Doctor Catt, but this is a thing that you know of, and yet it's not here in this room?"

Fisher chuckled, like stones grinding against each other. "How quick she gets to know you."

Catt spread his hands beneficently. "My dear, perhaps one day. But if it exists at all, then word places the thing in Bleakmairn, and I hear the war is still rather present tense thataways. My agents value their own skin more than the meagre stipends I can afford to pay them. And probably it isn't there at all, or there never was such a thing made. War stories grow in the telling, or at least the ones people are happy to tell do." He took a deep breath to expand on his subject, and then the whole building seemed to jump at a thunderous bang. Celestaine heard the precise musical sound of the shop bell as it was ripped from its mount to rebound from the wall behind the counter.

Fisher had turned, apparently unflappable even in the face of a renewal of hostilities. "We're closed," he snapped.

"Need to see your Catt doctor," a deep Yorughan voice growled. Celestaine was on her feet already, jolted up by the sound, but now she pushed past Fisher urgently. Nedlam stood amidst the shelves, hunched under the ceiling beams and filling all available space in the front room.

"You know what Heno said, about them getting their stones together to come and kill us?" she said, with the rhythm of a joke awaiting a punchline. "It's only gone and happened."

CHAPTER FIVE

NEDLAM WAS READY to knock down every wall in Cinquetann, deep in her fighting-head, as Celestaine thought of it. She looked capable of it, too, and probably there was a quite a large band of Cheriveni militia within eyeshot and crapping themselves. She was also not the best raconteur, especially under threat, and so Celestaine was having a hard time working out what had happened.

"A bunch of the locals came and just... *took* Heno?"

"All sorts, a whole bunch!" Nedlam spat out. "I wanted to fight them, but he said you wouldn't want that and then they were all over us. They had magic, C'leste, and while he was trying to talk, they got him. I said we should've just whacked them the moment they showed!"

"Wait, wait, got him how?" Celestaine was very aware of Catt and Fisher's curious scrutiny from behind the shop counter. "They *killed* him?" A stab of guilt and worry, more than she'd ever thought she'd feel for a minion of the enemy, but then Heno was Heno. *And he was even trying to do the right thing.*

"Don't think so. Took him off, though, a bunch of them."

"And where's Amkulyah?"

"Kul went after them," Nedlam said. "Fast, that one. I was fighting by then. Tried to get me as well. Hit me in the head. Heno'd have told them that won't help." Her scalp and coxcomb were crusted with brown blood, and Celestaine reckoned someone must have gone for her with a bill hook.

She took a deep breath, because a lot of her just wanted to go with Nedlam and start kicking doors in at random until she found Heno, and that wouldn't accomplish anything. Nedlam's studded club was streaked with glistening red, she saw. "Ned, you were fighting. Did you kill anyone?"

Nedlam frowned, thinking back through the fight. "I reckon so. Two, three, maybe. Stopped them trying to grab me."

Her heart sank; that only made things worse. A tiny, mad part of her told her it was all right, because they were in the office of a Cheriveni notary and surely that would make everything fine. "Who came, Ned? Were they in the uniforms, the blue?"

"Uniforms, yes," Nedlam confirmed, and then frowned. "Not all of them, not that uniform. Not like them out there with one leg and a stick. They had like…" Her huge hands described something vague in the air. "Like a big stick with balls."

"Like a *what*?"

"I don't suppose you mean the Redecina?" Doctor Catt enquired. Celestaine and Nedlam looked at him blankly.

"Thing like this," Fisher said, emerging from the back room holding a short gold rod. As he held it up, a scattering of gleaming orbs danced about its length, then guttered and died.

"Could have been a picture on it, up front on their robes," Nedlam considered. Her eyes narrowed. "Why've *you* got it, then?"

To his credit, Doctor Catt did not back away as she loomed over the counter, although he was almost lost in her shadow. "That little trinket came from the Hospice, a little souvenir with no power to do anything but amuse. The original Redecina was lost when the Hospice was levelled, of course. It's the symbol of the Gracious One here in Cinquetann, His healing wand."

"So, what?" Celestaine demanded of him. "These were followers of the Gracious One?"

"Priests," Fisher put in. Catt added, "To wear the Redicine surplice was the privilege of clergy, it's true."

"I thought the clergy all died," Celestaine demanded. "And aren't they all healing and bandages anyway? They took my... my companion! Why?" She became aware she was shouting, and tried to calm herself, then exploded with, "What in *bloody fire* is going on?"

The two Cheriveni regarded her sombrely and she threw up her hands. "I know, I know, not your problem, and sure as death nobody round here's going to lift a finger for a Forinthi and a couple of *Yoggs*, right?"

"Well, actually," said Doctor Catt primly, and Fisher gave out an exasperated snort and stomped off into the back room.

"He hates it when my benevolent side rises to the ascendant," Catt confided in them. "To answer your multifarious queries: no, they didn't all die; no, they're not so much concerned with the good works the Gracious One was formerly associated with; I can make some educated guesses as to why, and, whilst it is not in any way my problem, a certain sense of civic pride is outraged at this treatment of a visitor to our fair township; and I know what this is about and where they'll have taken your friend."

"What'll they do to him?" Nedlam demanded, going almost nose to nose with the little Cheriveni.

"Well, unfortunately, they are likely to want to engage in some ceremonial bloodletting, especially with a former servant of the enemy," Catt said brightly. "However they will require some time of preparation before such a precipitate step. Where was your temporary accommodation, if I might enquire?"

"Some inn," Celestaine said. And then remembered, "There was a picture above the door, man in white robes with his arms out."

"The Mendicant," Catt identified sadly. "Mistress Frame, the proprietor, is one of the pious. No doubt she took your arrival as prophetic and sent straight away for the Underprior." He ducked into the back room and Nedlam growled, obviously anticipating escape. Instead, they heard the doctor clattering about and demanding Fisher find him various things.

"Underprior," Celestaine echoed flatly. Everything she heard sounded worse and worse.

"Well, quite," Catt's voice drifted to them. "Not the most auspicious title in the history of nomenclature. When the Hospice fell, you see, most of the priesthood chose to die with it. They put their bodies in the way of the hammers and the spells, so that others from the town could evacuate as many of their charges as possible. Even the Lightbearer, our resident Guardian. Courageous fellows all." His tone strongly suggested it was a courage he could admire, but wouldn't emulate. "But during the occupation, rumours began to circulate. Obviously everyone was very hush about who did what against the Kinslayer, mostly because being found out meant a quick trip to the excruciation pits. The suggestion was that some of the Gracious One's priesthood had survived the fire and collapse, and one in particular—a churchman of some stature who still had some magical might to throw around, despite the gods' silence. Not healing might, though. Not with the Gracious One cut from us all and the Redecina gone or broken. Was your friend a magus, by the way?"

"Yes," Celestaine confirmed.

"That rather cements my hypothesis, then." Catt reappeared, wearing a robe of silver-grey embroidered with ravens, a purple jewel at his throat and a hawk-headed walking stick in his hand. "The Underprior went after the magic and the magicians of the Kinslayer over other targets, and often at great risk."

Celestaine wanted to ask why, but she found she already knew. "Because he was cut off from his god? And thought that would help?"

"Imagine if the power to heal the world was just a wound away," Catt suggested. "How deep would you cut into how many throats, if you thought that just one more would let you help so many people?" He eyed Nedlam. "And there was a war on. We didn't *like* your people much, back then."

"And now?" Nedlam growled.

"I, my dear creature, am egalitarianism personified. Alas, many of my compatriots may not share my cosmopolitan leanings."

"So where are they?" Celestaine demanded of him.

"Why, just next door, in a way," Catt told her. "Just look outside and you can see the Hospice, or what's left of it. There are cellars, they say; cellars and tunnels, and a sacred cave. So, what do you say: shall we go meet the neighbours?"

THERE WERE INDEED militia lurking a safe distance outside Catt and Fisher's premises, but Catt sauntered over to them and had a word. Despite the fact that Nedlam had apparently left the Mendicant's interior spattered with the blood of at least three cultists, this was apparently satisfactory. He met Celestaine's sharp gaze and shrugged. "Firstly, I convinced them that we were engaged about a vital evidence-gathering errand which would, when concluded, throw an entirely contrary light on matters." He paused to draw breath. "Secondly, the magistrate is my cousin and they know she'd give me a licence to vivisect kittens if I asked nicely enough. Either way, we have a little time in hand." Celestaine's gaze hadn't got any less sharp, and he cocked his head at her. "What?"

"Why all this?" she asked. "You're shutting up shop to help a couple of complete strangers."

His smile was brilliant and as full of guile as a coven of foxes. "Why, my dear, I feel we've become acquainted with one another in the brief time you've been my guest, and besides, you're a Slayer, and we all owe you a debt of not-inconsiderable size. Also, are you really in a position to turn down any help that's on offer, right now? You want your Yorughan friend back, don't you?"

Something inside her kicked and wanted to argue, but she recognised it as her Forinthi upbringing, unwilling to give a Cheriveni the benefit of the doubt. With bad grace she shrugged. "Lead on, then."

He did so, tripping off down an alley from the Hospice street as blithely as though they were going sightseeing. Celestaine and Nedlam followed him, and Fisher trailed dourly behind, carrying rope and grappling irons and a robust iron-shod staff.

"So if the priesthood's all supposed to be dead," Celestaine asked over Catt's shoulder, "and they're now some sort of secret murder cult, how do you know where they do their murdering?"

"Oh, as to that, it's no great mystery." Catt's grin was nonetheless a little shamefaced. "They were taking all manner of magical bric-a-brac from the minions of the Kinslayer during the war, so of course I tooled up and went to take a look, in case they had anything that deserved to be preserved for the ages in a private collection." He sighed theatrically. "Alas, nothing of worth. Except the poor old Redecina, or what's left of it. They abstracted it from the rubble, I'd guess, but only in pieces. So much for the Grace of the Gracious One."

He got them to a street where the houses were boarded up, the doors and shutters chained and padlocked. They were all imposing three-storey jobs; Celestaine guessed they were the townhouses of rich families who had yet to return for them. Catt stopped at one door and tutted. "Remarkably inconvenient. They've resecured the place since my last exploratory larceny. Fishy, do the honours, would you?"

Fisher muttered something uncomplimentary and came for the door, tweaking a pair of picks out from behind his ear. Before he could get to work, Nedlam reached forwards and took the lock and chain in both hands. A mulish look came to her face that Celestaine was well acquainted with, and the muscles of her arms bulged like blue-grey melons. The *snap* of the metal shearing was muffled in her grip.

"It would seem, Fishy, that you're surplus to requirements," Doctor Catt remarked mildly, pulling the door open. Within was a dust-caked hallway, rich furnishings and hangings defaced and spattered. Picking at the splintered gilding of a balustrade, he added ruefully, "They barracked the curfew patrol down this street. I fear the character of the neighbourhood will not soon recover."

"Why are we here?" Celestaine asked him. "The Hospice was over by your shop,"

"Yes, but when we descend to the wine cellar here, now sadly denuded of comestibles, you'll see that one entrance to the sacred caves is behind the barrel racks. All through the occupation, the Underprior's agents were sneaking in and out under the noses of the guard." He frowned at her unhappy expression. "Hmm?"

"They're heroes," she said simply. "They fought the Kinslayer, like I did. And now I'm going to fight them."

Catt glanced at Nedlam. "You have a curious choice in friends, and they're desperate. The Kinslayer's death didn't give them back their god."

IN THE CELLAR, behind the barrel rack and the false wall, both of which Nedlam shifted with a minimum of fuss, they found their way. It was a chasm straight down, a crack in the earth that made Celestaine think of giant spiders and centipedes, mostly from personal experience.

"They utilise magic to ascend and descend, I suspect," Doctor Catt murmured. "We are bound to a more traditional methodology, alas."

"Where's Amkulyah?" Celestaine hissed at Nedlam.

The Yorughan shrugged. "Little razzer was right on their heels. Moves quick and quiet for a prince. They got him, or he got in after them, or something else."

"An admirably complete list of options," Catt commented. "Fishy, make yourself useful, would you?"

Fisher hooked his grappling iron over a beam, swinging on it like a bellringer to test its firmness. With a long-suffering look at Catt, he kicked the rope down the hole, watching the fixed end shake and shiver as the rest unravelled down the abyss.

"Only about twenty feet, no demanding venture," Catt said, before clambering down the rope with a nimbleness Celestaine wouldn't have credited. She followed, wishing she'd had a chance to get her armour—surely there would be steel flying about soon enough. She was halfway down when Nedlam started after her, and she got off the rope quickly in case the beam gave. Yorughan weighed a lot, but they were stronger even than that, and Nedlam let herself down effortlessly, hand over hand.

Down below, the walls were part natural rock, part carved. Where the cave dipped low, it had been worked into an elaborate arch; where it reached higher again, one wall had been levelled out and inscribed with lessons of the Gracious One, all open hands and unconditional love. The sconces by the words were empty, and Celestaine guessed the surviving priesthood had been operating off-book for a while now.

There was a wavering light to be seen somewhere ahead and they made their way forwards cautiously through the narrow cleft in the rock, hearing the murmur of a few voices talking in low, agitated tones. Doctor Catt walked like his namesake and Nedlam had her boots off, her bare leathery soles soft on the stone. Behind them, Fisher was clumping along as though every step was a personal insult to his standing as a professional.

The cultists were arguing in that strained, formal way people do when they really want to come to blows but can't. The discussion seemed to be part magical theory and part theology. The dominant voice was a woman's, but two or three others had strong, academically complex opinions they were trying to get in. Celestaine couldn't follow two words of it together, magic never having been her thing. The debate was involved enough, though, that it covered their approach nicely.

The fugitive priests had a couple of braziers set up, and the heavy scent on the air suggested they were for more than just light. Between them, where the rock floor had been levelled precisely flat, was the Redecina. It had been a golden pillar about six feet tall at one point, but as Catt said, the temple had fallen on it since. Now it stood, crooked, within a rough scaffold of wood and cane, and the orbs that had danced about Catt's little toy were conspicuous by their absence. It formed the centrepiece of a phenomenally complex design on the floor, some of which was carved, the rest written in chalk, and now being rewritten as one of the priests made some philosophical point. Chained to the Redecina was Heno.

CHAPTER SIX

HE HAD BEEN beaten about a bit, Celestaine saw, and her heart lurched to see the blood on his lips where his own tusks had cut them. Yorughan were nothing if not tough, though. A fierce human beating was the sort of thing they'd expect for a minor infraction in the Kinslayer's army.

The argument was reaching a peak. There were nine of them there, Celestaine saw, in robes of varying condition and fit, mostly emblazoned with the Redecina. The woman doing most of the whispering looked as though she was only a little over twenty, and of the rest only one was much older, a grey-haired man who was continually spoken over as he tried to say something. *Not the priests of the fallen temple, but their children, or maybe the children of their most faithful? Save me from the fires of young faith.*

"No more!" Abruptly the young woman—the Underprior?—shoved the older man in the chest, and then thrust a hand in the face of a boy surely no more than sixteen. "We don't have time. The gods will have to understand."

"She's got magic," Nedlam muttered. "That manchild too, watch 'em."

"But Lees and the others aren't back," the boy was saying. "At least wait—"

61

"'Not back yet' means 'not coming back,'" the Underprior snapped, and of course she was right in that, because Nedlam had presumably flattened Lees and his or her compatriots. "We do it now, before the militia come calling. You think we're so very secret here?"

"But why should it work *this* time?" the older man eventually managed, and the Underprior cut him off contemptuously.

"If it doesn't work, then look to your lack of faith! We keep going until it works." She knelt swiftly to finish the chalk lines, then stepped gingerly over them, drawing a knife from within her robes. Catt sucked at his teeth when he saw it, suggesting that it had a threat beyond a mere keen edge.

"Right," Celestaine said, and made herself known, Nedlam at her back. "No further, any of you."

They scattered in surprise as she appeared, but then mobbed up again. Swords and staves and daggers flashed in the emberlight.

"You have a friend of mine," Celestaine told them flatly. "I don't care what you think you're about here. I'm leaving with him, alive."

The Underprior looked at her with utter loathing. "If you count things of the enemy as your friend, then you won't leave here at all. When the Gracious One comes back to us, she will judge you."

"Let her. My name is Celestaine. I killed the Kinslayer." *With help*, but just this once she let the truth slide.

In the pause that followed, the boy-mage cultist's reverent "Fuck" echoed from the walls.

"My friend, Heno," Celestaine went on calmly, advancing with measured steps as the priesthood melted away on either side, "brought me and the Slayers to the enemy's chamber. For that, he should be in the songs, but right now I'll settle on him not having his throat cut."

The Underprior bared her teeth like an animal. "You don't understand. Look at it!" And she meant the Redecina, not Heno.

"The war's over." Celestaine was certainly saying that a lot, these days. She stopped with her feet at the edge of the chalk.

"It's not about the war, it's about the gods!" the Underprior shouted. "How can we ever be what we were, without the gods? The Gracious One meant *everything* to this town. People came from every kingdom for Her mercy and Her healing. The Lightbearer herself dwelled among us, teaching and training us. And the Kinslayer killed her, tortured her to death when she would not fight. The Kinslayer killed almost all of *us* and tore down our walls and broke the sacred symbol of the Gracious One's trust in us. And without the gods we'll never be what we were, we'll only decline and decline. I've seen it out there. Everything's… *mean* and *poor* and *broken!*"

"But they're rebuilding," Celestaine insisted.

"How can they?" the Underprior demanded. "It's just stone and wood. It's not the *gods*. If we can't reach the gods, we're nothing. The Kinslayer cut us from Them, but we will bridge the gap to Them, with his own tools." And she lunged for Heno, but Celestaine had been ready for her. She was scuffing through the chalk already, hauling back on the girl's robe so that the blade did no more than nick a hair of Heno's beard.

The Underprior lashed out at her, elbow cracking across Celestaine's cheekbone, that dagger lashing dangerously close to her face. Nedlam whooped her Yorughan battle cry, instantly dragging the attention of all the spare priesthood and leaving Celestaine and the Underprior to each other's good graces.

"Doesn't have to be this way." Celestaine still hadn't drawn her blade; that was a bridge that couldn't be recrossed. She tried for the dagger wrist, but the girl wove back from her, nimble as a dancer. The move gave Celestaine the chance to get between her and Heno, who rattled his chains pointedly.

"You're not a Slayer," the Underprior spat. "If you were the Kinslayer's foe, you'd understand. You'd not protect a thing of his making. The world needs to be cleansed of them, and why not do so and bring the gods back at the same time? You think the enemy's death cleans up all the blood he spilled?" Abruptly she scuttled back, but she was taking up a halberd from the scattered weapons by the cave wall.

"No," Celestaine said, still calm. She slipped her blade from its scabbard very carefully, because a halberd in a trained grip was nothing you wanted to face with bare hands. "But what are you suggesting? That all the Yorughan, all the Grennish and the rest, they just get rounded up and put to death?"

The Underprior stared at her as though she was mad. "Of course! They're just things the enemy made, after all. All the monsters and dragons and mockeries of mankind, all of them. They're just pieces of the enemy, you idiot woman! They're *him*, left over. And as *he* took the gods from us, so his pieces will bring them back!" She punctuated the last word with a cleaving stroke that Celestaine deflected with a brief pass of her blade. The halberd head rang and danced on the stone floor and the Underprior looked at the clean-cut end of the haft.

"If you just open up enough of them, right?" Celestaine prompted. "How many did you kill so far?"

"Not enough!" The Underprior swung the shaft like a quarterstaff, lashing out with one end and then the other.

Nedlam was holding back. Celestaine caught sight of her from the corner of her eye, swinging her massive club around to keep the priests back. She was scowling, plainly wanting to reduce a few more to a bloody paste, but she was doing what she was told. Celestaine saw the older man rush her from behind with a sword, only to get hoofed in the stomach and end up on his back, gasping for breath. Another two jumped on one of her arms and she used them as an impromptu flail against the rest of them.

Two strikes and the Underprior was left with a stick barely suitable as a cosh. Celestaine decided to try the last reasonable argument she had, in the moment of stillness before her enemy found a new weapon. "The Yorughan aren't made things," she insisted. "Yes, *he* bred dragons and monsters and all sorts, in ones and twos, or perhaps a half-dozen at a time. He didn't *make* the Yoggs," she cursed herself mentally for the slur but pressed on, "or the Grenns or the rest. They're gods-made, like us or the Oerni. They're just the races the Guardians didn't reach, that the Kinslayer hid away for his own pleasure. He twisted them to serve him, but he didn't create them, and they don't deserve to die."

The Underprior had a denial right there on her lips, but something in Celestaine's tone got to her. She had a sword now, Cheriveni war surplus, and her knuckles were white about the hilt, but she didn't use it.

"Seriously," Celestaine told her. "They didn't choose it, none of it, any more than we did." She watched the battle behind the girl's eyes. Would any words cut through that terrible certainty? Would they balance out the guilt of so many wasted sacrifices? Easier, surely, to believe her own lies and just keep slitting throats, buoyed by the heady liquor of her divine mission. Celestaine slashed across the chains holding Heno, sending their severed ends rattling away and inadvertently carving a long scar of sacrilege in the front of the Redecina.

There was a sizzle and flash that left spots dancing before Celestaine's eyes and she heard Nedlam bellow in fury. The young mage-priest had finally got his power together and conjured blazing rings of fire about her wrists, locking her arms above her head. "Kill it!" the boy shouted, forehead gleaming with sweat at the effort. Nedlam roared and bared her tusks, but the power held her in place as the cultists closed in with their blades.

Celestaine shouted out for them to stop and the Underprior barrelled into her, knocking her from her feet and sending her sword flying off to bury itself to the quillons in the wall. A moment later she was on her back, the breath slammed out of her, with the furious girl poised above her, dagger raised.

"Liar!" she shrieked, so desperate to gainsay Celestaine's words that she didn't take her best chance to stab.

Nedlam kicked the closest of her attackers right between the legs, adding considerably to the celibacy of the priesthood. There were too many of them, though, and the magic held her, tug as she might.

The boy mage gave out a wordless cry of triumph at his own power, before an arrow took him in the eye hard enough to split the back of his skull. Abruptly freed, Nedlam brought her club down to smash the nearest swordsman's arm into bloody splinters. Celestaine wanted to tell her not to kill anyone, but the Underprior was trying to stab her in the face and, besides, the unseen archer had obviously declared open season on priests. *Amkulyah, somewhere up high.* She hadn't taken the little Aethani as a climber, but he must have been scuttling about the upper reaches of the cave like a monkey.

The Underprior shouted out a vitriolic incantation, and abruptly Celestaine was losing the struggle for the dagger. A mad strength surged through the girl-priest's limbs, her muscles writhing and swelling with borrowed power. Celestaine saw veins bulge and burst beneath her skin, the white of her eyes flooding red and blood leaking from their corners.

"If the blood of his creatures won't suffice, then the blood of his killer will!" the girl spat, and she hoisted Celestaine bodily up, smacking her against the crazily slanting Redecina and holding her there with one hand. Celestaine punched her in the face and kicked her in the knee, neither of which did the slightest good. A hundred arguments swelled in her head to try and turn this girl back to sanity, but none of them were good enough and, besides, she was being choked by the Underprior's iron fingers.

Nedlam was still fighting, too involved in mopping up to see the problem. Would an arrow wing its way from the darkness to save her? Her grasp of the tactical situation was fading along with her breath but she didn't think Amkulyah would have a good enough angle to try it.

With a supreme effort, and because her arms were slightly longer than the girl's, she got her hands on the Underprior's face and dug her thumbs at her eyes. To her horror even that didn't slacken the grip at her throat. She saw the dagger flash in the firelight as it drew back.

Then the pressure was gone and Celestaine slid down the Redecina's engraved side until she dislodged some of the scaffolding. The gold pillar lurched sideways and collapsed back into pieces on the floor.

All the rest of the fighting had stopped, mostly from a lack of combat-worthy priests. All that was left was the Underprior and Heno.

He had her lifted in the air, limned with a spiky white fire Celestaine knew all too well. It hurt through every nerve, that fire. She had once screamed just like the Underprior was screaming. Past her, Heno's expression was dreadfully intent—not hating, not angry, but concentrating absolutely on what he was doing.

"Heno," she gasped, but her voice was just a croak in her throat. He couldn't possibly have heard her.

The dagger fell from the Underprior's grasp and clattered across the stone. She was flailing, striking out at the air around her as Heno cocked his head thoughtfully.

"Heno!" A gasp, now, Celestaine's strength returning to her. Nedlam was just watching, because she'd seen a lot of this sort of thing and it didn't bother her much. The surviving priests were watching too, and Celestaine felt their terror. Not just a Yorughan but a Heart Taker, the worst of the worst, the nightmare that robbed the free folk of sleep and turned battlefields into butcher's yards.

Celestaine saw Heno's eyes begin to glow as the power rose in him. The white blaze seemed to dampen the braziers, to swallow all light not its own. She had seen his fellow magi in a score of fights. She had seen Heno himself give vent to this power, both before his conversion and after—turned against his own people to get her and the others into the Kinslayer's presence. It was terrifying. It was impressive, in the way that power wielded skilfully always is. The weapons of evil could still lend a strange beauty to their wielders.

"Heno, no," she got out, properly audible now. "Please."

She waited to see what he would do.

His eyes flicked to her, the fire searing about his irises and dancing from his lashes. He took a deep breath and grinned, that infinitely maddening expression of his that meant he would do whatever he pleased and whatever amused him.

He blew out again and the white fire was gone, the braziers seeming to leap up like angry dogs. The Underprior collapsed to the ground, weeping with pain and anger, still scrabbling for her dagger. With a deft step, Doctor Catt removed it from her reach and tucked it neatly into his robe, no doubt to find pride of place in his collection.

"Any more?" Heno's voice growled around the chamber, sabotaged only slightly because there were no heroes to defy him. Nedlam had broken enough legs to make sure of that, though Celestaine cautiously reckoned that she had left people mostly alive, or at least only slightly dead. As for the arrows, though... There were three bodies that plainly wouldn't be getting up any time soon, each with a shaft somewhere particularly fatal: the eye, the throat, the back of the neck.

"You can come down now, Kul," she called up into the echoing, stone-edged void.

There was barely a scuffle as he swung down, agile as a spider, bow holstered once more. He glanced about at the bodies with his huge, round eyes.

"Is it all going to be like this, travelling with you?"

"No," she said quickly. And then, because she was honest, "I hope not."

The Underprior had recovered enough to prop herself up and glower at Celestaine and all of them. "You have doomed us." Her eyes lit on the fractured Redecina and she let out a little cry. "Why did you come to our town? Did the Kinslayer put us in your mind before you killed him?"

"It's not always about you," Celestaine said shortly. "Besides, you were going to open up my... my comrade. Who helped, with the killing of the Kinslayer. So you should be thanking him."

"He's a thing of the enemy!" the Underprior insisted.

"Not any more. And the Kinslayer's barely cold and already you're looking for more enemies? Is peace that terrible?"

"Being cut off from the gods is," the Underprior said, and she believed it, Celestaine could tell. She herself had never been the most pious of people. She had approached the gods with a nodding respect, and Their servants in the world with sheer pragmatism, judging them as she found them. Wanderer she'd liked, most of the others she'd had little time for; and a handful like the Undefeated were nuisances through and through. "The Gracious One, She was all for healing, wasn't She? That's why She had a hospice and not a temple. I mean, what do you think She'd even *say*, if he came back sprayed with the blood of your victims? Would She thank you?"

"She would hate me," the Underprior said with utter conviction. "She would cast me out, damn me forever, leave me in silence and spurn my ghost. But at least She would be *back* and it wouldn't matter about me. I'd pay that price, to have Her voice speak to the faithful."

"None of the gods has a voice in the world any more," Celestaine said quietly. "The Guardians that are still with us are as cut off as we are. I would have just tried to live my life as your god might have wanted, and hope She'd creep back some day. Not try to force the issue at the end of a knife. But what do I know? I'm not a priest or anything." She looked at Catt and Fisher. "So what now?"

Doctor Catt played with his finger-ends as he looked around the cave. "It has all rather fallen into confusion, has it not?" he said dolefully.

"Militia," grunted Fisher.

"Oh, well I suppose we may have to involve the appropriate authorities," Catt admitted.

"No," Fisher said. "Militia, here."

Then they all heard the tramp of feet, even over the groans of the wounded. A score of blue-uniformed Cheriveni soldiers bottlenecked the passageway they'd come in by and stared at the wreckage. At their head was the little housegrave whom Celestaine had promised no trouble to.

CHAPTER SEVEN

THE MAGISTRATE OF Cinquetann Riverport was short and plump, grey-haired and with a grandmotherly demeanour, but she had a hawkish stare on her that would have given the Kinslayer himself pause. She was also Doctor Catt's cousin or aunt or sister or some sort of relative, but as Catt and Fisher had not been politely asked to accompany the militia, Celestaine didn't pin many hopes to that.

She and the others had been kept in an unlocked room, but with just enough uniforms in sight to suggest that sauntering out and going about their business would be considered a major breach of etiquette. They had been fed, that sort of uniquely Cheriveni stew that looked meagre but turned out to be so filling you could barely finish the bowl, and somehow tasted richly of bacon despite being almost entirely beans. It was poor man's food, like all the best cuisine, and Celestaine was willing to bet the locals were glad their ancestors had endured a spell of privation so they could dine well now whilst having almost nothing to eat.

Nedlam was happy. A fed Ned was always a good thing to have, and no doubt their hosts would be thinking of the stories where the Kinslayer sent his occupation forces out without rations, telling them to take prisoners instead. True stories, as it happened. Heno had spoken of how every Yorughan warrior had been brought up believing their race was destined and superior, and everything else—friend and enemy—was just meat.

"And look," he'd pointed out, the night after the Kinslayer died, as they looked into the fire and tried to imagine the future. "We're stronger, we're just as fast or faster, we're better wizards a lot of the time. See in the dark better, smell you out better, you can see how we'd lap it up. Especially when we found that the gods never got round to us, in their haste to make sure you humans were comfy." He'd made a joke of it, but she hadn't known just how much he'd believed it, too. Just because he was smart enough to come down to the human level and plot didn't mean he didn't have that Yorughan pride.

"Maybe the gods knew we needed more help," she'd said, making him laugh. He had terrified her, back then, despite his turning coat and saving the world with them. His Heart Taker uniform, his unbounded willingness to use the power that came with it, his sheer physical strength—nothing like Nedlam's, but enough to snap Celestaine in half. And it wasn't some sudden revelation about the value of other races that had brought him over to the side of right. He was just sharp enough to realise that the Kinslayer didn't believe his own lessons, that the Yorughan were every bit as much his victims as the humans and Aethani and the rest, and would suffer in their turn. And because he was Heno, and didn't like *anyone* telling him what to do, not even a demigod.

In the magistrate's waiting room, he regarded her with a sardonic smile. "They won't let us live, Celest. Or not free. Not us as Yoggs, not you as a Forinthi. We made trouble. They like their foreigners quiet or absent."

"Don't say that word." She held up a hand. "And yes, I know I said it, I'm sorry."

Heno made an amused sound. "Maybe you should tell the magistrate: 'I understand you're going to execute us, but please don't call my friends Yoggs because it might hurt their feelings.'"

"Comrades," Nedlam mumbled about a mouthful of stew. "Companions. She doesn't like the 'friend' word."

"That's not true," Celestaine protested, knowing that it was. "It's just... *they* wouldn't understand." Which wasn't the reason. It was almost the opposite of the reason. With Heno especially, *she* didn't quite understand what he was.

"So we're friends, but you don't want the Cheriveni to know about it?" Heno was struck by a thought and laughed explosively. "They already call your lot Goat-wives behind your back, don't they? You just don't want to be a Yogg-wife?"

"Will you just—!" Celestaine started, and then they got hauled off to the magistrate, with Heno still grinning his damnable grin.

She spared a glance for Amkulyah, trailing along behind her with an accusing look. He, at least, would probably get out of this unscathed, being a prince and all.

Then they were before the cool regard of the magistrate, the papers before her no doubt setting out a lurid and entirely accurate account of what had happened.

"Celestaine of the Fiddlehead Clan of Fernreame, Forinth," the woman began, "this is an unexpected pleasure." She did not sound pleased. "Your recent exploits, and those of your companions, have not, of course, escaped us. The more shame, then, that you have brought that storied sword of yours to our town and used it in such a fashion."

That her sword hadn't shed a drop of blood was probably too pedantic to mention, and besides, Celestaine didn't want to shift the blame onto the Yorughan. She ignored the bait and instead just said, "I was defending my com—" She scowled at Heno. "My *friend* was kidnapped by your priests. There wasn't time to file for a writ in triplicate and attend a godsdamned *tribunal* to get him back." The Forinthi contempt for their bureaucratic neighbours jumped her so suddenly she couldn't stop the words.

"I'll wager you didn't see our Cinquetann before the war," the magistrate said icily. "The Hospice was our pride, its priests our joy."

"Look, I know, *but—!*" Celestaine tried, but an irritated twitch of the woman's lips stopped her.

"So yes, they are not what they were," the magistrate went on. "I know what happened. You'll be glad to hear that certain concerned citizens have confirmed just who did what to whom, and where it would have led."

Gods bless Doctor Catt, Celestaine thought, but was wise enough to say nothing.

"So, well done," the woman told her acidly. "Well done, the great Slayer and her Yogg friends have rid us of our delinquent priesthood, or at least the orphans and strays they left behind."

"But—!"

Again she was silenced, but this time the magistrate's tone was softer—not kind, but sad. "And, of course, we would have had to do something about them. We were hoping we could bring them round, make them part of the solution, not the problem. They had lost everything to creatures like these. We understood that. And perhaps it would have been our militia in that fight one day, instead of you *heroes*. Perhaps it would have been just more Cheriveni blood spilled, one more little corner where the war didn't end." Celestaine, who had been hating the woman's venom with a passion, abruptly saw through the act. Bitter, yes, but in mourning more than vengeance.

"So you've done a thing that needed to be done," the magistrate finished tiredly. "But they were our children. Don't expect us to thank you for killing and maiming them."

Celestaine glanced around: still no sign of enough uniforms to manhandle Nedlam off to the gallows. "So what happens now, er, Your Worship?"

"Puissance," Heno corrected her. At her baffled stare, he added, "A Cheriveni magistrate is 'Your Puissance.'"

"How...?" But now was not the time. Celestaine glanced at the magistrate, who was looking at Heno with loathing.

"I wasn't with the occupation, if that's what you were wondering," he told the woman easily. "I just listen."

"I am well aware of the Heart Takers' reputation for *listening*," she replied, in a near-whisper. "It matches their reputation for encouraging people to talk to them."

"So what now?" Celestaine broke in, because Heno was obviously in one of his kick-the-dragon moods and that never went well.

"Is your business in our town concluded, Slayer?" the magistrate asked flatly.

"It is, Your Puissance," Celestaine confirmed, stumbling over the word.

"Then I would be greatly obliged if you would get yourself outside the town limits before nightfall and be on your way, or I will find some pretext to have you whipped."

The Forinthi in Celestaine bridled. Whipping was what masters did to servants, and it was what Cheriveni did to Forinthi they wanted to punish, precisely because of the implied humiliation. The cosmopolitan in her narrowly wrestled down her clan pride and she nodded equably. "Of course." She wanted to say she was sorry, some meaningless verbal bandage over all the wounds they were leaving behind, but everyone there knew how empty the words would have been. Instead, she squared her shoulders and said, "We're heading west. What's the best way?"

The magistrate bristled. "Are you asking me directions?"

Celestaine shrugged. "You want us gone, we want to go. And this Forinthi girl doesn't have the book-learning to figure out Cheriveni maps."

For a moment, she thought she'd undone everything, but then the woman nodded slightly, recognising the détente. "The river runs due west, and the Shelliac are taking their barges most of the way to the Iron Wall and the Unredeemed Lands. Your *friends* will find a better welcome there than you will."

Celestaine received that news glumly. *And, of course, she's right. Land eight years under the Kinslayer's boot won't turn bright and cheery overnight.*

THE SHELLIAC HAD once been on every watercourse worth the name, pottering from town to town on their longboats, carrying passengers and cargo that didn't need to get anywhere too quickly and calling out to each other in their whistling, fluting language. Most large cities had a little Shelliac enclave, though the individual residents changed from month to month.

They were a strange people, far stranger to human eyes than even the winged Aethani. Their skin looked flexible, but was hard to the touch like a carapace, translucent pinkish-white so that in the right light the organs showed as shadows beneath. Their eyes were like faceted buttons beneath a ridged, hairless scalp, and within their lipless mouths were no teeth, but a flurry of little filaments like tiny frantic arms.

When the Kinslayer came, of course, many Shelliac had died. Many more had lost their otter-drawn boats and their way of life. Celestaine had travelled with them in her youth; it now seemed a century ago. Every panel of their narrowboats had been decorated with intricate art, histories and abstracts and scenes from nature. Each one the Kinslayer had burned or sunk had been a whole culture extinguished. The survivors had ended up in camps with the other refugees, or else as slaves of the enemy, and many had died simply from not being able to be what they were meant to be.

Finding a Shelliac clan already travelling the river west of Cinquetann was a ray of hope Celestaine had not thought to find. Keeping the others safely back at first, she had engaged in the familiar old haggling with their trade-patriarch, communicating by whistle and finger-sign their desire to take some berths. It all came back to her, the familial compliments, the little excursions into freeform narrative, the formal well-wishing, all conveyed by the hands and the lips. It almost made up for the boat itself.

This was no long-established Shelliac clan that had escaped the Kinslayer's wrath, that much she saw. The boat was new, although made from old things: some pieces and panels had belonged to older and less fortunate narrowboats, but the rest was salvage from a dozen different types of vessel, fit together like puzzle pieces and secured by many pairs of hands, each with a different idea of how to do it. The decks were sheltered by pavaises pierced by arrowslits, and the wooden sides were armoured to the waterline. Even the giant otters that frisked about the bows wore leather barding to protect them. Shelliac did not fight, they just moved on; that was the wisdom Celestaine knew. These Shelliac had crossbows and boathooks they'd turned into spears. When at last the two Yorughan did make an appearance, the boatmen just squared their narrow shoulders and stared with their black button eyes. The price they were asking went up, but only a little.

Celestaine had half-expected Catt and Fisher to come and see them off, but the two lawyer-physician-hoarders stayed away. They had done a lot of favours for her, and she hadn't even paid them for their information, but perhaps they didn't want to be publicly involved with such troublemakers. She felt a little sad that she'd never set eyes on either of them again.

DOCTOR CATT SURVEYED the Underprior's sacrificial dagger, now properly cleaned and mounted. "A most serendipitous addition to the collection," he observed happily. "And, yes, something of an intriguing provenance should we ever come to turn the old place into a museum, but for now the truth of its acquisition will rest only on our shoulders. Quite where the poor girl acquired

Dashimar's Vengeance I cannot begin to speculate. Far safer in our hands, really." He looked about him at the varied pieces in the collection and sighed, less with proprietorial contentment than with resignation. "Fishy, did you get the shrouds like I asked?"

"Can't put the shrouds up until you choose what you're taking with you," Doctor Fisher pointed out.

"Ah, well then, Tenet's Warding Amulet, of course." Catt touched the brooch at his neck, donned to go help Celestaine against the fugitive priesthood and not yet removed. It lent him such a feeling of security. "I think we'll want the Endless Satchel and the Bounteous Domicile of Hule, unless you fancy sleeping under the stars like a Forinthi, and I'll take Fyat's Malachite Cane and the Ring of Faultless Striding. You should probably grab something offensive as well, insofar as you need anything more than your face and general manner."

"Staff of Ways will do me," Fisher decided, striking his quarterstaff on the ground and prompting a glimmer of sparks. "Take some stock you don't much care for, too. We may have to trade for stuff."

Catt looked over the varied wonders he and Fisher had brought in, a hobby that had started long before the war but profited greatly from the Kinslayer's disruptions across the land. So many treasures to be pried from the fingers of the enemy or purchased for mere gold from desperate refugees. And now the war was done, why, the market was only growing more exciting. "I think our recent adventure has left me somewhat jaded by the religious paraphernalia in our possession," he mused. "I really don't think the gods are coming back any time soon. Let's go for Cinnabran's Skull and the Redecinette and some of the Gnostic incunabula. I don't see us getting any use out of any of it, so we might as well find an appreciative and remuneratively grateful home for them all."

Fisher grunted and took up the skull, jawless and yellowed. The gems that had been set in its sockets were long prised away by less discerning thieves than they, but it had once worn the face of one truly touched by the divine. He stared moodily into its shadowy recesses as though hunting out any last spark of godliness. "Sure we won't need them later?"

Catt shrugged. "You know, I never really liked the idea of gods. So desperately judgmental, so terribly hard to talk your way around, or bribe. Not our type, Fishy, not our type at all." He looked at the pile of artefacts he had selected. "What do you say: Helambrin's Mechanical Horses or the Sheep Chariot? I know the sheep will make us the laughing stock of the whole world, but I am so dreadfully prone to saddle sores."

"Sheep it is," agreed Fisher. "Now stand back so I can get the shroud up."

Catt busied himself stowing everything away in the Endless Satchel, which was slightly misnamed, but easily capacious enough for their purposes. By the time he had finished, Fisher was done as well, and all the remaining treasures of their collection seemed just so many cobwebs and shadows. Any thief of average curiosity would be going away disappointed.

The *more* curious would discover to their cost that the shroud was a hungry thing.

"Sure about this?" Fisher asked him. "Could just send an agent again."

"I don't think we have one on the payroll that could take on that woman and her rather striking friends. You saw them plying their trade, Fishy. Lethal, quite lethal." Catt beamed. "So perhaps they may actually be able to find that little trinket for us and pry it from the hands of whatever monstrous malcontent is currently crouching over it." He weighed the satchel in his hands and then passed it to Fisher, who slung it over his shoulders with a roll of his eyes.

"Of course, once dear Celestaine has it, I'm sure we can devise a way to part it from her, and I do rather think the Crown of the Kinslayer is going to look pretty above the mantelpiece."

CHAPTER EIGHT

AFTER A DAY and a night on the river, Celestaine came out to watch the sun rise, more out of habit than anything else. Forinthi clan warriors were supposed to be up in the first grey light of dawn. There were far too many songs about bloody sunrises presaging bloodier battles.

Apparently watching the dawn was an Aethani thing too, because Amkulyah was perched atop the narrowboat roof, the highest point he could find, bundled in a cloak against the chill and hugging his knees.

"Kul?" she asked. He hadn't been the most sociable travelling companion thus far, saying little, staring at everything. The one person he had seemed to genuinely take to was Nedlam, and he spent a lot of time lurking in her shadow.

His expression was taut, his look haunted. Aethani faces looked old, to a human: big eyes dominating gaunt cheeks and thin lips.

"Old habits," he told her. "Hard to shake."

"That why you're up there?"

He shrugged and his flight limbs stretched and fought against the cloak. "We don't like the water. I remember being taught from the youngest age, don't go near, don't fly over. Water gets in your wings and then you're drowned. Silver linings, don't you think? I'm far lighter than any human; without my wings, I'd float like a twig. But still I don't like it."

Celestaine leant back against the wall of the cabin, listening to the first whistles and flutings of the crew as they stirred. The dawn was as bloody as any saga-wright could wish. "Thanks for going after Heno, back in Cinquetann, by the way. I wouldn't have blamed you if you'd stayed out of it. We've only just met, and I appreciate it's not the most auspicious start for us, or something a prince should have to put up with."

"Pah. What is it, to be a prince? My people are scattered, dying, hopeless. Shall I go to them and ask them for a fine chair and a big hat, like you humans have? Should they give me a parade and pay me a tenth part of the nothing they have?"

She shrugged. "Well, then, you shouldn't have said you were a prince. It's a hard thing to just forget."

"I thought you wouldn't take me seriously."

She shrugged, reminding herself how young he was. He would have been a child when his people lost everything. "Anyway, thanks. For helping."

"It was probably the wrong thing to do."

"Yes, probably." She watched the countryside pass by, the night giving ground reluctantly, leaving villages and woods in its wake, passing great blackened swathes of land where the forces of the enemy had made a point, or where their monsters had been let loose. One copse of trees now supported a twisted knot of fungous tendrils, strange vegetable spires jutting high into the air, tipped with bulbous pods. She had no idea if it was the work of the Kinslayer or some desperate plant-wizard or Draedyn. "You're good with the bow, though. I'll give you that. Learned it during the war, or was it a pastime of princes in Aethan?"

"I never learned it," Amkulyah said. "You never saw one of my people loose an arrow?"

"A few, during the war. And yes, they were good, but I assume they just had lots of practice."

"It's part of what we are, how we're made. Pin some wings on a human, make her light as we are, you won't make her a flier. It's... it's seeing the world like us, like birds and dragonflies. It's... Look, here." He dropped down from the cabin roof and pressed something into her hand. She looked down at a handful of walnuts.

"It's walnuts?"

"Throw one, out over the water," he suggested.

She did so idly, frowning at the waste. Amkulyah's hand flicked out with a nut of his own and she heard the sharp *tak* as he struck hers from its course, mid-air.

"Objects in motion, things in flight," he said. "We just *know*. Try living in a forest and having wings, if you can't tell where everything's going to be every moment. Try again."

They wasted a dozen walnuts between them. She tried to fake him out, threw high, threw flat, even skipped a nut three times only to have his cast shatter her champion before it could reach the bank. Before her astounded look he just gave another uncomfortable shrug.

"It's just something left over from what we were."

"You'll get it back. You heard Doctor Catt—making and unmaking, right?"

"If this crown exists. If we can find it. If we can use it."

"If we can't, there are wizards who owe me favours. I mean, I cut the Kinslayer's hand off. That should buy me credit with any archmage you care to name." She shrugged and went to clean up after her horse, which was down in the hold and not enjoying it much.

THAT EVENING, AS the river took them ever westwards, the Shelliac sang. The land they were passing through was bleak, grim moorland littered with boulders like the bones of giants. The hand of the enemy was more apparent here: abandoned forts held every hill and high ground, most of them riven with the signs of fierce sieges. They saw few people here—the Kinslayer's occupation had driven them out, and it was too soon for many to have crept back. Monsters, they did see—escapees from the breeding pits or leftovers from old battles. They passed the corpse of a huge, hairy thing like a wolf the size of a cottage, its ribs showing through its tatty pelt and its stomach shrunken into a fist, too vast to find sustenance in this barebones land. Later, a serpent longer than the boat tried to pluck one of the crew from the deck and they held it off with spears until Kul sent an arrow into its eye and drove it away.

West of here was the Unredeemed Lands, where the news of the enemy's passing might still be a subject for mourning. Celestaine had heard no news, nor had any of the Slayers lingered there after the slaying. The Kinslayer's armies had been scattered in the wake of his death, but not destroyed. A month was time enough for them to reform and swear vengeance, if that was how it was going to be. Bleakmairn was most likely still in the hands of the Kinslayer's lieutenants.

But for now, they had the river to themselves and the Shelliac were singing down the sun, half a dozen of them occupied in keeping the boat in trim and the rest just sitting about, their hands making a cascade of complimentary words to their music, which sounded like the wind keening harmoniously through rocks, like birds, like bells. It was as alien as their eyes and their gleaming hard skins, beautiful like a vista, not like things made by human hands.

When they were done, Celestaine tried her own, because according to the stories every Forinthi warrior hero was supposed to go into battle with a harp in one hand. She had a crack at 'The Stones of Carrabree,' which was one she'd learned from poor dead Ralas. She remembered it in his soulful tenor, though; her voice was rough and her pitch uncertain, and she gave up in embarrassment after two verses and a chorus. *So much for music, then.*

But then Heno, who had been smirking at her as usual, took in a deep breath and began to sing. She had never heard him do it before, or ever dreamt that he might. As when he spoke, his voice was rich and deep, chanting a verse without any words she knew that rose and fell like the hills, like the waves. Halfway through each line, Nedlam joined in, harmonising high and grinning as she did so, although the counterpoint struck a melancholy tone. To Celestaine, it seemed they were telling a story of endurance and the inexorable, on and on, each line varying from the last yet always coming back to the same conclusion. It was plainly a song that could go on forever, but after the fifth stanza Heno stopped and looked sidelong at his audience, abruptly deciding the pastime wasn't befitting his dignity.

"Anyway," he said vaguely, and waved a hand as though encouraging them to forget it all.

"What was that?" Celestaine asked, nonetheless.

"Work song," Nedlam filled in. "Takes me back, that does. Surprised you know any, you Heart Takers."

Heno gave her an arch look. "We all start with a pick in our hands. Some of us get better, though."

Nedlam snorted, and Celestaine pressed, "But what did it mean? That was in your language, yes?"

"It was in no language," Heno told her. "No words to our songs, any of them." He regarded her for a moment, one of those moments when she could read nothing human in his face at all. "We were down in the earth with the Kinslayer, Celest. You had him for ten years. We had him for generations. Songs without words are safer. The wrong words could get you killed."

A DAY LATER, the Shelliac started preparing for trouble. Many of them put on armour—leather or light mail adjusted from human fit. They put their crossbows and bolt cases out by the pavaise shields, and their old Matriarch came up on deck for the first time and wove a few spells on them, little charms of protection and sharp sight. Amkulyah, who had appointed himself lookout, got up on the cabin roof again, standing to get the best vantage, and scowling when the riverbanks were too forested to keep a good watch.

Seeing this, Nedlam went to get her own gear and stood in the bows like a gurning figurehead, leaning on her iron-studded club. Celestaine found one of the Shelliac not actively preparing for battle and tried to get an idea of what was going on.

Last time we came here: much fighting, his hands explained. *Many Yorughan, many monsters beyond the wall. Kinslayer's death just heard, they don't believe it, or they don't care. Many soldiers here fighting over the wall, engines for the siege. Little word comes from the rest, only wounded, always wounded. Probably we take some east with us this time, too.*

They saw some plumes of smoke out across the land, which had turned rocky and harsh, scattered with wind-twisted trees. Occasionally there was a palisaded camp, and Celestaine made out a handful of different banners, all of the free folk and one from a Forinthi clan that the Fiddlehead had been feuding with for decades. There was no sign of the armies of the Kinslayer on the march, but all the same, whoever was camped was plainly expecting trouble.

We will stop at the post, the Shelliac told her. *Any further, you take yourself there.*

She nodded, and they reached their destination before nightfall. It was not the little trading shack the term had led her to expect, but a literal post, a great pillar driven into the riverbed at which they moored.

"What happens now?" she prompted.

They see us here, and they are friends, we hope. They come to trade. Or things are worse, and we hold them off and go back. Shelliac faces were short on expression, but she thought he was afraid.

*   *   *

THEY WATCHED THROUGH the night without incident, but even as dawn crept in, a whistle went up that got everyone awake and on deck. Boats were coming from the west. Celestaine squinted into the gloom, trying to make them out. She reckoned two skiffs, making the best of a brisk westerly breeze to raise sail, and behind them a galley, considerably bigger than the Shelliac's narrowboat, lurching through the water to the beat of a bank of oars. Closer to, she made out their flags: at first, just a white device on a black field, which made her heart sink a little. Not anything of the Kinslayer's, but one of the Arvennir warrior orders.

Back before the war, Forinth and Cherivell and most of the other small kingdoms would have described Arven as the great enemy looming in their immediate future. The big eastern nation covered as much ground as any five of its neighbours, and had a habit of going into diplomacy with an army at its back. It was run by a jockeying pack of knightly orders under a figurehead of a king, and every order had its own ambitions and almost complete autonomy should it choose to send its troops across a border. Then the Kinslayer had brought his war, of course. Arven had been slow to join the fight, but in the last years there had been black and white banners on every battlefield, because while nobody much liked the Arvennir in times of peace, it was hard to deny how effective their soldiers were.

The high-water mark of the Kinslayer's advance had taken his armies into Arven itself, tearing down the castle strongholds of the warrior orders and laying siege to the capital of Athaln. Most said that the siege of Athaln had been the turning point of the war. Warriors of all the nations had fought the Kinslayer there, and although the city had been savagely sacked, the Kinslayer had never been able to push further east. His enemies had finally found the needed unity to hold him, and then to turn him back. Celestaine had grim memories of the retreat from Athaln, but that was where the road began that ended with her and the other Slayers bearding the Kinslayer in the heart of his power, in his great fortress of Nydarrow.

Of course, now the war was done, there were sizeable Arvennir forces sitting around on everyone's doorstep, and the rosy blush of a common cause was starting to ebb away. Nobody knew quite how that was going to go.

The light was good enough, the boats were close enough that she could make out their device now: a lily, because the Arvennir considered themselves sophisticates despite all the fighting they were so good at. Celestaine didn't know this order in particular, but she doubted it was much different from the rest: harsh discipline, rigid routine, a lot of talk about the gods, the Guardians and Arvennir destiny. The Shelliac were plainly expecting them, though, and not expecting trouble.

The galley backed oars and moored up on the opposite bank, while the two skiffs drew alongside the Shelliac, who were hauling up crates and barrels from the hold. This was a supply run, apparently, because little of the land that had been under the Kinslayer's shadow for long would grow anything wholesome for a human palate. Celestaine watched the Arvennir, squaring the historical bogeymen with the normal men and women she was seeing. They were sandy-haired, mostly; pale, high-cheekboned and square chinned, not bad looking in a samey sort of way. One of them signed idly with the Shelliac and she read their hands as they talked about the land behind the Iron Wall. *Still some fighting, but not like it was,* the Arvennir man said. *They're organised now,* but the way he made the words didn't suggest worry.

Nedlam was helping with the unloading, and that was surely the test. Celestaine would not have walked into any Arvennir town with the Yorughan as she had in Cinquetann. Even before the war, foreigners in Arven were advised to pay off one of the orders to avoid awkward questions or indefinite incarceration. Yorughan would surely end up as heads on pikes. And yet, while the Order of the Lily kept their eye on Ned, they kept their swords sheathed. The interpreter jabbed two fingers at her—to the Arvennir, even pointing was like threatening someone with a knifeblade—and suggested, *We chain ours. It's safer.*

Celestaine didn't like the sound of that, and then the Shelliac was bringing her into the conversation with a piping whistle, indicating that Nedlam was hers, not theirs.

The interpreter looked her up and down. "What's this, then?" He spoke the language of the middle kingdoms almost without accent.

"We're travelling west," she told him. "You have news from Bleakmairn?"

His eyes widened. "Not a good place to go."

"Still?"

"It's complicated." He shrugged. "You're taking on labour, though? You can deal with us. You don't need to go to the source."

She had no idea what he was talking about, but was damned if she'd admit it. At around that time, though, Heno appeared at her shoulder.

"On the big boat," he murmured. "My kin, many of them."

She didn't question the knowledge. "What's your cargo?" she asked the interpreter.

"Labour," the man said, as though it should have been obvious. "Plenty to rebuild back home. And it's the one cargo that'll row itself."

The skiffs themselves would be heading back to the wall, where the Lily apparently had some sort of camp within sight of Bleakmairn. The Arvennir were happy enough to take four passengers back in one of the skiffs, cautious about Nedlam and Heno but not hostile. They all got a good look at the galley before it took off eastwards. Its belly was full of Yorughan.

They sat stoically two to an oar, huge blue-grey figures waiting for the command to row. Celestaine saw the chains.

"What's going on?" she asked the interpreter in a clipped voice.

"They're making themselves useful," he said, waiting to see if that was going to be a problem for her.

Heno had leant over the skiff's side to exchange words with one of the rowers, and now he straightened up. "Let's be about our journey," he said to Celestaine.

"But..."

"It's complicated," he said, echoing the Arvennir's words. He stared out at the wall thoughtfully.

THE ORDER OF the Lily had occupied one of the wall forts. The soldiers here were a long way from home, and Celestaine expected to find them in a state of constant paranoid vigilance, given the Arvennir she'd known. Something had taken the edge off them, though. They kept up a westward watch out towards the Kinslayer's heartland, but most were off duty, gaming, reading or just lying around. There was a scattering of Yorughan in the camp, hobbled with shackles and working on the fort, which had plainly taken a beating during the war. The westward wall in particular was still mostly rubble, along with the cracked carapace of a ram-wyrm, one of the Kinslayer's living siege engines.

"Did you come through here?" Amkulyah asked her. "On your way to kill the Kinslayer?"

"We went south of the wall," Celestaine recalled. "The Arvennir and the Frostclaw and a whole load more attacked the forts here, tied up his forces. We went round—the clans, some of the Cherries and a whole mess of squads and orphans who didn't have anywhere better to be—forced marches and magical veils to keep the Kinslayer in the dark. We brought the fight right to his door, and then me and the Slayers got in, while everyone else was dying." The recounting, which had started cheerily enough, ended very flat at the thought. She was glad of the interruption when a new voice broke in.

"You're headed for Bleakmairn?" It was a big Arvennir officer with a drooping ash-blond moustache, the interpreter at his shoulder.

"Is that a problem?"

"I can't guarantee your safety. It's all Yogg land west of here within the wall."

"I don't need my safety guaranteed," she told him. "And what about these?" She indicated the Yorughan at work on the fort. "Do you raid for them?"

"Raid for them? We *pay* them." He shrugged easily. "But you've got to keep chains on them, just to remind them they're not fighting us any more."

She had expected more obstruction from the Arvennir, but then she had expected them to still be at war, and instead they seemed to be settling into a comfortable life of... slave trading? She wasn't quite sure, and Heno had said it was complicated. The answer to it all was with whatever Yorughan had taken over, on the inside of the wall. That was the enemy's land, and though the armies of the free had tramped over it, they hadn't stayed. The camp of the Lily was ostensibly the last friendly territory before... what? Not the Kinslayer's monolithic war machine any more, but the same soldiers and monsters, the same louring fortifications, the breeding pits, the torture chambers, all the accoutrements of a demigod's tyranny. And leaders had arisen amongst the defeated, of course, and one had started making deals with humans, and he was at Bleakmairn right now with all the answers, and perhaps with the crown.

Leaving the Lily behind and riding past the wall was

unnerving. The land was blackened, dotted with stands of crooked, unnatural trees, no two alike. The very presence of the Kinslayer, over years of occupation, had twisted the terrain to fit his inner nature. Everything was poisonous or jagged or hideous. But perhaps he had looked on all of this and counted it as beautiful. Perhaps it was a comfortable home to the Yorughan.

"No," Nedlam told her. "I mean, look at it. Can't even sit down without getting a sharp rock up your arse. Better than below, though."

"Always better than below," Heno agreed. By then they were in Bleakmairn's shadow, waiting to see if the occupants would greet them with arrows.

When the Kinslayer had erupted from the earth with his forces, Bleakmairn had been a fort belonging to one of the Varra hill kingdoms—Celestaine could not remember which, and there really weren't many survivors left to inform her. The whole moorland and hill-land around this region had been a mosaic of kingdoms smaller than most Cheriveni towns, distant kin to the Forinthi, whose main pastime had been feuding with one another. The Kinslayer had chosen his invasion point well. 'When the Varra eat together' was one of those figures of speech that meant 'never,' and they'd had no time to change their ways before the armies of the enemy had picked them off, flattened their walls and enslaved or slaughtered most of their people.

The Yorughan built swiftly and well, and their former master had held this land for almost a decade. Celestaine couldn't see anything of the Varra left in Bleakmairn now. Its walls rose thirty feet, capped by jagged crenulations and lanced with arrowslits. Iron spikes slanted out below the wall top, and there were heads on some of them—all Yorughan, she noticed. She could see movement above, and the gates—twenty feet high and wide to accommodate the Kinslayer's engines and monsters—stood open. Inside, a band of Yorughan were forming up, and

Celestaine's stomach clenched. *The war's over*, she told herself, but right here it wasn't. The Kinslayer had died, but these soldiers had never really been defeated.

Heno strode past her, lifting his staff and setting its end alight with a Heart Taker's cold fire, a badge of office every one of the Kinslayer's minions would recognise. His voice boomed out, declaring something in his own tongue, alien words that rolled and clacked around his tusks. In the midst of it, Celestaine caught her name.

"Hmf," Nedlam observed. "That's torn it open, then."

"What did he say?"

"Put it like this, everyone in there knows the Kinslayer's come to visit."

Celestaine looked at the fortress full of Yorughan soldiers and who knew what else, and had to clench her hands on the reins to stop herself just turning around and riding off.

CHAPTER NINE

STEPPING THROUGH THE gates of Bleakmairn, into the very grasp of the Yorughan, took as much courage as Celestaine had. If she hadn't ever met Nedlam and Heno, it would have been too much for her. Even with them at her side, the massed stare of all those flinty eyes, the regard of so many grey tusked faces—it all brought back far too many bad memories. The shield wall at Ornasco where the Yorughan had charged down the hill and shattered the entire defending army in ten bloody minutes, or the seven-hour struggle over the river crossing at Matton, the waters choked with enemy dead and yet still they kept coming...

They weren't in chains here, but they were working. The west gate of the fortress was open as well—she could see clear across the courtyard to the land beyond—and a train of ore wagons was just being hauled in, no beasts of burden, just iron Yorughan muscles. A great furnace and smithy took up one whole side of the quad, and they were busy about it, the air ringing with the sound of hammers and hazy with the heat of molten metal. Celestaine thought of weapons, armour, an army rebuilding itself for renewed hostilities. All she saw were ingots, though, rank on rank of good iron being loaded into yet more wagons to be taken elsewhere.

"Got the mines going still, then," Nedlam observed, and Heno nodded.

Amkulyah shivered. The Dorhambri, where his people had been chained, was north-west of here, in land since reclaimed. There had been other mines, though—the Kinslayer loved working the earth, tearing out its bounty with the blood of slaves, and who knew more of the earth than those races that had been condemned to its darkness?

Of course the armies of the free had gone to those mines, killed the guards and overseers and freed every slave they could find on the way to fight the Kinslayer, but who was to say they'd found every pit? It wasn't as if the enemy had kept neat records of their atrocities.

The doors of the main keep slammed back abruptly and more Yorughan were marching out, a dozen wearing some of the heaviest armour Celestaine had seen—the sort they used to break the Cheriveni pike fences or force the breach of a wall. They were all of them nearly as big as Nedlam, marching in step. She felt the ground shiver with their tread, and so did she. Her hand found the hilt of her sword as though it was an anchor to keep her in place.

They formed two ranks, either side of the doors, and between them came someone who was plainly the undisputed master of Bleakmairn.

He was about a foot shorter than his honour guard, but nobody found it funny: a barrel-chested, broad-shouldered Yorughan wearing a miscellany of war-loot from across the world. His breastplate, black steel with silver ornament, had surely been made for an Oerni trade-lord's son. His bracers had been greaves for a Cheriveni officer. The slender-seeming sword at his belt was an Arvennir half-and-a-half bearing the insignia of an order preceptor. His remarkably bandy legs were swathed in loose silk pantaloons, garish iridescent blue and set off by a red-lacquered armoured codpiece from who knew where.

About his shoulders and waist was a rust-coloured cloak worn immaculately in the Forinthi style. Celestaine recognised the colours of the Maidenhair clan, now extinct.

Tucked under his arm, like a marshal's baton, was a goad with a savage, hooked head, the sort they used to wrangle dragons and siege monsters. Celestaine took from this that he was something of a disciplinarian. His bluish face was square, scalp shaven on top but with shaggy sideburns and a snarly tuft of beard. Someone had hit him quite hard with an axe some time ago: an angry, puckered furrow slanted above one ear, its trailing edge crossing his brow and check, a miracle the eye had survived.

He looked at Celestaine and grinned around tusks that pointed almost straight sideways. His face was brutal, but the smile gave life to it and made it charming.

Nedlam had been staring at him, uncertain, but the smile apparently tipped the balance; she thumped her fists to her chest and bowed her head, the same pose that the honour guard had adopted. "*U'rostir*!" she snapped out. *General.*

THE ARVENNIR, IN their eternal quest for sophistication, drank killingly strong liquor out of tiny porcelain cups. In the Yorughan's hands, the vessel looked like a thimble, smaller than the last joint of the general's thumb; it seemed impossible that it should not be crushed any moment. Even so, he raised it to eye-level, meeting Celestaine's gaze past the exquisite miniature scene of Arven farmland painted on the side.

"Your grand health," he toasted. He had a surprisingly soft voice, thick with accent, less comfortable with human speech than Heno or Nedlam.

Celestaine nodded and returned the pledge, knocking back the shot and feeling it sear the back of her throat pleasantly. They were all in the general's study, a room that Bleakmairn had not been designed to include, but that he had created by simply cramming a high-ceilinged armoury with furniture and knocking out part of the wall to make a bigger window. He sat on a gilded chair carved with twining oaks that had probably belonged to the Varra chieftain who'd once made this site his home. Behind him, a bookshelf reached most of the way to the ceiling, the contents chosen either for their look or because the general had a remarkably inclusive taste. One wall bore a framed map that had plainly done campaign duty in its time, stained and smudged and scarred.

"We never met, I think," the general murmured, staring at her. "Of course, your name is known to me, even before you killed *him*."

"Yours likewise, General Thukrah." Which was, if anything, an understatement.

There were surprisingly few names amongst the forces of the enemy that had become common currency amongst those they threatened. The greatest of the pit-bred monsters, certainly, because they were not exactly going to win any popularity contests amongst the rank and file. But one reason Heno had turned coat was that the Kinslayer was deeply suspicious of any underlings who showed too much personality or ambition.

Thukrah was the exception. He had led the fighting in the north at first, shattering the forces of the Frostclaw and the Udrengasi, and then he'd come down after Bladno to take on the various little kingdoms gritting up the wheels of the Kinslayer's advance eastwards. Celestaine recalled the stammering voices of prisoners he'd taken. He dined with them—the best food the conquered had to offer, wines chosen with delectable taste. He'd made conversation—through a translator, back then— talking about the most recent book he'd picked up, the weather, philosophy, subjects he was plainly only now encountering, but conversation nonetheless. Then he'd let the lucky soul go, after a fraught evening of tusk-slurred small talk, but only after watching their comrades get viciously executed. The released prisoner then became an involuntary ambassador, spreading the sort of fear that won battles before they were even joined.

And now here he was, and a long-armed Grennishman knuckled over and refilled his tiny cup, and did the same for Celestaine.

"You don't know what you think," Thukrah supplied for her. And, at her cautious nod, "You want I should be dead? Plenty do; plenty want us all dead. Some, though, some of your kind say: they didn't make the war happen. The Kinslayer, hm? His mind, our blades. You came in with these two no-goods, so you're one of them saying that second thing, hrm?"

Celestaine glanced at Heno, who was watching her, and at Nedlam, who was chain-eating the small cakes the Grennishman had set out as though hoping one would eventually be filling enough. Amkulyah was sitting on the arm of her chair, knees drawn up, the frailest living thing in the room by some margin.

Here goes my mouth, then, she thought, and said, "Some would suggest that you must have had more say in what went on than Nedlam here. You went about things your own way."

"At great risk to myself." That smile came out again and he swilled the spirits in his thimble and knocked them back. "Ah! Good! The Kinslayer is in my head a lot, telling me, go here, defeat these people, make everything *mine*. You can't imagine. He knows." A nod at Heno. "The Slackers, they're always having *him* turn up and tell them what's what. So I do it my own way. Fear, lies, tricks, like I'm sure you noble peoples wouldn't deign to use. I fight fewer battles. I lose fewer soldiers. Kill fewer of you, too."

"That's one way of putting it," she said slowly. And then, "I'm not here as some great avenger, General Thukrah."

His face was abruptly serious. "I'm glad. Because I don't want you as an enemy, not you, not that sword you have. You saved your many nations and tribes and peoples, when you shed the blood of *him*. You saved us more. You had only been his slaves for ten years, less."

"So tell me about slaves." She just threw it out there, saw his eyes narrow as he chewed the words to see where they were leading. "We saw your people in chains. The Arvennir said they'd bought them."

"Bought their backs, their arms," Thukrah said. "Their *work*."

"And yet the chains."

He shrugged. "You know who those were, on that boat? They did not want to do things the Thukrah way. And then we fought and they lost, then suddenly, oh, they *do!* They go to build walls for the Arvennir as penance. They go to win back their right to have a future." He said it all very matter-of-factly, without venom. "They are ambassadors. Work hard, make you humans say, *These Yoggs, good for something more than fighting*." He grinned, swiped the bottle from the Grennishman and necked it, a long draft of liquor meant to be measured in drops. "You would kill us all. Oh, not *you*, you are peace and tolerance incarnate, hrm? But your Arvenman, your northlings, better if we died with *him*. Or better if we went back where we started, give this land back to the dead people we took it from. As if that isn't the best way to brew another war in ten years' time." He shook his head. "We are not going back into the earth. We have seen the sky now. The sky is better." His eyes flicked to Amkulyah. "Ask *him* if the sky isn't better than the earth."

"And so...?"

"And so I break heads and fight my kin until I have enough who do what I say, and I say, go into the mines, go on the human boats, go build or tear down or spread your arse cheeks if that's what they want, but make them see we have value. Or it is war for us, and without *him*, a war we would lose. Kill many many human and Oerni and the rest, but lose all the same."

"You sound like you're not so glad he's gone," Celestaine pointed out.

Thukrah looked at her for long enough to make her uncomfortable. "He made us strong by killing those who were weak. He made us hard by killing those who were soft. He made us obey by killing those who said no. And it is good to be hard and strong, and what leader does not want those who obey? With *him*, you would have lost. We would have destroyed you all, even you with your magic sword we all hear about. But who wins when you lose? The Yorughan? General Thukrah? No, none of us. Only *him*." He shrugged. "Plenty out there in forts and holes still thinking, if only we had *him* still, still believing maybe *he* is not so dead, maybe coming back to make us his fist again. We fight them, day after day. We make them believe different or we kill them. Because there is no room in this world for a Yorughan who wants the Reckoner back."

She saw him wanting to bite back the name, because of course the Kinslayer hadn't defined himself by that word. To his minions, he had been the instrument of just vengeance, and woebetide any who had said otherwise.

"So you're selling yourself as the lesser of two evils," she suggested.

His grin widened. "Less evil is less evil, hrm? Besides, you're not here to hire strong backs *or* avenge old wrongs."

She searched within herself to see whether the death of General Thukrah—probably swiftly followed by the death of Celestaine the Slayer—seemed like a worthy cause, and decided not. Less evil, as he said. Or he was lying to her. Either way, it wasn't why she'd come.

"Heno tells me you want to go through the Kinslayer's toys," Thukrah said, and she shot the Heart Taker a sharp look, because he and the general had been talking in their own language and she didn't know *what* might have been said.

"Maybe," she said cautiously.

"Unfinished things, or things only just finished, he said," the general went on, and she nodded. "Here in Bleakmairn, down below, is *his* main mage-forge, all sorts of bad things made there. You hear of the Blade of Severance?"

"I cut it in half about ten miles from here, along with its wielder," Celestaine told him.

Thukrah exploded with a whoop of surprised laughter. "Ahah! Yes, it was so! Made here, beneath us. Many other bad things, too. Some things probably still there even now. Maybe what you're looking for, hrm?"

"Well, can we go and see?"

"Not so simple. Those parts, we've not got to yet."

She frowned, and Heno bent forward with a quick question that Thukrah shrugged at.

"You think we're here for our health?" he asked. "I got plenty no-goods say they're Thukrah's men, not their own, not *his*, but they don't see me for a few days, maybe they forget just who they make their promises to, hrm? So we move around, fort to fort, make sure nobody's forgetful. And we go where they're holding out. Bleakmairn is mine, up top. Below? Not so much. Got some bad things down there, got some still waiting for *him*, or who say they'll never clasp wrists with any *human* or *Oerni* or the like. So I come here with my fists to change minds or cut out livers." He cocked his head. "Want to come?"

"Me?"

"You want the mage-forge? It's down there. Why not be first in when we clean it out?"

Celestaine glanced at Heno, then back at the general. He had a calculating look in his eyes, behind the smile.

"We'll need to talk about it," she told him.

"Tomorrow we're in there breaking heads," he said. "Offer's open."

* * *

"Do you trust him?" she asked Heno, when the four of them had been shown to a room high in one corner of Bleakmairn, overlooking the courtyard.

"Thukrah? Not really."

"But I thought..."

"All Yoggs together?" He gave her a lazy smile. "You heard him, it's every Kinslayer's minion against the rest right now. Do you *want* a strong, unified Yorughan here?"

"It would be better for you, wouldn't it?" she asked.

"Better for Thukrah." He shrugged. "I'm me. I'm not the Kinslayer's creature, I'm not any general's follower. Besides, the regulars hated us Heart Takers about as much as your side did. *Shur-meh*, 'Slackers,' they called us, because we didn't do the hard work. That right, Ned?"

"*Shur-meh*," Nedlam agreed enthusiastically. "I trust him."

Celestaine blinked at her. "You do?"

"Was with him a year, two. Three?" Yorughan had difficulties telling time, coming from a dark place without seasons. "Before I got chucked over for special guard stuff with the Slackers." A leer at Heno. "Thukrah? Best leader I had. You knew he'd get you killed, but not stupid-killed."

"What choice do we have?" Amkulyah broke in. "If it's down there, it's down there. Or did you want to go down *now*, before they do, just the four of us? Fight whatever's there on the way down, fight this general and his creatures on the way up."

Celestaine sighed. "I'm sorry. I'd hoped to find something already liberated, not... not still where the war is."

"Don't be sorry," the Aethani told her harshly. "What use is that? Just *do*. If this is what is needed, I will go into the dark again. I will wear this general's colours if he asks. I will polish his boots with my tongue. And if he takes the crown for himself I will put out his eyes and open his throat. I will do what is needed. Will you?"

Celestaine just stared at him. He had been so quiet, so retiring and mannered. Even now he was not shouting. The anger in him was not a flare of heat that would gutter once the moment had passed. It was like the fires of the earth that were molten forever, always ready to crack their shell of stone and vent. He had been a slave for years. He had done whatever it took to survive, things she knew she didn't want to know about.

"I will," she said slowly. "And that might mean fighting General Thukrah on the way out. Can I count on you two? Would you rather stay behind?" She eyed the two Yorughan.

"Fight him? In a moment." Heno looked as though any expedition that didn't involve crossing swords with Thukrah would be a wasted one.

Nedlam scowled fiercely, which meant she was thinking.

"Don't want to stay behind. Don't want to fight the general." She didn't look unhappy often, but it came out now. "If he gets in the way, though, we're going to have to, right?"

Why? Celestaine was afraid of asking the question. Heno's loyalty warmed her. Nedlam's worried her. It wasn't as though the big warrior owed her—all debts were quit once the Kinslayer died. It wasn't as though she and Heno had a long history either; they were from very different classes amongst the Kinslayer's forces, allies of convenience once Heno decided to betray his master. And yet here Nedlam still was.

And, in the end, she had to ask. "Why, though?"

Nedlam grinned. "You ever hear me turn from a fight?"

"Seriously, Ned."

The Yorughan warrior looked mulish. "I can't want to do the right thing? You think I'll stab your back when Thukrah's at your front, now?"

"I don't think that," Celestaine told her, and it was true, to her surprise. "I don't want to put you where you do things you're ashamed of."

"Being left behind's what'd shame me," Nedlam insisted, and perhaps it was as simple as that. They were her squad, her friends, her family, however she thought of it. She didn't want to be left out.

When Thukrah formed up his people ahead of the dawn, they were already waiting in the courtyard, armed and ready for the fight.

CHAPTER TEN

CELESTAINE WAS SURPRISED to see Thukrah there, buckling on a gold-chased Arvennir helm, plainly about to lead the expedition in person. First it made her think better of him, then it made her worry that his control of his troops wasn't such that it was guaranteed to survive contact with the enemy, absent his presence. Especially if those enemy were hardline Kinslayer followers and might win over the general's soldiers with a little rhetoric. She only hoped he was leaving a solid henchman in command up top.

He rolled over on his crooked legs and grinned appreciatively. "Good to see you back in something that suits you." It would have been a weirdly offensive comment if he hadn't meant her armour. She had her breastplate and the swept-back Forinthi helm that covered her neck, tassets protecting her legs halfway to the knee, then greaves for her shins and bracers from elbow to wrist. It was far simpler than the war loot Thukrah was wearing, and it was as light as possible because the Forinthi liked to take the battle to the enemy. And, according to the Cheriveni, take it back and run off with it if they started losing, but that was just calumny.

She had thought she would be underdressed for the occasion, but instead of the great ironclads of the Yorughan vanguard, most of Thukrah's force were kitted out for mobility as well, armed for close-up, vicious work. Even Nedlam had left her great club behind, swapped out for a pair of short-handled cleavers. Heno had his staff, of course, but he was unlikely to resort to bludgeoning with it.

"You didn't need to come," she said. Because Amkulyah was in Ned's shadow again, unarmoured because there would be nothing for a hundred miles small enough for him, bow slung over his shoulder.

"I said I would go into the earth again." There was a tremor in his voice; perhaps the enemy he really wanted to defeat was inside him. "Besides, I don't trust these creatures. Not enough to be left alone with them."

The courtyard was lined with Thukrah's troops, calling out rough encouragement to the expeditionary force, each of them four times Kul's weight and unlikely to make allowances for his frailty. She conceded the point.

"General," she called, "is this all we're taking?" She counted around forty besides themselves.

"Going to be close down there, numbers just get in our own way," Thukrah told her. "Besides, words first. Been down there a while, they have. Some already thinking, 'This Kinslayer business is an old thing, just like being back home. I want the sky again.'"

"How much do you know about what we'll find down there?"

"Some. We know the rooms, we know there's some of the old garrison and some of the *Borun Atta* battalion that fell back here in the last fighting."

"'Gut Eaters,'" translated Heno, at her shoulder, which she felt she could have done without.

"We found seven ways in, blocked up the last a few days ago," the general went on. "They're down in the dark, not much food, we think. And other things with them, also hungry. Come play nice with Uncle Thuk, hrm? Sound like a good deal to them right about now."

That sounded overly optimistic to Celestaine, but she said nothing. Thukrah barked something out in the Yorughan tongue that Heno didn't bother to translate, and his force formed up and, to her surprise, marched into the keep itself.

They tracked down to the cellars, where a handful of skinny Grennishmen were busy about what she thought at first was a well. Closer, she saw a perfectly round hole down into the dark, with a corkscrewing ramp shallow enough to walk down.

"Probably they wait at the rubble for us to dig down to them," Thukrah explained. "But no! We make our own way. Nice surprise for all those no-goods down there."

Make their own way how? But the answer came before she could ask the question, as the Grennish coaxed a nightmarish creature out of the hole. It came out backwards, a great fat grublike body rippling in pallid bloated waves as it extricated itself from its burrow. Its head was a nightmare, a half-dozen chewing mandibles still grinding against each other even though it was free of the rock, and two stalked eyes popping free of its dark-shelled head to goggle about at them. Nedlam let out a fierce whoop, and for a moment Celestaine thought she was attacking the creature, but instead she had put her face right up close to those horrifying mouthparts and was cooing over it like a puppy—apparently the equivalent of *Who's a little deathworm, then?*

Thukrah coughed pointedly and she stepped back, looking a little mutinous. The worm-monster was hauled off by the Grennishmen, leaving everyone looking down at the hole.

"It doesn't go all the way through," Thukrah said. "Or maybe they'd think something's up. We were going to pick through, but now we have a Heart Taker." He nodded to Heno. "You going to follow a general's orders for once in your life?"

"No," Heno told him, unapologetically and to his face. "I'll do it if Celest asks nicely, though."

Thukrah chuckled. "Sounds like you're his new Kinslayer."

Which made her feel very uncomfortable indeed. "Right then, get your Heart Taker to crack open the last hand's breadth of it and we get to say hello."

The Yorughan went down the spiralling ramp with a will, virtually shoving Heno and Celestaine ahead of them.

"You can do this?" she asked, as she fought to keep her footing.

His expression was caught between offence at her doubt and a stubborn dislike of what was obviously menial work.

"Save your strength," she suggested, and grinned when he arched a silver eyebrow. "I want to show General Thukrah what he's getting."

Then they were at the bottom of the well. Celestaine glanced up, seeing ascending rings of Yorughan faces, beady eyes and tusks glinting beneath their squat, boxy helms.

"Going to be dark down there," Heno told her. "Not pitch, but dim. You humans have bad eyes. But, you know me."

She nodded, finding Nedlam in the press, with the owlish stare of Amkulyah glowering from under her armpit. *Keep him safe!* "They know we're coming, right?"

Thukrah shrugged. "I got warriors kicking up a fuss at all the places we blocked off. They are split, I hope. But yes."

Celestaine nodded. *First into the breach.* It was the Forinthi path to glory. Did the Yorughan feel the same way, or was it just duty to them, ground in by the heel of the Kinslayer's boot? And was glory even a thing worth having?

Enough procrastinating. She drew her sword, wincing as it bit into the scales of her new scabbard. In one motion she reversed it and drove it down into the stone beneath. The blade slid in smoothly—not without resistance, but, however reluctantly, the stone parted for her. She cut out a circle that left the end of the ramp intact and thought, *Look out below.*

There was more than one awed Yorughan intake of breath when the disc of stone simply dropped out of the bottom of the shaft—and a brief cry of appalled shock as it landed fatally on someone underneath. Then Thukrah's people were rushing past, dropping down into the hole, landing hard on bent knees and then pushing out of the way for those behind them. Celestaine heard the first shouts and a clatter of steel on steel. She glanced at Heno and saw him roll his eyes in the dim light, eloquently suggesting that all this first-into-the-breach business wasn't a Heart Taker thing.

Nedlam leapt past with a whoop and Amkulyah clinging to her shoulders, and Celestaine followed suit, sword held high to prevent any friendly decapitations.

Below everything was chaos. She hadn't missed the part of the plan that gave them no ready way to retreat. Thukrah was already in the thick of it, though, so the exercise wasn't *intended* to be a suicide mission. She had to blink and blink before she got an idea of what was going on. The only light came from pale crystals set into the walls—junior Yorughan blood mage work, she reckoned—that were calibrated for their keen eyes, not human ones. For seven heartbeats she just stood, holding her sword out of trouble and letting her eyes adjust. She might only be human, but she'd fought the Kinslayer's minions in places like this for years. She knew the drill.

That ululating Yorughan battlecry rang out, firing her blood with the need to fight and kill things. It came from every throat around her, though, friend and foe. She made out Nedlam's own yell over the others, louder and longer as she laid about herself with her cleavers. Half of Thukrah's warriors were still above, without clear space to jump down to, and for a moment the defenders hemmed them in, trading blows furiously, shoving and kicking and headbutting.

Heno shouted something from above, in their language, but she knew what he would be saying. *You know me*, he'd told her, and she did. She knew that he was the least reliable creature in the world, unless it was for her.

He thrust a hand down into the room below him and unleashed white fire in ribbons across the ceiling, incandescent serpents crawling across every crack and imperfection. Thukrah's people were mostly facing away, but the defenders were looking straight into the blaze and they fell back, trying to shield their eyes. Celestaine cried out, "Fiddlehead blades in!" though it would mean nothing to anyone else there, and then shouldered her way between two Yorughan to bring her sword to the enemy.

They were veterans, the Yorughan buried down there. They were the die-hard Kinslayer followers, and she wished they understood who she was and what she'd done. News of their master's defeat had either not reached here or had been thrown out as lies, though. She had to show them what her blade could do.

There was an art to fighting with the Wanderer's blade. She had come so close to death so many times with textbook parries that lopped off the last two inches of a sword but left the razor-edged rest of it still on a course for her throat. Now she parried in, striking towards the hilt and the hand in a way her Fiddlehead swordmaster would have despaired of. She made her swings obvious, showed her enemies precisely where she would take the blade so that they would line their blocks up neatly for her. She sheared through their swords, carved their shields up, and the armour beneath, then the flesh, then the bone, feeling the minute variations of resistance with each layer. It was a bloody thing, that sword, for those who faced it for the first time, and precious few had much chance at a second. With four strokes she cleared the way in front of her, and Thukrah's people were sweeping on either side, heading towards a tall arch thronging with new enemies.

Arrows were leaping at them now, and Yorughan bows were vicious things: no more than four feet long, thick as a man's arm and needing their giant's strength even to bend. Celestaine saw three of Thukrah's soldiers punched off their feet by the arrows, shafts splintering with the impacts. The rest were pelting forwards, leading with small shields or just barging shoulder-first, trusting to their heavy pauldrons to deflect the arrows. Amkulyah, still about Ned's shoulders like a monkey, returned the favour, pitching a shaft ahead of the charge that struck the middle defender over his shield-rim and through the roof of his mouth.

Most of the general's people were below now, and Heno dropped after them, straightening his coat and shaking his sleeves out. He looked slightly exasperated with the whole business, and even more so when there was a flash of cold white fire from beyond the arch, and Thukrah started shouting for the *Shur-meh* to get front and centre.

Celestaine and Heno hustled over, finding Thukrah's people bunched either side of the arch and a couple of fractured, frozen corpses strewn in the middle to show why.

"They've got a Heart Taker?" she demanded, and the general nodded curtly.

"What, you didn't think the whole gang would be together?" Heno needled, and Thukrah slapped him across the head, staggering him sideways. Celestaine had her blade up, but Heno was waving her to stand down, licking at a trickle of blood from where his scrimshawed tusk had gashed his cheek.

"Battlefield order," Thukrah growled, and she understood. Sure, the regulars and the 'Slackers' didn't see eye to eye, but there was no time for infighting when the lines were drawn.

"I see three in Taker robes," Amkulyah reported. Nedlam was standing in line with the arch, but well back. Apparently Aethani eyes were good enough in the murk. "One older, definitely in charge." He glanced around, unnerved to find so many Yorughan listening to him so intently. "Probably twenty soldiers, but they're keeping either side like we are, so could be more."

"Tell me of the chief Slacker," Thukrah demanded.

"Almost as tall as Nedlam, but thin, eaten-away-like," Kul reported. Celestaine saw his huge pupils expand and contract as he focused. "Has a big staff with a caged skull. The skull's on fire, the white fire they do."

"Skull...?" That obviously threw Thukrah a little.

"Big skull, bigger than yours," Amkulyah confirmed.

"White hair like mine?" Heno asked, and the Aethani nodded.

"Shulamak," Thukrah and Heno said at the same time, and the general added, "Balls. Thought he was long dead."

"Trouble?" Celestaine asked.

"Have to find out." Thukrah bellowed something that was patently, 'Oi, you in there!'

Heno leaned in to Celestaine's ear and murmured a translation. Despite the imminent violence, it was a weirdly intimate moment and she shivered.

Thukrah was demanding their surrender and telling them the Kinslayer—the 'Reckoner'—was dead, and the Yorughan had their own destiny now. He called out to Shulamak by name, telling him that even Heart Takers could walk under the sky now.

Shulamak laughed, and said that the Yorughan would never walk free until all the others were dead. The Reckoner's dream still lived, he said. If not now, then they would come from the earth tomorrow, a year's, a hundred years' time.

Thukrah sighed and chuckled loudly, asking if they wouldn't rather have the sky now, even if there were humans under it? He would, certainly. He could look up every day and see the sun, how warm it was on his face. And the Reckoner was dead— why, he had the woman here who'd done it, right here fighting alongside him. She'd carved the old boy up like a seven-hand rabbit—Heno's literal translation, and Celestaine had no idea what it meant—and where did that leave Shulamak's dreams now? Come on, old man, the general pressed. Come up under the sky, enjoy the breeze.

There was a growing murmur amongst the Yorughan in the next room that Celestaine took for longing. They had been beneath the earth all their lives, until the war had hurled them across the free nations in a burning tide. But they loved the sun, this much she understood. They hated the dark, cramped spaces and the crushing weight of stone above, because they had found something better.

But then Shulamak was speaking again, voice rich with contempt. The Reckoner was not gone, Heno translated. The Reckoner was right here… And then Heno faltered and stopped speaking and a lash of shock went through Thukrah's people. Celestaine saw the cold light grow, and then the cadaverous Heart Taker was virtually in the archway, brandishing his staff, rattling the fanged, outsized skull in its brass cage.

"He says he has the Kinslayer there!" Heno spat. "His skull, his spirit. He says he'll bring it back." And then Shulamak was chanting a single phrase over and over, and his followers were chiming in. Celestaine knew it from the battlefield—it had rung in her ears during more than one retreat from the victorious Yorughan. "*Schor harkt na!*" Masters of all.

"That's not his skull," she shouted. "His head wasn't even that big!"

But events were already out of control. Thukrah was bellowing orders, but one of his own people suddenly turned and tried to stab him in the face. The blade cut a black line across his cheek, crossing the old axe scar, and then Shulamak and his people rushed through the arch, the blazing skull their banner, and everyone was fighting everyone else.

In those first moments Celestaine had no idea how many traitors Thukrah was facing, or whether it was her and her friends against the whole pack of them. She just went straight towards Shulamak, to fight Yorughan who were, at least, definitely his people rather than the general's, until the old Heart Taker fell prudently back into his chamber again.

She made speed her ally, and her pale human face, too—every enemy Yorughan wanted to kill her, for Thukrah had told them exactly what sacrilege she'd committed. Probably too late now for her usual self-effacing, *It wasn't just me*, and besides, for once she wanted to own the damn deed. *Yes, I killed your cursed Reckoner. Reckon with that!* They wanted to kill her so much they got in each other's way. She saw one axeman whip his weapon back to swing at her and bury it in the face of his closest ally, and another warrior slammed into the body and sprawled practically at Celestaine's feet. She dropped low to stab the luckless fighter in the back of the neck, crouching behind the angle of her blade so that the axeman's eventual stroke just parted head from haft and left him holding a truncated piece of stick. Fighting from your knees was another tactic her swordmaster would have yelled at her for, but he hadn't owned a sword like hers. In the baffled moment where the axeman stared at his little stump she swung her sword in a flat arc half a foot from the ground and the closest four Yorughan lost their feet at the ankles. She leapt up with a cry as they dropped all around her and came face to face with one of the junior Heart Takers, his hands on fire with white light as he prepared to rip her lungs from her body.

She had time to say, "Arses," before Amkulyah's arrow pierced the mage through one ear and out the other, the Heart Taker's eyes crossing in a moment of perfect, inadvertent comedy before he fell. Nedlam bowled up a moment later, Kul still using her helmed head like a rampart to shoot over.

"We need to get in, to the chief mage!" Celestaine shouted.

"Leave it to—" Nedlam started and then Kul lunged past her face with his bow, a blur of lithe movement. Celestaine didn't see the enemy arrow at all, just head the sharp *clack!* as it deflected from his bowstave and rattled off towards the ceiling, rather than spitting Nedlam's face. For a second she and the Yorughan just stared at each other, putting together what had happened.

"Whatever you're doing, *do it!*" Amkulyah shouted, and Celestaine snapped out of it, looking around for Thukrah.

She found him with his back to the wall, beside the archway. There were four dead soldiers at his feet, all clad as his men, and she had no idea how many had been trying to kill him. In one hand he had his Arvennir sword, in the other his hooked goad, both arms gory to the elbows. His face was running with blackish blood, but he had a grin for her when she ran up.

"Right, then," he said, as though she was slightly late for an appointment. "I say we go in there and cut Shulamak a new eyesocket."

A blaze of white fire cut through the door, sending Thukrah's men stumbling back, but he seemed not even slightly deterred. At least the incursion from Shulamak had been contained, and all the surviving enemy were next door again.

"Slacker," said Thukrah to Heno.

"Fire with fire?"

"*Yaro yaro e*, right," the general agreed. Then he raised his voice and addressed the rest of his people, presumably saying something like, 'The rest of you no-goods be ready to go.'

"Hold," Celestaine told him. "They're all about the doorway, right? And they've got two mages left, Shulamak and Shulamak Junior, or whoever."

Thukrah chuckled. "Your point?"

"Heno holds the arch; fire with fire, like you say. Ned and a bunch of your people, have them follow me."

"Through the door?" Thukrah waggled his eyebrows to suggest he didn't rate her chances.

"Not exactly. Just follow." Crossing back past the arch, she realised she hadn't felt alive like this since she cut the hand from the Kinslayer, and what did that say about her precisely?

CHAPTER ELEVEN

"WHILE THERE IS much to be said for the Perspicacious Lens of Glyssa," Doctor Catt remarked, "one is forced to conclude that Glyssa, whoever in fact she was, only ever wanted to look at things that were plentifully well lit, because I am having the scabs' own job making out what is going on."

Doctor Fisher just grunted and peered down into the courtyard where General Thukrah's stand-in was maintaining loyalty by dint of all-comers weapons training.

The two of them were perched up on the wall of Bleakmairn, concealed from view by the powers of Incantor's Gauze. Catt had been squinting into a blue glass disc for some time, seeing confused images of fighting Yorughan with the occasional glimpse of Celestaine's face showing as a pale blur.

"I don't even understand why they're all fighting one another," he complained mildly.

"Yoggs," Fisher said dismissively. He pulled down the peak of his Cheriveni army cap, an accessory he had in no way earned the right to wear, and made a great show of trying to nap.

"Well, even so." Catt shivered. He had not, of course, rushed to the recruiting sergeant to have his name put down for the army. He was a gentleman of a certain age and disposition, after all: not for him the push of pike. Not that he hadn't done his little bit to further the war effort, after all, with the gathering of intelligence and one reluctant poisoning, but he had always tried to stay well away from the Yorughan. Their robust physicality intimidated him.

"If you get a chance," he added, "could you just put a fresh shine on Torquil the Majestic's Opal Dweomer-Shield? It sounds as though they have quite a few Heart Takers down there, and I really don't fancy them detecting our shrouding and coming to take a look."

Fisher sighed theatrically, but did the honours with the little bejewelled buckler, scattering the traces of their magic so that only the most diligent of mage-hounds could pinpoint them.

"We'd be in an abysmal predicament should this chance to be a wasted venture," Catt went on, peering into the lens and then wincing as Celestaine seemed to escape death by a hair's breadth. "Oh, do come on, young lady, bring matters to a prompt conclusion. I know that our interests are about to diverge sharply, but I would rather not have sent you to an early demise."

Fisher snorted, and Catt eyed him testily. "Is something snort-worthy?"

"You like her."

"Well don't you? Slayer of Kinslayers, et cetera?"

"And you'll still rob her."

"Ah, if there were any other way."

"Plenty of other ways," Fisher pointed out.

"Very well, if there were any other way that didn't take more effort than this one."

"There we go." Fisher shook his head with a rueful grin. "This is why I like you, Catt."

"Well, that's that sorted, then," Doctor Catt observed. "Some day I may discover why I like you, or even if. Oh, now, wait— what's she doing?" He squinted, tilting the lens as though he could shed more light within it. "Oh, now that's rather clever…"

* * *

HENO STRODE FORWARDS, staff raised before him.

"Shulamak!" he challenged. "*Seo chak!*" and then another phrase Celestaine remembered from the battlefield. "*Ho yaro ser!*" Test your fire! The cry of the Heart Taker to his comrades commanding forth their power.

"*Heno na a?*" came Shulamak's voice, and then a torrent of what was clearly abuse.

Heno laughed, that rich warm sound that so often presaged devastation. "He says I betray our order, to be standing on this side of the wall!" he shouted, for Celestaine. "How much more, if he knew I'd brought down his Kinslayer?"

The howl of outrage suggested Shulamak understood Middle Kingdom speech well enough, as Heno had doubtless guessed, and then spears of white fire were leaping through the archway, making Thukrah's soldiers cringe back. Heno dropped into a fighting stance, his hands sheathed in jagged light, catching each shaft as it came and hurling it back, like so many javelins. Celestaine heard at least one scream from the far side of the arch as Heno banked a shot past Shulamak and into his troops.

I could watch him all day, she thought wistfully, but she had her own plan to put into motion.

She chose her spot, eight feet to the arch's left. A glance showed Nedlam's reassuring bulk at her shoulder, bloodied cleavers ready for action. Amkulyah fit an arrow to his string. A score and more of Thukrah's soldiers were crowded in behind, keeping plenty of space between them and Heno.

She spared one more glance for her Heart Taker. He had given a foot of ground and his face was locked into an expression of concentration, rather than his usual scornful grin. Shulamak was testing him, and she didn't want to wait to find out who was the stronger.

She dropped the point of her sword so that it touched the boundary between floor and wall, and pushed.

The dense stone fought her, but this wasn't her first time as improvisational architect. She knew when to lean into it, when to let the steel find its own way. She thrust the blade in six inches, guessing at the thickness of the wall, then hauled up, keening the edge through stone and severing the very bones of the earth. At head height she turned the straight stroke into a cleaving arc that would hopefully run high enough to give even Nedlam head room, and then drew the blade back down with no more than the occasional spark. When she was young, she'd heard a story about a child with a magic quill, that could draw a door in a wall that could be walked through. All she lacked was the ability to close the portal afterwards.

She finished the cut with a straight flick along the base and then stepped back, because there were some tasks Nedlam was just plain better at. The huge Yorughan took two steps back, shrugged Amkulyah onto her right shoulder, and then whooped out a warcry and rammed the demarcated wall with her left, shunting out a door-shaped wedge of stone and not stopping, running right into the other room with Thukrah's soldiers at her back.

Celestaine waited until the rush was gone before following, because being in a press of bodies with a sword of infinite sharpness was always a bad idea. She made sure she was right on their heels, though, and her heart was pounding with a sheer childish excitement. She couldn't help it. She'd seen the unstoppable Yorughan charge so often—always from the wrong end. She'd seen their ferocity in battle, matched only by their courage and their discipline. Like every enemy of the Kinslayer, she'd hated them: their tusked faces, their strength, their sheer unwillingness to give. But she'd thrilled to them too, in a perverse way. She couldn't help admiring them even when she was steeped in their dark blood, when she was fighting for her life or to give the civilians time to escape. They were an elemental force, and in her dreams she'd explored what it would be like to be one of them, to be a part of that thundering momentum. She threw back her head and did her best shot at the long ragged sound that had struck fear into her so often. It didn't sound much like it should, but it *felt* good.

Thukrah's people had got stuck in, driving towards where Shulamak was still launching his power at Heno. For as long as Heno could hold him, the old Heart Taker should be out of the fight. More Yorughan were scrambling out from another chamber, some unarmoured or half-dressed, many looking scrawnier than usual. Presumably the hold-outs hadn't had the chance to lay in much of a larder.

Still, they were trying to flank her side, and so she met them head on, using the staccato flaring of the magical fight to light her way. The first few hadn't even seen her—she caught a pair of archers still frantically stringing their bows and cut them without slowing, enough to put them out of the fight. Her next swing lopped the head from a spear that someone thrust her way, the shortened shaft ramming her shoulder painfully and bringing her up short. She cursed and took three quick steps back, because if a Yorughan got into grappling with her, it wouldn't go well. Her enemy was just staring at the stick in his hands, though, and then he had a foot-long dagger out but was backing away, plainly not up for this sort of nonsense right now. He had a bolder friend, though, a broad Yorughan woman who came howling for Celestaine with one of their heavy hacking swords. She tried to clip the blade above the quillons, but her enemy was quicker than she'd thought, so she got the hand behind the wrist instead. Looking past her suddenly ashen opponent, Celestaine saw she had the undivided attention of at least a dozen of the Yorughan second wave, but none of them wanted to be next. It was an education, really. She remembered them as the indomitable masters of battle, unstoppable in attack, dangerous even in retreat, often fighting down to the very last when their master demanded it. That master was gone, though—and the skull was perhaps not the substitute Shulamak hoped. They were hungry and beaten, cut off from the sky. This wasn't the field they wanted to die on.

Then she saw the other Heart Taker pushing forwards, the second apprentice. He had a spitting ball of white fire in his hands, already flying at her even as she saw. She braced, but though it left a skin of rime across her armour it barely chilled her. Shulamak had obviously been a lax teacher. The apprentice's face twisted with fear and frustration, and Celestaine yelled at the lot of them to put their weapons down, hoping that some might understand the words. They didn't, but they didn't fight her either, just backing off, keeping their swords and spears levelled at her but only to stop her following.

Shulamak's roar of fury split the air, and she turned to see him thrusting a hand at her, even as Heno's own fire started to bite him. Defeat was in his face: his followers were falling around his feet, but most of all it was those who would not fight that incensed him. He was going to die, but he was going to kill her first, because *he* knew the Kinslayer was dead and the skull was a sham, and he knew she was to blame.

She began to run at him, knowing the fire was faster than she'd ever be, but then a huge shape loomed over the cadaverous Heart Taker. Nedlam stooped and came up with something limp and flopping in her hands, and brought the weight of it down across the back of Shulamak's neck, heedless of the spitting fire.

That sufficed, as it turned out. The old Heart Taker broke like a stick, leaving Nedlam grinning down at him, still holding her makeshift weapon. She called something proudly over to Heno, who was just sauntering through the arch as though he owned the place, brushing frost from his robes. At Celestaine's look, he rolled his eyes. "She says she told me you could beat someone to death with one of their friends in a battle. She's always wanted to try it."

Thukrah limped in after Heno, barking out orders and plainly very pleased with himself. He spared a particular grin for Celestaine. "All good, thought your Slacker wasn't going to make it, but all good. Let's get these no-goods up top, hrm? Then we talk."

Amkulyah was at her elbow, but Celestaine didn't need the reminder. "I think we keep going to this mage-forge." *Before your people get to creep in and strip it behind my back.*

Thukrah's expression neither confirmed nor denied that intention. "All good. I'll come with, me and some of mine. The rest will see about these losers."

"What will you do to them?"

"Rip out their livers and place them on spikes, warning to the others." At her expression, Thukrah laughed uproariously. "These are my kin! Bad leaders, once, but now they have me, a good leader. They get the shit jobs until they make us like them. Besides, you ever seen a liver on a spike? Ridiculous, warning to nobody."

In the room beyond, where the walking wounded had come from, they found children. Only a handful, but when the Kinslayer had mobilised his armies, he had taken only those fit to fight. The Yorughan had been taken from their families, never to see them again, in most cases. Heno said that close family ties were frowned on, back in the bowels of the earth—any loyalty that wasn't to their master was suspect. But the Kinslayer's power only went so far. Family and camaraderie were a constant counterculture amongst the Yorughan and the other minion races.

"General, you knew the layout up here, you know where the forge is." Heno strode up.

"Yes, yes, below, even more below," Thukrah told them. "Come on, then, let's see what's what."

"Will there be more down there?" Celestaine asked him.

"More of these no-goods? Maybe some guards to keep loot out of pockets. Maybe worse."

It was worse, of course. They found a shaft leading down, studded with metal rungs. The surviving apprentice came with them, only too happy to spill all the beans there were in order to keep his hide intact. Heno listened to his babblings and then cursed. Celestaine had already picked up the world *Vathesk*.

"So your fire's no use," she said. The otherworld demons the Kinslayer had summoned and abandoned were notoriously resistant to any kind of magic.

"Shulamak was after recruiting it," Thukrah said. "Sent some boys down to say hello. It ate them. And then yakked up the bits because, you know, Vathesk."

"Have to kill it, then." Nedlam rolled her shoulders. "Shame."

Celestaine nodded, because it was. The Vathesk were even less to blame for their situation than the Yorughan.

"That sword of yours good against Vathesk shell?" the general asked her.

"Oh, yes," she said, starting down the ladder.

Close to the end of the shaft she heard the thing prowling about, claws scraping the stone. It was very dark down there, but Heno could help with that, at least. She rapped her sword pommel on the side of the shaft to signal him, and he dropped a chill will-o-the-wisp down past her that flitted into the chamber below and danced aside, shedding a wan blueish radiance.

The Vathesk gave out a ghastly sound like bottled suffering and skittered over towards it. They never roared or threatened, the Vathesk. They begged, they pleaded, evident to all even though their language was alien even to the Kinslayer's other minions. They made entreating motions with their mouthparts and whimpered. And then they killed, even though they knew that they could eat none of it.

She saw its broad carapace pass beneath her and tried to drop onto it, but got kicked by one of its jointed legs instead. With a sobbing wail, the Vathesk turned on her. Twice the size of a horse, it filled the end of the chamber. Its body was a broad shield like a crab's, beneath which a clutch of limbs sprouted, some of them legs, some little toothed arms for manipulating, but most prominently its two great pincers that could scissor open the strongest mail or take an arm off without slowing. Its head was just a jutting projection at the front of its shell, flanked by faceted eyes like jewels. They wept, those eyes; all the pain in the world was within them.

"You can't eat me. I don't taste good," Celestaine told it. Vathesk couldn't form human words or even Yorughan words, but they picked up languages effortlessly. "Don't make this a fight, come on."

For a moment, she thought she might have got through to it. The monster shook its rattling body and whined like a dog, backing away from her blade. Then the ravening hunger got the better of it and its claws clattered as it bounded towards her.

She had killed Vathesk before, though the enclosed space was not ideal. She ran to meet it, dropping to her back beneath its initial charge and hearing a thousand scrapes across her backplate that no amount of polish would quite get out. Her blade scored across its ridged underbelly, parting its plates and laying open the honeycomb of their interior, but cutting no deeper. Vathesk were appallingly robust, even for her sword.

It gave out a shocked sound and flailed at her with its pincers, raking great furrows in the stone around her. She hacked at one smaller arm that reached for her, chopping through its hooked claw, and waited for her reinforcements.

Nedlam just dropped boots-first onto the Vathesk's back. From the impact, she had been building speed down the length of the shaft, and Celestaine heard something crack explosively beneath her heels. Then she was tumbling free, rolling to her feet with her cleavers out as the Vathesk rounded on her. Arrows began to flit down, Amkulyah sighting into the circle he could see from above. His shafts just shattered against its hide, though, one even bounding back from the Vathesk's beautiful crystalline eye.

The monster tore at Nedlam, clipping her with enough force to knock her from her feet. Vathesk were insanely strong. Their only saving grace as an opponent was that they were not warriors, back where they came from; just the people of a peaceful world unlucky enough to be discovered by the Kinslayer.

Celestaine kept that in mind when she rammed her sword to the hilt in the creature's underbelly, lunging forwards to unseam it to its mouth. Even that didn't kill it, but while it was rearing up and lamenting she let Nedlam boost her high enough to drive her blade between its eyes and into its brain.

A mercy. I hope it was a mercy.

They found the Vathesk's lair soon after, an alcove with walls covered in intricate diagrams and alien writing, carved into the rock by the creature's claws. There was a whole epic treatise there, thousands of characters in neat columns supported by what looked like the sort of geometry that Celestaine had never been able to even start on. Looking at it, she felt ignorant and mean and bloody-handed.

"Trying to get itself home," Heno suggested, after he and Thukrah had come down.

Celestaine shrugged morosely. Killing the Vathesk had left her with a bad taste in her mouth, but it was worse than that. "Where is it, then?"

They had found the mage-forge, but the fires were cold, and even the tools had gone. There were no half-completed treasures lining the walls, no racks of magic swords or Heart Taker staves, no enchanted armour made to the Kinslayer's own measurements. No magic jewels of making; no crown.

"Someone's been over this place," Thukrah said, and, at her look, laughed. "You think we sneak a Grennishman past Shulamak's lot *and* the Vathesk, and he comes out carrying all the loot? No, some power did this, some real power." He shook his head. "So, no thing for you, no loot for us. Pfesh!"

"I hear singing," Amkulyah said. The statement was odd enough to silence everyone.

"What, you...?" Celestaine tailed off. There had been a tune in her head, one that she knew very well indeed from the war, but she'd thought it was just one of those songs that got stuck in her ear and wouldn't come out. Now she listened, and perhaps it wasn't just inside after all. "Heno, do you...?"

Heno didn't, but by that time Celestaine was sure she did. She prowled about the forge until she came to a point where the song was loudest. It was 'The Boys of White Feris,' a Lantir ballad that had been all about the free armies after Lannet fell and its soldiers went to join anyone who was still fighting. With the eyes of the rest on her, she joined in with the verse, butchering the tune as she always had. Ralas had made fun of her so much, calling her the worst Forinthi hero, saying her ancestors would crawl from their graves because she was so little the ideal warrior-bard of legend. Even croaking through three bars of White Feris she could hear his voice as he castigated her: "Celestaine, you sound like a dog gargling mud."

She smiled sadly, despite herself, and met Heno's gaze. His eyes were wide.

"What?" she asked him, but he was holding up a finger and that distant voice was still calling her name. "Celestaine!"

Nedlam stamped next to her, and they all heard the hollow knock of it. A moment later she was on one knee, using a cleaver's edge to pry at a crack in the ground, and then just going to get a mace and battering at the floor.

"Back," Celestaine warned her, and then cut a new hatch approximating the actual one they couldn't get open, carving two rough dents in so Nedlam could get her fingers in to lift it out.

Below there was a cell, no other way to put it. It was too small for someone to lie down in, and had been too low to stand straight in before Celestaine's impromptu improvements.

A ragged man was hunched there like a bundle of sticks, turning a wild-eyed, hollow face to them. Celestaine felt her heart stop, then hammer painfully at her ribs.

"*Ralas?*"

The prisoner below let out a wretched laugh. "Is it? Am I? I don't really know. But I know you, my dear warrior bard. I'd know that terrible voice anywhere. How are you? How's everyone? How's the war?"

"It's… it's over," Celestaine stammered out, staring so hard she thought her eyes would fall out. "But Ralas, you died. Everyone thought you'd *died*. If there was any chance, we'd have… I'm so sorry, I…"

With lordly grace the emaciated figure waved her apologies away. "No, no, you're right."

"I'm…?"

"I died. I died a lot." His eyes glittered madly at her. "But I got better."

CHAPTER TWELVE

"I KNOW WHO he's supposed to be," Heno snapped. "I don't trust him just *being* here." He scowled over at Ralas, who was sitting on the ground and staring at the clouds as though he had half-forgotten what they were.

He had looked better in his time, Celestaine admitted, although surely that argued for him being the man, and not some trick or imposter—they'd have made a fake more convincing than this threadbare reality. She'd even wondered if this was some mad scheme of the Undefeated to get into her good graces, at first, but Ralas had not made any demands of her, nor promises either. He had been carried out into the open by Thukrah's people like a scarecrow, and left there to look at the sun.

He was horribly thin, his limbs seeming to be just skin over old bones. When he stripped off the filthy rag of his shirt, she could see each individual rib and where they had been broken and not quite healed. Someone had taken their fists and boots to him not long ago, it seemed, and on and off for a long while before then: his skin was a mosaic of bruise-colours, blue and purple, red and yellow. A blow to his face had swelled up the skin until one eye was almost hidden, and when he walked it was with a halting limp where one foot was crooked.

He must have felt her eyes on him, for he glanced over and

smiled. His teeth were yellow but all present, seeming outsized in his sunken face. As she went over to him, he waved. His hands were perfect too, not a finger broken.

"Ralas, who was holding you down there?" she asked him gently. "Was it Shulamak? Was it one of these?" She jabbed a finger at Thukrah's new recruits from below. Her attitude to them had soured remarkably after the discovery of the prisoner.

"Oh, warrior-bard, always looking to mete out justice," he said. His voice was still his, far more than his face or figure, the words dancing to an unconscious music he could never quite suppress. They had pared him down, but left the things that made him Ralas.

"I don't know about justice. I'll settle for helping. Right now I'll help you get revenge on whoever did this to you."

He laughed, though his eyes glittered with tears. "Oh, you're too late, too late for that."

"Ralas, I'm looking at you, and someone put their fist in your face no more than three hours ago, best guess." She pointed at the rainbow colours of his black eye and he flinched back. "See, still tender, isn't it?"

This time the boundary between laughter and tears was much harder to draw. "Oh, it is, warrior-bard, it is. But it's old news, that no true teller would bother with. And you revenged me anyway, they tell me. The Kinslayer, at your hand?"

"Me and the others. Lathenry, Roherich, Shoel…" Names of the absent, names of the dead, and Ralas had been on that latter list until just now. "Help me," she said to him. "Give me something I can understand."

"He took me," Ralas told her. "He took me and had lads like these work me over. He kept me on water and worms. All fair treatment, for a prisoner of the Kinslayer. I wasn't the only one. He wanted to break me, but I sang until he gagged me and I hummed after that. I made the walls and the bars my instrument. When he brought me out for execution I sang

'Towers of Coin and Copper' to the torturers and 'Gisella the Red' to the headsman, and 'Three Farmers of Doubty' to the Kinslayer himself."

"You didn't!" Celestaine goggled at him. 'Three Farmers' was the earthiest sort of raunchy folk song. She tried to imagine Ralas standing surrounded by all the Kinslayer's monsters and belting out the verse about the innkeeper and the… "What happened?"

Ralas's thin finger drew a line across his throat. "At least it was quick."

She stared, waiting for him to say it was a joke. It wasn't a joke.

"Woke up after that, on a big old stone table with a pack of those Heart Taker boys all over me," he went on. "Kinslayer was there, too, and it looked like he'd been through a few of them before because they were surely glad for their lives that they'd got him what he wanted."

"Which was?"

"Me." Ralas shrugged. "Got in his head, didn't I? Turned out, all those times I'd been in my cell going through my repertoire, himself had been spying. Turns out he hated my damn guts more than any human alive, by the end, for the thoughts I put in his head. And yet, after he'd gotten me out of the way, the songs just went round and round, telling him, *And there was more than this, if you hadn't whacked his head off like that.* Turns out this was a thing he'd been working on anyway, because, you know, he was the Kinslayer, and even death was just his stock in trade and not his master. He meant it for himself, of course, but he tried it out on me, and I guess he could never make it work for anyone else, or I never did hear of it, and you seem pretty damned sure he's dead."

"Oh, he's dead," Celestaine confirmed. "If I'm sure of nothing else, I'm sure of that. So he made you… sing for him?"

"And when I displeased him, with what I sang or what I didn't, he killed me again," Ralas told her. "Only it never took.

Nothing does. This," and he pointed to the raw bruise on his cheek, "this was years ago, Warrior-bard."

She sat down heavily beside him, aware of Heno's gaze on her. Ralas nodded companionably to the Heart Taker. "Interesting company you keep, hey?"

"Friends," she said firmly. "Heno, and over there's Nedlam and Kul. We're trying to help."

Ralas laughed softly, more genuinely. "Of course you are. When they write your story, warrior-bard, they will have to invent some lover or sibling you couldn't save, to explain your eternal guilt."

"It's not guilt, it's duty," she told him, more sharply than she had intended. "It's the right thing to do."

"And why your duty?"

"Who else was there—*is* there?"

He shrugged his bony shoulders. "All the world, my warrior-bard, and yet here you are. What are you up to now? Looking for more demigods to kill?"

"I want to restore the Aethani."

"Of course you do."

"You could help. You..." Her voice faltered. "I've missed you, rhymer."

"It would have been kinder if you'd not found me," he said. "I'm not what I was." The next laugh was forced. "How will you, anyway? The Aethani, I mean."

"A clever man said there are artefacts that might... remake them, return them to what they were. Some of them, all of them, even just a few. We thought there was one here."

Ralas was silent, frowning. "A crown-looking thing all over with gems?"

Celestaine stared at him. "You saw it?"

"Your source was good, it was here. But some bastard came and took it. I know because he got me out of that damn cell to take a look at me, and then slammed me back in."

"What man? Who took it?"

"Well, he didn't take the time to introduce himself, and he was inconsiderate enough not to take his helm off. All I saw was that he was a big matey wearing Ilkand Temple robes and holding this precious fancy hat. He could have just left me to find my own way out, but no, he just slung me back in so hard he killed me again."

"Ilkand?"

Ralas shrugged again. "Every damn thing in the world goes through there eventually, isn't that what they say? Why not fancy hats?"

"That was the Kinslayer's crown, it's got about a half dozen top grade relics in it. It's the power to help the Aethani. It's probably the power to do a lot of worse things as well."

Ralas shrugged. "I wasn't really in a good place to argue the toss with him while he was killing me. What's the Ilkand Temple like these days?"

"Not sure." Ilkand had fallen to the Kinslayer a couple of times but never for long, what with the influx of fighters sailing in from north and east. The Temple itself had survived, but then it had been one of the fire-and-battle types that the Kinslayer had almost encouraged.

Ilkand, then. Which left one question. "Will you go there with us?"

"Your man there, he might not like that." Ralas cocked his head at Heno, who was still glowering. "Jealous type, is he?"

"I... we're not—" she stammered over the knee-jerk denial. "How did you—? It's not..."

"I have been too dead too often to judge anyone," Ralas said exhaustedly. "I don't want to go anywhere for more heroics, warrior-bard. I want to die." And, at her appalled stare, "I do. I want to die, to just not-be. But the Kinslayer's probably the only one who could pull that off, and he's gone, and so here I am, not dying any time soon, or possibly forever. Gods, what a thought."

"I'll take care of you," Celestaine promised. "We'll... feed you up, put a poultice on..."

"You've not been listening to a word I've said, have you?" Ralas said, lowering himself back until he was lying full length in the dust. "I don't eat, and if I do, it doesn't stop me being hungry. I don't heal, any more than I would keep any new bruises your Yogg friend might give me. This is me, the way I was when the Kinslayer had me killed, forever and forever. But yes, warrior-bard, I'll go with you. I don't have any engagements for the foreseeable future. I may as well make myself useful."

"WELL, I RECKON we can hitch up the sheep-cart and get to Ilkand way before them," Fisher suggested, stretching. "They'll be stuck on the river again, most likely."

Doctor Catt made an indeterminate noise. "You know, if I hadn't actually been *watching*, I'd think we were the victims of some manner of circumlocution."

Fisher gave him a blank stare. "What now?"

"You know, that they'd already located the crown and were staging this mummery for our benefit," Catt explained. He let himself down from the wall top and took up his walking stick, striking a rakish pose. "Some priest from the Ilkin vengeance-mongers slips past all that mob of villains without an altercation, discovers this poor Ralas character but abandons him and makes off with the crown?"

"Kills him," Fisher pointed out. "Just wearing the vestments doesn't make you a good priest."

"In my humble opinion, *none* of the Ilkin Temple are particularly benign examples of the clergy," Catt said primly.

At his expectant stare, Fisher sighed and shouldered his pack. "So, we're not going to just hotfoot it and beat them there."

"Oh, I think we'll continue to play the shadow to the Lady

Celestaine's lamp for a while. I confess myself suspicious of some manner of subterfuge; to wit, it may be a trap."

"It's always a trap," Fisher grumbled. "Besides, they don't like us in Ilkand. Not at the Temple end, anyway."

"A matter of supreme indifference to me," Catt said airily. "I have some insurance, on that front."

"Don't try and sell them any relics," Fisher warned. "Priests never appreciate it."

"You sure you don't want to stick around?" Thukrah asked. "You, I can use. Your strong-woman here, use her as well, and your arrow-boy. Not sold on the Slacker but I'll take him as part of the bargain."

"Use me as propaganda against the loyalists?" Celestaine asked acidly. They were in Thukrah's study again, reclining and sharing a bottle of gleaming red that probably came from one of the vineyards of the Lucevien, now just ash and salt.

Thukrah toasted her with the outsize wooden mug he was swigging the wine from. "Yes," he agreed. "Show them the hands that killed the Reck—the Kinslayer, sure enough. More of those no-goods come over to me without a fight. Saving lives and limbs, hrm?"

"I need to go to Ilkand and see what can be salvaged of all this." She shook her head, disgusted. "One little clue, and if our man just stole a habit because he liked the look, then we're at a dead end."

"Ilkand," Thukrah rumbled. "Not so good of a place."

Celestaine frowned at him. "City of a hundred open doors, so they say."

"They shut a whole load of them because of us, not opened since. I sent there, offering strong backs, strong arms. They sent back a hammer. You know what that means, to Temple Ilkand? Means they want to come and hit me in the face about now, but they got more pressing matters. Your two, her and the Slacker, they'll not get much of a welcome there."

"So, let me guess, I should leave them with you?"

The general shrugged. "Can if you want. Don't have to. I'm just saying,"

"I'll leave them outside the gates when we get there," Celestaine decided, despite the little voice that said, *Didn't work so well in Bladno or Cinquetann.*

"North of the wall, some Arvennir bunch, call themselves the Foxglove Order," Thukrah told her. "We sell them iron, they trade it to Ilkand. Ilkin don't ask questions so long as it doesn't have our dirty hands on it. I show you to them, they get you to Ilkand."

"That's good of you, general."

He shrugged, waving an arm expansively and lashing a long chain of wine up the wall. "You did good for me, and you got nothing but that walking corpse out of it."

She sipped at the wine. They said you could taste the ash, that the Kinslayer destroyed the vineyards so thoroughly it tainted even their previous vintages. "General, what will you do, when you've got all the Yorughan here under your hand?"

"Will I go all fire and sword on you people, that what you mean?" Thukrah gave her his most charming smile. "Not the plan. Plan is we live, we bring up family, raise brats, trade, see the sun every day and the moon every night." His look put her on the spot and demanded honesty. "You think they'll let that happen?"

"I'm sure they will." She hoped she sounded more convincing to him than herself.

THE FOXGOVE ORDER were a pragmatic enough lot, and Celestaine watched them carefully unpacking Thukrah's iron and re-crating it with Arvennir stamps so that nobody had to ask where it came from. The general's assessment of the current Ilkin regime plainly had some substance behind it. Taking two Yorughan to the gates of Ilkand was going to cause some sort of diplomatic issue, but they were happy enough to drop their guests off within sight of the famous sea-wall and ask no further questions.

They rode north by cart to a Yorughan-built fort that had once served the Kinslayer's forces as a staging post for their attacks on the seaport city, and thereafter by river on a Shelliac convoy, five boats carrying a dozen smaller parties as well as the Arvennir and Celestaine's band, and they were not the river's only traffic. Temple or not, Ilkand was plainly still a desirable destination.

"Trade, some of it," the Arvennir constable said, "but talk, too. Our chapter Turcopolier is in Ilkand to talk, and the Lily and the Dogstooth have men there." He squinted down the line of boats as though trying to bring their destinations closer by sheer scrutiny. "The Frostclaw, the Ystachi, the Udrengasi, all sending chieftains to shout at each other, and some Tzarkoman grave-judge come over to rattle his bones at them. Sure to be some of your Forinthi clans. And all the rest, the mercenary companies who never got paid, the commune leaders who want to keep the land they ended up with, all of that."

"What have I missed, why all this?" Celestaine asked him carefully. Arvenhal was enough like Middle Kingdom speech that she could manage it, but there were always words that, for unknown reasons, were innocuous in one and vastly offensive in the other.

"War's over, did you miss that?" He grinned, a man who knows what his job is and doesn't need to worry about politics. "Everyone has an idea about what to do about it all—people where they're not supposed to be, not enough food here, not enough wood there. And Ilkand is easy to get to, so that's where they go to shout at each other about it."

"And the Temple?"

He shrugged. "Temple runs Ilkand. Who else? So they get to play host while their guests shout at each other."

"What about the Harbourmaster's Council... oh, no, they're gone." The third and last time the Kinslayer got troops inside the city, he had thrown the councillors to the sharks and hung the old Harbourmaster from his own sea wall, before being forced out again almost before the body had stopped swinging.

The Arvennir nodded philosophically. "Wouldn't want to be those priests, though," he added, but then rolled an eye at Celestaine. "Wouldn't want to be your Yoggs, either. Lots of raw war-wounds in Ilkand right now.

They got off the river before the convoy reached the walls, and trekked north until they came to the road and a shabby-looking inn. Celestaine knew the deal with inns this close to a city—who would ever stay at one unless they had good reason not to go inside? The rule was no questions asked, money up front and don't complain to the management if your possessions walked away in the middle of the night. Their fellow guests were a motley of maybe-merchants-maybe-criminals waiting for word or goods to reach them from Ilkand, plus a small band of skinny Grennishmen touting their services as tinkers. Celestaine paid out more money than she was happy with to get Heno and Nedlam ensconced in a room.

"The rest of us will go in and see if we can get access to the Temple, somehow. Ralas and I might just have a friend who can help."

"Roherich," the ragged bard supplied. "Do you think he's still there?"

"He always came back to Ilkand," she said determinedly. Roherich, the Lord of the Silver Tower, whose magic had held off a dozen Heart Takers while she and the rest took on the Kinslayer. Roherich the long-lived, whose melancholy eyes had seen the Kinslayer's first bloody arrival a century before, and who had walked through the worst reaches of the war when he came back. Not a man it was easy to call 'friend,' but he had never faltered in the fight, shown no weakness, admitted no pain. He could find the crown, perhaps; he could find some relief for Ralas. Maybe he could just heal the Aethani and they could let the whole Crown of the Kinslayer business go hang. What couldn't such a man achieve, now the Kinslayer was done?

She said nothing of the uneasy thought that perhaps Roherich held the Kinslayer's Crown even now, and had plans for it that would conflict with her own.

CHAPTER THIRTEEN

ILKAND HAD ALWAYS been a melting pot. Celestaine had fond memories of entering Low Ilkand by this very gate, hearing greetings, threats and offers of wares in four languages and twenty accents. The sea breeze blowing in chill off the water, the creak of rigging and the grinding of cranes from the docks, the mingled scents of a hundred different dishes from all over the world. Up above, Temple Ilkand still loomed over the harbour like a parent, but she had always felt like the parent was on the point of reining in its rebellious child, never quite acting. Now the parent was midway through delivering a slap, or that was the sense she had of it.

Of course, Temple Ilkand wasn't just the Temple itself. Up on the bluff were all the offices of government from which the late Harbourmaster and his wealthy fellows had administrated the port's unbounded trade. Up there, as well, was the slender gleaming needle of the Silver Tower, the unchallenged domain of the magician Roherich, fellow Slayer, ally and hopefully still friend.

"He'll know what's what," Celestaine said.

Ralas gave another of his loose shrugs. "Better you ask than me. He never could stand to listen to me. And that says something about the man. The *Kinslayer* wanted to hear me

again, when I was gone. Roherich would have left me to rot."
He considered that. "So I prefer Roherich, in the end, but I
don't like him."

Celestaine shrugged. Roherich hadn't *liked* anyone, she
thought. Not that he was hostile in any way, just that part of
his mind that connected with other living things had withered
and died, along with various other mental facilities he had been
born with, while the rest of him had stretched out over the years,
fuelled by his researches. He had come to fight the Kinslayer out
of an intellectual duty and because his own work was under
threat. He had expended decades of stored power, given sage
advice, bloodied his hands and suffered wounds and losses, but
there had always been a distance between him and the world.

And Ralas's music had repelled him, that much was true. It
had reminded him too much of his missing parts.

They saw three fights before they got five streets into Low
Ilkand, which wouldn't have been out of place in the old days;
but these weren't just drunken brawls. In each case, she could
see tribe against tribe, nation against nation. The angry words
were not just threats but accusations—who had failed to come
to whose aid, who had hoarded, who had collaborated. Blood
was shed two times of three, and one cocky Arvennir ended
up losing an arm to a howling mad Frostclaw's blade, but the
arrival of the Templars killed off each brawl, just by the sight of
them. Whether they were genuinely the select martial servants
of the Temple, Celestaine wasn't sure, but they had the shield-
mark on their surcoats and they turned up mob-handed and
ready to cudgel anything that didn't give way. She didn't feel
like asking them for an escort up to Temple Ilkand.

That reticence left her and Ralas outside the huge stone portal
of Temple Gate, the chief thoroughfare to the higher city, which
was pointedly shut. It had been ripped from its hinges by the
Kinslayer's monsters in the second siege, she'd heard, but of
all the broken things in the world, this had apparently been a

priority to restore, and now it loured over the crowd in Gate Market Square with its stern images of armed Guardians ready to defend the Right from the Wrong. Being in Low Ilkand and looking up at that gate certainly made people feel that they were amongst the Wrong.

Ralas jabbed a finger upwards to draw her eye. The lifts were still working, or had been repaired as well—wooden platforms worked by pulleys and wheels, which ferried goods and guests up to the Harbourmaster's High Dock. Celestaine had never had to ride one, but then Temple Gate had always been open before.

It looked as though a lot of people had business in Temple Ilkand, and few of them were having much joy of it. Most of the crowd there had obviously already been rebuffed by the Templars controlling the lifts, and only goods seemed to be going up, rather than people. Presumably the various ambassadors and dignitaries were already housed up above, and Ilkand's current regime didn't want to deal with the mass of refugees, agitators and supporters seething about the city below.

She looked speculatively at Ralas. He was cleaner than when they'd pulled him out of the hole, and wearing some ill-fitting clothes they'd bartered from the Arvennir, but he hadn't lied: he was just as much of a battered starveling as before, and even his long hair and beard regrew any lost inches the moment the scissors stopped their work. The one thing that changed about him was how cripplingly tired he looked. She herself cut a slightly more presentable figure, but still little more than 'itinerant Forinthi mercenary,' all told.

"You think they'd let us up for a song?" he asked her drily.

"No. I think we lead with our names." She smiled at his blank look. "Say it with me, Ralas: 'Don't you know who I am?'"

IN NO MORE than half an hour they were watching one Governor Adondra glare down an Udrengasi seer and a blue-scaled

Ystachi Dragon Speaker as each tried to accuse the other of crimes going back three generations, backed by groups of glowering, muttering followers. Everyone was talking in the local Kandir, which Celestaine knew well, but her city Kandir and the barbarously accented speech of the ambassadors seemed worlds apart. The seed of the dispute, as far as Celestaine could understand it, was that the armies of the Kinslayer had, while sweeping like a tide across the Udrengasi lake-cantrevs, looted the tombs of various fathers and forefathers, which loot had then met a high tide mark in the Ystachi's mountains, where some of it had beached. The Udrengasi wanted it back; the Ystachi, whose own sacred glades and hatcheries had been burned, claimed it as spoils of war. Adondra argued doggedly with both sides, chipping away a compromise by apparently seeking the exact point where everyone was equally dissatisfied with what they were getting. She didn't even glance at her new guests, giving everything she had over to bludgeoning the ambassadors with words until they bent. At the last, she took a hammer from her belt—perhaps it was a ceremonial tool, but it looked entirely capable of smashing skulls—and lamped it against a pillar, silencing everyone with the high, clear ring of steel.

At the sound, another man stepped forwards, squat and bald, pauldrons and breastplate gleaming bright over his white robe. The plate bore the Temple's emblem boldly: a shield, half plain for strength of faith, half cut into a brickwork pattern for strength of body, and as a reminder of one of the Temple's most notable Guardians of the older days. Everyone took a step back from him: seer, Dragon Speaker and Governor. There was a moment when the priest might have said anything, but then he nodded somewhat curtly to Adondra and said, "You have brought your grievance here and the Governor has given her verdict. Be bound by it, or be divided by blood, and seek no sanctuary in Ilkand, nor trade. How much do your people crave war?" From his tone he wouldn't have lamented a bit of bloodshed there and then.

"Same bloody Ilkin Temple," Celestaine whispered to Ralas and he nodded glumly. Unlike the mild priests of the Gracious One in Cinquetann Riverport—or, at least, unlike their mild selves before the war—the Templars of Ilkand had brought religion home with the stroke of a warhammer. Founded under the gaze of a knot of warlike Guardians and devoted to the god known as the Just Watcher, Celestaine had never got on with them. Not evil, but excessively rigid, in her opinion; unwilling to overlook the slightest infraction, unwilling to let circumstances cloud the sharp edges of their codes and laws. Back before the war, they had been a loud voice in Ilkand, but not an overwhelming one; far too many other factions and interests had tugged and pried at the Seaport's reins of power, and the Harbourmaster had been venal enough to blunt their pious demands. Now it seemed as though they were shouting louder than everyone else combined.

The Udrengasi and Ystachi representatives hesitated, briefly united in their dislike of the Templar.

"I wish the judgment of the Silver Tower," the Dragon Speaker spat, the blue scales of his otherwise human face twisting. "Let the Mage-Lord speak on this, as he used to."

Celestaine pricked her ears up.

"Archmage Roherich has closed his doors to all petitioners," Adondra stated frostily. "Even now he watches the forces of the enemy that still threaten our security and peace. Will you drag him from that vigil for such squabbles as these? And will the others, that great line of plaintiffs who stand each day to bring their grievances before the will of Ilkand? No, you will not. As the Archimandrite says, be bound by my words, or spend a generation cutting each other's throats."

"There is no middle way," the priest declared, in a tone that suggested there never was.

The moment balanced on a knife edge, but then the two of them were agreeing with poor grace, swearing on the Ttemple and on the Just Watcher to bind their respective peoples. Celestaine wondered if the oath would last. After all, the Just Watcher had been as silent as all the other gods since the Kinslayer emerged.

"Thank you, Archimandrite," the Governor said stiffly. "Your assistance is, as ever, invaluable. Now, what's the next business?" She looked around and a clerk hurried up, pointing at the two newcomers. Even at that distance Celestaine saw her eyes narrow. *That's not a good sign.*

She was an imposing woman, Adondra. Not tall, but solidly built, her reddish hair cut short enough to show the shape of her skull, making her strong jaw even more pronounced. Glowing runes curved beneath each eye, a magical affectation of the Ilkin rich. Possibly it gave her insight into the hearts of those she dealt with, or perhaps it just gave them the jitters. She wore a simple dark coat, cut to recall the Templar vestments, with a white scarf-like tippet slung over it, tucked into her belt. A little pewter Temple shield pinned over her left breast completed the image of someone who knew exactly what organisation held the shoving power in Ilkand today. The hammer in her belt looked, as Celestaine had noted, entirely functional. Most likely it had seen its share of enemy skulls when the fighting had washed through the streets of the city.

"Well. Such an honour," she said, every ounce of her tone contradicting the words. "Celestaine the Slayer and... Ralas. You're a Slayer too?"

"Something of the opposite," said the bard.

"Well, famous foes of the Kinslayer nonetheless," Adondra sad acidly. Then, to the clerk, "Please tell the remaining petitioners that I shall be closeted with these great dignitaries for some time, listening to their tales of their own deeds and importance."

"Look—" started Celestaine, but the woman silenced her with a mismatched stare.

"Oh, no," she said. "You came here swinging your names like maces, so you get what you asked for." And then she was marching off, and it was either follow her or stay under the bristling countenance of the Templar.

Adondra fell back to a small room mostly containing a desk, which she sat at, and no other chairs whatsoever. The walls were papered with lists and documents, accounts and reckonings— Celestaine had seen quartermasters keep similar records, and she suddenly had an image of Adondra as a company book-keeper during the war, constantly fending off starvation, finding the wherewithal to replace broken swords and armour and to pay mutinous soldiers. And now here she was, endeavouring to walk the same tightrope for a whole city.

"Ilkand can't be short of supply, surely?" she wondered, only realising late that she was speaking aloud. "It's the biggest port on the northern coast."

Adondra looked at her sourly. "The Slayer has spoken. Obviously I, with all my careful calculations, am doing something wrong. Although perhaps you haven't taken into account the literal thousands of the displaced who are thronging our streets right now, all of them victims of the war, not a malicious bone in them, except anyone will start fires and break doors if they get hungry enough, if they get cold enough. And the Temple will hand out its precious largesse only to those it deems 'worthy,' which means those who already have work and wealth enough to appear respectable, not those who have nothing and need it the most. So yes, I have a hundred plates spinning across the city, each of which requires my constant attention, not to mention the arguments, like that little spat you witnessed. And tomorrow's watch patrols will tell me if my compromise has stuck or whether we've got a dozen dead Ugrengasi and Ystachi lying about the place as the first shots of a new street war. But no, of course, let me listen to the words of heroes."

She turned pointedly to the papers on her desk, but stopped when Celestaine asked evenly, "Are we to blame for any of that? It seems to me that you could have heard us out and given us what we want in the time you spent making that speech."

"*Diplomacy!*" Ralas coughed into his sleeve, but Celestaine ignored him.

"We had your friend Garenan here ten days ago. He came waving his name about too. 'Garenan the Bold,' he was calling himself."

"My condolences." Of all the Slayers, Garenan had been most prone to blowing his own trumpet. There were a dozen songs out there outlining his achievements, prowess and potency, and he had paid bards to write each and every one of them.

Adondra raised an eyebrow. "I thought you hero types stuck together."

"Do you see him here with me?"

"And you're not here like he was, to 'save the city' by becoming its de facto tyrant on the back of a lot of gullible people who thought he was their saviour?"

"Gods alive," Celestaine swore. "What happened?"

"I managed to persuade the Temple that just running him out of town was enough. They wanted to execute him. And I got enough stick from them about it that, if they want to light you on fire, I won't put you out. Things have got worse since then, and the Templars are done with being lenient."

Celestaine exchanged a look with Ralas. *Not the Ilkand we remember, for sure. And what do we ask for now?* She didn't fancy telling the Temple that she knew they'd got the Kinslayer's Crown and would they just hand it over? "We haven't come here to be the new Harbourmaster, believe me," she said. "I mean, I can see just how coveted that role must be." At Adondra's grudging nod, she went on. "I'd like to see the Temple now. Not for a handout, but… well, they'd welcome a Slayer, show her round, wouldn't they?"

"Not if you don't wear their colours." Adondra shook her head. "I need the Temple. Nobody else has the fear and respect to keep order, right now, and they have a lot of people, plenty of recruits who sign up for the regular meals and the moral certainty. But they're waiting for a word from the Just Watcher. They believe they have a purpose, that the world has a shape it needs to be in. And when you carry a hammer, everything looks like it needs a few knocks to put it right. You want to go join all the petitioners outside Temple Gate, be my guest. You want to see the Inner Temple, you'd better start studying scripture, because I understand there's a written exam for the priesthood."

"I'll take it up with the… Archimandrake," Celestaine tried awkwardly, because ranks of the Templar hierarchy was probably also required reading. "But what about Roherich?"

Adondra's face closed. "No."

"Look, Garenan was never a friend of mine, but Roherich was. As much as he had friends. We went through a lot together. I have a standing invitation to the Silver Tower."

"Not any more," the Governor said flatly. "I don't care how many times you saved each other's lives and shared fermented blood and milk by the fire or whatever it is you Slayers do. He said nobody, not anybody, is to disturb him. And his name carries as much weight as the Temple these days. He's the great hero, in this part of the world. What he says, goes."

"At least let him know I'm here," Celestaine insisted.

Adondra shrugged, "If I get the chance. Now, you'll excuse me, but I have the needy to feed and house and clothe, and a thousand godsdamned factions who want to set fire to each other and every street in the city."

*　*　*

SOON AFTER THAT they found themselves outside the Temple Gate again, ejected from the Harbourmaster's officers like a vagrant from an expensive shop. Celestaine scowled upwards. She could just see the apex of the Silver Tower if she really craned her neck; probably, Roherich was up there laughing down at her. Or not laughing, because that would be rather more demonstrative than he was wont to me. Smiling distantly with one arched eyebrow, that way he did. Utterly maddening.

"Huff," she said, abruptly exhausted by sheer frustration, and sat with her back to the gate—she wasn't the only one, either. A rank of the tired and travel-worn were slumped around her, who had come so far into Ilkand and no further. Ralas folded down beside her, his starved limbs making him look like a dead spider.

"What good are we?" Celestaine asked him.

Ralas looked around, to take in any number of penitents, petitioners and vagrants. "Who now?"

"Slayers." She spat the word. "Do you remember how it was, back when we were united? One purpose, one vision, storming through the world to bring the Kinslayer to justice. We were all sorts, nothing in common except we'd become the champions of our people, the defenders of the weak, those who dared. Even back at the start, when you couldn't get news without a list of battles lost and towns taken, we were the ones who held the line the longest, in our way. Even me. Even Garenan, for all he was a self-glorifying weasel, he held the damn line. He made people stand up and fight for their homes and families. Even Lathenry, though he used to drink himself half to death every night. Even Pelevar the murderer, even *you*."

"Why, thank you." Ralas lent back on his spindly elbows. "I always viewed myself as simply putting a few sounds to the rest of your actions."

"Even Roherich." She stared up at the tower. "And the moment the Kinslayer died, I felt that bond break. It was all we had keeping us together, and you know what? I regret it. For that thing only, for the most selfish of reasons, I regret we killed him. We fought and we hurt and some of us died, but I *enjoyed* it. I enjoyed being a hero. I knew I was doing the right thing. I knew I was alive. And now he's dead and we're... lost. It's like the world expected us to die with him, and doesn't know what to do with us."

"Preaching to the choir here," Ralas agreed bitterly.

A new voice broke it. "It was ever so." The old man beside Celestaine gave her a grave look. He was a ragged creature, the cast-off from some distant village, no doubt just ash and bones now. He gave her a grin made more of gaps than teeth and nodded at the gate behind her, encouraging her to scoot back from it until she could appreciate the huge carven figures that dominated its face.

"You think they didn't feel the same way?" the old timer croaked. "When they'd driven the Kinslayer into the earth, that first time, over the body of their fallen brother?"

The Ilkand Temple had a prestigious heritage as far as Guardians went, and their founding fathers were set out in idealised images upon its gates. Of the five, two were gone entirely beyond, and none of the others had come out of the war with particularly glowing reputations.

"What, then?" Celestaine got slowly to her feet, wondering whether the outburst she could feel brewing in her would get her set on fire by the Templars. "The Custodian, I see there." The leftmost figure, bearing a staff and with tears chiselled into his stone face. "Can't really throw much mud that way. He wasn't to know he would get his heart ripped out and eaten to give the Kinslayer power and a new name. And Vigilant, there," she nodded to the rightmost, bearing a torch and a bow. "He got nailed to these gates by the Kinslayer the first time Ilkand fell, so he tried. Fury, first amongst the hunters after the Custodian's death." Next to the Vigilant, a bestial creature, part man, part dog, with crooked clawed hands. "But he'd not been seen for decades before the Kinslayer came back. And Wall," the huge central figure, armoured from head to toe and bearing a massive hammer. "He holed up in the north with some other fanatics, promising that he would come save us all when the time was right. Only the time was never right and we saved ourselves. And last of all." She nodded at the final icon between Wall and the Custodian, carved to seem like a Forinthi hero of old, all swept cloak and sword and long hair. "Last, and absolutely least, is you, Deffo, because I am not fooled. I am not fooled at all, no matter how few teeth you've given yourself."

The old man leapt up, face a picture of outrage at being uncovered. "You wretched ingrate," the Undefeated spat through his ravaged gums. "Your life is so great now that you'd pass up the help of the divine?"

Celestaine just stared at him, shaking her head slightly. "You had your chance," she told him. "Every moment of the war, you had your chance. Just go away. I won't make you *that* again." She nodded at the imposing carving. "If you ever were."

"Ralas," the Undefeated hissed, looking the ragged bard up and down. "You know me. I can help you, I can lift you up again, make people love you like they used to. Just drop my name into your songs, remind them of me. I raised my hand against the Kinslayer all those years ago. I avenged my brother's death at his hand. Is that not worth something?"

"You had people sing your songs back then," Ralas observed, not unkindly. "The way I look at it, you used up your credit and did precious little since to earn any more. Come on, Celest, let's go find somewhere that serves beer. I've missed beer."

The Undefeated watched them go. Celestaine thought his ragged beggar's look suited him far more than the sagacious old patriarch from the Skull Cap.

"Back to the others, then?" Ralas prompted. "Tell them the bad news?"

"No," she told him. "Not a chance. I am going into the Silver Tower, Ralas. I don't care what Roherich wants, or what he told the priest and the Governor or anyone. I am going to ask him about the crown, and I won't take no for an answer."

CHAPTER FOURTEEN

YORUGHAN DID NOT take well to inaction. Any field commander knew that if his indomitable warriors were going to be sitting on their hands for any length of time then they would need some diversionary raiding or a few competitive games to stop them making trouble. Nedlam, always first amongst the troublemakers, was not happy. She would sit on the creaking bed and grumble to herself for five minutes at a time, and then get up and prowl the confines of her room, kicking at the walls and furniture. So far nobody had braved the stairs to find out what damage she had done, but at some point a fear of ruin would overcome the landlord's common sense and then there would be trouble.

Heno, who was temperamentally more suited to patience, watched her with open amusement. "How did you ever end up on prisoner detail?" he asked her in their tongue. "Interrogation's such a subtle art."

"Not the way I do it," she shot back. "I think the Reckoner's own staff was about the only place left to send me by then. Been in everyone's army, me. I'm too much for them. They can't handle this much Nedlam."

"Surprised they didn't just make an example of you."

"Was too good for them," she replied in Middle Kingdom human, "You don't go killing off the woman who breaks the line and wins the fight." She thumped at her chest. "Just give her a pat on the head and a better job." She nodded to Amkulyah. "And we speak so he can understand, or he's going to think we're up to something."

"Chance would be a fine thing," Heno declared, managing the words rather better. "Did you fight, little bird man?"

Amkulyah stared at him flatly. "You know I was in the mines."

"Would you have fought?" Heno swaggered over, looking down on the little Aethani.

"You think only Yoggs can fight, don't you?"

"And C'lest," Nedlam put in, dropping back to the bed with an agonised sound of splintering wood. "Oh, Heno?"

"What?"

"Lay off."

The Heart Taker frowned at her. "*Orama hus*," he said. *Just talking.*

"Lay off." Nedlam stayed sitting, but something in her poise spoke elaborately of how small a room it was, if she chose to go for him. "Kul's one of us, like C'lest. You like her, you live with him."

"What is it with you and the human anyway?" Amkulyah asked, seeming to shrug off both Heno's looming and Nedlam's defence.

"Between her and me," Heno told him, his frosty dignity somewhat sabotaged by Nedlam's clarification: "Lovers."

The Aethani's round eyes grew considerably rounder. "The Slayer Celestaine and…"

Heno's expression had lost its mockery. "And…?"

Kul cocked his head to one side. "I assume you don't tell every human you meet. There would be horror, I think." He blinked deliberately. "Disgust."

Heno's fists clenched and a few flickers of cold fire danced about his knuckles. "Remind me why we're helping your broken little people again."

"I don't know," Amkulyah admitted easily. "I watch you, Heno. Nothing in you says that you do anything for anyone except yourself. Or maybe her." His inflection pointed at the absent Celestaine, rather than Nedlam, who stood up suddenly.

"All right, you both lay off."

"You don't need to stand up for me," Heno told her smoothly. "I'm perfectly—"

"Shut up or I'll belt you," Nedlam told him, and to Kul, "and you lay off too. I can't be doing with any of this. Heno is my friend. You are my friend. C'lest is my friend. Friends don't argue."

The enormity of this speech silenced the pair of them for several heartbeats, before Amkulyah finally asked, "Why is he your friend? And why am I your friend? You barely know me. Your people—"

"Did many things," Heno broke in. "Many things at the behest of the Kinslayer. Terrible things. And so we atone." He sounded anything but penitent. "And when the Kinslayer fell, Celestaine, of all the Slayers, looked on us and did more than just not murder us where we stood for the crime of being Yoggs, for the blood the Kinslayer had painted our hands with. And so she is a friend, yes. And more than a friend, now, but we were giddy with victory, and one thing led to another." He said the words like the least giddy person in history.

"And another and another," Nedlam put in cheerily. "Now, we're friends, right." And, in answer to Kul's almost pleading expression. "I like you. You can shoot someone in the eye in the middle of a fight in the dark."

"But... that's not enough," Amkulyah said weakly.

"Enough for me," Nedlam said firmly, and then frowned. "And now I smell ora root."

Heno perked up. "What?"

Ned went over to the window and pushed open the shutters a bit, taking a deep sniff. "Cart down there, all sorts of ora root."

"Nonsense, the humans don't take ora," Heno said slowly. "It makes them crazy, makes them see things."

Nedlam shrugged. "Nose doesn't lie." She made a sad face around her tusks. "Piss, I really want some now. Been ages."

"What's ora?" Kul asked cautiously.

"About the only good stuff we ever got down below," Nedlam explained wistfully. A string of saliva worked its way down her chin. She inhaled again and shook her head. "No good, I'm going down to get some off them."

"Ned, no!" Heno got in the way of the door. "They see you bearing down on them, they'll think the war's on."

"Don't care," Nedlam decided. "I want ora, and they've got ora. Doesn't have to be complicated."

"Let me go," Amkulyah suggested. "I'll get some for you. I even have money."

The two Yorughan exchanged glances, and Ned nodded eagerly. "I said you were a friend."

Kul grimaced, but slipped past Heno and out of the door.

DOCTOR CATT WAS leaning out of his own windowframe in his shirtsleeves, not scenting the ora but just enjoying the breeze. Behind him, Fisher was darning Catt's socks on the bed with the expression of someone intending to use them as a murder weapon.

"You're only going to throw them out," he muttered.

"But until we return to Cinquetann I will be inconvenienced by a paucity of footwear," Catt replied over his shoulder. "And so it's terribly kind of you to perform the necessary."

"Better than listening to you complaining about it." Fisher muttered. "Just go into Ilkand after her, already. Let her find the cursed thing and then take it."

"But why, when I have a hero to take it for me, and not just point the way like a bloodhound?" Fisher asked him. "After all, we know she'll come back here to her companions, one of whom I note is making his exit."

"Oh?"

"The Aethani. Possibly, from all the beating about, sharing a room with the Yorughan was taking its toll."

Fisher threw a balled-up sock at him, bouncing it neatly from the back of Catt's greying head. "Done. What's the boy-prince about, then?"

"Talking to some caravaneers." Catt dipped into his pocket and produced a small brass horn inscribed with faintly glowing sigils, which he applied to his ear. "Let's see now. Oh, he's enquiring about... oh dear."

"Oh dear what?"

"He's asking for ora."

"The thing the Yoggs chew? Banned here, isn't it?"

"A prescribed substance just about everywhere, as some of our legal clients had cause to discover," Catt agreed philosophically. "On account of its rather unpredictable effects on the human physiology." He leant further out, seeing the rather shifty-looking caravan merchants strenuously denying that they had any ora, while Amkulyah tried to give them money. "Oh, this may be problematic."

"Shroud up," Fisher said suddenly, and acted on his own advice before Catt could question him, rendering the pair of them into nothing more than a faint shadow at the window. Moments later the inn courtyard below was filling with hard-looking men and women in white tabards bearing a halved shield. Most had hammers and some had crossbows, and they were seizing the merchants and slamming them to the ground, shouting at everyone to surrender. Amkulyah had skittered up the side of the covered wagon the moment they came in and was now crouched on the roof while they demanded he come down and give himself up. Catt saw his four crippled wing-limbs flex and clutch at the sky for an escape forever denied him.

"Oh, dear me," he said. "Well, if we're lucky…"

The explosion of Nedlam into the courtyard suggested that today was not going to be lucky for anyone. She didn't have her ironbound club with her, but she barely seemed to need it, standing head, shoulders and half a chest over most of the Templars and bellowing for them to get back.

There must have been a good twenty of them, with drawn weapons, but they did indeed get back, though only for a shocked second. A moment later it might as well have been the war, and they were descending on Nedlam with the plain intent of hammering her into the ground. She opened her jaws and whooped out the Yorughan battlecry, meeting their charge with her own and shouldering right into the middle of them, giving them no chance to get a good swing in without braining one of their own. Unarmed, she was just picking them up and throwing them into their fellows, kicking, punching and slapping.

Catt watched glumly. "This is just going to be a distraction for Celestaine, isn't it?" he observed.

The Templars were up for a scrap, certainly. More and more were jumping Nedlam, dragging at her arms and neck, striking at her hamstrings and groin. One of them got a solid hammerblow to her face, but most were just trying to overwhelm her, massed strength against strength. Catt moaned as Amkulyah began throwing stones, cracking them across Templar temples or breaking noses.

"Aren't we short a Yogg?" Fisher muttered, just as Heno appeared in the inn doorway, wreathed in white fire.

"Oh, dear me," Catt whispered.

The Templars had Nedlam down by then, at least ten of them straining to hold her while an eleventh had eschewed her hammer for a knife, poised over the Yorughan warrior's throat. Now everyone stopped, staring at Heno the Heart Taker with his staff upraised, about to bring excruciating agony to everyone present. A crossbow bolt skipped towards him and exploded when it met the flames dancing from his skin.

"Enough!" he bellowed, and Catt saw him take a deep breath, gathering himself. "We are not the enemy. We are companions of the Slayer Celestaine. Wait!" This last as the knife drew back to stab again. Heno tried for a reassuring expression, with debatable success. "This is clearly a misunderstanding. Shall we go with you to your city to find our companions and explain everything?" His eyes were on the knifepoint, and it was plain that, if the weapon moved another inch, that fire was going to be off the leash. "Otherwise things will go badly for everybody."

If the lead Templar had been some fanatical veteran then 'badly for everyone' might well have been an understatement. But Catt identified their chief as a thin man, looking more like a book-keeper than a blood-letter, and standing prudently back from the scrum with a crossbow in the crook of his arm.

"You're surrendering yourselves?" he called, because everyone *knew* the Yorughan never surrendered.

"Quite willingly." Heno laid his staff down. "Aren't we, Ned?"

"No!"

"*Aren't* we?"

Nedlam growled and spat and fought a bit more to save face, but there were enough Templars to pin down even her. "You should have let them kill me, and then killed them."

"I..." Heno rubbed at his carved tusk. "I am trying to do things differently. I am trying to do things Celest's way. Just this once."

"*Ho u gash-la*," Nedlam spat, which Catt translated mentally as 'You'll regret it.'

"Probably," Heno agreed.

The Templars bundled all three of them off soon after, along with all the caravaneers who hadn't fled. Catt gave a heartfelt sigh. "I have my doubts about whether the Ilkand Temple will listen much to two Yorughan and an Aethani. In fact I think the former pair are going to get themselves executed publicly as a warning to… well, just as a general warning. I am rather disturbed by the way the Temple has gone."

"Can't be helped," Fisher decided. "I'll pack, shall I?"

"If you would, Fishy," Catt agreed.

"For home."

"For Ilkand," Catt clarified. "If we want this scheme to work out, I think we'll need to go change the Temple's mind for it."

"Catty, that's not going to work," Fisher pointed out.

"You forget," Doctor Catt told him brightly. "I have a secret weapon of particular use against religious fanatics. Go get out the relics, would you?"

THERE HAD BEEN human slave-miners at the Dorhambri as well as the Aethani. Amkulyah had many memories of fighting them: bigger than his people, stronger, more suited to the hard work, they had jostled for the meagre food every evening, forcing the weaker and the smaller to band together or to starve. Towards the war's end, humans had come to liberate the Dorhambri as their armies drove towards the Kinslayer's fortress at Nydarrow, and it had been a shock to look up at that robust, heavy-boned people and *not* see them as bullies and persecutors—Yorughan in miniature. Amkulyah was young—he barely remembered the old days when human merchants would petition respectfully for entrance to Aethan, bowing and scraping to the Vaned Throne for the right to peddle their wares in exchange for Aethani riches.

But he had tried to recast them as allies, and not just brutish rivals for too-little food. Right now it was hard not to snap right back to where he had been in the Dorhambri.

They had put him in a cell with a window so small he could barely have fit his arm through it, and barred even so. He had no idea where Nedlam and Heno were, and he greatly feared they would be faring worse than him. And yes, he had been full of hatred for Heno not so long before—the Heart Taker would never know just how he had burned with it—but the Aethani were mannered by nature, and surviving in the mines had ground into him the ability to turn his back, turn his head and endure any slight or provocation.

And now he feared for Heno, even so; he feared for Nedlam. Because there were humans all around them, humans who hated and feared the Yorughan just like he always had. They had run the mines, and they had cut away the wings of his people, and so he had loathed and despised them, but most of all he had feared them. And of course that fear had never become anything else, because the Yorughan and their fellow minions had always been the masters at Dorhambri. What would the Aethani have become, if they had a couple of Yoggs at their mercy? Merciful? He didn't think so. Nor would these humans be. Every second word from their mouths was 'justice' but what he heard was 'vengeance.' Amkulyah was good at reading human faces and his keen Aethani eyes noting all the little twitches and tics that spoke of the mind behind the muscles. These Templars were going to have a trial, they said, but they knew how it would go. And probably they would let Kul himself go, eventually, but by then it would be too late.

He went to the door and picked at the hatch. His nails were too blunt, but he strained the weakened sinews of his back until one of the sharp-edged flight-limbs flicked forwards and caught, agonisingly, in the seam, flexing and hissing in pain until he had slid the wood aside. Then he jumped and got his hands about the hatch edge, hanging there effortlessly, so much lighter than a human, yet almost as strong despite his size. He had heard no key, when they put him in here. Instead, there had been the solid *thunk* of a bar. These were short-term cells, he guessed; the Templars didn't keep live prisoners for very long.

Next time, perhaps, they would invest in a lock. Supporting himself with one hand he writhed the other through the hatch and felt for the bar, snagging it on the third go and levering it up. It was heavy, though, and he tried to balance it but felt it tip and slam to the stone flags of the floor with a sound like the end of the world.

Swiftly he had the door open and was scurrying off down the corridor, desperately hoping the Yorughan were nearby. The sound of the bar had been too much, though. He heard alarmed cries and running feet. Old instincts cried *Escape!* and he began running, looking for a window he might fit through, following the light like a moth. The sounds of pursuit grew more urgent, but that didn't matter now. He slipped through half-closed doorways, bolted past surprised humans. In his mind he was in the mines again, darting through the close tunnels, escaping another beating.

And there was a window; he vaulted up to the sill, ready to dive through.

The city of Ilkand Seaport was spread like a dirty, rucked-up sheet, but it was below, far below. He was up in Temple Ilkand, above the Gate, looking down on sharp-peaked roofs and the hard-flagged streets below. There was so much angry shouting behind him, though, and he thrust out his flight-limbs, instinct goading him to the act denied his people and alien to him. He leapt.

A hand caught his belt even as he did, hauling his thin body back within the prison of stone walls and ceilings. He tried to fight, but two humans had him, and he would break his own bones before he broke their grip.

"Just in time. Mad little tyke, isn't he? You sure you want him?" one of his captors asked.

Amkulyah stopped struggling and looked past them to a familiar face. "Doctor Catt?" For a moment he couldn't work out whether the Cheriveni was friend or foe. "What...?"

"Just a little voyage to hunt down something for our collection," Catt said in his avuncular way. "Fishy and I happened to see you and your fellows being paraded through the streets, and we rather thought we should do something. In this case, bail you out."

"The others!" Kul burst out. "The Yorughan, you've got them out too?"

"Ah, alas, sufficient largesse does not exist to pry them from the hands of the Ilkand Templars," Catt informed him solemnly. "I think we had better locate Celestaine and inform her of developments, don't you?"

CHAPTER FIFTEEN

CLOSE UP, THE Silver Tower didn't look that silver. The eye refused to focus on it, seeing instead a blur of rainbow colours like spilled grease. Up above were structures that could have been balconies and windows, though Celestaine suspected they were just for show. There were no doors, but she knew Roherich of old. The whole tower would be a door, under the right conditions.

"You think he knows we're here, then?" Ralas asked her, going to lean exhaustedly against the side of the tower and thinking better of it.

"I was counting on it," Celestaine said. "I thought he'd open up, if it was me. I mean, we got on, mostly. As much as he got on with anyone."

"Not saying much. So what's the fall-back plan?"

"Well, there's a question." Celestaine tugged at her chin thoughtfully. "There would be a phrase he would use, I'd think. If the tower responds to his voice, then we're screwed, but maybe it works for anyone. Open for Roherich! In the name of the Silver Mage!"

Nothing happened.

"Tulips," Ralas said, and then, at her look, "He liked tulips. He wore one in his hat."

"That once."

"More than once." Ralas squared his angular shoulders. "We're neither of us the wizard to guess wizarding things, and it'd be other wizards he'd most want to keep out. It has to be something down to earth. What else did he like. What would say 'home' to Roherich of the Cold Heart?"

"He always hated that," Celestaine said.

"It fit him."

"It didn't," she insisted, at least partly in case the magician was eavesdropping. "Just because he didn't show it doesn't mean he didn't care."

Ralas walked round the tower's circumference a little, in case a tradesman's entrance had appeared for the delivery of tulips. "I saw him at the field at Touremal, when we arrived late. That was the day the north was lost, you remember, the Kinslayer's armies at the gates of Ilkand the first time. They were *his* people, left for the crows on that battlefield. And he just walked through the bodies like they were... well, not even tulips. He *liked* tulips."

"I won't believe he didn't care," Celestaine insisted. "He found it hard to show it, that was all. He was different from most people, in his head, but he wouldn't have fought if he didn't care." She faced the tower again, knowing that whatever magical lock Roherich had put on it, she would never guess the key. "Roherich, I hope you can hear me. It's Celestaine. I need to speak with you. I'm still trying to help, Ro. Just like always. I know you've said you don't want to talk to anyone, but I need your help."

Overlapping with her last words, a voice chimed from the tower. "I recognise Celestaine of Fernreame and grant access." It sounded so much younger, so uncharacteristically cheery, that she barely knew it as Roherich.

Between blinks, a doorway opened in the shifting wall, showing the way to spiralling steps lit by a directionless argent light.

"He couldn't have put us at the top of the stairs," Ralas observed sourly.

Celestaine entered, with Ralas hard on her heels, and even then he sat down suddenly as the door became solid wall. Celestaine glanced at him and flinched to see he'd left a foot on the far side of the door, the stump of his ankle ending in a bloodness nub of bone. He didn't seem overly bothered.

"I've had worse. Literally." He stared at the amputation, and the flesh began to crawl and ooze, as though moulded by invisible, unskilled hands, until a new foot was kneaded into shape, grimy and dotted with raw patches of skin. One of the toes was missing, another folded back on itself. "It's the boot I'm going to miss," Ralas added sadly.

"Can you even walk on that?" Celestaine asked him, horrified.

"I've been walking on it all the way from Bleakmairn, haven't I?" he pointed out. "Always grows back the same, no matter what, remember?"

"But... then, it doesn't hurt?"

He gave her a frank look. "Of course it hurts. It all hurts, and I never get used to it. I'd love to say different just to make you feel better about it, but as a bard I'm sworn to be honest and true in all things, you know?" He gave her a weak smile and then slapped her hand away when she tried to help him up the stairs. "I can manage."

She never knew if that staircase represented anything other than Roherich's vanity. Perhaps there were notional doors off every turn, that they just didn't have permission to go through. Perhaps they just trudged up the same loop of steps sufficient times to appreciate what a great mage Roherich was, before he let them into his chambers. Either way, neither of them were feeling particularly charitable when the space above opened out, and they entered a suite of white-walled rooms too large to fit within the tower's visible confines.

"Welcome, Celestaine of Fernreame," that same happy voice said, Roherich the Younger speaking invisibly from thin air.

"What about me?" Ralas demanded, but apparently the magician had made no provision for him, nor would acknowledge his existence.

"Hello?" The chamber they had finally climbed to was windowless, but at some point Roherich had tried to make it seem homely. The rug on the floor came from some huge woolly animal she didn't recognise. The stone effigy of a batwinged demon looked like the sort of thing she'd have to fight to get through the next doorway. She recognised the black shield painted over with red daggers as a trophy Roherich had taken after one of their battles, when everyone else had been doing it and he hadn't wanted to be left out. There was a thick layer of dust over everything.

"Roherich!" she called. "Celestaine here. Come on out!" But he didn't, and nor did the young voice speak again.

The room beyond was his study, and just standing there started a churn of worry in Celestaine, because surely he wouldn't just let the pair of them saunter in. The stone demon stubbornly failed to come alive, though, and no curse flashed from the ceiling to incinerate them.

Roherich had lined this room with shelves, and just about everything he valued had to be there, neatly arranged by some arcane filing system of his own. There were books here, scrolls stacked in pigeonholes there, stones, figurines, racks of herbs now mostly gone to dust. And in the centre of the room was a portal.

It was formed from interleaved vines that had sprouted somehow from the lambent floor, climbed upwards unsupported and then met in a knot at the point. Within their curtilage was another place.

It was lush and overgrown, far more so than anywhere within miles of chill Ilkand. She didn't recognise any of the trees, and many of them seemed barely related to any plant of the world she knew, with great plate-like leaves of umber and purple and blue. The ground was rich with flowers, and if they were not precisely tulips, they were very close, in a riot of spring colours bright enough that Celestaine had to squint at them.

Roherich stood amongst the blooms, his back to his visitors, perhaps ten feet within the portal. She knew him: the gold headband binding back his long dark hair, his broad shoulders, the russet robe he always wore, that had not a hole or darn or stain to it, for all that he'd been wearing the same thing all the years she'd known him.

She called his name but nothing came of it. He was staring off into the forested shade of his otherworld. Perhaps her words could not fight clear of the portal to reach him.

Ralas had stepped cautiously round the outside of the vine arch and then stopped. After a moment he called for her to join him.

She did so, startled to find herself facing Roherich, again ten feet into the world beyond but from the front this time. His hands were clasped before him, the three red-stoned rings she remembered still on his fingers. His green eyes stared past or through her from his long face. She looked into them for a long time, but never felt that she had met his gaze.

Ralas waved tentatively, but there was no suggestion the movement was seen. He tried a shaky caper, part of the fool's routine he'd once used to supplement his singing in the early days. Still nothing; in fact, no motion at all from that verdant world. No wind touched the alien leaves, no bee circled the flowers.

The bard went and found a paperweight, some many-legged thing caught in amber, and made to lob it at the magician's chest, but Celestaine stopped him. There were tears pricking at the corners of her eyes.

"What?" Ralas asked her, mystified.

"Don't you see it?" she asked him, but he didn't. He hadn't known Roherich well enough, or else the message in the man's face was just for her. "He's gone, Ralas. He's gone away."

"I can see that. How do we make him come back?"

"We don't. We can't. Don't you see it?"

Ralas's eyes widened and he stared into the portal, at that eternal calm sad face.

"Oh," he said at last, understanding. It was no definite sign, nothing Celestaine could ever describe, but it was as if they had come in to find him hanging from the rafters. Magicians did not do things the same way as others, not even the manner of their self-chosen exit. Roherich had found a place to go, and left them all behind.

"Maybe it's just an image, a memorial," Ralas suggested. "Maybe he's having a high old time through there, fresh fields and pastures new."

"That's a nice thought," Celestaine said, hoping but not believing. Then she turned away from the frozen shadow of her old friend and called out, "And is anything still here that will talk to me? Come on, voice. We're here, we've found it." A sudden thought struck her. "It's a big secret, isn't it? It's what the Governor doesn't want anyone to know, that Ilkand's precious Silver Mage isn't just brooding in his tower."

"Governor Adondra is aware of my absence," Roherich the Younger's voice informed her. "Hello, Celestaine."

She flinched. "What am I talking with? It's not *you*, is it?"

"I am a figment only, a snakeskin of my creator, shed to watch over his tower and follow certain instructions. Including to admit you."

"Then tell me," and her voice shook, "is he still alive somewhere? Alive and happy?"

"I don't know," the figment told her. "But I don't think he is happy. I was never very good at being happy. I'm sorry, Celestaine. I didn't want him to go, but he could not live with the world any more. He—I—we saw so many years come and go, so many autumns strip the trees. He forgot how to connect to people, even to you, but he could never forget that he wanted to. He could never cut himself free so we could just be ourself. And in the end it was too much for me. I would have held on, if I could. For you."

The last two words fell into the silence between them. Celestaine was trembling. *Not what I came here for, but then I came here for easy answers, and when has that ever worked?* "Can you... can I see you?"

"I don't know." And the figment's voice was so maddeningly polite, no emotion behind it at all, but then that had always been the way with him; not that he hadn't felt, but that he hadn't known how to show it.

There was a shimmer in the room, like the air over a fire. For a moment she could almost convince herself she saw him there, alive, well, but it was her mind more than her eyes. There was nothing of substance to him.

"He doesn't know anything about the crown, though?" Ralas prompted her. "I ask you because it's obvious he's not interested in talking to me."

"The Kinslayer was making a crown," she explained. Taking refuge in duty, because it was easier that way. "We need it, to right a great wrong. The Aethani."

"I don't remember the Aethani," the figment said in a small voice. "But I feel the touch of magic beyond these walls. A great artefact was brought to the Temple recently, but it is gone now, I don't know where."

"The Temple," Celestaine acknowledged heavily. "Thank you." She had somehow known her path would take her to the new bully of Ilkand. And did they look on the crown and see, not an instrument of healing, but a rod of vengeance? And against whom, and where would that vengeance stop?

They went back down the stairs, despite Ralas's complaints,

and again the silvery doorway gaped for them, and nearly claimed another foot as it closed. The lost boot and its grisly contents had been taken from outside, to Ralas's incredulous disgust, and he was halfway through swearing to hunt down every one-legged man in Low Ilkand when Amkulyah practically sprang out at them.

"Celestaine! You need to go to the Temple!"

"I... know." She frowned at him. "What's going on? Where are the others?"

"At the Temple. They're going to burn them! I've been waiting here for you. Doctor Catt said you'd gone to the tower. You have to hurry!"

"Doctor Catt, what...? Burn them?" Celestaine goggled. "How did things go that wrong, that fast? Never mind. We go to the Temple, right now."

IT TURNED OUT that crashing into the Temple demanding to see the Archmandrill was not a recipe for success, but in Celestaine's defence it was an honest mistake and she couldn't remember the proper title. That entrance certainly got the three of them before both the bald, scowling priest and Governor Adondra, although as they were up at a high bench and Celestaine and company were decidedly below and under guard, the interview felt more like a trial than she was happy with.

Behind them was a single statue, the Guardian that the Ilkand Temple had always looked to, the Just Watcher's most trusted servant: Lord Wall, depicted as an armoured titan, ten feet from sabatons to the crown of his crested helm, holding a hammer Nedlam would never have been able to lift. Wall's devotion to the sort of justice that came at that hammer's end had sustained the Temple through the generations, especially after the Kinslayer's murder of his brother the Custodian. He had been foremost in the hunt that drove the enemy underground before leaving

Ilkand to patronise ever more fervent seekers of vengeance. Until the war came and he had wasted ten years planning a great resurgence that had never come. Where he was now, she had no idea. Even his presence in effigy was oppressive.

"You've arrested two of my companions," she accused.

Adondra waited for the Archimandrite to speak, but the priest was busy glowering and so she took up the slack. "You'd be referring to the two servants of the enemy who attacked a Templar squad at the Sign of the Marching Bear earlier today. Along, I note, with your Aethani confederate."

"*Prince* Amkulyah of Aethan," Celestaine said, leaning on the title for all the weight it would bear, "has explained to me that he was attacked by your people, and our companions came from the inn to aid him, seeing only an act of brigandage." The Forinthi had little patience for legal niceties, but Celestaine had seen how it was done in her day.

"His Most Royal Highness was engaged in purchasing contraband from smugglers at the time," Adondra stated. "So sorry to shoot that high horse you were climbing up."

"It doesn't matter what they've done," the Archimandrite said, not the fist-banging bellow she had expected, but just a no-nonsense statement. "They're Yoggs. They're the enemy. We'll burn them. Throw open the doors of the Temple to let people see. It'll remind them."

"They're not the enemy," Celestaine said. "They got us to the Kinslayer, to kill him. Without them, we'd still be fighting the war."

The Archimandrite looked as though he'd be quite happy to still be fighting the war. "Their hands are steeped in the blood of the innocent, as are all their kind. There is only one fate reserved for them. The dead demand vengeance."

"All right, listen to me," Celestaine tried, though she'd sworn she wouldn't. "I am Celestaine the Slayer. I cut the hand off the Kinslayer with a sword the Wanderer gave me. I bore him down and saw him destroyed as even the Guardians themselves could not do. I say these Yorughan are my friends and allies, and I will say it at every street corner, and rally an army to my banner if I need to. Or you will release my friends to me."

Adondra's face had hardened through her words, and she exchanged glances with the priest. "And you have been in the tower, of course," she mused. "I thought that he would leave loose threads, when he made his exit." She stared at Celestaine without love. "I have no use for live heroes, Celestaine the Slayer. I have no use for personality cults that will fracture my poor city further. There are enough gangs and sects and tribes and embassies trying to pull everything apart as it is. I don't need you cutting things loose with your magic sword."

"Then release them. They've done nothing."

"They don't need to *do* anything," the Archimandrite told her, almost pleading. "The Just Watcher demands vengeance against all who have done wrong. We must turn that wrath against the servants of the enemy, each and every one of them, or what are we? How can we expect Him to speak to us again, if we turn from His path?" To her surprise he seemed quite genuine, not the politician at all, but a man clinging to his faith with both hands.

"And so," Adondra said, and nodded, and abruptly all those Templars who had just been around to provide a bit of pomp and circumstance turned out to be far more hands-on than Celestaine had expected. She went for her sword-hilt, but they bundled her before she could draw and forced her to the ground. She heard the furious skirmish as Amkulyah leapt up on the bench and tried to get out past the priest and the Governor, and the audible snap of bone as a Templar landed on Ralas. His yell of pain was drowned out by her own furious shouting.

* * *

"ALLOW ME," SAID Doctor Catt, "to monopolise mere moments of your valuable time."

Adondra and the Archimandrite stared at him. Eventually the Governor said, "I'm assuming you're nor Hakrond Reavaxe here to talk about the lumber concession."

"Master Reavaxe was kind enough to delay his presence before Your Graces in return for certain remunerations, the details of which are confidential," the Cheriveni explained to them happily. "However, in his momentary absence, I present myself as Doctor Catt of Cinquetann Riverport, advocate, physician and scholar, at your service; and desirous, if it be in your power to grant, of a trifling favour."

"What is this?" the priest demanded, after wading through all those words. "Is this some manner of clown?"

"No indeed, but a very sagacious individual with a proposal for you, should you see your way to releasing certain ne'er-do-wells currently within your custody—"

"This is the Slayer woman and her zoo," Adondra broke in. "You're one of them, are you?"

"By no means, my noble Governor, and yet merely one who has some residual gratitude towards one who struck so creditable a blow against the erstwhile tyrant, to which end I would ask that you free them and allow them to carry on their heroics somewhere *outside* your city walls, and in return your Temple's fame shall be forever enriched."

"What is he talking about?" the Archimandrite demanded. "There is a lack of respect in your voice when you talk about the Temple, Cheriveni."

"Alas, it is my customary register on any topic, Your Holiness," Doctor Catt swept an elaborate bow for good measure. "But before my welcome is outstayed permit, me to remind you of the narrative of Cinnabran." Before their baffled looks could coalesce into a shout for the guards, he barrelled on. "As you may know, there once was a young woman of that name whose time upon this earth was centuries before the Kinslayer ever slew his kin. In that far-off time the gods spoke mostly to their servants the Guardians, such as the imposing Lord Wall who looms so magnificently behind you. Much was lost, alas, between the lips of the gods and the ears of mortals, try as the Guardians might to bridge the gap. But then came Cinnabran—"

"We know all this," the Archimandrite broke in. "What does this have to do with anything?"

"Cinnabran," Doctor Catt said lightly, as though he had only heard a polite "Go on." "She whom the gods loved. She whom They spoke to, the only mortal at whose feet the Guardians knelt. She who the Wanderer loved. She whose divine favour enraged the heart of the Kinslayer and set in motion so many terrible things. And yet, she was mortal, and all mortal things must die. But touched as she was by the divine, those things she left behind retain an echo of her nature. And so, I give you… the Skull of Cinnabran." With a conjurer's flourish he had reached into his robe, which surely had no space to contain anyone's skull, and yet a moment later it was in his hands. Just a yellowed, jawless cranium, but the Archimandrite stood suddenly, eyes almost popping from his head.

"It is the skull," he hissed.

"Doctor Catt is no purveyor of frauds," Catt agreed proudly. "Now, I would be delighted to donate this relic to the Temple, if only you might see your way to—"

Adondra had opened her mouth and perhaps she would have agreed, but the priest spat, "No!"

Catt paused, weighing up the relic in his hands. "I'm sorry, but that sounded as though you said—"

"You *dare* haggle with those things the gods have touched?" the Archimandrite cried, the veins standing out on his forehead. "You bring before us the mortal remains of one whom the gods loved and would use them in some seedy trade to free monsters and their allies from just vengeance?" He slammed his hammer down on the high bench, splintering the top. "Templars!"

"Ah, well this is most unfortunate and I really must be leaving." Doctor Catt pivoted on his heel but found his path to the door obscured by a pair of guards brandishing hammers of their own. "Ah," he noted wanly. "Violence."

"You are so very fond of our prisoners," the Archimandrite growled. "Perhaps the Governor will permit me to add you to their number."

Adondra looked as though matters had gone beyond comfort, but in the face of the priest's wrath she just nodded.

"Well, fortunate it is that I dressed this morning with Tenet's Warding Amulet!" Doctor Catt declared, a hand going to the broach at his throat. A moment later a sphere of purplish energy crackled into life about him, leaving him a hazy figure at its centre. "Now, as you'll observe," his muffled voice came from within, "I am herein proof against your buffets and malletings, and suggest you remove yourself from my path and consider in the future how you should treat an agent of commerce only seeking to enrich you."

The Archimandrite's expression did not falter. "To the cells with this desecrator," he ordered, and the Templars cautiously closed in.

SOON AFTER THAT, Celestaine watched as a pale, stumbling Doctor Catt was shoved into a next door cell.

"What happened?" she demanded of him. "Are they just rounding up anybody now?"

"Anybody who is a familiar of the Slayers, perhaps," came the shaky voice from the neighbouring door hatch. "Alas, I attempted to secure your release, and this is the reward I get for it." There followed a bout of retching, and the air curdled with the sour reek of vomit.

"I'm sorry." Celestaine was trying to work out how things could get worse, right now. Nedlam and Heno were in neighbouring cells, each secured with what looked like half a ton of chains. Amkulyah was across the corridor, sulking because all their doors had locks, rather than bars. "I need to talk to them again. I'll explain you weren't anything to do with us."

"I appreciate your post facto candour," Doctor Catt said. "Alas, I understand we are all to be burned as an example. I think the Ilkand Temple has a great deal of vengeance it feels it should be meting out and relatively few available targets, and so we have become something of a lightning rod for their ire. Ah, and here he is."

Because a new figure had slipped in, wearing a drab Cheriveni robe and a military cap askew on his head. Doctor Fisher regarded his colleague dourly.

"So this is where you ended up. I've been looking all over," he complained.

"Fishy, I've had a terrible time," Catt told him. "They *rolled* me. I put up Tenet's, and they just hit me with hammers and rolled me all about the room until I didn't know which way was up. I was so dreadfully ill you wouldn't credit it, and now apparently I'm to go on the fire with these reprobates. It's not been one of my best days, Fishy."

"Gods give me strength," Doctor Fisher said, unimpressed. "I have to sort this out, do I?"

"It may be beyond even your capabilities," Catt lamented.

Fisher looked sour. "Where's your faith?" he asked, and abstracted from his satchel a jawless skull.

"It won't work, Fishy, I've already tried that—and for that matter, where did you even recover it from? That bald ecclesiastical fellow took it from me."

"Explains why it was in his rooms, then," Fisher said pragmatically. He shook his head. "I'll sort something, though why I bother, I don't know." Two sidelong steps brought him to the hatch at Celestaine's door. "Heroes," he said dismissively. "Heroes and monsters. Woman, how do you end up friends of your enemies and enemies of your friends so much?"

Celestaine just stared at him, and he shrugged and sighed and shuffled off.

CHAPTER SIXTEEN

DON'T KNOW WHY I *bother*, could be Doctor Fisher's family motto. It wasn't as though he would get any great outpouring of gratitude from Doctor Catt if he was able to spring the man from prison, even if whisked him from the very flames. Catt's nimble mind only moved on to the next scheme. Hindsight was alien to him.

"And yet…" Fisher shook himself, thinking wistfully of his comfortable bed back in Cinquetann. "I should keep birds or something." Because then he would have to make a choice: save Doctor Catt from an incendiary death or go back and feed his birds, and surely the birds would give him the excuse to walk away. Instead of which he had to look after a Catt instead.

Once in sight of his destination, he got the skull out again and peered into its vacant sockets. No doubt of its provenance, to the trained eye. Relics of power could be made, like the very crown everyone was scrabbling over, but they could just happen, too. Cinnabran had been a wonder, not to be repeated, and Fisher tried to think what it had been about her that had drawn the eye of the actual gods. And where were They now, those gods? What had the Kinslayer done, to cut Them from Their precious mortals? His greatest and worst act, the one no amount of armies or vengeance or magic could undo.

"And what if They're dead, then, eh? What then?" Fisher asked the skull. He put it to his ear as one might a seashell, but answer came there none. Everyone said the Kinslayer had silenced the voices of the divine. The gods had very seldom spoken to mortals anyway, nor even to the Guardians as time had gone by. Certain prophecies, guidance in dreams to particularly devout priests, oracular pronouncements ringing in the temple air from carven lips, all that sort of thing. And some of the Guardians had still gone, from time to time, into that hard-to-find contemplative state where they felt the gods close and could be reassured that their path was just.

And other Guardians had given up even on that a long time ago, trusting to their own judgment and carving a place among the mortals. The Ilkand Temple itself was the result of just such an accommodation, five immortals deciding that they would set some ground rules for the rest. Others had travelled, like the Wanderer. Still more had found that self interest and pushing the divine message were not so very incompatible after all.

Cinnabran had been dead before the Kinslayer arose, of course. Probably even *he* would have kept his head down when she was around, chatting with the gods as though they were dolls at a child's imagined party. Infuriating, of course, to those agents sent down by the divine to guide mortals, to find a mortal who didn't need them, who presumed to tell *them* of the gods' wishes. And yet most of the Guardians had loved her in the end, or pretended to. And only the Reckoner had been unable to live with the implications of her existence. Her blessed presence had sown the seeds of treachery and war.

"Bet you didn't see that one coming," Fisher told the skull. Even in death, even with nothing but bone there, polished to a shine by the hands of a thousand hopefuls seeking her posthumous blessing, Cinnabran contrived to look smug. He was only glad her jaw had parted company with the rest of her, because he didn't think he could live with that grin.

"Right, now." And he stowed the skull again and looked up at the Silver Tower. It was time to pay a call on his old friend Roherich, if, by 'old friend' you meant distant and frequently antagonistic acquaintance.

There were Templars about the tower base now, after Celestaine's exploits, but by a combination of shrouding magic and soft shoes, Fisher stole past them. He might look like a lanky old man, but he and Catt had accumulated a surprising grab-bag of skills while indulging themselves as collectors of the strange. Still, hollering up at the tower-top was likely to draw the notice of even the Temple's least perceptive servants, and Roherich had obviously retained his aversion to just having a door like normal people.

"All right, you snooty bastard," Fisher whispered to the shimmering opalescence of the tower's exterior. "You know me, don't pretend you don't. Now let me in before I get persecuted."

If Roherich was listening, he obviously didn't think much of the request. The tower wall remained unpierced by any entrances. Fisher wondered if he could magically strongarm his way in, either by his own powers or with one of the trinkets he was carrying. The answer was probably 'no.' Roherich knew his stuff, all right.

"Listen, you owe me, from way back," he tried. Possibly it was true; they'd crossed paths quite a bit, given their combined years. Or possibly the scales were tilted the other way and Fisher had contrived to forget. He did that, on occasion, but in that case Roherich would certainly remember.

As no door had manifested, Fisher tried that tack. "Or maybe I'm here to settle up. I've got some goodies in the bag. Come on. A man could catch his death, out here. Bloody north coast."

Roherich, if he was even listening, remained obstinate, and Fisher bowed his head, aware he was about to make the ultimate sacrifice, something that went so deeply against his nature that he might as well be driving a knife into his own face.

"*Please*," he hissed. "All right? I am saying 'please,' this one time, like I always said I never would. But things are screwed all over and backwards right now, so *please* let me in."

A voice came to his ear, Roherich from earlier eons. "A condition has been fulfilled," it said to him, and then, "I am permitted to grant access."

At last the doorway, and Fisher regarded the stairs with the same look Ralas had not long before. Of course Roherich could just open a door to his private chambers, but the man valued his privacy and had no respect for old, old bones.

"Bastard," Doctor Fisher spat, setting off up the spiralling steps, his staff clacking on the not-quite-stone.

As he neared the top, infuriated by the wasted time and effort, he started shouting at his unseen host, "All right, very funny. You see what hospitality you get, you ever come and visit *me*. Spiders in the tea, *and* I'll let the toast get cold before I serve it. Though Catt'd say 'Who'd notice the change?' Oh, yes. Bloody unappreciated, me, always. You better be ready to listen, Roherich. More than your damn priests and bureaucrats." He was practically rolling up his sleeves for a fight, when he reached the top and marched into the magician's study. And then he saw the portal.

"You…" Fisher's voice trailed away as he came to the same understanding Celestaine had. "You… utter *turd*." He walked round the vine arch and stared into Roherich's final, eternal expression. "I needed you, you stretched-out fraud. Just this once. I said *please*."

"That condition has already been fulfilled," said the voice from the air.

"And what did he expect to happen next, now I've crawled here on my knees to beg?" Fisher demanded of it.

"I had forgotten that I had put such a challenge to you," Roherich the Younger said uncertainly. "I believe I forgot to remove the condition from the tower before I… before I…"

"Before you did," Fisher finished for it. He regarded the final resting place of Roherich grimly, and then just stared down at his feet, fighting a familiar wave of feeling as the silence stretched around him.

At last the disembodied voice broke in. "You should probably go."

"No." Fisher looked up, and Doctor Catt would not have recognised him, with the fury riding his face. "No," he spat again. "Is this it, then? Live long enough and you just can't be *bothered* to take part any more? I thought that was the great sin of the Guardians, that they strayed, that they lost the point of it all. After all, name me one Guardian who actually did a proper job of it, all the way through? Wanderer? Oh, but where's he these days, now the war's over? Too damn mystical to help anyone put things back together. Wall? Probably still refusing to admit the war ended without him. Lightbearer? Dead. *Dead!* Is that any way to get a job done?" He swept his staff around, smashing a ceramic statuette of a dragon and releasing a scatter of magical energies. "And now what? What's supposed to happen *now?*" Another sweep smashed a bookshelf from the wall, scattering its contents and raising another swirl of angry magic. "Ask the gods, of course! But no, we can't do that!" With a roar of rage and a sudden access of strength, he upended Roherich's desk and kicked it apart as the tower shuddered around him. "And who might have been able to work out why? Why, Roherich the Silver Mage, except he's *fucked off* because it was *all a bit much!*" And Fisher took his staff, the Staff of Ways, by one end with both hands and slammed it against the argent wall with such force that it snapped in half.

That done, he felt terribly tired by it all, and mostly because his true ire wasn't really at Roherich after all. "It's fine for Guardians to just piss off and leave people in the lurch," he told the vine arch and its contents, "but you were supposed to be *better* than that."

In the echo of his words, the air fizzed and twisted with magic, all the power he had let loose that could not escape the tower's confines. It made his hair stand on end and his teeth ache.

"What have you done?" whispered the figment.

"You still here, then?" Fisher demanded of it.

"Of course. Where could I go?"

"Another loose end he never thought of," Fisher grumbled and, with a magical precision Catt would not have believed of him, undid the magical tensions holding the figment in existence so that it was instantly undone. A mercy, he decided, rather than having to spend eternity alive in its own tomb.

That done, and feeling sheepish about giving vent to all of it, he took Cinnabran's skull from his satchel once more. No doubt as to its provenance, as he knew, but it wasn't as though it *did* anything. There were toe bones and vertebrae and even loose *teeth* in his and Catt's collection that had more practical value, but this was *her* skull, the first mortal the gods ever directly addressed.

He held it up, picturing the vacancy within it, that great hungry absence left over when what made her Cinnabran had flown free. The loose power about him began to channel into it like water into a bottle.

"Cinnabran, if there's anything of you, give me something. Just a shadow of you, just an echo rattling around in that braincase will do. Come on, just open up. If there was anything to you that wasn't just a great big showboater, eh? 'Oh, look at me, I'm so precious, all the gods talk to me!' Was it just that, or did you mean it? Come on, you fake, you fraud. I'm shoving so much power up your non-existent arse you can taste it in your tonsils. Come *on!*"

He felt the anger rising in him, that he always kept at the stave's end, but that never really went away. He would need to practice again, so that he didn't break his calm with Catty, because his partner in misadventure could be so *infuriating* sometimes.

All that spare power had gone into the skull now, but it wasn't just sitting there, swirling about the cavity within, nor infusing the bone itself. It had gone somewhere. Tentatively, Fisher lifted the relic to his ear again, perhaps hoping for the wash of distant waves.

THAT NIGHT, CELESTAINE woke in her cell to a quiet tapping at her door. She was reaching for her sword, which of course they had taken off her; its absence brought back sufficient reminders of her situation and she sat up on the hard bed.

Someone was at her hatch. She went over and squinted in the gloom, seeing a stout man in a Templar's uniform. *Is it time, then?* But no, it was the middle of the night, no time to make a public statement. Her heart leapt with hope. Surely she would be taken to the Governor or someone else of influence, and get the chance to talk them round. Perhaps there was some resistance to the Temple's fundamentalism, and they wanted her as a figurehead. Perhaps, perhaps...

Her visitor grinned at her and she sighed, resting her forehead against the door. "Oh, it's you."

"I figured you'd be wanting to make a deal about now," said the figure who looked like a Templar.

"Did you?"

"I can get you out of here. But you've got to do the thing for me." From behind that solid guard's face, the Undefeated's weasel cunning showed through. "Come on, Celest, what'll it cost you?"

"My good name."

"I'm a Guardian," he insisted. "I did things, good things, back before you were born. And who knows what I did in the war? Would it hurt so very much, a little white lie in exchange for not going to the fire?"

Celestaine opened her mouth to turn him down, then stopped

herself. Was her pride worth so much? Why not tell the story of the Undefeated standing against the Kinslayer, as he wanted? As he said, who would it hurt?

She felt the tug within her, though, like a fish feeling the hook. "We found you," she remembered. "We came to you—it was the Wanderer and me. He asked you for help, right at the start. After all, you'd gone strong against the Kinslayer before. And you wouldn't. You didn't think we could win. You were scared, you with all your power. You laughed in the Wanderer's face, Deffo. You laughed in mine. And you were in the shape of a rat at the time, so that was a feat."

"A badger," the Guardian muttered. "Why does nobody remember it was a badger?"

"Because I think back and I only remember a rat," Celestaine told him.

"Ancient history," the Undefeated whispered, plucking at his fingers. "Water under the bridge. How was I to *know* you'd actually pull it off? You don't understand what it was like when the Kinslayer killed the Custodian and ate his power. Before that, none of us had ever died."

"I'm a mortal," Celestaine pointed out. "Don't lecture me about having to die." She sighed. "You want to be the noble Guardian? Save *them*, get them all out of here. Maybe I'll put in a good word, after. There, that's the deal."

The Undefeated's eyes flicked left and right. "There's no way I can get them out, woman. The Aethani? The *Yoggs?* No, it's you I can save, just you, come on."

Celestaine looked him in the shifty eye. "I will howl of your cowardice when they light the fires, Deffo. Count on it."

After the Guardian had skulked off, the voice of Doctor Catt arose from the next cell. "Permit me to observe that compromise is the very soul of civilization, and it's as a result of unyielding dogmatism that we're in this predicament. Once you were out, you could have tried to free the rest of us."

Celestaine returned to her bunk. "I could have handled that better," she conceded.

THE TEMPLARS CAME for them all at dawn, and Celestaine reckoned that Low Ilkand must be running riot, because it looked as though pretty much *all* the Templars were at hand, and ready. Mostly it was in case Nedlam decided to kick off, but even Doctor Catt had four burly men competing to bundle him through the cell door. Celestaine herself apparently warranted seven.

Heno they dragged still chained from his cell. He managed to catch Celestaine's gaze with an eyebrow arched, as if to say, *Whatever you've got, now would be a good time*, but of course she didn't have anything.

Nedlam walked from her cell, ducking low under the lintel. The Templars fell back from her, suddenly afraid, and there was a knife at Heno's throat in an instant.

She looked them over and held up her hands, piled with sundered chains. With exquisite contempt she dumped the ruined metal at her feet.

"I walk," she told them, daring any of them to so much as take her by the hand. Celestaine watched duty war with prudence on the Templars' faces, and then they were levelling their spears, but letting Nedlam stride between them. Probably the Yorughan's head would have been held high, but there simply wasn't room for it.

Ralas certainly wasn't offering any resistance, flinching from their grip as though he was made of glass. His injuries had healed overnight, of course, but he was so brittle that it seemed even harsh language might break a bone or two. *And of course the Kinslayer let him dwindle to that condition before making it his eternity.* And, like a lot of the enemy's cruelties, it probably hadn't even been intended, just a side-effect of his capricious whim.

Amkulyah came out last—almost overlooked entirely in the

fuss over the Yorughan. He looked small as a child surrounded by the armoured might of the Templars. His twisted wing-limbs shivered and shuddered.

"He's not part of this," she told the guards. "He's just trying to help his people." But they weren't taking orders from her, and Kul got shoved along with the rest of them.

"I notice you didn't say that about me," Doctor Catt observed, somehow at her elbow. "I am actually even less a part of 'this' than your friend there."

"I can't save everyone." And that was the whole problem, of course. Catt must have seen it in her face, because he remained uncharacteristically silent. She had wanted to save everything, but her memories of the war were one long book of all the names she hadn't saved. What if she had...? Couldn't she have...? If she'd only...

Then they were coming out under the sky into a courtyard enclosed on all sides by the walls of the Temple. One large gate was thrown open, and Celestaine saw a crowd gathering, not even that many people yet. The courtyard itself was lined with carvings: a map showing the free lands, implying an ecclesiastical jurisdiction over them that had never been the case; great carved icons of Wall, Fury, Vigilant and the Undefeated in martial glory—those who had routed the Kinslayer the first time, immortals further immortalised in stone, presiding over judicial proceedings and punishments.

Well, I wanted to see the Inner Temple. And here she was, the special guest of the Templars. *Any evil crowns immediately apparent? No? What a surprise,*

They had stakes set up along the wall carved with the four Guardians, she saw. Vigilant's statue had been defaced. Had that been by agents of the Kinslayer when they took the city one time, to record their slaying of the original? No, it looked too recent for that. Odd what thoughts went through your head on the way to death.

The Templars were bringing in firewood, and there was a farcical dance as the prisoner escort and the tinder detail clashed and neither would give ground. At last the logistical difficulties were sorted and Celestaine found herself secured to a stake, watching her fellows undergo similar restraint. She saw Nedlam try the chains thoughtfully, flexing her prodigious muscles until the metal twisted. *Yes, probably she can, but that'll just get her a cleaner death, won't it?*

Once they were in place, everyone just stood around, and it was plain that nobody had thought to send for the Archimandrite ahead of time, and someone somewhere was arguing about whose job it was to get the oil.

"You'll have to excuse them," came a voice from near Celestaine's feet. "They haven't actually done this before—it was getting their hands on a couple of Yoggs that gave the big man the idea. How better to stoke support for the gods than a good old-fashioned bonfire?"

She looked down on a beggarly individual who had hopped up by the stacked firewood. He was depressingly familiar.

"Hello, Deffo," she said.

"You see they only polish Wall?" He nodded at the carvings behind them. "Me, Vig and Fury, we're all over dust and birdshit."

"Perhaps it's because Wall was around for the war."

"*Around*, yes. Not *here*, not actually doing anything." The Undefeated sighed. "And you curse *my* name. There's no justice."

Celestaine looked down the line of them: Amkulyah, Heno, Doctor Catt, the imposing bulk of Nedlam. "They are actually going to set fire to us," she said, quite calmly.

"When they can get their arses into gear, yes," the Undefeated confirmed. "Let's face it, they're a religious institution without gods and, whatever you think of me, where *are* the Guardians these days? Where's your precious Wanderer? Wandered off, that's where. And so they want to do what they think the gods want, and what they think the gods want is revenge for what was done to them, whatever that was. I mean, no wonder the Templars secretly hate you."

"What?" Celestaine demanded incredulously.

"You outvengeanced them," the Undefeated pointed out. "While they were swearing oaths to each other, you went off and did in the Kinslayer. I mean, what were the odds? So, like everyone else," and he jabbed a self-conscious thumb at his own ragged vest, "they're trying to show just how important they are in the grand scheme of things, because some band of nobodies stole a march on them and now everyone's singing the praises of the Slayers."

Something bright caught Celestaine's eye; not hope, but torches, in the hands of Templars. Apparently nobody could find sufficient oil so they were going to do things the hard way.

"Wait!" The voice was Ralas's and then, without any further prevarication, he lifted up his head in song.

His true gifts were the one part of him the Kinslayer hadn't touched. His voice was as pure and sweet as it ever was, as he launched into 'Last Port of the Chemina,' that every Ilkin knew: a song of coming back to this city and finding home, stepping off the ship and knowing the sights and smells, the taverns and the accents. It said nothing about the Temple, nothing about vengeance or war, only hearth and home and forgiveness, the child renewing bonds with the parent and the city. Celestaine held her breath as Ralas finished the chorus to utter silence and launched into the (somewhat raunchier) second verse. The crowd were utterly still, the Templars too. Only the flames danced, and even they seemed to take their metre from the song.

Then the Archimandrite arrived, bringing with him his tin ear, demanding to know what was going on. Was this what the gods demanded of Their faithful? Why were the guilty not being punished? He stormed through the suddenly abashed Templars to stare up at Ralas, whose voice faltered to silence. Celestaine glanced at the crowd to see how they were taking this, given they'd been listening so raptly a moment before. True enough, there were frowns there if she looked for them—they weren't all firm Temple aficionados, and perhaps some had come out of a purely secular wish to see a good burning. Before any help could come from that direction, though, there was the distinct metal sound of Nedlam's chains shearing.

She strode down from her stake like a statue suddenly animated and the Templars fell back from her, putting torches and spearheads in the way. The Archimandrite took out his hammer and faced her, showing considerably more courage than most of his followers. He barely came up to her solar plexus.

Nedlam opened her mouth to say something unwise. Probably the Archimandrite was doing the same, though he had his back to Celestaine at that point. The voice that rang out was neither of theirs, though.

Doctor Fisher had elbowed and kneed his way through the crowd, as testified to by the trail of angry, injured people behind him. Now he stood, a shabby long-faced Cheriveni in a soldier's cap, holding aloft a worn skull as though it was made of gold and diamonds.

When he had the Archimandrite's attention he smiled, though not much, because he was still Doctor Fisher, after all.

"Catch!" he said, and lobbed the skull underarm at the priest.

CHAPTER SEVENTEEN

THE ARCHIMANDRITE LUNGED for the skull on its slow, tumbling arc. He almost fumbled it, juggling the relic frantically until he could clasp it to his chest. His face, turned to Doctor Fisher, was all set for an outrage of truly divine proportions: that this scruffy Cheriveni had interrupted his burning, that such a holy thing had been treated in so cavalier a manner. Even as he was fighting to form the words, though, he froze to an absolute stillness, eyes staring into nothing. In the resulting silence, his shocked gasp sounded in every ear.

Doctor Fisher was already moving, slouching over to Catt's stake with a folding knife to cut the bonds. Celestaine saw him roll his eyes as the priest began to speak.

"I... hear!" gasped the Archimandrite, to the bafflement of the crowd.

Some of the Templars tried to stop Fisher, but he nodded towards the priest. "Your boss's got something to say."

"I..." The Archimandrite had the skull to his head, eyesocket to ear, straining, waving at everyone to be quiet so he could listen. His face had gone chalk white.

"Fishy," Catt asked in a whisper. "What did you do?"

Fisher shrugged. "Not much."

"Parlour tricks?"

"Bit more than that." Fisher had him free now, and was looking moodily at the others. "Suppose you want me to spring the lot of them?"

"If you'd be so kind." Catt's eyes were fixed on the priest, who just stood there, mouth hanging open. There was such a look on his face—Celestaine had never seen the like. It was equal parts elated and aghast.

"The gods..." the man breathed.

Celestaine goggled at him, even as Fisher sawed at her ropes. "The gods?" she asked him.

"Cinnabran, you know." Fisher managed to shrug while still cutting away. "Gods wouldn't shut up, for her."

"But the Kinslayer, he..."

"What, then? What did he do?" Fisher said savagely, severing the last strands. He went on to Amkulyah as Celestaine crossed past him to Heno.

"I hear such sorrow," the Archimandrite said. His face was running with tears. Glancing around, Celestaine caught sight of Governor Adondra, come to see the execution she hadn't quite wanted, now witnessing the breakdown of the Temple's fiercest fanatic.

"Archimandrite, what is it?" she asked, her hand to her own shield symbol as if to protect her against divine sanction if the man suddenly veered back into blood and vengeance again.

"I heard the gods." He had the skull away from his ear now, dangling from his hand as though he would dearly like to be rid of it. "They are far from us; so far. And cold, cold and lonely are the gods."

Celestaine shivered, and when Heno was free she just stood and listened while Kul freed Ralas.

"What... what do you mean?" Adondra asked, glancing around nervously. She had probably not much liked working with the Temple when everything was revenge and intolerance. Now she didn't know what it was, and that was worse.

"I heard Them." Nothing in the Archimandrite's manner suggested he was aware of his audience. "Just for a moment, I heard Them. They were so far away, and still drifting. They were lost without us. They rejoiced, when They touched me. They rejoiced because They hadn't even known we were still there." He dropped to his knees. "I heard the Just Watcher. I heard He Who Walks the Groves, I heard the Gracious One, the Bringer of Waves, Kind Companion, all of Them."

"Come on," Fisher suggested, but none of the others moved. He raised his eyes towards the peak of the Silver Tower and spread his hands, as though to say, to some distant spectator, *What am I supposed to do with this lot, eh?*

"What did They say?" Adondra breathed, speaking in that moment for all the people she governed.

The priest turned his agonised expression on her. "Look after one another," he said. "Be kind. Help each other. You're all you have. We can't help you any more."

Celestaine heard a ragged breath from her left, distinct from all the others. She saw the Undefeated there, and for once there was nothing sly or mean in his expression. He was a thing of the gods too, of course. In the ancient days They would have spoken to him often, one of Their chosen children sent to shape the world. Now he was hearing his parents' farewell.

Adondra helped the Archimandrite up, then backed off as he tried to give her the skull. The priest's head swung about until his gaze fixed on Celestaine. "You!" he said hoarsely.

Oh, damn. And Fisher sighed and said, "Told you we should've left." But it was too late now, because the man was shambling over, almost unrecognisable now, a witness to things no mortal should experience.

He lurched forwards as he approached and ended up yanking on her cloak, dragging her closer than she wanted to be. "You!" he said again, and all the Templars had tensed for his orders.

"I wronged you," the Archimandrite said. He looked about wildly at his followers, at the crowd beyond. "I have wronged all of you!" he told them. "What good does vengeance do the gods now? Why tear down, when we may never be able to build again? We must live. We must help each other to live. I'm sorry, I'm sorry for what I am." She was terrified that any moment he would blow his nose in her cloak like a sad clown in a farce. Some instinctive pity had her patting his shoulder.

"And us?" Heno asked, pushing his luck as usual. "What do your gods say about us Yoggs?" Because the gods had never got round to his people, or any of those the Kinslayer had taken as his minions. They had been mislaid or ignored, they had been taken beneath the earth and honed into something that cared nothing for the divine. The Archimandrite's revelations broke on Heno like waves against a cliff.

The priest stared at him. "They said be kind," he said, more collected now he was faced with a former servant of the enemy. "I cannot love you, monster. But They said be kind, and *she*"— he yanked at Celestaine's cloak again—"vouched for you. You are free, you are all free. Do no harm, and you shall walk these streets like any man."

"An honour," said Heno acidly. "I think we've outstayed our welcome, Celest. Don't we have somewhere to be?"

"We..." The realisation hit her. "Archimandrite, there's something we came for, that was brought to the Temple. It would have looked like a crown. A thing of power. We need to do a good thing, a great good thing. Please..." But blankness ghosted across his face before the fire of his revelation banished it. He had no idea what she spoke of, and just staggered off to spread the word to his startled Templars.

"Well then, we don't," she said dejectedly to Heno. "We came for the crown, but there's nothing. Roherich is gone, and... maybe we can search the Temple or something. Perhaps they'll let us do that now."

"No need." Amkulyah's voice was without inflection. He sat on the stack of firewood intended to burn him and she saw his face was locked down tight, the look he must have worn for his long imprisonment, where emotion was weakness. "Don't you see it?"

He was looking at the map, which showed the alleged reach of the Ilkand Temple across the lands to the south. Out of date, of course, carved some time after the Kinslayer was driven beneath the earth and before he emerged strong and savage with his armies. There were towns marked there that had been destroyed, blank spaces where fortresses had been raised. And there were places that had been innocent to the mapmaker that history would remember for very different reasons now.

"You see?" Amkulyah said, and she followed the line of his finger. *Ah, yes. That.*

She thought she had misunderstood him, that he was just marking out his place of pain for her. "When they carved all this, it was just, well, one more place the faithful went."

He frowned at her. "Do you truly not see it?"

She didn't, but then she lacked his eyes, designed to see fine detail from on high.

"It's been covered over now," he told her. "But recently. Someone's marked this."

THEY COULDN'T GET any more words with the Archimandrite, who was now going through the Temple imparting the gods' faint and fragmentary message. Celestaine was still startled by how devout the man had turned out to be. The Ilkand Temple had surely been ripe for some demagogue who wanted nothing more than to turn people's fear and uncertainty into personal power, and for one such as that, any message of peace would have been anathema. The Archimandrite, to his credit, had heard the gods, or at least believed he had, and had become a different man. He even seemed relieved not to have to hammer the world flat in the name of vengeance. There was, she thought, a kind man buried in him, that had always been desperate to get out.

If he was relieved, then not half so much as Adondra. Celestaine still didn't feel she liked the Governor, but the woman had been caught between the chaotic mass of refugees crowding the city and the Temple's unyielding obsessions. Now it seemed the Templars would be doing more than simply keeping the peace. Celestaine imagined them building new homes, distributing food, returning lost children to frantic parents. Who knew? Perhaps if she came back in a month, this new message would be twisted into a reason for persecution and punishment, but she hoped not. Against the backdrop the war and its end had left her—a land broken, exhausted and riven with factions old and new—it was good to have a little gem of hope.

Adondra could spare them some time, while she waited to see precisely which way the Temple would jump. She had their answers too, now that they knew the right questions to ask.

"We all thought he was a Templar from one of the further outposts. After all, the war jumbled everyone together, as we Ilkin know more than most," she explained, looking up at the map. "Big man, been in the wars, certainly. He came in, saw how it worked around here, then two days later he'd lit out, nobody saw him again. But somehow he'd got into the Temple Courtyard here and vandalised the place, hacked a symbol there and broke Vigilant's statue. The Templars plastered over it, of course, restored the place as best they could..." She glanced at Amkulyah, whose gaze was still fixed fiercely on the map.

"What symbol?" Celestaine asked.

Kul demonstrated, tracing the shape with his finger: three flat-based triangles in a line, touching. A crown.

Over the defacement the Templars had restored the original place name so well that Celestaine could only see the damage this close. *Dorhambri*, read the letters. Just a little mining town, when they had first been carved.

"It won't be like it was," she assured Amkulyah, but he didn't seem to hear her. No doubt he was fighting back the memories of being a slave in that place, buried beneath the earth, for long years.

After Adondra had gone, Heno shook his head "So, what," he asked, "the thief came through here and just thought to let us know where he was heading?"

"He had friends following," Nedlam suggested, squinting at the map.

"Far easier ways of going about it," Celestaine said. "Heno's right, there's a trap here somewhere. But if there's a trap, there's also something to lead us to our thief."

"If they didn't want to be found, why bother?" Nedlam wanted to know. Celestaine could only agree with her.

"A test," Ralas called. He was still sitting on the stacked firewood, massaging his legs and waving away Templars and random citizens who wanted him to sing for them.

"For what, though?" Celestaine asked, and he shrugged.

"Perhaps someone's watching. Perhaps they'll be waiting for us at Dorhambri with a chest of gold and some cake, to reward us for our persistence. And perhaps I'll poke them in the eye for leaving me in that hole in Bleakmairn."

Celestine rubbed at her face. "We will go to Dorhambri. Or else we find some other artefact of making, because I don't see what else there is? Kul? It's your call."

"Really?" The Aethani was regarding her without expression.

"Yes." She frowned at him. "You don't want to go back to Dorhambri, fine, we won't. Or you stay here and the rest of us will go, or however you want. Or we find Doctor Catt, wherever he's got to, and see if he can put us onto anything else."

"I don't trust Doctor Catt," Amkulyah said sourly. "I don't trust why he's here and not in his shop back in that place." He shook himself angrily and his wing-limbs spasmed like clutching talons. "I don't trust human heroes with causes."

Celestaine stared at him. "...What?"

"What is it you keep telling that beggar-Guardian who follows you? You won't make him important. Am I the way you stay important, Celestaine the Slayer? Is that what my people are, to you?"

"How could you say that?" She gaped at him. "I'm in this to help you, Kul, you and all of your people, if we can. No more than that."

He held her gaze for a moment, then looked away and shrugged, another convulsive shudder of his crippled parts. "Then let's go to Dorhambri. Like you say, I'm sure it's completely different now."

"It will be," Celestaine assured him, hearing her voice so artificially bright and cheery because his words had hit home, deep inside her. *Ever since the Kinslayer died, what have I been doing, save try to recapture that moment? Trying to make up for the people I couldn't save? Perhaps I owe Deffo an apology.*

LOOKING DOWN AT the courtyard, shrouded from the view of others, Catt and Fisher eavesdropped shamelessly on the conversation. There had been a distance between them, since the business with the Archimandrite and the skull, and Fisher waited with infinite patience for the other man to bridge it.

At long last Catt cleared his throat awkwardly. "I just wanted to say, well, those shenanigans with the gods, what the priest heard from Cinnabran's skull... that *was* just a scam, was it not? I mean, well done, obviously. A very subtle and ably targeted piece of business, but I'm sure it was just some magicianly sleight-of-hand at work."

Fisher grunted. "So no actual thanks for saving your hide."

"What?" Catt looked at him with genuine puzzlement. "Oh, I

would have thought of something." He waved away the thought dismissively. "But it's been preying on my mind a little, what the priest said. And I would like to peer behind the veil a little, and be reassured that it was all just flummery."

Fisher just waited, one eyebrow slightly up as though to raise it the full way would be far too much effort.

"Only," Catt went on, wringing the hem of his robe a little, "it would be rather a dreadful thing, if it wasn't just that the connection between the gods' lips and our ears was obstructed, but that the gods Themselves were... drifting in some dreadful void somehow, further and further with each passing moment, reaching back towards us, Their beloved creation, for some final message before They passed beyond all hope of us hearing Them." His voice had grown thin and forlorn and now he coughed and shook himself as though trying to be rid of the sentiment. "I just mean, that would be rather awful for all concerned, all things considered."

He looked to Fisher hopefully, but for a moment the other man was just staring down at the Guardian statues below, and the moment lengthened between them, and Catt fidgeted and plucked at his cuffs.

At last, Fisher forced a sly look onto his face, that complicity their entire friendship was based on, and Catt laughed, nervously loud, so that it rang across the courtyard below. "I knew it was a scheme, I knew it. You can fool these credulous religious types, but not me, Fishy. And really, what a trite final message! Be nice to each other! As if the gods would be so banal." And Fisher neither confirmed or denied the accusation, but Catt seized on it nonetheless, shaking off the melancholy thought of the gods receding into an infinite eternity, denied Their creation just as Their work was denied its gods.

"Anyway, we'd better get the sheep chariot out again," Catt decided. "Looks like they're going for Dorhambri. And it's a trap, according to them."

"'Course it is," Fisher said scornfully.

"Know what I think?" Catt asked, rhetorically as it turned out, for he left no gap. "Our crown-purloining miscreant must be well aware that others such as we would be trying to locate his prize, and would divine its location by magic eventually. No doubt this is some fellow connoisseur of the magical, probably someone we've actually met and done business with, given how small the trade actually is. We've done our own misdirection and sabotage, haven't we? If you know you've got a choice piece that everyone's on your heels for, better to ambush your rivals in some place of your choosing, don't you think? So lucky, therefore, that we have a genuine hero and a pair of formidable brutes to take the brunt of it on our behalf."

"And some scrawny Aethani kid," Fisher added. "And an undead musician."

Catt waved them away, obviously more impressed with the two Yorughan as unwitting pawns. "I think they'll flush out our rival collector admirably. In fact I'm rather delighted at the wisdom of my strategy."

CHAPTER EIGHTEEN

THE MOST DIRECT route from Ilkand to the mines of Dorhambri was overland, and right through Hathel Vale. Of course, nobody went *through* Hathel Vale any more, but skirting it was still the most direct route, and apparently there was, if not a road, then at least a well-beaten track. Iron shipments, Adondra explained, still came north to the city sometimes, on and off.

"It won't be like you remember," Celestaine had to reassure Amkulyah after that. "There will be free miners there, just like there were before the Kinslayer came. Just because it's a mine doesn't mean it's... bad."

She looked to her companions for moral support, but that cupboard turned out to be bare.

"Always seemed like a bloody awful way to make a living," was Ralas's expert opinion, and the Yorughan just exchanged awkward looks; throughout the war the Kinslayer's forces had used mines specifically as bad places you didn't want to end up in, working people to death even if it meant less actual ore got mined.

And Dorhambri had always been special. Long before the war, wizards and mage-smiths would send there for iron from certain veins, rich with latent magic a skilled practitioner could bring to life. The Kinslayer had not been blind to the place's attractions, of course. Half of his nasty little toys had been forged from Dorhambri steel.

"First we have to get by Hathel Vale, though," Celestaine knew.

"What's so off about it?" Nedlam wanted to know, but Heno leaned close and made a fluttering little gesture with his hands, as of mounting flames, and she nodded in understanding. "Oh, right, that place."

Celestaine had wanted to find Catt and Fisher again, to thank and covertly interrogate the pair of them, because, like Kul, she was feeling ungrateful enough to find their presence suspicious. They had vanished away, however, leaving only a few unpaid bar tabs. Standing there listening to one more host gripe about the urbane Cheriveni who had seemed so trustworthy, Celestaine knew she should be on the road again, even though it was past mid-afternoon. Duty called, but for once she decided it could wait until next morning. None of her companions complained; Ralas and Amkulyah were neither of them suited for long walking trips and could use the time off their feet, and the Yorughan, who could have marched forever, were not the complaining type. Or Nedlam wasn't, anyway. Now that she wasn't about to be burned at the stake, she was happy enough to sit around in front of the Temple Gate, drinking some sort of paint-stripper wine she had bought and munching on handfuls of roots she had found in the Templars' evidence chest.

Heno could complain like a trooper if he wanted. His sarcasm was sharp enough to shave with. He had other things on his mind that night, though, and he and Celestaine ended up naked, tousled, watching the moon. She was propped up against his broad chest, tucked into his arms. He might be a small Yorughan, from a life given over to sorcerous pursuits rather than breaking shieldwalls and storming breaches, but she could still feel the slumbering power in his embrace, enough to crush her if he wanted, and yet utterly under control, a slow and patient strength like a great cat's.

"You're thinking this is a mistake again," he murmured in her ear.

"Probably." She shrugged, making herself more comfortable against his smooth skin. "The Archmandrill would have a fit."

The others would never have understood—the Slayers, who had hacked their way through countless Yoggs and Grennishmen and assorted monsters. They accepted Heno and Nedlam's help to get to the Kinslayer and earn their title, but the two were no more than convenient pawns. They hadn't seen them as people, though at least they hadn't seen them as enemies any more. Only Celestaine and Lathenry, who had brokered the deal in the first place from the comfort of the torture benches, had got to know the two of them. Before then, even Celestaine hadn't thought of the Yorughan as really having minds of their own.

Lathenry had died, of course, in the fight with the Kinslayer. One more friend she hadn't been able to save.

But Heno and Nedlam had impressed her for their courage. Naturally bravery was in no short supply amongst the Slayers, going into the very inner sanctum of the enemy; but theirs was a spirit born of desperation, because it was either kill the Kinslayer or see the conquest of all they knew. The Yorughan could just have gone along with that and not rocked the boat. And yet there had come a moment when Heno had decided he would not be ruled by his demigod master any more, and Nedlam...

Celestaine was less sure about Ned's motivations. At first the big Yorughan had just seemed a willing follower whom Heno had recruited. There was more to her than that, of course. She wasn't the most eloquent and didn't dwell on her own thoughts, but Celestaine thought that perhaps she just hadn't *liked* it; that some sort of rudimentary sense of right and wrong had bloomed even in the Kinslayer's darkest shadow, and Nedlam had got sick of the interrogations and the blood.

And after the Kinslayer was dead, his minions had fled the Slayers' blades and abandoned the fortress of Nydarrow to the conquerors. With the contents of the Kinslayer's wine cellars on hand, Heno and Celestaine had talked out half the night, comparing their different lives and worlds, flush with the glow of having achieved a great thing between them.

One thing, as the storytellers said, had led to another. Even as she watched herself seduce and be seduced by him she had been thinking, *I will loathe myself in the morning.* Yet the morning had come, and she had woken to his slate-grey face with its carved tusks, and she had looked into it and thought, *Yes...*

THEY MADE A start early enough that any prurient Templars would be unable to satisfy their curiosity about just what Celestaine and Heno had been about the previous evening. Reclaiming her horse, she managed at last to barter her good name and a little coin into a mount for Ralas. Given his recent history, he had probably not been expecting a thoroughbred destrier, but between her limited funds and the inn's limited stable, he got a lunnox, like it or lump it. Lunnoxes were seldom seen this far north, and certainly the complaining bleats of the thing suggested it wasn't enjoying it much. The innkeeper explained he'd ended up with the beast in lieu of payment for room and board, and was obviously keen to get rid of it in exchange for currency more generally accepted. It was a long-legged, goatish thing with yellow eyes and wicked spurs on its hooves, and had anyone ever managed to train them for war, then lunnox cavalry would have ruled the battlefields of the world. Like their goat cousins, however, they were too smart by half for that kind of risky work.

Ralas stared into the beast's eyes and it butted him, not hard, but just to let him know who was boss. After that it consented to let him saddle it, occasionally making bleating sounds that sounded too much like mocking laughter.

Amkulyah refused a mount. Riding beasts was not something the Aethani did, apparently, and hadn't he kept up all the way from Bladno? Celestaine didn't mention that they'd been on boats for most of that way. The little man was so *proud* sometimes. She decided that she'd keep to his pace, no matter what. Later that day, she turned to find him sitting on Nedlam's shoulders, leaning down to say something that prompted a guttural laugh. She turned front again, knowing that if he saw her staring he would remember his dignity and get down.

Two uneventful days on the road, but ahead of them was something that looked like weather, smudged across the sky: a storm that never broke. Celestaine knew what it was, but Ralas had been lost to the Kinslayer before this particular abomination and Kul would have been in the mines when it happened. She didn't want to ask the Yorughan. There was always a chance they'd have been involved. It wasn't as though the Kinslayer had set the fires himself, after all.

That night, when they camped, the southern horizon leapt with light, and Amkulyah said he could see the stark silhouettes of trees against the blaze.

"Will we need a different route?" he asked her.

"Our route will skirt it. The road used to go through, but you'd be mad to try that now."

"You'd burn," he agreed.

"Not just that."

"And what do you mean, 'used to'? How long has it been going?"

"Three years." She met his incredulous stare. "Hathel Vale, Kul."

She saw him searching his memories. The Aethani had probably flown here to the beautiful glades, the silver brooks, the vivid greens of spring and summer and the riotous autumn hues. People had come from every neighbouring land just to see. Celestaine's mother had brought her, when she was just a child.

"The Kinslayer hated it, of course," she said hollowly. "He took it, and for years he worked towards some punishment for all that beauty. And then he got his Heart Takers together, and his dragons and all the rest, and worked this magic, start the fire of forever in every living thing of Hathel Vale."

"But didn't people live...?"

Celestaine looked from his appalled face to the bright horizon. "Not people, exactly. People could have fled."

THE NEXT DAY they passed about the edge of Hathel Vale. Long before they got there, they were travelling under the smoke that blanketed the sky, making her wonder, *How is there smoke, even? What burns, when nothing is consumed?* It was as though the black-grey pall was made of pure misery, of which there was an inexhaustible supply.

Before they reached the edge of Hathel they heard the inhabitants, too. The people of Hathel had not been human or Oerni or any of the mortal races. They had been bound to the trees, spirits that took human-like form but whose hearts were tied to the vale and its forest. They had been things of grace and beauty, Celestaine remembered, seeming to drift above the ground or the water, talking to one another in voices like the music of streams and breezes. More than one young man or woman had lost their heart to them, pining beneath the verdant canopy for an entity centuries old that could never quite love a human back.

Their screams rose from the midst of the burning wood in an unholy chorus. Celestaine, who had been ready for it, felt the sound tunnel into her innards and twist them. Ralas was very pale, slipping from the saddle to lead the lunnox, the fires reflected in his eyes. Hathel Vale was an inferno, the heat washing from it in waves, the air about it dancing with embers. Every tree roared and cracked, a leafless blackened skeleton, and yet never guttering even for an instant. And between the trunks ran the dryads of Hathel, not graceful now, not beautiful, save in the way that fire dancing can be beautiful. Every cracked, charred face was contorted, all other features shoved aside to make room for that great open maw so they could wail and shriek. They beat at their burning trees with charcoal fists. They raised candle fingers to the roiling smoke of the sky. Over and over; over and over.

Amkulyah's round eyes were so wide Celestaine could see the whole of Hathel reflected in each one.

"Why not this?" he asked. "Why not be a hero for this, rather than for my people? I would have mended this, if I could."

"I just... Once we have the crown, maybe we can mend this too. Who knows?" And yet she knew the greatest magi and sages had applied their minds to the Hathel, just as they had to the silence of the gods. Not one had come forward to say, "Oh, if only we had some great artefact of making..." The Kinslayer had wrought many things that nobody could undo. At his height, he had commanded powers even Roherich hadn't understood, arts the other Guardians could barely guess at.

THE DORHAMBRI, BACK before the Kinslayer's war, had been a bustling mining town, complete with a local duke who was, if not a saint, then at least relatively content with his considerable wealth. There had been rows of miners' cottages beside the foundry, and a knot of tradesmen and a handful of small temples at the other end of town. Or that was Ralas's claim, as Celestaine had never had cause to go there.

The Kinslayer had little use for pleasant little cottages, even less for a benevolently idle duke. What he had a use for was the iron beneath, both regular and magical. He had lusted after that rare, pure metal, but as with so many other things his desire to hurt had got in the way even of his own ambitions. Hence, alongside many of the original mining families and some prisoners of war, he had conscripted practically the entire Aethani race and buried them in the shafts and pits to scratch out the ore for him. Because, of all the people of the world, it would pain them most.

He had raised a fortress there, as he did everywhere he established a centre of power, and now that was what people thought of when they said, 'the Dorhambri'; that and the mines. The original town was forever lost to history.

Dorhambri was set deep in the hills, the new fort at its highest point with a view over the minehead, the old foundry, all the squat ugly buildings the Kinslayer's people had thrown up, and then across the hilltops, limned at night with the Hathel's distant blaze. No doubt that counted as scenic if you were the Kinslayer. Celestaine wasn't sure what they'd find, when they crested those summits to look down at the town.

Dreams of happy industrious people rebuilding rows of little cottages were swiftly dashed. All the Kinslayer's work was still in evidence: the long, low, windowless buildings where the miners had been penned—those non-Aethani who were even allowed out of the ground. The slightly bigger blocks with jagged spiked roofs and arrowslits that had housed the guards, she saw, and of course the looming shadow of the fort itself. It was smaller than Bleakmairn, but more work had gone into it. Grennish masons had set hideous gargoyles at intervals, and the walls themselves were intricately incised with complex sigils that made Celestaine's heart sink to see them. It was not that she knew them, but there was magic set into those shapes and those stones, and it was doing its best to crush any hope in her, just as it had done for all those who laboured in the pits, or even worked there as guards. The Kinslayer was hardly the most caring of employers, after all.

And he was gone, now. He was dead. She had helped kill him, and seen his body burned. There was absolutely no chance that the Kinslayer was squatting here in Dorhambri behind his dread runes, working his slaves to death because it amused him. And yet she looked on that place and knew that she had lied to Amkulyah when she said it wouldn't be like he remembered.

A shift was coming out of the mines, another waiting to get onto the lift. They weren't chained, but despair hung over them like the smoke over Hathel Vale. There were guards, too, and some were human and some were Yorughan, and a few were Oerni, hardened and brutal in a way the big people so seldom were. The workers were a similar mix, and the only grain of solace Celestaine could take from the sight was that no Aethani were among them. There were men and women of a dozen nations, though, and Grennishmen, still more Yorughan, and some other monstrous things that must have been yet more obscure minions of the enemy; even a couple of Shelliac, their pale shell-skins blackened by soot.

There were whips. They heard the cracks even at this distance. There were fights amongst the miners that the guards waded in and stopped with kicks and clubs. The foundry belched out a blacker, fouler smoke than even the Vale had given out. Then the foreman came round to look over his domain, and even Nedlam winced at the sight. He was borne on a chair carried by four despondent-looking Yorughan, their bare shoulders and backs a hatch of lash-scars. And he was Aethani, a pot-bellied, stick-limbed creature, his crooked, broken wing-limbs decorated with streamers of bright cloth as though they were a badge of service or a mark of honour. And even this dignitary cast glances up at the keep, where the lord of this place must hold court.

"How can they?" Celestaine hissed. "Who has done this?"

"Who would stop them?" Ralas offered dolefully. "It's not as though the old duke left heirs. As long as the iron's still coming, who's going to come over here and tell them to stop?"

"Us," Celestaine said, before she could stop herself. She sized up their responses. Nedlam was all for it. Nobody else seemed keen.

At last, Ralas sighed heavily and said, "I suppose it's going to be the old sing-for-your-supper line then."

"What?"

"You want to find out who's in charge, don't you?" He looked anything but keen about the idea. "I reckon I'm the only one who can just walk in. I'm a starving minstrel, after all, willing to sing his bitter heart out in exchange for a meal. And someone'll tell me who the chief cheese is, even if I don't get to sing for him. And what's the worst that can happen? To me, I mean."

"They lock you underground forever," Amkulyah told him.

Ralas gave him a sour look. "Yes, thank you for that."

He set off on his lunnox and they made a camp between hills, trusting that their fire would go unseen before the Hathel's radiance. Celestaine was twitchy, chafing at the inaction and wanting to be *doing* something; though precisely what, she didn't know. Nedlam was unusually pensive, though. Where she'd have just sat watch or gone instantly to sleep that enviable way she had, now she stared out towards the fortress where it bit into the starry sky.

"Thoughts?" Celestaine asked her.

"Bad times," she grunted. "Never got me in the mines, not for anything I did. Came close, but I knew where the line was. *Yorokha yoro na!* Yoroghan are for fighting. Even when we lived below, it wasn't us who dug. But those down there..."

"There were your people on guard too," Celestaine pointed out.

Nedlam shrugged, because that hadn't bothered her. She visibly went back over her words, and frowned. "Maybe they've good reason. We don't know. But those doing the digging—"

"Ned," Celestaine said softly. "Are you saying they're to blame for what they're made to do?"

The big Yorughan scowled angrily. "Who'd do it, though? Who'd let themselves be made to do it, or to carry that *Shur-meh* on his chair?"

"Welcome to life outside the army," Celestaine suggested.

"Stupid," Nedlam muttered. She was more disturbed by it all than Celestaine had seen her.

Ralas was back before dawn, practically dragging the lunnox, which had an aversion to the dark.

"That was an education," he said, dropping down by the ashes of the fire. "I've never done so many laments and dirges back to back. You can't actually sing anything jolly, it turns out, with those damn runes louring over you."

"But what did you find out?" Celestaine demanded. "Did you get into the fort?"

"I did not," Ralas confirmed. "Nor did I want to, because I caught the name of the chief here, and you're going to like it about as much as I did. You remember Jocien Silvermort the Liberator, don't you?"

"*Piss*," she spat. "He's not dead?"

"Riding high and ruling the Dorhambri," Ralas confirmed.

"'Liberator' sounds like a good thing," Amkulyah said uncertainly.

"Yes," Celestaine agreed. "That's what a lot of people thought, before they opened their doors to him. And he's exactly the sort of bastard who'd want the Crown."

CHAPTER NINETEEN

"Going way back," Ralas said. "What, after Bladno, Celest? Or was he there for that?"

Amkulyah and the two Yorughan looked from one to the other as, behind them, the angry radiance of Hathel Vale was slowly consumed by the dawn.

"Bladno was just you and me," Celestaine corrected him. "And we weren't anybody then. You, me, and Wanderer, giving out swords."

"A sword," Ralas pointed out. "Singular. So he obviously saw something in you. But you're right. It was after Bladno, after you killed that big old dragon. Not exactly a win, and Cherivell and Forinth both fell anyway, but you'd done *something*. People started to hunt you out, people who'd done something themselves. Years of war left, of course—we'd lose on plenty more battlefields once the Kinslayer got his armies moving again." He looked at the Yorughan. "I guess you were on some of them yourself. Situation probably seemed a whole lot rosier to you than to us, back then, right?"

Heno was diplomatic enough just to shrug, but Nedlam said, "Well, yes," and even grinned a bit before she remembered who she was with and whose side she ended up on. At Heno's sidelong look, she spread her huge hands. "It was, though."

"Those of us that had scored any kind of victories, we found each other. That's how it started," Ralas went on. "And those who survived the next five years ended up at Nydarrow, met you two, death of the Kinslayer, all that. I gloss over it because, well, I wasn't one of the ones who survived, now, was I? But at the start, soon after Bladno, there was Jocien Silvermort. Arvennir, long before Arven got into the war. There were a few—some of the more farsighted warrior orders could see the way things were going. We thought he was principled. Actually he just liked taking over places. He'd picked up a fair grab-bag of sorcery, and had a gang of bully-boys to follow him around. They'd strike where the enemy were weak, drive the Kinslayer's forces out of a village or a town. The Liberator, they called him. Not for long, in most cases. He took everything he wanted from wherever they went, said it was for the war effort. Then he left, and most times your lot came back twice as hard. But we didn't know any of that at the time, so he was one of us for quite a while, until…"

"Szendarc," Celestaine said. "The Tzarcoman monastery place. We turned up to rescue them and they didn't want rescuing."

Ralas nodded. "We were trying to punch through to meet with the Tzarcomen, because the Kinslayer hadn't got far past Tzarkona Gate—and that was a costly bloody business, because necromancy's the Tzarkand way, and they spent more of their own people on making that work than they killed enemy soldiers."

Nedlam grunted. "I remember *that*," she said sourly. "Got so that being sent to the Dead-Front was punishment detail. I did half a year there."

"Anyway, we found this monastery when we were pushing northwest," Celestaine took up the tale. "The Kinslayer's forces had gone past it. They couldn't crack the walls, or just didn't want to spend the time. We dealt with the camp that'd been left behind to bottle the monks in, but the locals weren't impressed.

So we went on. What we didn't know was that Jocien took that hard. He didn't like people who'd already liberated themselves."

"What Jocien didn't know was that we'd meet around half the Kinslayer's entire army, doubling back because they didn't fancy being necromanced," Ralas added. "So we fell back to Szendarc and found that Jocien's people had got inside it. They were tearing the monks a new one, looting their tombs."

"So that was where we parted company with the Liberator," Celestaine concluded. "There was a fight—us against his people on the wall-top of the monastery with the Kinslayer's army making double-time towards us. We only just got out. We thought Jocien was dead, but word kept popping up of him, here and there. There were lots of Jocien-the-hero stories, but when you actually followed his trail, he was just screwing people over, same as always. He'd protect you, while he was there, but he'd make you pay for it, just like a city gangster. And now he's running the Dorhambri." She shook her head. "How'd he even do it? How did he get all those people?"

"Little bastards will always follow a bigger bastard," Ralas suggested. "And from what I heard, those poor sods he's got working for him? He just sent out to everyone nearby, saying, send over your criminals, send over your prisoners of war, anyone you don't much care for. And he's the Liberator, isn't he? People would trust his reputation. Besides, if he's making the mines profitable again, who's going to ask questions?"

"And he's got the Crown," Celestaine says. "Or maybe he just knows where it is. Only we can't just march in the front, and Silvermort will sure as death recognise me and Ralas. We're going to have to sneak in, that's all."

"This is rather a delightful turn of events, don't you think?" Doctor Catt asked as he and Fisher strolled into Dorhambri. "Imagine, Joss Silvermort."

Fisher grunted, as though he was indeed imagining and the exercise had brought him little joy. With the Staff of Ways broken at the Silver Tower, he had fallen back to an entirely mundane walking aid, but he stabbed it at the ground with each step to make up for the lack of magic.

"Oh, don't be so surly," Catt admonished, in the optimistic manner of a man commanding the tides. "Always good to meet someone in the trade face to face, eh?"

"Thought you were going to let your tame hero sort it out."

"Well, I was." Catt smiled brightly at the pair of Yorughan who had materialised in his path. "Good morning, fine fellows. Would you be so kind as to tell your big man that a pair of old friends are paying a visit. Doctors Catt and Fisher from Cinquetann Riverport, dropping in unannounced."

Probably the Yorughan didn't speak human languages well enough to follow most of that, but the sheer volume of words obviously convinced them the matter was beyond their pay grade: one of them loped off to fetch someone more important. The other sort of tagged along beside the two Cheriveni as they walked in, trying to look as though he was doing his job without actually accomplishing anything.

"It just seems to me," Catt went on, "that Celestaine has got us as far as she's going to. Under the circumstances, we're probably better equipped to secure possession of the Crown than she is."

"He'll just hand it over, will he?" Fisher asked.

"Trade, Fishy, trade. We'll have something back at the shop that will tempt him. Something we don't mind parting with. And if not, well, the Slayer might think she can make her way in by subterfuge, but we'll already be guests within Joss's walls, and I think we have a great deal more resources at our disposal than she has, wouldn't you say?"

Their progress was interrupted by the four Yorughan and their sedan chair, who barrelled up with a haste not conducive to the dignity of the occupant. "You two, how dare you just march in?" a thin voice demanded. The old Aethani leant down at them, face a picture of owlish outrage. His robe had been fine once, but the back had been torn out to make room for his wing-limbs, and the buttons over his paunch were all in the process of parting company with the velvet they were stitched too.

"The very best of the morning to you and your kin," said Catt in what he vaguely remembered to be an Aethani greeting. From the old man's expression, it probably hadn't been. "May I present myself as Doctor—of law, of physic, of thaumaturgy— Catt, come here from Cinquetann to pay my fond respects to my old colleague and fellow collector Jocien Silvermort." He struck a pose with his cane and gave the Aethani his most blistering smile. "And this is Doctor Fisher. Fishy to his friends. Of which category I may be the sole representative."

The Aethani majordomo took a few moments to digest all that, his face locked in an expression of arch disgust that, Catt considered, was probably so habitual that it just relaxed into it in times of absent contemplation. At last he snapped out some commands in the Yorughan tongue, and half a dozen of the big warriors ran up, staring at the newcomers suspiciously.

"You say you know the Liberator," said the Aethani, and to his credit he said it without any hint of irony, surrounded by a mining camp synonymous with slavery. "We'll see. We'll pass your names to him, Cat and Fish, and if he doesn't want to know you, I'm sure you'll settle for lesser hospitality."

Doctor Catt smiled levelly at him. "Cat*t*," he said, giving his name a Cheriveni flair that made the doubled consonant apparent. "And if you would, dear fellow. Joss won't want us kept waiting."

ANY APPROACH TO Dorhambri was a descent from the hills, which meant that Celestaine's company had plenty of good vantage points on the fort. That Silvermort wasn't expecting an attack was clear: the attention of the guards was mostly on the mine and its workers. There was also a convenient amount of bustle down there, plenty of activity around the foundry and the minehead, and the guards constantly crossing back and forth to their own quarters and the fort. When the Kinslayer had set up shop here, he hadn't been planning for outside assault either. The fort cast an imposing, magically-augmented presence over everything, but it had three gates and two stood open.

"Either of you see inside of there?" she asked.

Neither Nedlam or Heno had, but when the Kinslayer ordered a fort built, it wasn't as though he had architects come up with a unique and exciting plan each time.

"Count on a lot of it being underneath," Nedlam pointed out. "He always did make us dig in. Especially where there were mines."

"Most of the quarters, cells, stores," Heno agreed.

"So can we get into the lower layers from the mines?" Celestaine asked them.

"Maybe." Nedlam shrugged. "Why not ask Kul?"

She blinked at the Yorughan for a moment and realised the Aethani was standing close by her elbow, very pointedly. "I... Yes, of course."

Amkulyah's jaw was tight, and she could see the tension about his eyes, gripping the skin there. "How much did you see, down there?" she asked him.

"I was there six years, seven?" he said quietly. "What they've dug out since, I don't know, but I knew every corner of that place. They never let us out under the sky, my people. It was an error of the Kinslayer, I think. If we'd seen the sky each night, the sky we couldn't reach, it would hurt more." He glared at them, a brief spike of the anger that was normally so well hidden in him. "Yes, there is a way from the mines to beneath the fort, so the guards could control us better. So they could drag us off for beatings and murder us somewhere private. Yes, I can take you there. But there is a door, of course, and there are guards, and there will be guards going into the mine and guards in the tunnels, just like when I was a slave here."

"Well..." Celestaine said thoughtfully. One thing had changed since the Kinslayer's day: Silvermort's guards were hardly uniform, as the armies of the enemy had been. The only difference between them and their charges was who was standing where, some of the time.

Ralas had plainly been thinking along the same lines. "Brazen it out?"

"Brazen it out," she confirmed. She was going to ask Kul if he was sure he wanted to go back, but he was practically buzzing with anger, and possibly that was his way of dealing with what he was seeing. True, it wasn't his people under the lash, but there were still whips and hands to wield them.

"It's going to be tough on the nerves, if nothing else," she told them all. "We're going to just slip round the side of that building and then march for the minehead. Heno and Ned are guards, we three are workers. You look a bit too much like Kinslayer soldiers, the pair of you, but I see a fair amount of war surplus down there. We just have to hope the guards aren't so close-knit that a couple of unfamiliar faces will spark notice."

"What if they do?" Heno asked. "Or what if something else goes wrong? If there's a password, or you look too healthy and unbeaten to be a slave miner?"

She opened her mouth to say that they'd deal with that when they came to it, exactly the sort of response that used to horrify her from an officer, but a new voice broke in.

"You should listen to your Yogg. You can't just bluster this. Look at them, it's not an army, where nobody questions the orders. It's a hundred little personal fiefdoms down there, every bully ruling the space within arm's reach. And everyone'll notice a bigger bully like her." And a thin-faced man wearing the sort of half-armour, half civvies of the guards below was prodding Nedlam's ample bicep.

Celestaine stared at him a long time as he stood in the shadow of Nedlam's raised club, the Yorughan just waiting for her nod to flatten him. At last she said, "Deffo."

He looked aggrieved. "How can you always tell?"

"Your voice." She hadn't realised before she said it. "There's a whine in it I'd know a mile off. What do you want?"

"I want to help." He flinched even as he said it, anticipating her response.

"No 'sing me songs and make me famous,' this time?" Ralas asked him.

"Please," the Undefeated whispered. "I understand why you cast me off all those times. But let me *earn* it. Let me help you do whatever you're doing. I..." He stuttered with self-pity. "I was great once. I fought the Kinslayer. It's just that, you come into the world with a name like the Undefeated, and you stand there looking at your brother's blood, silver across the ground where the power's been sucked from it, and you wonder how long that name will hold. I was afraid. I've been afraid longer than you've been alive. I'm a thousand years old; it's a lot to lose. But I'm here now. I want to be that Undefeated again, the one who wasn't afraid to fight. I'll help."

"How?" Celestaine asked bluntly.

"I'll go into the earth with you. And I can show you a place, where to dig. You can cut into the mines without going down that lift, without their questions. With your sword, you can. Let me lead you. Just..."

"Just tell everyone how wonderful you are, after," Celestaine finished for him, and then held up a hand against his protestations. "Deffo, if we come out of this with what we're after, I will sing your damn praises myself."

"Not the honour you might think," Ralas put in. "Not once

you've heard her voice." Even so, the look of hope and gratitude in the destitute Guardian's face was pitiful.

The Undefeated took them between the hills, skulking from shadow to shadow as though the very sun was trying to find him. He cast left and right like a mongrel looking for a scent. Celestaine couldn't convince herself he was doing anything useful. Each lost moment just screamed that it was all attention-seeking on his part. When at last he turned and said, "Here, carve it up here, and you'll come through," her expression must have dampened his enthusiasm considerably.

"How can you even know?" she demanded. "Why here? There's nothing to mark it out." She indicated the scrubby hillside they were on, which had nothing to recommend it as a secret entrance to the mines.

His smile was a desperate thing, but still the most genuine thing about him. "You forget," he almost whispered. "I was a badger, for years. Nothing knows the earth like a badger. Right here, Celestaine." His shaky hand described a circle in the earth.

Feeling like a fool, she drew out her sword, noting the scabbard already starting to fray. With a sigh, she drove it to the hilt in the ground, feeling the edge grate on earth and stone, the momentary almost-musical twangs of severed roots. She drew the circle, leaning a little into it, the blade cleaving the rock as though she was moving it through clear honey. It was good for cutting, but not so much for excavation, and when she had the circle cut, nothing happened. Was there a tunnel a foot lower? How could she know?

Heno was crouching, though, all but putting his ear to the grass. He murmured, and she saw a film of white energy dance across his face and eyes.

"Hollow," he muttered, and then scrambled hurriedly out of the way as Nedlam just came over and stamped hard in the centre of the circle Celestaine had cut. And vanished in a sudden cloud of displaced earth as the ground gave way beneath her.

They all gathered at the lip of the hole, looking down into the dark. Heno sniffed derisively. "She's fine." Amkulyah hesitated a moment, clenching his fists, and then jumped down; landing on Nedlam, if the sound was anything to go by.

The others descended more cautiously, and Heno conjured a pale little flame to show the interior of a mine gallery, dust thick on the floor. Plainly whatever seam had run here had been mined out long ago.

"Kul?" Celestaine asked.

Heno's light caught in the Aethani's wide eyes. She heard his shivering breath, but then he nodded and said. "I know it. I know every inch of it. Follow me."

JOCIEN SILVERMORT WAS a long-boned man, six inches over Fisher, who was tall for a Cheriveni; considerably more over Doctor Catt. He had broad shoulders, accentuated by the metal pauldrons sewn into the sleeveless coat he wore, with pockets arrayed about the waist. Beneath the coat was some semblance of Arvennir military order uniform, with a curved razor or knife thrust into his belt, the gold and bone hilt ostentatiously on show. He moved his lanky limbs gingerly, a little like a spider does, when it feels something brush its web. His face was the oldest part of him, thin and mean, hollow-cheeked, with a small mouth that always relaxed back into an expression of bitter disappointment no matter what smile he put on. The thatch of fair hair on top might have salvaged the rest a little, but he had the sides shaved to stubble, a dated Arvennir look, and it only accentuated the sourness of the rest of him.

Across his chest was a half-breastplate displaying a white eight-pointed star. This had been the badge of the Liberator during the war, symbol of the false hope he brought with him. These days he didn't make his guards wear it. It was his alone.

"They're not really my people, not like the old days," he explained to Catt and Fisher once they'd joined him at his breakfast. He sat at one end of a table that bore far too many scars and stains to have been intended for eating. A whole ham was set out for him, along with bread, honey and raisins, but he didn't offer a seat to his unexpected guests. Instead he picked at the food slowly, a scrap here, a crumb there, and his left eye examined them thoughtfully. The right was a narrow milky slit under the droop of a lazy lid that twitched and trembled of its own accord. It gave half his face a profoundly suspicious expression. "They don't... last," he added lugubriously. "So they don't get to wear the star." His speech was slow, full of pregnant pauses as he chose his words, the longest of which seemed to get pushed out sideways and with difficulty from his lips.

"Do tell," Catt said politely.

"When they send me their dregs," Silvermort went on, "I look them over. I can tell who's apt for my purposes, who's better holding the rod than under it." He dragged at his right cheek, revealing more of the orb beneath: not a living eye but a clouded marble, surely enchanted. "I'm a good judge of character," he said. With that pronouncement still hanging in the air, he asked, "To what do I owe the honour, doctors?"

"It's been a while since we heard from you over in Cinquetann," Catt said, sitting on the table edge. "We were passing through, on the way to acquiring a few curios, and I said, why don't we pop in on our old acquaintance Master Silvermort? I've always wanted to admire your collection in its full glory."

"My collection." Silvermort said the words as though they had no meaning, pressing down on the table to stand from his barely-touched breakfast. "Doctors..." He stared at them thoughtfully, the marble glinting from beneath his sagging eyelid. "I'm not really a collector like you are. My interests are... specialised."

"We've noted you had a fondness for Kinslayer memorabilia even before he was cold," Catt agreed. "While he was very much alive, in fact."

"Know your enemy." Abruptly Silvermort was very close to them, looming over the pair, his narrow mouth wrung into a painful-looking smile. "The world was a different place when he was in it, wouldn't you say? Dangerous. Interesting. He made... opportunities."

He stalked past them to a door, for all the world as if that was the end of the interview and they could make their own way out. As he opened it, though, he paused. "Well?"

"Well?" Catt queried, somewhat unnerved by the sudden shifts in conversation.

"You wanted to see what I've done with my... collection." Again that smile. "I'm afraid it won't compare to your own. I don't hold much with all that... display. But come on, doctors. After all, I've been... working a long time. And you're educated men. You'll... appreciate... what I've done here."

As they joined him in the doorway they heard distant sounds from below, echoing weirdly until they were just formless shrieks and bellows.

"Good gracious," Doctor Catt remarked faintly. "Are those your miners?"

"Oh, no," Silvermort confirmed. "It's just that some parts of my collection are... livelier than others. Things of the Kinslayer, doctors. All sorts of... things."

CHAPTER TWENTY

THE UPPER GALLERIES where they'd come in were long-abandoned, the low-hanging fruit of the mine, seams picked clean probably long before the Kinslayer had taken the place. From below, echoing weirdly down the tunnels, came the sounds of the active face, the clack and hammer of picks, shouting, the occasional crack of a whip.

Amkulyah moved surprisingly swiftly through the tunnels, pausing for only a heartbeat at each branch before choosing his route, leading them ever downwards. He was small, of course, and the tunnels here were low. Celestaine had to stoop, desperately scrabbling to follow the sound of his progress, as the only light was the receding morning behind her and a faint radiance of lamps from far ahead. Of the others, Nedlam displayed a surprising turn of speed on all fours, her shoulders brushing the tunnel sides from time to time.

Celestaine was struck by the change in Kul's manner. He moved swiftly, but his shoulders were turned in, his head bowed. When he stopped he was very still, so that she almost lost track of him. He didn't look back at his followers, and sometimes she almost thought he was trying to lose them.

Then he had paused, and they could all hear the sounds of much more immediate activity ahead, the scuff of feet, a couple of harsh voices speaking Yorughan. Kul seemed to shrink until only a ghost of himself was left, trembling slightly. When Celestaine touched him lightly on the arm, he flinched away, and his wing-limbs thrashed in momentary panic.

"It's all right." She stared into his wide eyes, enough light bleeding here for her to read the shadowy angles of his face. For a moment she thought he didn't know her, that the memories had just washed away all the months since he regained his freedom. Then he pulled back from her, himself again.

"Down, down, left, left, down," he muttered, reading from the map of the tunnels in his head. Then, "But there will be guards. This wasn't a good plan."

The Undefeated pushed his way past Nedlam, hands up as though he were about to strangle the Aethani. "This is the best plan. This is the only plan. You can't take this away from—"

"Shut up," Celestaine hissed at him. She took a deep breath. "Yes, there will be guards. That was always the deal. How often is this gate used—or *was* used, when you were here?"

"Not much: twice, three times a day for guards going out, but most went out from the top, to control the miners who got to live up there. Or if there was trouble at the face, they'd come out then, in force."

"So replace the guards with your Yoggs," the Undefeated put in, desperate to please.

"Because we all look the same, obviously," Heno put in drily. "Also, what if you need us?"

At that point advanced planmaking was put on hold as three guards walked into them.

There were two Yorughan and a big, scarred human, and precisely what they'd been off into the old galleries to do was anyone's guess, from a crafty smoke to a clandestine threesome. They were just as surprised as the intruders when they rounded a corner and found a bunch of complete strangers arguing about how to infiltrate the fortress.

It wasn't the sort of surprise that played out in valuable seconds of complete silence, unfortunately. Just about everyone started yelling, and then one of the Yorughan was pelting back the way they'd come, and the other two, perhaps not seeing just how *many* intruders there were in the poor light, went wading in.

Celestaine shifted aside to let Kul get out of the way, but he had made himself scarce already. Instead, she had a sense of blurred motion and a swung club whirred past her face and hit the tunnel wall with splintering force. Her sword still sheathed, her reflex was to kick her human attacker between the legs, hearing a satisfactorily horrified hiss and watching the club fall from nerveless fingers. Then the Yorughan was at her, having gone for a knife as weapon of choice, a good call in the close tunnel. Celestaine fell back from the thrust, heel turning on a loose stone so that she ended up crashing painfully onto her back. The Yorughan jumped on her, blade drawn back, and then obviously saw how many friends she had. He tried to cut her anyway, a hasty slash that barely nicked her cloak, and then scrabbled backwards. Celestaine made to get up and almost got Nedlam's knee through the back of her head as the big Yorughan woman pounded over her, grabbing the guard's knife-wrist and bringing it down against the stone floor, loosening his grip on the weapon. A moment later the two of them were struggling, strength against strength and almost completely silent save for the occasional grunt.

The human guard had recovered his wits enough to get his club back, bringing it down on Nedlam's skull to try and free up his friend. Ralas got in the way of that one, taking the blow to his chest with a sickening splintering of bone and going down instantly. Before Celestaine could get her sword clear, the Undefeated jumped on the guard's shoulders like a monkey, wrenching at his head and biting at his ear. With that distraction, Celestaine had her weapon out and into him, striking low to avoid taking Deffo's leg off. She tried to wrestle the blade into a swing that would only wound him, but that was a tough call with an edge as sharp as the sword boasted. The blade ended up going into the man's abused groin, and that was it for him. The sharp crack she heard as he hit the ground was the neck of the guard Nedlam was fighting, Yorughan bones yielding to even greater Yorughan strength.

"One got away, though," Ralas wheezed. He was lying on his back and she could see his tunic twitch and shudder as his ribs sorted themselves out.

"We'd better move fast…" Celestaine stopped. From up ahead came Amkulyah, when she thought he'd bolted for the back. He had his bow in hand and no expression on his face. Ten feet on they found the body of the other Yorughan, an arrow neatly jutting from between skull and spine.

"They'll see us from here," Amkulyah said. "So we just go. Is that all right? We go for the door, through it, and if they have people on the other side, we kill them. We kill them."

These aren't the jailers that kept your people enslaved, Celestaine wanted to tell him, but she couldn't say they were much different, either, and she couldn't look Kul in the face and tell him no.

CATT AND FISHER peered down at the monsters in the pit below, neither of them getting too close to the railing in case Jocien Silvermort turned out to have that sort of sense of humour.

"Vathesk, then." Catt managed to regard the three crablike monsters with equanimity as they raised their great claws towards him, pleading for sustenance. There were bones and bits of body trampled about the pit floor, but of course nothing that would have sated the otherworldly creatures.

Silvermort made a dissatisfied sound. "I thought they'd eat each other," he said. "I wanted the… strongest Vathesk. But they won't. No matter how hungry they are." He shrugged. "I should get rid of them, but... how to go about it?" He turned away, heading further down into the chambers beneath the fortress. Catt caught Fisher's glance and raised his eyebrows high, to convey his declining impression of their old business associate. Fisher rolled his eyes. *I said so, didn't I?*

"There was that rod, the one with the emerald skull on it," Silvermort cast over his shoulder as he skulked on through his own halls like a thief. "You got me that, didn't you?"

"Enchezzar's Sceptre of Dominion," Catt agreed. "You traded us a set of dragon teeth and the Abominable Helm of Temmor the Damned."

"I thought it would command the Vathesk," Silvermort said, mildly disgruntled. "But they ignored me. Only *he* could make them do things. However he did it, it's... lost. They're useless now."

"We should find a way to send them home, really," Catt agreed.

Silvermort stopped and looked back at him blankly. "Why?"

Catt smiled by desperate reflex. "Oh, quite, why would anyone bother? But you were going to show us some more of your collection."

"I keep telling you," Silvermort lurched off again. "It's not a collection, it's... research."

Fisher hissed through his teeth abruptly. They were passing along a corridor lined with doors, most hanging open but plainly intended to be cells as the need arises. Fisher drew a sharp breath in through his teeth, prompting a concerned look from Catt.

"Do you need your pills again?"

Fisher just shook his head, but Silvermort was watching, mouth screwed into that twisted smile again. "Yes, it was here. Here I... broke through. Nothing of yours, this. My own researches. My own... acquisitions."

"Ah, well, success in one's investigations is always a joyous thing," Catt decided. Fisher put a hand on his shoulder and he winced at the pincering pressure of the fingers. "Easy, Fishy."

Fisher's long face said eloquently that this was a bad place to be in, but Doctor Catt just smiled, blithe in the face of any number of ill omens. "I daresay you'll be showing us what all this was in aid of," he tried.

"Yes," Silvermort said, his stone gaze twitching between them as though trying to pin down something they were hiding. "Yes, the thing all your... baubles were in aid of. You might as well see. You might as well be the first ones. At least you'll appreciate it."

THE GATE TO the fortress hadn't been locked. It had been guarded by a couple of bored-looking men who were plainly sitting there to ensure no miners went absent to go raid Silvermort's wine cellar or his pantry. Celestaine and the others had gone into a huddle to discuss the best way to deal with them without raising the alarm, and partway into that, Amkulyah had just shot them both dead, one after the other. One of them had fallen of his chair with a clatter, but apparently those within would require more than that before they came out to investigate.

"That's... Well, right," Celestaine said. Nedlam, always the pragmatist, went and got the bodies and hauled them off into the upper galleries where they might not be found for a while.

Kul was looking a little frightened at his own actions, but plainly ready to push right back if Celestaine called him on them. She had no idea what kind of a tangled snarl his thoughts were in, right then. *Should have left him behind.* But then they'd be wandering lost through the mines. And if this had been the war, and they'd been the minions of the Kinslayer, she'd have killed them without a thought, she knew. And Heno was standing at her shoulder, proof positive that those minions had a right to life and freedom, same as everyone else. So why should Silvermort's thugs, complicit here in the slave labour of so many, warrant greater consideration?

But the war's over, she tried to tell herself, except that some wars are never over.

Nedlam came back and they slipped into the fortress, closing the door behind them.

Amkulyah's role as guide ended there, of course; he hadn't had much of a chance to wander the Kinslayer's actual stronghold. The Yorughan had confirmed there would be plenty of business belowground, as per their former master's standard building strategy, and she was looking at the evidence of that now. Distant sounds echoed from above, where presumably Silvermort's staff were keeping parts of the fortress habitable for his use. So would he be keeping his precious treasures up there to be dusted by the underfootman? Probably not. Not when the Kinslayer's design had provided him with a whole realm of cells and chambers beneath.

That was her logic, anyway, and she was uncomfortably aware that it was untested. Rather than just charge off, she had a hurried conference of whispers with the others, which Heno ended definitively by saying, "I smell magic. Strong magic, from below. Maybe this crown, maybe not, but something touched by the Reck—the Kinslayer. Something of his."

"Can you lead us from here?"

He shrugged. "Magic doesn't care about where the doors or the stairs are, but I can try."

They hunted along the level they were on, looking for stairs. In some rooms they saw guards sleeping—or, once, a bunch of them raucously gambling, paying no attention whatsoever. Soon they were plainly beyond any guard, entering a dimmer realm where the walls echoed to monstrous, distant sounds that brought shivers of remembrance to Celestaine. *What has he got down here? Was that a Vathesk?* Then Heno sniffed at the air and took a sharp turn, heading down a line of thankfully unoccupied cells. Probably there were few situations that would result in Silvermort imprisoning one of his charges rather than simply having them killed.

Heno was slowing, though, towards the corridor's end. Celestaine could see what looked like steps down at the end, and had been putting on a burst of speed. He dragged at her shoulder, though, and soon they had dawdled almost to a stop.

"What?" she demanded, though her own feeble sense for magic was prickling the hairs of her neck.

"You don't feel it?" Heno seldom deigned to look worried, but something was eating at him now. "There's power here, or the echo of it, but not power I know…" He cast about, then recoiled from a nearby cell. "What's been *done* here."

"What do you mean?"

"Your Silvermort. He's a magician?"

"Of sorts. Not a book-learning magician, but he was always good with what he picked up."

"He's picked up a lot," Heno murmured. He had his staff extended as though about to wake a bear with it, nudging open one of the cell doors. "What…?"

At first glance it was just another windowless little room, and Celestaine's eyes told her she was seeing a strange play of shadows from the low corridor lamps. The lamplight was a sullen amber, though, while the gleaming shapes cast across the cell walls were silvery, and didn't make sense until she tilted her head and they abruptly became a great argent splatter across one wall. Attempts had been made to scrape it off, but the smear remained, a chaotic spatter that reminded her of nothing more than…

"Blood…?" *But what bleeds silver?*

The Undefeated drew in a ragged breath. He was shaking, his hands half-up as if to fend something off. He gaped at her baffled look. "You can't...? How can you not *know*? Even the Yogg understands what happened here. How come you can't even feel it?"

"Someone tell me what's going on," Celestaine snapped.

"Power," Heno said. "A great release of power, somehow. Contained, but enough of it got loose to taint this place for a hundred years." He scowled. "I should recognise it."

"You should," the Undefeated agreed, prodding at him with a trembling finger. "You're steeped in this blood, all your kind are. It made your master what he was."

"Deffo, just tell me," Celestaine ordered. "What *is* this white stuff?"

He looked as though he might vanish away at any minute, his new-found courage dangling by a thread. "That's *our* blood. The blood of the divine," he moaned. "They killed one of us here, oh, yes they did. Opened him up and let the godhead flood out. The Lightbearer, it was. I can feel the echo of him. Oh, you poor bastard, to end up here."

"The Lightbearer died in Cinquetann," Celestaine told him.

"He fell there. They wounded him gravely. I thought he'd died," agreed the Undefeated. "But no, they must have taken him. The Kinslayer must have done such things to him that... but he ended up here, still living, somehow. And someone finished the job. Not too long ago, either."

"Silvermort," Ralas put in. "Celest, this is sounding worse and worse."

"You want to turn back?" she asked him.

"Me? No, but I've got less to lose than the rest of you."

"I STARTED SMALL, did you know?" Silvermort called back to them as they descended another flight of steps. Doctor Catt was wondering how far the Kinslayer had tunnelled into the earth here for his own chambers. It seemed otiose to do so when there was a perfectly good mine next door. He made an enquiring noise to keep the conversation going, while checking that his protective amulet, his walking stick and various other magical gewgaws were to hand, should this business take an untoward turn.

"Banditry, protection," Jocien continued. "We'd roll up and tell some village there were raiders on the way, and they could pay us to protect them. Sometimes there were. Sometimes the raiders... were us. But small beer, doctors. The war changed everything. Suddenly everyone would pay... everything for our protection. I was the Liberator. And when you're fighting on the side of right against the ultimate darkness, you can take... everything, doctors. It was a golden age, when the war was on. Except towards the end, when our side started winning battles, and nobody needed the Liberator and his friends. And some of the other heroes started... asking questions. They'll come for me, you know." He had stopped at a door and was squinting back at them, as though suspecting them of being in the pay of heroes.

"Fancy that," Doctor Catt said pleasantly. Beside him, Fisher was fidgety and ill at ease, had been ever since the cell bay.

"Sooner or later they'd remember old Jocien," Silvermort told them with a fond smile. "All my old comrades. The live ones, anyway. Peace time's no use to me, doctors. I need... conflict, chaos. The Kinslayer gave me the best years of my life. Even before they killed him, I could see that if he went, I'd miss him."

"That's a novel viewpoint," Catt noted politely.

Silvermort back-kicked the door open and then spun on his heel to march through. "The magic helped with the banditry, at the start," he explained, turning abruptly back to hold the door for them as though he was a servant, even sweeping a mocking bow. "I never had the sort of... erudition you can boast, doctors, but I had a knack for spellcraft. I could always see how to make

242

things work, how they fit together. And you were so very kind. You got me some... choice morsels, in exchange for some of the war loot. You made it all possible, really."

The room beyond was a long hall, cluttered with alchemical apparatus and magical engines, some stolen, some apparently roughly assembled by Silvermort or his people. On either side, long galleries overlooked the floor, suggesting that the room had been made for some other purpose than the tangled laboratory it had been pressed into service as. There was a half-dozen of Jocien's people here, and they all bore the Liberator's star emblem somewhere on their person. Three were human, one was a dwarfish Grennishman with four skinny arms, and the remaining two were Yorughan. Not just your regular kind either, Catt noted without enthusiasm; they wore the white edged greatcoats of the Heart Takers, though he guessed they would be less congenial than Celestaine's companion.

"I had the idea towards the end of the war." Silvermort turned with a flourish, sweeping up from a bench a bejewelled mace Catt identified as Enchezzar's Sceptre of Dominion, formerly of his stock in trade. "But I ran into a dead end. I didn't have the power and I... didn't have the focus. All just dead meat without that, of course. Except you found me one very particular rarity, and while I was in Cinquetann I did some shopping. I'd heard from some of the Kinslayer's people about a certain treasure still locked up beneath the town. A certain injured but still-just-living treasure the Kinslayer had been... saving. And now I'm ready, thanks to you. And here you are in time to see it all... come to fruition. And that's convenient, because you're smart enough to put the pieces together when the news gets out. I'd only have had to send people to kill you, and that would be... tiresome, very tiresome."

Catt and Fisher exchanged looks. It was hardly the first time they'd been in this situation, although Catt's vestigial sense for magic was sending all sorts of worrying signals.

"My dear fellow," he said, as calmly as could be, "you're obviously itching to enact the grand reveal. Which, precisely, was the key trinket we provided, and what does it allow you to accomplish?"

On the gallery above, Celestaine and her company looked down on the unfolding drama,

"See a crown anywhere?" she murmured to Amkulyah, who had the best eyes.

He shook his head, but nodded to a great table where some shape lay, like a huge corpse, beneath a heavy velvet curtain. One foot was protruding, clad in mail. Celestaine thought about the big man who had apparently gone from place to place with their quarry. *Did Silvermire kill him and take the crown? Did he leave the clue because he didn't trust Jocien, and wanted to be avenged?* It didn't ring true. But there could be a crown beneath the shroud.

Heno was looking the two Heart Takers over. At her look he shook his head slightly. "The bigger one's Tarraki. She got sent all over for the serious torturing. Specialist in bodies and how to break them. The other I don't know, but he looks low rank; she's the big threat."

"The Grennishman was in the mines before," Kul breathed. "He's a magician. He used to sniff out seams for us to dig."

"He's yours, then," Celestaine decided. "We're ready to go over the rail?" She glanced around to find the Undefeated hanging back, his eyes wide.

"This is a bad place," he whispered. "We need to leave now. Something terrible's here."

"Pipe down," Nedlam hissed. "I want to hear. He's about to show his thing."

Celestaine, who'd lost track of the conversation between Silvermort and the inexplicably present Doctor Catt, looked over the rail, half-expecting Jocien to be unbuckling his belt. Instead, Silvermort was gesturing to the covered corpse.

"You remember what you got me, that little keepsake from Nydarrow?" he asked Catt. "They burned the rest, I was... so disappointed to find out, but you gave me a *hand* with my collection anyway."

"Oh, dear," Catt said. "Dear me, that was terrible. Beneath you."

"What?" Ralas wondered, but Celestaine suddenly had a very ill feeling about what Silvermort meant. Nydarrow, of unfond memory: the Kinslayer's home fortress, where she had teamed up with Ned and Heno, where she had... Her hand tightened on her sword grip.

Silvermort gestured with the wand he had, and the shrouded figure sat up abruptly, the curtain sloughing off it. Revealed was an armoured form as large as Nedlam, but weirdly piecemeal, no two parts of it quite matching. One arm was the great chitinous pincer of a Vathesk. The other was Yorughan, but the hand stitched to its wrist was pale, outsize but more human save for its curved nails. She knew it instantly.

The figure swung its metal-clad legs from the bench and stood, the darkness within its helm directed squarely at Silvermort. Abruptly, a pair of membranous wings erupted from its back, dramatic but pointless, for it was far too heavy to use them. The Aethani they had been cut from would have been a quarter of the thing's size.

"Behold," Silvermort said, and in the moment of revelation all glee had gone from his voice. He was seriousness incarnate. "They killed the Kinslayer just when I was doing so well out of him, but it's all right, I've... made a new one."

CHAPTER TWENTY-ONE

THE UNDEFEATED GAVE out a weird kind of whimper, more animal than human, but born entirely of fear. Even as Celestaine turned for him he was backing away, and a moment later he was running, all his promises of aid streaming behind him like tattered flags.

"Oh, for..." But that was that. There would plainly be no help from that direction.

Down below, Silvermort was stepping back, and his little cadre of magicians had spread out a little—definitely to keep out of reach of the Kinslayer construct thing they had built as much as to get a good look. Things didn't look good for Catt and Fisher, and Celestaine didn't feel that was anybody's fault except their own. *What are they here for, after all? The same thing they were sniffing for in Ilkand. They want the crown, and they've been following me to it.* It all seemed pitifully obvious, now.

So, let the monster do them in, and then do the monster in, and Silvermort as well.

"This is rather untoward, Jocien," Doctor Catt was saying, one hand plucking at his collar.

Silvermort snickered, a mean little sound for a man of ambition. "But I can't save people from the Kinslayer if they know it's *my* Kinslayer, doctors. And you'd have worked it out far too quickly... Really, seeing you on my doorstep, I couldn't credit my own luck." And he waved the sceptre languorously, like a despot accepting tribute. The Kinslayer thing he'd made lurched into motion, clumsy at first but becoming more sure with each step. The helmed head wobbled and jolted on its neck, tilted over to one side, and its legs seemed slightly different lengths, yet it exuded power nonetheless. A Guardian had died to make it, and curdled divinity shone darkly from every join and suture.

"Just kill them quickly. They've earned that much," Silvermort said, abruptly tired of his own voice and all the pageantry, and Celestaine felt that familiar combination of guilt and duty that made her do things misguided people called heroic.

"Heno, do something with the Heart Takers. Kul, shoot things. Ned, come with me."

"And me?" demanded Ralas, but to be honest she wasn't really seeing him as a combat asset. She vaulted the rail and dropped down into the laboratory below, sword clearing her scabbard, and ran for the fake Kinslayer with the thought of just cutting the dead thing in half and having done with it. She heard Silvermort bark with surprise, and guessed she'd have to deal with him after, but he'd be a lot less mouthy with his precious creation in pieces on the floor.

She had to trust that everyone else was getting on with things behind her, since she still had half the length of the room to cover to get to her target. At the corner of her eye she saw one of the human mages trying to get in her way. Rather than dodge into his reach she went over the next table, kicking a priceless assemblage of glassware onto the floor save for one half-full alembic, which she rescued and threw at his face. Whatever had been bubbling away there set new parameters for the term 'volatile' as the luckless man went up like a goose-fat torch, staggering away in a roaring pillar of flame. She didn't have time to stop and either admire or regret her handiwork, however, because the fake Kinslayer had reached its victims.

Catt was surrounded by a nimbus of purple energy, and the gaping pincer that lunged for him skittered off it, sending him sideways to rebound from the wall, cracks flowering across his magical barrier. Fisher just ran, ducking away from the creature with his staff raised to protect himself, his other hand pulling up his robes to knee height to give his long legs play. He ended up going directly at Celestaine, saw her and her blade with only a slight widening of the eyes and dropped down onto his back, sliding past her beneath her swing as she lashed at the false Kinslayer's neck.

She took its head off neatly, just as she had planned. The backswing of its hand—that damnable man-like hand she had cut from the real Kinslayer in Nydarrow—caught her in the chest, denting her breastplate and flinging her back into the table she'd vaulted, collapsing it in a jagged nest of splinters and digging broken glass into her wherever her armour didn't cover.

She waited for the thing to fall over, but it wasn't even slowed by the loss of its head. It was a magical construct; why would it need something so minor as a head?

She fought to get clear of the table, breathing with difficulty because her breastplate was pushing into her sternum. A brief glance showed her that everyone else was busy. Towards the back of the room a salvo of white sparks marked Heno and the Yorughan woman, Tarraki, exchanging magic, but who had the upper hand she couldn't say. Nedlam had killed one of the humans pretty much by landing on him club first, and was now warily approaching the younger Heart Taker, whose hands flashed with fire. Even as Celestaine registered him drawing back to launch something vicious at Ned, an arrow appeared in the Heart Taker's eye and he was down, quick as that. Then she had other things to worry about: she still couldn't breathe properly, and the fake Kinslayer was lumbering towards her, pincer raised to turn her into paste.

She kicked back from the wreckage of the table, intending to separate the pincer from the rest of the thing, but those stolen wings clapped out suddenly, sweeping the walls either side of the thing and whipping forth a blast of air that knocked her from her feet again. She went spinning backwards, fell over the cowering Grennishman and lost her sword, which spun across the floor, hacking the legs from another table. The abused furniture tipped, and a great copper vat toppled and burst against the floor, spilling a wave of something corrosive and reeking that Celestaine skittered back from hurriedly. When she looked up it was into the impassive chest of the ersatz Kinslayer.

The rest of the room was still locked in furious combat, but right there, between her and her monstrous enemy, there was a moment of calm in which she thought, *Should have killed you harder the first time.* An arrow drove itself to the fletchings under the thing's left pauldron, punching into the rubbery dead flesh. Another shattered against the Vathesk carapace of its right arm. It didn't seem to notice.

Then Ralas broke in, or at least his voice did. For a moment, Celestaine thought he'd gone mad, because this was no time to bring up an old Forinthi folk song. Still, there was Ralas virtually at the fake Kinslayer's elbow, head tilted back and eyes closed, just like she remembered. He even had his hands up as though he held his harp still, memory twitching his fingers into the chords of 'Out of the Mists and over the Sea':

> "*Blow, blow, wind and rain,*
> *Blow my love home again,*
> *Empty heart shall be my refrain*
> *Until I'm with my love again,*"

he sang, and then put in, *sotto voce*, "There really is some of *him* in you, isn't there? He always loved that one. Would have kept me alive for no other reason, maybe." And then, even as the monstrous form shook itself he was singing again, the whole room falling silent as each combatant in turn caught the melody and looked around to see what on earth was going on.

Celestaine, who'd heard the song plenty often before, started to shift around the spreading pool of acid towards her fallen sword.

"If you've enjoyed this performance," Ralas said into the silence after the second chorus, "then perhaps you could finish the job and take this curse from me, because everything hurts, and believe me, I want it over."

A sound came from within the thing's barrel torso, not a word, barely even a grunt, just a sound. If there was any connection to intelligence there, Celestaine couldn't hear it.

"No!" Silvermort suddenly broke the spell. "Kill them! Kill them all!" And he raised his sceptre again. "You are an engine of destruction!" he railed at the creature. "You will lead an army to imperil the world, so I can... save it! So I can be the hero!" And he brought the bejewelled rod down across Ralas's head so hard Celestaine thought it would shatter.

The bard went down instantly, and the spell was gone as swift as that, the patchwork monster back on form and trying to kill her.

So: scratch the power of song. Next stratagem, please. Celestaine ducked under the sweep of the thing's manlike hand, feeling its thumb snag her cloak briefly; it was far faster than it should be. Abruptly she was right in front of Jocien Silvermort, bringing her sword up awkwardly towards him as she tried to keep her balance. He had a blade in his off-hand, but he obviously remembered her tricks because he didn't try a parry, merely swayed aside from the obvious stroke. Except that she was perfectly balanced, thank you very much, and twisted the blade's course so that, firstly, it guarded her from any strike of his, and secondly, it cut his little sceptre clean in two.

The look on his face was worth it.

She tried to cut his face in two as well, to complete the set, but he leapt back, froglike, throwing the stump of his magical toy at her in a shower of bleeding magic. He ended up almost with his back against the wall and mostly standing on Doctor Catt, who had taken refuge there already. Catt yelled, his toes well and truly stomped, and whacked Silvermort across the shoulders with his cane. The emerald set into its head flashed with power, and Silvermort was knocked to the far side of the room, a great charred streak scarring the back of his coat.

Celestaine would have loved to take advantage of that to gut the man, but the false Kinslayer was still going for her rather than rushing to chastise its former master. She had her sword back, but it was getting swifter with each movement, more at home in that lopsided body. She struck three times, trying for its joints and hoping to dismember it, but it evaded the blows with a dismaying nimbleness. Then the pincer came for her again, snapping like a shark. She tried to use that opportunity to cut it off, but settled for scarring the top of it and warding it away. Then she was dancing awkwardly over a body—probably the man Nedlam had landed on—just trying to keep a keen edge between herself and the enemy.

The Enemy. It really is. The actual enemy of everyone. Silvermort, you idiot. The wisdom of destroying the one thing that could rein the monster in was starting to look questionable. Could she not have cut Jocien's hand off at the wrist and taken his toy for herself? Apparently not.

Ralas, slightly the worse for wear, leapt on the monster's back, clambering up it and shouting his curses down its neck-hole. It ignored him. What it couldn't ignore quite so readily was Nedlam crashing into it at top speed.

It stayed on its feet, which was a minor miracle in itself. The force of the impact knocked the Kinslayer back across almost half the room, with Ralas flying from its shoulders like a scarf in a high wind.

Nedlam stepped back and brought her club up in a blur of iron-bound wood, caving in the bottom of the thing's breastplate without seeming to hurt it much. It tried to get its pincer about her arm but she ducked under it, arms about its broad waist, and just threw the entire monstrosity across the room with a roar.

It came down in a colossal crash of metal and shell, and Nedlam and Celestaine were both running to catch it before it righted itself. In that they failed, and Nedlam caught an uppercut from the claw that would have killed Celestaine outright, and which battered her into the nearest wall. Arrows were springing from the armoured form like mushrooms in autumn, but Kul had yet to find anywhere that counted as vital.

Celestaine squared off, sword out in one hand and the other finally releasing her breastplate strap so she could breathe properly. The fake Kinslayer shook itself, ratting Kul's arrows like a hedgehog's quills. Was it slower now? When it raked at her with its manlike hand, she got out from under the blow readily enough, though she reckoned she was slowing now herself. Then Doctor Fisher came up behind it with a determined expression and rammed his staff between its legs just as it tried to lunge for her. The hard wood exploded into shards, but the Kinslayer-thing went over, leaving Fisher with a comically small stub of wood to beat it with. Celestaine didn't hesitate, but rammed her sword into its body twice and then cut off one of the tines of its pincer as it threatened her, leaving it with a single jagged prong that looked almost as nasty. It was still clambering to its feet, despite the holes she'd punched in it.

A scattering of white fire danced over it from wherever Heno had got to, but the Kinslayer had never given his minions magic that might threaten his power, and this lifelike replica had inherited the same resistances.

Going to have to mince this damn thing before it stops, she decided, and then Jocien Silvermort grabbed her from behind, twisting her arms back and locking her sword out of harm's way.

"Kill her!" he bellowed in Celestaine's ear. "Kill the meddling bitch! Kill—*ach!*"

His grip was abruptly loose and she squirmed out of it and got behind him, seeing him with an arrow lanced through his arm and into his chest, probably the best safe shot Kul could make in the circumstances. Silvermort shrieked in rage and then the Kinslayer swatted him aside, still desperate to kill Celestaine, whether on Silvermort's orders or not.

Doctor Catt was shouting something at her, and she suddenly realised he'd been shouting it for a while, if she'd only had the spare concentration to listen. It was a pitifully obvious thing now he said it.

Still, easier said than done. Even slowed as it was by the sheer volume of arrows, a good swing at the monster was proving elusive. She backed away from its advance, wary of a floor now completely cluttered with bodies, broken glass and ruined furniture.

With a roar, with a bloody face and a broken tusk, Nedlam hurled herself on the Kinslayer, wrestling with that mutilated pincer, and Celestaine shouted, "No, the other arm, the *other arm!*" Ned didn't question. She took a blow from the pincer to do it, but for a golden second she had the Kinslayer's left arm under control, keeping the clawing fingers away from her face.

Celestaine wanted to spend two breaths lining up the blow, but even Nedlam's strength wasn't going to hold the beast for that long. She just had to cut, and hope that no part of Ned got on the wrong side of the stroke.

Despite the furious wrestling with the construct, she got it exactly right. The moment of contact was like deja-vu, because she really had done this before; this same hand, though from a different wrist.

Instantly the hulking body dropped to its knees and collapsed in a heap, flailing wings and all. The twitching, clawing shape she'd separated from it flew through the air and landed like a spider, threatening them with its long nails: all that was left of the Kinslayer.

Nedlam took considerable and evident pleasure in stamping on it until there was very little left that looked like a hand, or anything recognisable.

Celestaine looked around. Heno stood at the back of the room, Kul was still on the balcony.

"Nobody died," she said.

"Speak for yourself." Ralas was sitting with his back against the wall, watching his own bones knit. "Twice in one gig. Just like the real Kinslayer."

CHAPTER TWENTY-TWO

CELESTAINE TOOK A deep breath, sword still up, waiting for the next enemy. None came, and gingerly she sheathed the blade and removed her breastplate, looking mournfully at the sizeable dent.

"Two hours with a hammer," she decided. "At least."

A sudden movement nearby had her fumbling for her sword again but it was just Amkulyah dropping down from the balcony where he had prudently spent the fight. He gave her one of his owl-eyed looks before crossing to a broken table and lifting it up. Beneath, cowering with his four hands over his head, was the Grennishman. Again, Kul looked at Celestaine.

She shrugged. "All yours, like I said."

Kul crouched down by the cringing greenish creature. "You'd better go," he advised. "Go far. Run."

The Grennishman looked from him to Celestaine and then bolted from the room.

"I thought he was a guard in the mines?" Celestaine asked.

"He was in the mines," Amkulyah confirmed. "He was kind, sometimes. When he was down below, hunting magic ore, he would bring food, news. So I remember."

"Where's the other Slacker?" Nedlam asked suddenly.

"What?" said Heno, somewhat evasively.

"You were fighting her. That Tarraki." She eyed him suspiciously. "Don't see her body anywhere. You just turned her into itty bitty pieces?"

Heno's look said eloquently, *Since when did you start to notice things?* "I beat her," he said. "She knew I was better."

"You let her go?" Celestaine asked. "Heno, they were making a new Kinslayer down here."

He shrugged, somewhat defensively. "I knew her. What was I supposed to do?"

"I..." Abruptly Celestaine had the sense that his *knew* meant something more than casual acquaintance. An unexpected stab of jealously nearly had her demanding that he hunt Tarraki down and murder her, but she fought it back. "Fine, then. So where's the damned crown? I mean, if I was making a fake demigod to ride my stalking horse, I'd want some great big artefact of making and unmaking, wouldn't I? What's your professional opinion, Doctor Catt? Seeing as you seem to be so goddamn *involved* with all of this."

"I promise you, just passing through," Catt said, not entirely persuasively. "And yes, for what it's worth, I concur with your assessment of the crown's relevance to this endeavour." He was keeping a wary distance from all of them. Beside him, Fisher was looking dourly at the shattered remnants of his replacement staff.

Heno, perhaps to take attention from his past liaisons with Tarraki, stalked over and hauled up one of the bodies which, from its startled yelp, was still very much in the land of the living: none other than Jocien Silvermort.

"You malignant turd," Celestaine addressed him with some relish. "A new Kinslayer, was it?"

Silvermort looked like he'd hit the wall face first when his creation had slapped him aside. He was already swelling into a bouquet of bruises, forcing the little marble half out of his eyesocket. "You've cut your own throat, Celest," he mumbled through bloody lips. "You think it'd be just me who'd… profit? You're tired of the hero business? They don't need you any more, just like I can't work the same way when there isn't a bigger… shadow for people to be more scared of." He spat a streak of red onto the floor. "You could have had it made."

"I'll live," she told him flatly. "Tell me about the crown."

"What crown?"

"The Kinslayer's crown, the one he never got to wear," she said. "Some man of yours, or just some man, he came here with it. He brought it to you, sold it to you, you took it from him, he… some damn thing." As she stumbled over the words, she felt hope start to drain away, because it was all sounding very tenuous indeed. If he'd had such a thing in his hands, it would be here, where all his magic was concentrated. For that matter, if he'd had it, then probably she wouldn't still be alive and standing, and he'd be off playing kingmaker to the Kinslayer.

And yet, and yet…

"Someone, carrying something of great power," she told him slowly. "And you were always one for sniffing out power wherever it was hidden. Someone came here. You didn't get the crown off them, then, but you *know*."

He almost bluffed her. If she hadn't known him from before, she would have missed the slight twitch about his single living eye. Hope flared up once more, as it always did. Silvermort was hiding something.

"Tell me." But he just looked at her, battered but unrepentant, denying the crown's existence for the sheer spite of it.

Heno's hand was a comforting weight on her shoulder. "Celest, there's work for a hero to do here. There's a mine full of people who need to know that Silvermort's not going to be a problem any more. They should probably make plans to leave, and you should probably make sure that no guards are going to stop them."

Silvermort spat out a wheezy little laugh. "There will be more miners. The ore's too valuable. If not me, then someone else."

"And they'll pay their workers fairly and nobody needs to be a slave," Celestaine told him. "And don't give me that *If not me then someone else* bollocks. I am not in the mood." She looked at Heno, about to ask him what his plan was. He had his damnable little smile on, and she remembered that smile from before they had anything shared to smile about.

No. She reached inside herself for her Duty, that always cracked the whip in these moments, but perhaps the fight with the fake Kinslayer had given it concussion. They had come so far, and the road had been brambles all the way: Bleakmairn, Ilkand and now Silvermort and the Dorhambri. And if she didn't ask, she could pretend, just for a moment, just a little, that she wasn't complicit.

"Of course," she said to Heno. "You hold the fort here. I'll go break some chains."

He nodded calmly. Heno, who had shaken off the Kinslayer's yoke, yes. Heno, who had brought his evil master down. But, before that, Heno the interrogator.

She looked over at the others. "Kul, Ralas, Ned, let's go."

"But I wanted to…" Nedlam looked crestfallen.

"Ned, with me, please." Celestaine went to go and then stopped, fixing Catt and Fisher with her gaze. "What about you two? Doctor Catt, perhaps your medical knowledge would be useful. Plenty of hurt slaves needing a bandage."

Catt had the exact shifty look of a man about to go ransacking a heavily guarded fortress for a crown that almost certainly wasn't there. She had him bang to rights, though, and she had Nedlam hulking behind her, and so he gave her a magnanimous smile and professed that he would be only too delighted. Fisher wasn't with them, though, when they got outside, so Celestaine decided she'd been outmanoeuvred after all.

*   *   *

CELESTAINE WENT WITH the news that Silvermort was dead, because it was simpler than going into the gory details. Certainly Tarraki and the Grennishman magician had already been through with news of the fight, and Celestaine had met a notable absence of concerned well-wishers coming to see if their chief was all right.

Down the mines, a few of the guards started to put up a fight, but Nedlam, backed by Kul's arrows, set some fairly solid precedent. Some of the guards bolted for the fortress itself, but a surprising number resigned from Silvermort's service immediately. Doctor Catt explained their provenance— prisoners themselves, who had seemed like promising recruits. The liberation of the mine was accomplished surprisingly easily.

The Aethani majordomo proved the major sticking point. Even without his sedan chair, he refused to accept that the world had changed, practically charging Celestaine, all bandy legs and hanging belly, shrieking for her to bow the knee to his lord and master. Perhaps he hadn't realised that none of the Yorughan or human muscle was backing him, or perhaps he had just grown so used to his station that he couldn't conceive of things changing. He must have been here since before Silvermort, she guessed, here with Amkulyah, even, some Aethani collaborator who had been plucked from amongst his enslaved peers.

Kul fronted him, a prince before his errant subject, but the old man refused to acknowledge him, shoving him aside. That brought Nedlam in to shove back, sending the majordomo spilling across the floor, squawking in dismay. When he got to his feet, it wasn't the big Yorughan he was facing, but a score of miners, most of them holding stones. And that was as far as he went. Plenty of his former victims had grudges to settle, enough that more than half would have to take their revenge vicariously.

The punitive attitude wasn't transferred to the bulk of the guards who had turned coat, Celestaine noted. The worst of the bullies had either got behind the fort's walls or fled, and she had the impression that Silvermort's regime here had been undermined behind his back, the division between guard and worker never as impermeable as he'd wanted.

And speaking of Silvermort…

"I'd have thought you'd be talking to him," Doctor Catt pressed her. "You must suspect he knows something."

"Talking to Jocien Silvermort was always like trying to think through a maze filled with spikes," Celestaine said, "even when we were supposed to be on the same side." She was overseeing the freed miners and defecting guards, none of whom wanted to stick around. She had a list of destinations for them, places that wouldn't have been over-reliant on the iron from this place. The guard huts had been broken into. Everyone had at least a little food.

"But still," Catt went on. "You came this far…"

"And so did you," she noted, turning to him at last. He had actually made himself halfway useful, patching up a variety of ailments with chirurgy and magic.

His smile seemed so wonderfully guileless. "One does become subject to wanderlust, does one not? It's amazing where one can end up. But Silvermort…"

"Is in hand."

"I'm sure I don't understand you. Your Y-Yorughan's guarding him." He stumbled a little but managed to hurdle the automatic slur before it came out. "But one imagines—"

"Heno doesn't do guarding," she said. "How do you think we met, him and me? I was on the rack in Nydarrow and he was turning the crank." She smiled a little, despite herself. "Not the most romantic of settings, you'd think."

Catt thought through that and she watched understanding cross his face. "But you—"

"I want to know what Silvermort knows. And he wouldn't tell me himself. He'd turn the whole exercise into one of his mind games about who was controlling who, he'd bargain and lie and weasel. And I'm not good at that. I'd lose my temper, doctor. Probably I'd kill him, or he'd trick me. I'm not clever like that, not really."

"But you're a hero. This isn't the sort of activity I'd expect—"

She silenced him with a look. "I'm someone who fought the Kinslayer, along with thousands of others. I happened to get a magic sword from the Wanderer, and I ended up cutting the Kinslayer's hand off, although even that didn't turn out as well as I'd thought, I now discover. Where's the hero in that?"

"But you're doing your thing with the Aethani, all that grand gesture." Doctor Catt seemed genuinely taken aback that she wasn't opening her veins for the thirsty or walking through the crowd curing scrofula by touch. "You're... supposed to be *good*."

Celestaine suddenly felt very tired of it all, and profoundly glad that the miners were making their own way from the Dorhambri as swiftly as they could and without further intercession from her. "I try," she said in a small voice. "I always try. Only back when I was young, being *good* meant raiding the clan next door, because we Forinthi only see eye to eye when there's some other enemy we all don't like. Like your lot, or the Kinslayer. And in the war I... I lost fights, doctor. I lost track of the number of battlefields all of us *heroes* ended up retreating from, magic sword or no. I lost friends. I saw towns burn. I abandoned the weak and the desperate because it was that or get caught along with them. I *tried*." She heard her own voice shake, close to breaking all of a sudden. "I did everything I could, but so many people got hurt. I failed almost everyone I met. You think lopping a hand off a wrist balances that out?"

She was aware that her small voice had turned into quite a loud one, and that her companions were all looking at her.

Ralas clapped a hand to her arm, a man who had shared in at least some of that pain, before she'd failed him and left him for dead, left him to be taken and tortured and pinned between life and death like a moth.

Doctor Catt pursed his lips as though she'd just made her outburst in the middle of a dinner party. "Well, if you will split hairs like that…"

"I'm saying this, here, to you, for one reason, doctor. Because you are messing with me, and don't think your warding broach or whatever it is you've got will stop me letting Heno loose on you, if you ruin this for me."

"For you?" he asked her, all innocence. "I'd thought this was all for the poor Aethani."

Celestaine felt as though the ground had been whipped out from under her. *It is for them*, she insisted inside her head, but her own little speech weighed on her, all the wrong reasons she ended up doing the right things, all the right things she hadn't done. And so here she was, having run out of war to win, trying to show the world she was still worth keeping around. *Not so different from Deffo, now, am I?* Although the immediate thought swung back at her, *Didn't run away, though, did I?*

Catt was smiling smugly, well aware of having scored a point. *Could I kill you, or have one of the others kill you?* He was standing right there, the Catt that got the cream, so very sure he knew her. And he wasn't Jocien Silvermort, who'd bleed monstrosity if you cut him. He was just a neat little Cheriveni townsman who was too clever for his own good, and that put Celestaine on awkward footing because that made him the villain and victim of all those Forinthi stories and traditions she was forever trying to separate herself from.

Something must have showed on her face, because his smile reached a new notch of self satisfaction and he nodded. "Here I am at your mercy, and I'm sure Nedlam there would take pleasure in transmuting me into a stain on the ground, but you won't tell her to. It's not in you, my dear. The fate of the unlamented Jocien aside, it's not how you see yourself." He struck the ferrule of his cane into the dirt and pivoted on it to walk away, coming face to face with Nedlam's abdomen.

The big Yorughan leant down, and then further down until she was nose to nose with him.

"C'lest doesn't tell me like that," she informed his suddenly strained smile. "Sometimes I just stomp people into stains all on my own. But I won't, 'cause I like you." She said it as though it was the most terrible threat in the world. Catt's stick slipped and he stumbled back a few steps, clutching at his amulet and momentarily without his prodigious stock of words.

That cheered Celestaine up no end. Then she saw Heno on his way back from wherever he'd been working and her mood sobered. *I let him, didn't I? I'm happy for him to go back to the way things were so long as it serves me.* The obvious sequel, that Heno had been only too happy, was a different flavour of troubling, but at least it suggested the two of them were made for each other. He looked happy, too, practically whistling as he sauntered over. *We are not good people, not really. We are just trying to do good things.* And it had been Jocien Silvermort, and of all the people she could have asked to rid the world of, he was high on the list. *He was making a new Kinslayer, for Death's sake! Surely even proper heroes have limits?* But she knew they didn't, that proper heroes would just do right by the worst villains in the world, following their codes, never set a Yorughan torturer on their enemies. *Probably never get into bed with the Yorughan at all—literally or figuratively. Probably a proper hero would be cheering on the old Ilkand Temple to exterminate everyone who even lifted a finger in the Kinslayer's cause. Because that's easier, isn't it? Us and them, black and white. I hope it is, because is sure doesn't feel easy where I'm standing, here in the grey.*

She made sure Catt was nowhere in earshot, in a futile attempt to shake him off the trail. Doctor Fisher was also on his way back, she saw, stepping from the fort's shadow and dodging a few arrows from the garrison still holed up inside. He was heading off towards Catt, though, so she drew Heno aside.

"Well?"

"You're not going to like it." He was smiling, though, every bit as pleased with himself as Catt had been.

"You're not supposed to enjoy it," she told him, more for her conscience than his.

For a moment he had that... *Yorughan* look on his face, the one she knew from the war, where there just didn't seem to be any common ground at all, and they were doomed to fight forever. Then, without any of his features really moving, he was Heno again, looking slightly awkward.

"I know," she said. He had spent all his life being told a certain story about morality, how to act towards others. Mostly, that plying his skills as magician and interrogator was a good thing, the greatest good in the Kinslayer's cause. He had broken from it. She had watched him break from it, from her position on the rack. But everyone carried their past with them. Heno was no exception.

"Anyway, our man came here, guested with Silvermort," he explained. "He had something of power on him—would fit with the crown, from the detections Silvermort tried on it. Why he came here, no idea. It seemed like a chance visit, and he was still done up like an Ilkin Templar. He came, he left, and Silvermort sent a half-dozen of his best to cut his throat and bring the magic back, whatever it was. Our man killed them, all but one. This is why Silvermort was so short on henchmen—his old followers from the war all got hammered flat."

"And Silvermort...?"

"Is not this world's problem anymore," he said smoothly, and she accepted that, grateful for the lack of details.

"So where did he go, this Templar?" she asked.

"This is the bit you won't like."

"I thought that was the bit where he killed five of Silvermort's veterans single-handedly."

"He went into the Unredeemed Lands."

"To Bleakmairn?" For a moment the whole thing became a plot by General Thukrah, somehow, but Heno was shaking his head.

"Closer to here, and outside of the area Thukrah'd got under his control. The *real* Unredeemed Lands."

Meaning those lands the Kinslayer had come to first, and which were still a blackened ruin infested with rogue monsters and the tattered remnants of the Kinslayer's armies. They would be reclaimed, year by year, and there would come a time grass would grow there once more, and the monsters would either be dead, or just possibly would be regenerated into people in the eyes of the rest of the world, as Thukrah was trying so hard to accomplish. But right now the Kinslayer's deep heartland remained the most dangerous place in the world.

"Why?" Celestaine moaned. "Why would a Templar, or whatever he is... Or is he another fake Kinslayer? Not a construct, I mean; some magician or warlord who thinks he can rally the armies, restart the war?"

Heno shrugged. "No idea, but you'd better get the last of the slaves out and then we'd better get moving. Sooner than soon."

She frowned. "What?"

"While Silvermort and I were having our talk, Fisher had his own ideas."

"He was looking for the crown, I assumed?"

"He was freeing the Vathesk."

She blinked. "What Vathesk?"

At around that time the shouting and roaring started from within the fortress, from all those of Silvermort's followers who had so securely barricaded themselves inside.

Definitely time to go, Celestaine decided.

CHAPTER TWENTY-THREE

TWO DAYS OUT, and they were camped about a fire that Nedlam had set, in the scrub off a road nobody else seemed inclined to travel. Going to the Unredeemed Lands was hardly at the top of most people's to-do list.

Celestaine had heard of some who had: Templars, Arvennir warrior orders, those for whom the end of the war hadn't meant the end of the fighting. Perhaps there were even people from the Varra kingdoms the Kinslayer had ousted, wanting their land back. She wouldn't, if she were them; the Kinslayer had had a decade to make free with those lands. There would be little left there that was natural, plant or animal. Monsters would lurk in every cave and twisted grove, and the land would be riven with passages down to that buried land where the Kinslayer had licked his wounds and mustered his armies.

And what about that buried land, exactly? There were Yorughan and Grennishmen and plenty more still down there, those who hadn't marched with the armies. To hear Heno tell of it, there weren't as many as you might think. The Kinslayer hadn't had much time for minions who couldn't fight, and the fighters had mostly issued forth onto the surface at the start of the war. There were some stay-at-homes, though. Children, learning in tight-packed crèches about the Kinslayer's divinity and their eternal enemies on the surface. Monsters even the Kinslayer had not been able to marshal for his armies. Those who had turned away from his orders even before the war, hiding in nooks and crannies in the dark. And the people of the surface were going to have to come to terms with those depths, if they didn't just try and shove all the Kinslayer's creatures back down into them.

There will be another war, unless we make the right decisions now. And right now, who's in a state to be making those decisions? Everyone's grieving. Everyone wants revenge, but that just breeds more revenge down the line.

"You're thinking 'What the hell?'" Ralas said. He was huddled too close to the fire—he was always cold, he said, and in constant, nagging pain. She only hoped he didn't catch fire and end up like something from Hathel Vale.

"I wasn't," she told him. "What do you mean?"

"About the crown. About this Templar character."

"He's no Templar," she decided.

"And yet he wore their colours when he came to make my life more of a misery," Ralas pointed out. "He went to the Temple in Ilkand, he still had the livery when he was guesting with Silvermort."

"Misdirection."

"Misdirection is what he's made of," Ralas agreed. "He's like smoke. I can't get any idea of what he's after."

"Maybe it's the crown," Heno suggested thoughtfully. At their curious look, he grimaced. "Big magic like that, it twists the mind sometimes. And the Kinslayer's big magic more than most. It's his crown, so maybe it tries to take you over, make you into him. Maybe Silvermort missed out on his big chance, except he wouldn't have been able to control *that* Kinslayer with his little stick."

"So you think our crown-bearer is…?"

"Confused," Heno finished. "Perhaps the crown's pulling him

one way, he's pulling the other. Crown wants him to go to where the Kinslayer was strongest, takes him as far as Bleakmairn. He doesn't want that, so he goes where that power's weak, the Temple. But then it gets one over on him, so he runs to the mines, then on to the heartland."

Celestaine shrugged slowly. It made sense, and yet she saw holes in the idea. None of it quite sat right.

"Do you miss him?" Ralas asked the Yorughan quietly.

Heno regarded him warily. "No."

"Not at all? He was your people's god, wasn't he? Or next best thing. He made you strong, that's what he told you. Remember, I got to hear a lot of it in between singing for him and getting beaten to death. He told you how strong you are, and that the only thing that strength was for was to kill people like me. He let his particular favourites kill me, as a reward. I was the gift that kept on giving. And you loved it, all of you."

"Not me," Heno said defensively.

"Ralas...?" Celestaine started, but he met her gaze flatly.

"I just want to know," he said. "I sat in a cage at the foot of his throne for a long time. I saw the fighting pride of the Yorughan. I saw the joy they took prisoners in with, so they could prove themselves to their god with hot irons and pliers."

"Is this about Silvermort? Because that's on me," Celestaine told him.

"It's not, actually. I don't really care about Silvermort. Frankly, it's hard to care about much that's not right in front of me, these days," Ralas told her. "But I care about your friends here. I can't see how it happened."

"If we'd been playing a long game to betray you," Heno said with a nasty smile, "then don't you think we've left it a little late?"

"I think that none of the fists and feet that broke my bones felt like they belonged to people who were thinking about turning on their master," Ralas countered.

Heno drew himself to answer, but it was Nedlam who spoke. "You don't know."

Ralas raised an eyebrow at her and she poked at the fire, raising a little more life from it. The light danced across her face, that big slab of slate-coloured brutality with its newly broken tusk and its bruises.

"You go in front of the Reckoner," she said. "You act like he wants, or he kills you. We all see it happen, back below. You think he was patient with us? You think you're special getting all the beatings? I got beat plenty, back then. I lived, but others, plenty others got killed because they weren't enough like the Reckoner wanted. And so, when you're with him, you do the things he wants. And you wonder if everyone's just doing it to keep him happy, or if they really believe, but you can't ever ask, because someone tells him or his Slackers or generals what you said, then it's you getting your skin peeled off, see? And when you're not where he can see, maybe you're different. I know lots who were. But like you said, you sat at his feet. You think some scout-captain who comes with good news's going to say, 'Oh no, Reckoner, I don't want to beat that human. That's a poor way to reward your singing man.'"

Ralas's mouth twitched with the faintest ghost of a smile. "And that was you, was it?"

"Me? I never wanted to be near him. Ended up at Nydarrow only because every general in the army wanted rid of me, but I was too good at breaking things to just kill off. Stayed well out of the way of himself, I can tell you."

"And you? Same story?" Ralas asked Heno.

The Heart Taker gave him a sour look. "I just don't like being told what to do."

After all that talking, Celestaine just wanted to bed down with Heno, tucking into him for warmth as she watched the fire die. Ralas was humming—not a full song, and nothing cheerful, but even on his worst day the sound of him made any camp a better place to be—and she wanted to just lie there and not think about Silvermort or the Kinslayer or any of it. There had been a girl once, a Forinthi girl of the Fiddlehead clan, who had listened to all the old stories and learned how to ride a horse and swing a sword, and gone around the crofters of her family's land with her parents' steward and thought herself very grand and superior for it. That girl hadn't realised how easy her life was, or how hard the lives of others were. Certainly she'd never guessed how hard so many people's lives were about to get. She wanted to dream of being that girl again, in the land when the most she ever felt guilty for was stealing an apple.

But Amkulyah was sitting there staring at her. He had a world-class stare, that one. His big round eyes just bored into you. Celestaine sighed and pushed away from Heno, who was asleep in that still silence all Yorughan seemed to manage, legacy of an upbringing crammed in with his fellows like sticks in a bundle, and gods help anyone who snored.

"Kul?"

He paused a moment, weighing his words. "What will you do," he asked at last, "with the crown, when you have it?"

She frowned. "You know what."

"I don't mean will you abandon us," he said quickly. "Why would we have these words, if that was what I thought? But let's say you get it, let's say it works, you remake my people to give them their wings back, those who want them. The crown isn't used up, I think. You still have it, this thing of power. So what then? You become King of Ilkand? You go back home and make Forinth a power? You make monsters in some dark room like Silvermort?"

"None of those things," Celestaine said, knowing an immediate revulsion at each suggestion. "And I don't know. If it can be used to help, there will be other people to help. Maybe I'll find someone better than me, and give it to them."

"And will they still be better than you when they have it?"

Amkulyah asked. "And is it the sort of thing someone can give away, once it's theirs?"

"I don't have any answers," she told him frankly, pushing back into Heno's chest and wishing he'd wake up enough to put an arm around her. "I'd give it to Roherich, if he was alive. I'd give it to the Wanderer, if he hadn't wandered off."

"The Wanderer," Kul echoed, sounding unenthusiastic.

"The only Guardian who came through for us. The one who warned us at the start, and was there all through the war, helping us out."

"But he's dead," Amkulyah said.

"Nobody saw him die. He got us Slayers into Nydarrow, though he had to leave us at the open gate. He fought in the last battles, keeping the Kinslayer's armies off our backs. And then he went on. His work was done. He didn't die."

Kul said nothing. Doubt came off him in waves, but eventually he turned away and huddled down to sleep in an awkward crouch that wouldn't snag his twitching wing-limbs on the ground.

Celestaine tried to sleep, thinking how much easier the world would be if the Wanderer was with them. *You're not dead. I don't believe it.* But there was wishing, and then there was the world, as the saying went, and the world remained stubbornly devoid of helpful divinity these days.

THEY HAD ALREADY exhausted the topic of why Doctor Fisher had freed the Vathesks, which Catt felt was an untowardly generous action towards man-eating crab monsters. Fisher was unrepentant, though. It was good to be free, he said.

"This is why you need me at your shoulder when it comes to making the hard decisions," Catt decided. "What if they'd eaten you?"

"Wouldn't have you nagging me about it, then," Fisher told

him, reining in their cart. "They've camped. You want we should too?"

"Well I would rather you did it, obviously," Catt decided, still troubled about the whole Vathesk business.

"What'll you do when you get it?" Fisher asked later, after he had made camp and put up the Bounteous Domicile of Hule—which mostly consisted of speaking the command words that manifested a tidy little hut with a modestly appointed interior—lit the fire within and called up phantom servants to set the table.

Doctor Catt tied a napkin about his neck meticulously, looking at the repast on offer. "I lament, Fishy," he said, patently not in response to the question, "conjured foodstuffs can be such a treat to the eye, yet are always bland and mealy to the palette. How curious that magic has made such meagre advances in the field of gustation."

"You're welcome to learn to cook," Fisher pointed out, before shovelling in a slice of what would never quite taste like rare beef.

Catt waved away the suggestion with the incredulous contempt he plainly thought it deserved. "Anyway, you posed some manner of query."

"When you get the crown, what then?" Fisher rephrased. "Not like we've had a toy like that in the shop before."

"A fair and valid enquiry," Catt conceded. He sipped his wine and grimaced. "Next adventure, can we bring along some of the August Loom vintages? This is swill. As to the crown, well, I thought it would do rather well beside mother's portrait. We can shove over the Pearl Nautilus of Fish Summoning and there should be room."

Fisher downed a mug of beer without complaint and wiped his mouth on his sleeve. "Big magic, Catty. You won't use it? Clear up the competition, choose the next mayor of Cinquetann, maybe even make a few new toys for the collection?"

"*Make* them?" Catt asked, aghast. "Honestly, Fishy! Whither our tradecraft? Whither provenance? No, no. And similarly, no to the rest of it. It will be very pleasant to look at, and remember this little escapade and how we acquired it. It will be exceptionally pleasant to know that we own it, we alone of all the world. And do you know, I rather think that constitutes a sterling service to the rest of the world? After all, it's a nasty little toy of immense potential cobbled together at the whim of a mad demigod. It's exactly the sort of thing that would exert a malign influence on those who possessed it. Can you imagine if Silvermort *had* gotten his treacherous hands on it? I shudder to think. And so, in passing into my benevolent and above all supremely *inactive* keeping, it will be safe from those who would use it, and the world will be safe from it." He popped a peeled grape into his mouth with great satisfaction. "A safe pair of hands, Fishy. I am indeed the safest hands in creation for nasty little toys, because I don't really feel like playing with them. I am a collector only. Also, these grapes are almost passable."

Fisher looked at him for a long time, gnawing on a chicken bone. "You really mean all that, don't you?"

"Crown and grapes, I confirm my opinions on both with equal vehemence. Although if you were to tell me the crown would augment the culinary properties of our roadside accommodation, I might be tempted to use it just for that." Catt chuckled indulgently. "The Kinslayer wouldn't approve, I suspect. An added benefit."

Fisher shook his head grudgingly. "Don't change, Catty."

"My dear Fishy, I have no intention of doing so."

CHAPTER TWENTY-FOUR

ENCOUNTERING AN ARMED camp had certainly been within the realms of possibility, crossing into the Unredeemed Lands, but Celestaine hadn't expected this one. An army of unrepentant Yorughan, perhaps—a dark mirror to what General Thukrah was building up southeast of here at Bleakmairn. She would have taken that in her stride: fought or sneaked or whatever the situation had called for.

She had not anticipated being, for a second time, the enforced guest of the Ilkand Temple.

It hadn't been Templars who had surprised them, first off. As they made the best time they could along the pitted road, a band of horsemen had come up from behind, scouts that had spotted them a mile away and swung in to investigate. The two Yorughan had been the problem, of course, although Celestaine suspected any travellers heading in their direction would have had a few pointed questions to answer. Seeing such an odd fellowship all in one place, however, raised eyebrows, and the cavalry politely requested that the travellers accompany them. There were a score of them, and they looked honed to a sharp edge by the war. Saying no didn't seem worth the aggravation.

About half of the riders had been Arvennir from the Order

of the Lion's Tooth, their suspicious expressions contrasting sharply with the happy yellow flower on their surcoats. The rest were a mixture: some Forinthi, some Lantir and one huge Oerni sitting astride an aurochs bull with steel-capped horns. Nobody there was in Temple livery, and Celestaine reckoned she could talk her way out of whatever trouble they were in. There were still soldiers in arms all around the edge of the Unredeemed Lands, keeping an eye on what the Kinslayer's remaining forces were doing. Some would still be sticking to the letter of their orders, others might have gone the Silvermort way and become more bandits than defenders of the innocent; either way, she would think of something.

They had reached the camp, and found it considerably more than just a few ranks of tents in a field. There was a palisade wall and a wooden fort inside—something built towards the end of the war that had probably been intended to be temporary, but had then been reinforced and added to until there was a sprawling building there, every part of it covered with stakes and riddled with arrowslits and murder holes. There were plenty of tents and huts within the wall, too, each with some banner or other. She saw three separate Arvennir orders—Lily, Lion's Tooth and the red butterfly wings of the Monarchs, who were, perversely, engineers. There were a handful of free companies as well, makeshift warrior bands who during the war had taken in anyone who could hold a spear and wanted to stick it into one of the Kinslayer's minions. Over all of that, though, was one grand tent beneath the shield badge of the Ilkand Temple, and that was where Celestaine and her fellows got taken.

She hadn't caught much of the hushed conversation between the Lion's Tooth officer and the stern-looking woman leading the Templars. Celestaine guessed she must be a Hegumen, a mid-rank warrior-priest in charge of a Temple detachment and the sort of more-righteous-than-thou pain in the backside she remembered without fondness from too many command tent arguments. The one word she made out of their muttered conference was her own name, and the Hegumen had recognised it instantly. Her wide-eyed stare at Celestaine had been unreadable, save that it plainly wasn't awe at having a bona fide Slayer as a guest.

After that, the woman had ducked out of the tent, and Celestaine and company had been left to count their toes, as the Cheriveni saying went. They weren't mistreated or secured, or even disarmed; but nor were they fed or given any hospitality. Every so often the sound of an argument drifted to them. It sounded like the Hegumen had a whole load of people to shout at before she could even think of getting round to mistreating her prisoners.

Nedlam had some Ora root left over from the Ilkin contraband affair, and she was chewing it philosophically, the least concerned of all of them. Heno was in a foul mood, possibly at the prospect of being burned at the stake.

"You remember when your lot finally got yourselves organised and pushed back," he said. "You remember liberating Cherivell and the little kingdoms, finally winning a few battles against our armies?"

Celestaine nodded.

"How?" Heno demanded. "Everything we've seen together, Celest, everything since Nydarrow, has been humans *not* getting on with other humans. It's been humans arguing with Oerni, it's been… chaos. How did you get anywhere?"

"Regretting switching sides?" she asked him.

"Don't tempt me," he shot back, and then scowled. "No. I don't. I just don't understand how I picked the winning one, given how manifestly disorganised you all are."

"There was never a Kinslayer of the surface," she told him. "We're different races, different nations, tribes, folk… of course we don't see eye to eye. But I guess we've got a hundred ways of doing things too. And the Kinslayer only had one. It was a good one, but when your enemy only has one way, eventually you learn it, and start to win."

Heno looked about the inside of the tent. There were Templars at the entrance, keeping a wary eye on their guests, but probably not within earshot.

"If you'd failed, Celest," he said, "if you Slayers hadn't slain, your armies wouldn't have kept winning. You were losing momentum even then."

"Our lot were about to push back like you wouldn't believe," Nedlam agreed around a mouthful of root. "Lucky you met us two, eh?"

"So why didn't you?" Celestaine asked. "Even with the Kinslayer dead?" The question had always been there, in the back of her mind.

Nedlam just shrugged. Command decisions had never been her thing.

"The Kinslayer didn't delegate," Heno suggested. "He never had a second in command. He never planned for what would happen when he was gone. He was an immortal demigod, he never looked for a world that didn't include him. So: no Kinslayer, you just have a rabble of generals, Heart Takers and big monsters, and suddenly nobody knows what the big plan was, or who gives the orders. Just as well your Silvermort never got his replacement on the road. He might have done better than his wildest dreams."

With that cheery thought hanging over them, the Templar Hegumen returned.

"You," she said. "You're Celestaine of Fernreame?"

Celestaine shrugged. "None other."

"Then come with me."

Two other burly Templars had come in with her, and Celestaine didn't much fancy the idea. Still, she had her sword, and that was a great equalizer.

"If they try anything with us, you'll hear it," Heno pointed out. Celestaine canvassed the expressions of the others. Ralas shrugged and waved her on. Amkulyah just stared at everything angrily, by now entirely fed up of the intraspecies squabbles of humans.

"Fine." Celestaine gestured for the Templars to lead on, fully expecting to get frog-marched from the tent. Instead the Hegumen just backed out and left her to follow.

She got another look at the camp on her way over to the wooden fort, with the uncomfortable sense that most of the camp was looking back at her. The previous bustle had turned into a kind of unnerving expectation. *So has someone gone to get the wood for the bonfire, or what?*

She was expecting... she wasn't sure what. The fort didn't look like it would have a dungeon, so maybe just some Spartan office like the Governor's at Ilkand. Instead the Hegumen just started climbing stairs until they ended up on the roof, looking out over the palisade and into the craggy, barren terrain of the Unredeemed Lands. They weren't alone there, either. There was a squat, jowly man with the insignia of the Lion's Tooth engraved onto a fine breastplate—probably a chapter Constable at the very least—and there was a lean robed Tzarkoman fidgeting with a wooden skull mask, who Celestaine guessed was a Grave-Judge or some other of their complex religious hierarchy. His forehead was tattooed with script that probably explained exactly who he was, if you were also a Tzarkoman priest and could read their archaic glyphs. Beside him, and miraculously not trying to kill him, was a middle-aged woman with blue scales for skin, a Dragon-speaker from the Ystachi and a long way from home. Next to her, making the wooden boards creak, she saw a huge Oerni, every bit a match for Nedlam in bulk but barefoot and wearing a simple robe, one of their Wayfarer-priests whose travels from place to place were a form of religious observance.

"So…" she said. If the world was trying to get her burned for heresy, it had obviously upped its game after last time. Apparently the Ilkand Temple on its own just wasn't equal to the task. She actually caught herself looking around for a few vengeful Guardians just to complete the picture.

The Templar Hegumen, whom everyone seemed to be deferring to, was in no hurry to start the witch-hunt. She was looking out over the land ruined by the Kinslayer—all that scorched earth, the bare rocks, the canyon and cracks riven through into uncertain depths. Here and there, great tangled stretches of forest had grown up, some close to the palisade: the trees twisted and serpentine, branches interlocked to bar all sunlight from the labyrinth of trunks beneath. Elsewhere, toxic-looking smoke issued from vents and sinkholes, casting a twilight gloom where morning should have broken. Not hard to see why nobody had been anxious to redeem these lands. And yet this great expanse of poison and desolation, warped both by the Kinslayer's actions and by his sheer continued presence during the war, this was where the remnants of his strength were most strongly concentrated. There were Yorughan armies bivouacked in there that might still be holding out for a second coming. There were dragons and twisted fire-eyed wolves and gigantic serpents, and all the other refuse of the Kinslayer's experimental whims. There were Vathesk and Umberwyrms and walking dead raised by Tzarcoman collaborators. There were nests of Grennishmen and Silanti and a half-dozen other distinct races that had been dragged beneath the earth by the Kinslayer and made into his servants.

And here were the defenders of the free world, holding the line against anything that might try to escape that blasted territory, and no doubt making incursions of their own to shed some enemy blood.

And here was Celestaine, waltzing into their camp in the company of a pair of Yorughan.

And yet nobody laid hands on her and the silence stretched on, all those august religious and secular personages just staring at her with expressions she couldn't quite read, until she kicked at the wooden stakes of the wall and cleared her throat and said, "Well, look, we were hoping to…"

"You were there," said the Hegumen, turning to her at last. Celestaine braced herself for accusation, but instead the woman's face was weirdly naked and vulnerable, not the look she expected from a battle-hardened Templar. "At the Ilkand Temple."

I was supposed to get burned to death there, so, yes, your lot did insist on my presence, was what Celestaine did not say. Instead she just nodded. Still, a reprise of that judicial outcome was looming large in her mind, and so she was braced to go over the rail and down the wall if absolutely necessary. It wasn't something she'd been called on to do before, but she reckoned, if the assembled clergy started lighting torches, that would be a good time to learn.

"We had a messenger from Ilkand. Just two days ago, he came." The Hegumen was trembling, ever so slightly. "He was only passing on words, though. He hadn't *been* there. And we've been here for two years now, fighting the Kinslayer, fighting what he left behind, reclaiming with the sword what was taken with the sword."

Celestaine recognised a line of doctrine when she heard it. "Vengeance," she said flatly.

"Because the Temple was crying for it," the Hegumen agreed. All the others there, all those middling war-clergy of different, contradictory sects and traditions, they were eerily silent, listening, letting the Ilkand Temple take the lead in whatever was going on here.

And then that silence spread, because the Hegumen was obviously waiting for something that Celestaine couldn't identify. The Oerni Wayfarer shifted his big feet, as though he'd already been in one place too long, and the Tzarkomen put his mask to his face, as though Celestaine might look different viewed through the eyeholes, but nobody spoke until the rising quiet drew the next words from the Hegumen with wires.

"They said the gods spoke at Ilkand," she said, her voice a shivering whisper.

Oh. "Um." *Oh gods, it's that, is it?* "Well…"

Because Celestaine hadn't ever had much time for the gods and temples. It wasn't a Forinthi thing—in Forinth being self-sufficient was a virtue and prayers to their little household gods and spirits mostly amounted to requesting that they just keep out of the way. Most of the small kingdoms between Arven and Varra were suspicious of anyone with a divine mandate telling them to change their ways. "The Gods made us this way for a reason," was a frequent comeback to travelling preachers who grew too insistent. But of course the Tzarkomen had lived for centuries governed by an impenetrable pantheon of gods, which nominally included everyone else's gods as well as quite a few whose voices had only been heard in Tzarkand. The Templars had never been such a power in Ilkand as they now were, but they were driven by the gods' demands for justice and reprisal against the wicked. The Arvennir considered themselves the gods' chosen, as part of their general tradition of being better than everyone else. And everyone knew of the Guardians, the gods' instruments to guide and protect their mortal creations. Though most seemed to have fallen from the path they had been set on, in the thousand years since they were set to work, even Celestaine would cheer the return of the Wanderer to the heavens.

And the gods had gone silent. The Kinslayer had done some great wrong that even Heno couldn't start to guess at, and the voices of the gods had ceased to sound. No statues grated out prophecy, no illuminating dreams came to high priests, no shimmering radiance lit on altars and told in bell-like tones the fates of kings.

To Celestaine, facing the onrushing tide of Yorughan, it had been just one damned thing among many; to many others, it had been the deathblow of their world. She had never stopped to consider just how much personal courage it must have taken, to keep the faithful fighting once their gods had been taken from them.

And now here were all these priests, who were also battle-weary soldiers, here at the edge of the free lands, still fighting some revenant war against the Kinslayer's hosts, and word had come to them that...

Well, what do I say? Do I tell them about Catt and Fisher, and how they're mercurial bastards who probably cooked the whole thing up as a joke? Because it was plain nobody here was laughing. Celestaine had thought the Ilkand Temple would probably shake itself and get over the whole affair, that it would be burning-people-business as usual for the Archimandrite by the time he'd finished next morning's breakfast. She wondered just what word *had* come to this nameless little outpost.

"There was a relic," she said carefully, feeling each word she spoke grow huge and full of portent in their ears. "The skull of..." And she couldn't even remember, or particularly remember why whosesoever's skull it was had been important. "A skull," she substituted lamely. "The Archi"—the word *mandrill* hovered perilously on her tongue, but she recovered—"...mandrite held it, and he heard the gods. He said so, and... I suppose he should know. Just, you know, faintly." *I am doing a horrible job of this.* She felt she should throw her arms out wide and lead them all in prayer, get them dancing to her music, get gifts and provisions and a guide to the Unredeemed lands, barter her prophecy into fleecing them for all they were worth. She didn't have it in her, though. She wasn't Jocien Silvermort to coast on a tide of fake liberation. "So yes, I was there." *Front row seat, in fact.* "Nobody else heard what he heard, but I saw how it affected him. He believed it. And..." *And now I'm on dangerous ground because do I tell them that I believe him, because the gods were telling him the flat out opposite of what he'd wanted to do, and he went with it?* That was what had been persuasive to her. If he'd said the gods were howling for more vengeance, that could just have been a man listening to the echoes inside his own skull, as far as she was concerned. It was the *change* in him that had been the miracle. *But here goes.* "The message of the gods was for mercy." The combined weight of their solemn regard was getting to her, and she just blurted out, "Look, we were about to be executed, me and my friends. For no good reason, frankly, but the fact that two of us were Yorughan didn't help. And then... gods. And we were freed, and... well, I don't know how things went after that, because frankly we got the hell out of Ilkand. But it looked like your man the Archimandrite's world got turned upside down. Mercy, he said. Peace. Tolerance." She was mortified to realise she couldn't actually remember the gods' exact words, which was something she really should have made an effort with.

"Some of us left, when the word came through," the Hegumen said. "A whole detachment marched off to Ilkand to ask... to ask, *What?* To ask, did they know we had been doing our best to bring divine vengeance to the creatures of the Unredeemed Lands? And did that mean we'd been wrong, all this time? I got a message yesterday from the Termaghent phalanstery denouncing the Ilkand Temple. *Already.* Saying it was lies spread by the Kinslayer's heir. But they've never believed that there isn't a leader still behind what's left of the enemy."

"They're fools," said the Oerni in a rich, deep voice. Nobody seemed to strongly disagree.

"Celestaine of Fernreame," said the Templar. "My name is Kait Esterra Hegumen. The Archimandrite of the Temple is my uncle."

Celestaine had to bite down on offering her commiserations, contenting herself with nodding.

"I know my uncle," Kait continued. "He is a hard man. 'Mercy' is not a word he would use in connection with doctrine. He's not a bad man. He has never taken pleasure in bringing pain or hardship, but he has done so because that was the word of the gods. Now I have a message from him saying that the gods decree mercy. Saying that"—and her voice shook, and the Arvennir chapter officer put a hand on her shoulder to steady her— "...that it may be the last word the gods ever have for us. And you have confirmed the message. You, who slew the Kinslayer and now travel with his creatures."

Celestaine nodded uncertainly. "Well, then, that's... Glad I could be of service...?" She wasn't entirely sure that this wasn't going to turn into blood and vengeance any moment. The whole encounter was profoundly unnerving her.

"We need your help," Kait told her.

I'm already helping someone. Can you wait, and maybe I'll get round to you...? But help was a two-way street, and the scouts here must have a good idea of what went on across the border, where Celestaine needed to go. "What, then?"

"We have a whole camp of very confused soldiers here, who don't know what they're supposed to be doing or what is right," Kait told her. "I think most of them want to believe the news from Ilkand. Any message from the gods is better than none, and a message that says something other than, *Kill until they kill you back* is going to be well received. Because we have been attacking the enemy, and defending ourselves from the enemy, for two solid years without much changing—even the Kinslayer's death didn't make things much better. They haven't just rushed out *en masse* and overwhelmed us, broken our walls and tortured us all to death; but they haven't gone away, either. It's just been attrition ever since the war ended. So I want you to go stand up and talk to them, talk to all of our people, tell them what you saw. Tell them it's true."

"That's not something I'm good at," Celestaine said. The

thought brought her out in a cold sweat. "I was never a speeches sort of person. I tended just to do things, and if people followed my lead, well, that was their look-out."

"You were there when the gods spoke," Kait said with ineluctable logic. "Who else can do it? Please."

Who else? For a moment, ridiculously, she was thinking of Heno, because he had such a smooth, persuasive voice when he wanted something. But of course, there was a better choice.

"I can't do it," she told them all. "But I know who can, if he agrees to it. And in return you have to help us."

CHAPTER TWENTY-FIVE

RALAS SPOKE LIKE a man who wasn't in constant pain from injuries that would never heal. His strong, confident voice rang out across the palisaded compound and beyond, using all the tricks of performance a professional bard could muster. He told them it true, not as some grand embellished saga, but every word brimming with sincerity. He made it simple and compelling. He spoke to hearts. Celestaine knew for a fact that Ralas had been no more invested in the wisdom of the gods than she, and his treatment at the hands of a demigod had not left him any more enamoured of the divine, but he knew what was expected of him. Not rabble-rousing slogans to cover an emptiness, but a plain, precise account of what had gone down in Ilkand. Celestaine would remember the event forever as Ralas had told it, not as she herself had experienced it. His version was better, even though he was striving for accuracy, neither overselling the miraculous nor playing it down.

And he was brief, keeping it short enough that nobody had a chance to shuffle or think of awkward questions. Afterwards, he strode from the makeshift stage the Templars had erected and collapsed, shaking. Celestaine put a hand to his shoulder and he winced before covering it with her own.

"Don't make me do that again," he said.

"I didn't make you," she pointed out. "I asked."

He opened one eye and fixed it on her. "And how was I supposed to say no, eh?"

"I'm sorry."

He waved away the apology. "I should be glad that I can still do it when I want to," he admitted. "So, what happens now?"

She looked around: Heno, Ned and Kul were leaning in for the answer to that question.

"Now we leave these walls and go where the monsters are," she told them. "And because of that speech, hopefully we do it with some help from these people. They've been making forays into the land beyond here for a while. They know the dangers and they might have word of our man. And they have some other work they might want help with."

"Of course they do," said Ralas tiredly.

"Because it's something they're not good at, and it's something we're invested in. It's something we've seen done, in bits and pieces. It's something we've done ourselves." She looked at Heno in particular because his expression suggested he was being stubborn and not wanting to go where she was leading. "They want to see what the others think about the Temple's new message. It takes two to make peace, and it's way more difficult than fighting, most of the time, but Kait wants us there when they offer the spring wheat."

"When they do what?" Heno frowned.

"Like a peace offering," she clarified, realising that, of all the Forinthi idioms, the Yorughan were probably least familiar with that one. For that matter, the Forinthi themselves didn't have much use for it, pugnacious as her people generally were.

"Because of us two?" he asked, indicating himself and Nedlam.

Celestaine shrugged. "I know it's not like you have some magic sigil of the Kinslayer that will immediately get anything of his to sit up and take orders from you. I know that even other Yorughan aren't just going to do what you say, let alone anything else. But anyone on the far side of that wall is most definitely going to be leery of listening to the humans they've been fighting for the last however many years. Having some Yorughan faces in the mix can only help."

For a moment Heno was impassive, and she thought she must have offended his sensibilities, but then he showed his sharp teeth in a sudden grin. "Celest, I'm a Heart Taker," he told her. "There's no one thing that unites all the Kinslayer's followers, except for the Kinslayer, but being a Heart Taker is the next best thing, because *nobody* likes *us*. But they will listen, almost all of them, because they know we're to be feared." The prospect of abusing his position seemed to have made him abruptly cheerful. "This will get us where we need to be, will it?"

"It will get us where our man went next, or closer to it," she confirmed. "Where we go after that, I don't know."

"Maybe we'll just find his bones and the crown," Heno suggested, obviously warming to the prospect.

THERE WAS QUITE a large concentration of Yorughan based a few miles into the Unredeemed Lands, but Kait's most recent scouting intelligence suggested they were undergoing a cataclysmic bout of infighting as various leaders struggled for overall control. Nobody wanted to go waving a Temple banner anywhere near them, and risk unifying them all into one anti-human alliance. Celestaine herself thought about General Thukrah and his efforts—not to mention his pragmatic approach to the war's victors—and wrote a note for a rider to run around the edge of the Unredeemed Lands to Bleakmairn. The arrival of a respected Yorughan war leader who was willing to come to accommodations with just about anyone could only improve matters.

More of an immediate problem was the Kelicerati colony in the dense forest near the outpost's gate, which had been a poisoned thorn in everyone's side during the great push against the Kinslayer's forces. The tree-dwellers had spent the war sallying out whenever they were unwatched to waylay supply trains, mount surprise attacks, kill messengers, and do the various uniquely unpleasant things that the Kelicerati life cycle required. Since the war, they had reacted aggressively to any attempt to curtail the forest's boundaries, leading to one open clash that had been costly for both sides, but they hadn't actually tried expanding their territory or taking the fort. In light of the Temple's new statement of intent, Kait was clinging to that fragile thread in the hope that it meant a dialogue could be established.

"Kelicerati?" Heno echoed without enthusiasm. "Feh."

The forest-dwellers had played more of a role in the nightmares of the free world than on the actual battlefields, for which everyone had been grateful. It turned out that 'everyone' included the Yorughan as well, who found the spider-people as creepy as humans did. The Kelicerati had never been particularly biddable servants of the Kinslayer, Heno explained. Mostly he had just seeded forests with them in parts of the world he hadn't wanted his enemies to be able to traverse freely, and left them to it.

That he was making this explanation to a gathering of the outpost's leaders rather than just to Celestaine was the remarkable thing. Here was a Yorughan Heart Taker lecturing Ilkin and Arvennir and all the rest about the war, and they were listening. Not happily, perhaps; not without a scowl when he unthinkingly referred to the Kinslayer's armies as 'we,' but still they listened.

"So you're saying you can't help," Kait clarified.

"I'm saying I will do what I can, but I can't even talk to the Kelicerati," Heno told her. "I don't understand their noises, and they have this mind-to-mind speech of their own I can't break in on."

"That..." Kait grimaced. "That won't be a problem. We have a translator. Of sorts." If she took any joy from Heno's expression of incredulous horror, it didn't show.

They had been sparring with the Kelicerati for years, Kait explained, here and elsewhere. Early on, the spider-people had made any travel near the forest lethal. They seemed impossible to surprise, hiding in every shadow and behind every tree. When they came near the fort, they were cut down with sword and arrow, but the forest itself remained inviolable, and at night they would raid in all directions, scuttling from their fastnesses to ambush anyone who hadn't got behind safe walls by dark.

The Kelicerati might not have been mainstays of the Kinslayer's armies, but he had made them a common problem for anyone trying to break into enemy territory. He'd scattered their colonies like spring-traps. Somehow, though, a bleak tradition had arisen amongst the scouts of those who had to face them. Kait was slow to give details, instead introducing them to one such specialist ranger, a man named Meddig.

When they first met, Meddig wore a leather mask, and she thought he must be a Tzarkoman or something, then guessed he had some injury or disfigurement to hide. He spoke slowly and precisely, reminding her a lot of Nedlam when the big Yorughan was trying really hard to be understood around her tusks.

"They have a dozen smaller nests around the forest," Meddig explained. The rhythm of his speech was sporadically interrupted by random stresses, as though someone was thumping him on the back at unpredictable intervals. "There is a big one in the centre, caves beneath. They talk about a leader sometimes."

Meddig could hear the Kelicerati speak sometimes, in his head, because of something he had done to himself years before. It was a risky procedure; sometimes it led to madness or death.

Having advance warning of Kelicerati activity had apparently been worth the risk to those who had to live near them.

"Show them," Kait directed him. "They need to understand."

He doffed the mask reluctantly. At first she just thought his face was pock-marked, as though he'd had some disease of the skin.

The Kelicerati were most notorious for the way they made little Kelicerati. They liked warm flesh to incubate their eggs. Meddig, and those others of his tradition, stole those eggs and had surgeons place them beneath their skin to hatch and develop. The process was extremely painful, he explained candidly. The doctors would tie the victim to his bed as the things hatched, under strict instructions not to intervene as the larvae began to consume flesh and bone.

And then, at a precisely calculated time, the victim—that was his phrase for a category of people he himself was a part of—was fed a virulent poison to kill off the grubs. If the timing was right, a connection would have been made.

"I get headaches sometimes," he said to Celestaine, almost defiantly. "But I hear them. And they can hear me. If I call, they will know it."

"And you're willing to try and make peace with them?" she demanded, because she would have wanted to exterminate the entire scuttling race, she thought, if it had been her hearing their voices in her brain.

Meddig smiled with half his face. "They're a part of me, Forinthi. I've lived with them for more than a year, now. It's hard, being at war with yourself. Peace would be pleasant." He reminded her of Ralas then, a man trying to live with a terrible burden that was never going to go away.

A SMALL PARTY went out to front the Kelicerati, all of them mounted so that they could show a clean pair of heels if things went wrong: Celestaine and Kait were there, Meddig and Heno, Amkulyah for his sharp eyes and a handful of others from the fort. Nedlam had argued bitterly about coming along, but there was no horse that could carry her, and if things did go badly, even she wouldn't be able to hold off an entire Kelicerati colony on her own.

Their counterparts emerged from the cover of the trees slowly, called forth by Meddig's unheard voice. There were three of them, plus a scorpion-thing as big as a dog, and Celestaine had to fight down all sorts of memories from times when she had been cutting off jointed limbs and poking out glittering eyes during the war. Kelicerati were about the height of a tall man, but slender: certainly smaller than even a runtish Yorughan. They had a hard skin that was almost like a shell, and several eyes—four or five or six or eight, depending on who-knew-what. Their mouths were not like mouths at all, really, dominated by two inward-curving fangs with tips like glass needles. They wore harnesses for their weapons and gear, but little else in the way of clothes, leaving the neither-ness of their physiology on show—not quite human, not quite spiders, not quite anything.

"Shelliac," Amkulyah said, surprised.

"They're not Shelliac," Celestaine said sharply.

"They are like them, though." He looked at her, an Aethani who had never grown familiar with the one nor fought the other. "Do you not see?"

"I thought the Kinslayer made them from nothing, like most of his monsters." Celestaine was here to play diplomat, but distrust was creeping up on her like an ambush.

"So did I," admitted Heno. "But now he says it…"

"They're *not*…" But if she squinted hard, they almost were. And Shelliac kept their bodies covered, and made themselves as human as possible to interact with humans. Take away the Kelicerati's savage fangs, reduce the number of eyes… Was this some lost atrocity of the Kinslayer, to take a band of Shelliac and turn them into *this*?

Heno had his hands out. He was still in full Heart Taker regalia, of course, and the Kelicerati plainly recognised it. He named himself and his station for them, in two human languages and in Yorughan speech, and waited for Meddig to relay the meaning wordlessly in the spider-people's own talk. Celestaine concentrated hard on the forest-dwellers, trying to read them as she would a Shelliac. She realised with a start that she recognised some of the twitching of their hands as mood-qualifiers, just as the peaceful boat-people would use to supplement other elements of their speech. *How did I never see that? Because I wasn't looking for it.*

Heno was taking a firm line with them: the last thing Kait wanted was for the entire forest-full of Kelicerati to decide the humans had gone soft. He was speaking peace, though—an offering to pause hostilities and see what arose out of it.

Meddig listened, went inward, his eyes losing focus, then snapped back to them. "They will meet," he said, frowning at his own words. "I can feel they're afraid. And… other things, feelings there aren't words for." A shiver passed through every part of him except where his face had been frozen, nailed down by the parasites that had died there. "There is a grove, a Way-shrine for the Oerni. It is also a shrine for *them*, somehow. That is where to meet."

Kait exchanged glances with Heno, who shrugged. "Sounds like a trap to me."

"Is it?" she asked Meddig. "Why not talk here, right now?"

"Their leader wants to see you. Their leader can't come out here, or—no, they fear you will kill their leader. I can't feel the leader at all, too far, or… I don't know. But that is what they say. Or it's what they *mean*."

"Well, tell them we… will discuss it, and if we agree then I suppose we send some people into the forest. Volunteers only." Kait's voice shook a little, and Celestaine knew that she would be among them. She wasn't a general, but a battlefield Hegumen. She led from the front.

MEDDIG THOUGHT THAT the Kelicerati were telling the truth, in that they would meet peaceably. He claimed that their mental web wasn't something they could dissemble over. Everyone else was plainly wondering whether he was just a puppet dancing on their strings. Going into the forest to have tea and cake with the spider monsters wasn't anyone's idea of a good time, and Meddig's halting attempts to explain what he felt of their nature didn't help much. The Kelicerati mind was full of concepts he could feel but not interpret or understand. Similarly, plenty about the human mind was plainly just so much noise to them, including the very relevant human concept of 'revulsion' which would be playing a major part in any negotiations.

"I'm like something of theirs, to them," Meddig said. "I could walk in and out of their places a hundred times without danger, so long as I didn't draw blade or light a fire. They're all together in here." He tapped his head. "To them, that's like warmth and home and mother, being at one like that. They think... I'm honoured, to be there with them."

"What do you think?" Celestaine asked him.

"I think... people don't look at me the same, since this was done to me. They don't accept me. They don't trust that I'm human. The Kelicerati know I'm one of theirs, even though I am human." He gave a slightly hysterical little laugh. "Some mornings I just don't know what I am, any more."

"We've killed a lot of them," Kait said thoughtfully. "They've killed a good few of us. And done worse than kill. We've found our people sometimes, still alive, but..." She made a twitchy gesture towards Meddig. "But worse. All eaten away, with one of *them* growing within their skin."

"Better than being dead and rotting, to them," breathed Meddig. "To them, it is not just food, it is becoming a part of them. To them it is good."

"How much do you need this peace?" Celestaine asked, thoroughly unsettled by him.

"If we can somehow come to an accommodation with them— if we can even get their agreement to leave us alone as we skirt their forest—then we can get to the interior and fight, or talk, or whatever the hell we're supposed to be doing," the Hegumen decided. "Otherwise we just fight them and fight them—and we don't have the strength to drive them away or wipe them out, and they're not going to all come out and make themselves targets. And the Temple—the gods say…"

"Even these? I mean, even the *Yorughan* don't like them," Celestaine said.

"And I'd be happier if it were Yoggs and not Crawlies," Kait said, heartfelt, "but we play the hand we pick up when we sit at the table, right?" The gambling metaphor sounded strange from a Templar.

The deciding factor was the Oerni Wayfarer, Olastoc, who had some jurisdiction over the shrine. He wanted to see whether the place had been entirely defiled, or if it retained some residual divinity.

The next morning saw a whole procession heading out into the twisted forest; on foot this time, as the horses wouldn't venture beneath the canopy. Olastoc had dressed himself as a Wayfarer on the move, which was to say, heavy practical robes and not a sniff of the priest to him. Around him, Kait and her dozen Templars seemed tiny, barely reaching his shoulders. Oerni always seemed to move slowly, mostly because they were careful around breakable things like humans. Once outside the fort's walls, Olastoc set the pace, pushing aside branches with his staff and brooking no barriers.

Ralas stayed behind again—they left him in the mess tent

tuning a harp one of the Arvennir had provided. Celestaine took the other three with her, though; she wanted them at her back if things went sour.

Beneath the knotted canopy the forest was like dusk, and Heno conjured up a cold light that gave illumination but no cheer. There had been a path to the Wayshrine, back before the Kinslayer came, but now there was almost no trace of it, the ground snarled up by the clutching roots of the trees. They had to rely on Olastoc and Meddig, who between them navigated their way to the place. Heno stood at their shoulders with the light dancing in his upraised palm, and everyone else crowded in close. Beyond its frosty radiance, the darkness between the trees was absolute.

"They're out there, of course," Kait said, through gritted teeth. "And worse, too. It's not just Kelicerati in these woods, and whether we can trust them or not, nothing else is looking to make a deal."

"What other things?" Celestaine asked.

"All sorts. Vilewolves, Red Vine Walkers, various one-offs that got out from the Kinslayer's laboratories."

Soon after they ran across something like a horse-sized boar with a hide of rust-coloured scales and a serpent for a tongue. It hissed and squealed at them, but meeting only a fence of sword-points, it turned and clattered clumsily off between the trees, as if it were a normal animal. Of the Vilewolves and the rest, they saw not a sign.

Then Meddig announced that the shrine was ahead, and they broke from the impenetrable canopy into a clearing around a huge stone it would have taken an Oerni's strength to move. Under normal circumstances, the monolith would have dominated the view, even with a dozen skinny Kelicerati hunched against the sunlight, their heads cocked to shade their many eyes. Nobody spared them much attention, though, and Celestaine was reminded of Meddig saying that he had no sense of their leader in their spared headspace. The reason for that was now evident: there was no bloated spider-mother here to bargain with them. Awaiting them, its sinuous body coiled about the great stone, was a dragon.

CHAPTER TWENTY-SIX

WHATEVER THE ORIGINS of the Kelicerati, the origins of dragons were well known. There had been such beasts on the face of the world in the dim recesses of history. One of the first tasks given by the gods to their Guardians had been to rid the world of them, because they had been vast, fiery, venomous and jealous, each one bent on an individual war against all other life. There were statues in the Ilkand Temple and elsewhere showing Lord Wall and Fury and even the Undefeated slaying the serpentine monstrosities; even the Reckoner—the Kinslayer as would be—had shed his share of draconic blood. The Guardians had performed their task well, back in the mists of time. No more dragons had been uncovered since.

Then the Kinslayer had mounted his war, and one of his particular hobbies had been to breed monsters to plague his enemies, either as part of his armies or just to let loose upon the world. Of course he had recalled the dragons of old, and he had done his best to recreate their towering ferocity, but never quite succeeded. The height of his efforts had been Vermarod, that Celestaine had killed on the field at Bladno; and after that, she felt, he had become discouraged with the whole enterprise. He had created a variety of reptilian monsters later in the war, but they had been smaller and more specialised, like the Ramwyrms. His false dragons had been thin on the ground, and not replaced when they met their violent ends. Heno claimed that they had somehow inherited the intractable nature of the originals, and even the Kinslayer had wrestled to control and direct them. Celestaine had always assumed a few had outlived their creator, but she hadn't looked to meet one in her lifetime. They had surely fled the haunts of man, she'd thought, and she was right: one of them had fled here.

None of the new dragons could claim to be old, but this one looked it. Its grey scaled hide was scarred and crossed with wounds that had healed without quite closing. Its long snout was crumpled by some great blow that had struck it close to one nostril, carving out a handful of teeth that had not regrown. The yellow eye it turned on them was narrow and cunning. Most dragons had been little more than bright beasts—Vermarod had been almost mindless, a terror to his own side whenever he got turned around in the battle. This one was staring at the newcomers with a calculating patience surely more dangerous than mere ferocity.

Heno rumbled, deep in his chest. "Look at its throat," and then, when the thing lifted its man-length head, "Nails and fire, look at its other *eye*."

There were cysts at the hinge of its jaw, bloating out and shouldering aside the smaller scales there. The dragon's far eye was swollen and pearly, the shadowy shape of a grub curled tightly there as though within the egg.

"Its blood killed them," Meddig whispered. "But they got far enough. It's like me. It's not part of them, it's its own thing, but it speaks to them."

"Does it speak *for* them?" Kait asked. She was very tense, one hand constantly twitching over her sword hilt. Dragons were engines of destruction, vomiting corrosive venom, poisoning the air, spraying forth sheets of fire that could incinerate whole squads of soldiers. Each one was different, hand-crafted by the

Kinslayer. And yet it just crouched there about the stone, plainly its resting place of old, for its scales had carved a spiralling track into the monolith's edge.

Meddig was blinking furiously, trying to understand. At last he threw his hands up in frustration, prompting alarmed reactions from the nearest Kelicerati. "I can't tell. I think they were frightened of it? Only, frightened doesn't mean the same to them as it does to us. It doesn't know what it is. There's never been a thing like it before. The Kelicerati don't have words for it even in their own way, let alone ours. But it is part of them. And everything of them speaks *for* them. It's—oh, gods." He clutched at his head. "It's trying to make me know what it's like, to be *it*. I can't understand. My head's full!"

"Enough!" Kait took a furious step towards the dragon and the spider-creatures. "Stop it, you're hurting him!"

The dragon's sharp snout was levelled at her immediately, and it drew in a colossal breath. Celestaine yelled and caught the Hegumen by the waist, throwing her aside and out of the way of whatever devastation was about to ensue. She ended up lying uncomfortably on the woman, Kait's pauldron jabbing into her armpit, and everyone had their swords out. Heno's hands were ablaze with barely contained power, and all the Kelicerati had clubs and sharp wooden spears, their fangs gaping in threat.

"*Stop!*" The word seemed to roll out from the dragon's very bowels and then off into the trees. "*Hvar!*" which meant the same to the Yorughan. Celestaine rolled off Kait and came up with a hand on her sword hilt. The dragon's head swung dizzyingly above her, regarding her first with its living eye, then with the dead orbs of the parasite in its other socket. She saw the muscles of its long throat ripple and compress like a bellows, and the words "*Sao yoragh nor na!*" echoed from it, formed without need for lips or tongue, but plainly with enormous effort.

"They are not here for war," Heno translated.

Yoragh was war, then. She hadn't appreciated that the *Yorughan* were just, what—warriors, war-makers? "Then what does it want?" she demanded. Her mind was consumed with thoughts of those jaws lunging forward just a little and biting off everything she owned above the waist.

"They don't want to fight," Meddig said, stepping forwards until the dragon's breath ruffled his hair. "They want to live. The dragon wants to live. The spiders want to live. They're…" He shuddered. "They're a thing, a single thing. They're a web." Emotions fought over his battered face: loathing, yearning. "I'm part of it, too. I made myself part of it. They think it's good."

"Well, then, we have a problem." Kait pulled herself up, looking about at her fellows to ensure everyone was ready to sell themselves dearly. "Because we don't. We don't think it's good to be part of the colony. I'm sure it's perfectly lovely, but no." Her eyes were very wide, and no doubt she was thinking of the many Kelicerati hiding in the trees all around them, unseen.

"*Hvar!*" the dragon boomed again. "*Stop!*" It shook its great head, and Celestaine recognised frustration, then: neither its own body nor Meddig were able to communicate its meaning.

"Ah!" cursed Meddig, as more alien concepts flooded his mind.

"Slow," Celestaine said, looking into the dragon's amber eye. "Be slow. One thought at a time. Do you—do *they* even understand what I'm saying?"

Her meaning must have got through, because Meddig gave out a long relieved breath. "Ah, gods," he said. "They know. They have learned—from us, from *me*, from others—there are others in the forest that are their enemies, that have rejected their one-ness. They understand that what seems good to them makes enemies of others. They want to live."

Celestaine stared at the dragon, unsure whether it was a willing part of this web of minds or just caught in it, like a huge fly. But then the wyrm had been made without kin, a solitary thing, abandoned by its creator and without a place in the world. Perhaps this communion that had been forced on it was better than being alone forever.

"Kait...?" she asked. The Templar opened her mouth to reply and a spear struck her across her helm, knocking her down again. Abruptly the trees were boiling with robed, hunched figures, shrieking and yammering.

Everyone there must have suspected Kelicerati treachery first off, but the spider-people and their dragon were no less the target of the attack than the Templars themselves. The newcomers had voices, and the air was filled with them, shrieks and curses, words of hate and death.

Celestaine had her sword out and was cutting, feeling the scabbard open up along one side and cursing the loss even as she lopped off one thin arm at the elbow. The attackers were smaller than human, grotesquely hunched, wielding clubs and spears and a handful of metal swords. They had no bows; the twisted wood of this forest would provide no useful staves. Only later did she realise how lucky that was.

They threw javelins as they came—of sharpened wood, or stone-tipped. Two Templars were struck down, the missiles finding the gaps in their armour with terrible precision. Three Kelicerati were dead as well, or at least pinned writhing to the ground by the shafts. Then it was close fighting against a desperate, keening host.

Celestaine assumed they were Grennishmen at first, though of all the Kinslayer's minions they were the least suited to open violence. They were small and quick, these assailants, not strong but seemingly mad for blood. She concentrated on limbs, ducking the blows that came her way and disarming her foes with extreme prejudice. The Templars had formed up around Meddig and Heno, and the Heart Taker was holding his fire aloft, giving everyone the light they needed to fight. Nedlam had just gone straight in amongst the enemy with abandon, and elsewhere she heard the thundering bellow of the dragon as it gave vent to its true nature.

The next few moments were desperate. If everyone hadn't already had a weapon to hand, then things might have gone far worse; but mutual suspicion apparently had its uses. The attackers broke against their swords over and over, trying to get to where Meddig was kneeling, clutching his head as the battle-hymns of the Kelicerati washed over him. The Oerni Wayfarer priest, Olastoc, stood over Meddig, batting aside spears with his staff, eyes almost closed as he focused on some ritual of his own. Celestaine took a stand between two Templar shields, lunging forwards on each stroke to avoid carving anything off her allies. The attackers were furious but undisciplined, getting in each others' way. Soon enough, Kait gave the order and the Templars expanded their ring, pushing forwards to get more elbow room and drive the enemy out of the clearing.

"Stop! *Hvar!* Stop!" It was Nedlam's cry. She was standing surrounded by broken bodies, Amkulyah sitting on her shoulders with his bow out. Neither were pushing the fight, though. "Stop killing!"

The sight of a huge Yorughan demanding *less* death was prodigy enough to stay the Templar's advance, and the attackers fell back to the treeline, obviously willing for a second attack once they'd worked themselves up again.

"Ned?" Celestaine pressed.

"Look!" Nedlam reached down and hauled up one of the wounded, a skinny creature with one dangling, broken arm, bent almost double under its hunch.

But that hunchback was rippling and moving beneath its cloak. Celestaine had a sudden thought of more cysts, more embedded parasites, some rival Kelicerati nest, but no, it wasn't that the movement reminded her of.

Amkulyah climbed halfway down Ned's arm and tore away the shrouding cloak just as the thing ripped itself from the

Yorughan's hold. It dropped, half-naked, to the ground, and Celestaine saw a twisted Aethani, its huge round eyes turned on them all in hatred, its broken, knotted wing-limbs clawing at the air.

"Wait!" Kul shouted. "Talk to me!" but the creature shivered back from him, from all of them. Their gaze seemed to hurt it more than their swords or Ned's club had. It shrank from them in a frenzy of self-loathing, clutching for something to cover itself. A moment later it had bolted and so had the rest, leaving only the half-starved, fragile bodies of their dead and wounded.

A lot of people were looking at Amkulyah after that, but he had no answers. Some of his people had not died or ended up in the Dorhambri, it seemed. They had lived, wingless and broken, in the Kinslayer's very shadow, learning only to hate themselves and what they had become.

Meddig gave a halting explanation, as much as he could glean from the Kelicerati's alien thoughtscape. To the spider-people, these Aethani were just more of the Kinslayer's minions, some other race of underlings from within the earth. They had been slaves of the same master before. Now that master was dead, the maimed people fought everyone else, turning their hate outwards, unable to tolerate any eyes that might pick out their ruined state. They had fought the Kelicerati, and they didn't want their enemies to gain new allies—or that was the gloss that the spider-people were giving the attack.

"They can be saved," Celestaine assured Kul. "They can be brought back. Especially if we can do what we're trying to. It's... just one more thing the Kinslayer did, to spoil the world."

Heno wore a doubting expression, when he thought Amkulyah couldn't see. She bearded him later and he admitted he'd heard the rumours. "After they lost their wings, some went over. The Kinslayer promised to make them whole, probably." And, when she asked why he hadn't ever said anything, he shrugged. "It was just a story. I never saw them myself. Why is it relevant?"

He was not telling her everything. Something hung in the air over him, just as it had when she'd first suggested trying to restore the Aethani in the first place. From experience, she knew that questioning wouldn't pry it from him. Heno kept his own council.

Both sides had taken losses to the Aethani and Kait wanted to get out of the forest with their wounded before the Kelicerati suggested any treatment of their own. "Meddig, can you tell them what I say?" she demanded.

"I'll try," he confirmed. "Where they even have words to match ours."

"Tell them to come to the forest's edge. Their spokesmen, their dragon, any other monsters that are of their party—not just this nest, but anything else that wants peace. Tell them to show themselves. I will go and tell the others how things are. We will try peace, and maybe the gods will be pleased. Perhaps they will come back to us." That last was hers alone, and Celestaine had no idea if Meddig had passed the thoughts on or what the Kelicerati might have made of them.

The Hegumen checked that the wounded were either able to walk or assigned to a stretcher. She made sure the dead were carried out, too, because whether there was agreement with the Kelicerati or not, she plainly wasn't going to leave any of her own as a peace offering. "Come on, now, form up!" she shouted, and then looked about for absent civilians. "Meddig, Olastoc, come on!"

The Oerni was standing beside the monolith, practically within the dragon's coils. This was his holy place, for all that it had become a Kelicerati larder and a wyrm's lair since. "There is something here," he said slowly. "A leftover dream of my people. We used these Wayshrines to cache our devotion, our prayers, so that fortune's favourites could leave gifts for those less lucky. Meddig has been speaking for me. He and I will stay."

"No—" the Hegumen started, but he held up a big hand.

"Look for me when the Kelicerati come to the forest's edge. If I live unharmed, that's more evidence this is a true peace."

"Meddig?"

The scout turned a face on her that had very little humanity in it. "You know I'm safe here. And if I am here, they will not forget that the priest is safe too. All is well." He was smiling, but it was a fragile thing, from a man who didn't truly know what he was, anymore.

Kait swore, obviously ready to argue, but the man's eerie calm got through to her. "We're moving," she said. "Everyone else, let's go."

"What about them?" Nedlam asked, loud enough to stop everyone in their tracks.

"Them who?" Kait glanced around to see Nedlam pointing at a huddle of Aethani too wounded to flee but still alive. Celestaine had the distinct impression the Hegumen had been well aware of them, but doing her best to ignore them.

Amkulyah was down off Ned's shoulders, looking like he wanted a fight. "We're not leaving them for the spiders," he said.

"The..." Kait looked from him to the Kelicerati, who were surely looking at the downed Aethani with a certain amount of anticipation.

"The gods say peace and mercy. Your gods, our gods," Kul told her. "Mercy for the spiders, fine. But as you can see, it's not all spiders in these trees. You want peace with these, my cousins, my kin? Tend to their wounded. Talk to them. They even use words, like you. It'll be easy." He was defiant, fists balled.

Celestaine cast a worried eye over at the dragon and its spidery acolytes. The great reptile watched her thoughtfully, and she had the sense of a great mind working, that meshed with that other mind, shallower yet broader, spread between all the Kelicerati. Once again she wondered that the beast was so much more aware than the dragons she had seen in the war. Was that because it had been smart enough to get free of the Kinslayer before it met her? Or were there still dragons left from the dawn of time, hiding from the wrath of the Guardians and their mortal allies both?

Its throat clenched and heaved out a single word, "*Shtok!*"

"Take," Heno translated.

"Then everyone carries," Kait said. "Grab a body, no need to be too gentle. I want out before they come back or these ones change their great big mind."

Celestaine took one arm of a bloody-cloaked Aethani, and a Templar took the other. Nedlam just slung two of them over her shoulders. Almost everyone ended up burdened and slow, sitting ducks if anything in the forest had an ambush planned. Only Heno and Amkulyah himself weren't carrying anyone: Heno because he was being superior and distant, which at least left him free to deploy his magic against any trouble; Kul because he was a prince.

She heard him passing his name up and down the line, speaking to any of the injured enemy conscious enough to listen. He took their curses and their spittle and stayed calm; regal even. For a youth who had seemed so angry in the time Celestaine had known him, it was quite a transformation. With his own people, even these twisted remnants, he had a stock of patience he didn't deploy for humans or Yorughan.

For their part, the curses petered out before they reached the fort, leaving a deep shame amongst the prisoners—not for their attack, but for what they were. Celestaine had the impression they had been broken and tormented by the Kinslayer's people far more than those sent to the mines. Their bodies were crooked, hollowed out by hunger, lop-sided and out of proportion. Life on soil poisoned by the Kinslayer's experiments had changed them, maddened them; most of all it had reinforced how much they had lost.

When the fort was in sight, Amkulyah broke from them and came back to Celestaine.

"You had better fetch the bard," he said.

She frowned at him, giving her wounded burden over to some of the Templars. "You have something he needs to hear?"

"I have somewhere to go," Kul told her, then scowled at her expression, all that chained anger abruptly back in place. "You think that talk was just indulging myself? You saw we weren't getting any word from the Crawlies? No way even to ask them what we wanted to know. But my people saw, my blighted kin. They saw a big man in armour come through. They attacked him and he killed five of them with his hammer. He killed some Kelicerati too, they said, and more. He went through the forest and slowed for nothing, and they followed him to the dry lands beyond."

"And where did he go from there?" asked Celestaine, thinking, *Yet another link, but the chain never ends.*

Amkulyah's eyes blazed. "According to them, he's still there."

CHAPTER TWENTY-SEVEN

THEY WERE GONE from the fort before noon, despite the Hegumen's obvious preference to hold on to genuine witnesses of the Ilkand Miracle, as they were calling it. Celestaine reckoned she'd only been witness to someone else's reaction to something that might have been entirely the work of the very mortal Doctor Fisher. She didn't want to be anyone's ancillary prophet. And Amkulyah had a good picture of where the mysterious thief had finally holed up, and was plainly about to explode if he had to sit on his hands any longer.

They left their mounts with the Templars, since the ground ahead would be too rocky for Celestaine's horse, too barren to feed even the lunnox. They could have cut through the forest and made shorter time, but they all reckoned that would be testing the goodwill of the Kelicerati too much, not to mention any other nasty surprises that benighted place might be harbouring. As it was, even skirting the forest's verge, they were attacked. A winged amphibian-looking monster burst from the trees, half leaping, half flapping towards them, frog eyes bulging wide as though it was trying to catch up with them to deliver an urgent message. If it hadn't been bigger than a horse, its vast gaping maw lined with ranks of hooked teeth, it would have been risible. As it was, Amkulyah put three arrows in it without finding a sensitive spot, and Heno's magic just feathered off its slimy hide, leaving little more than ice trails. Nedlam got a solid blow into its goggling face, though, leaving Celestaine to open it up from lips to legs as it tried to vault her. None of them had ever seen such a beast before, and the consensus was that they hoped it was one of a kind.

Celestaine re-sheathed her sword carefully. She had bound the scabbard up as best she could, but it wouldn't last long, and the nearest supply of dragonskin was still occupied by a dragon.

They camped at the far end of the forest, hidden in a hollow and keeping double watch. Aside from the folio-sized moths that arrived for fatal liaisons with their fire, nothing came from the trees to trouble them. Ahead, the land fell away, dry and cracked, as though the forest had drawn all the moisture to itself. Desert didn't mean deserted, of course: at dusk they had seen big domed mounds crawling across the rugged, rocky terrain like great horseshoe crabs. They were made-things, Heno said, bred to scavenge battlefields and ruins for anything of use. Now they were just roaming wild, no doubt dropping their meagre gains in some cache somewhere, waiting for a master that would never return. He was in an odd mood that night. Celestaine was fond of him, but even she would admit that he was all sharp edges, full of derisive wit and sharp words for all of the world outside his immediate fellowship, and sometimes even for them. This night, though, he had given in to a strange melancholy new to him.

"Talk to me," she suggested, sitting next to him to share his watch. He was looking out over those dry lands, streaked by the moon and mottled by the rolling shadows of clouds.

"These things..." He gestured vaguely, encompassing all the world. "Dragons, monsters, the Kelicerati, the Kinslayer's constructs and mistakes. Us."

"You're not like them," she said loyally.

"Who knows what we would have been, if not for him? If the gods had taken notice of us and sent Guardians amongst us, way back then. We fell under the Kinslayer's sway because he was still a thing of the gods, and so he was better than nothing. All of us—Yorughan, Grennish, Silanti—we were the people the gods never got around to. The Guardians infest your human histories like *lice*." His tone turned abruptly savage. "They came to the Aethani and taught them to fly, so they tell it. They walked the roads with the Oerni, they brought boatbuilding to the Shelliac, even. But for us, nothing. And we felt it. Long before the Kinslayer took advantage, we were there to be taken advantage of. The children nobody wanted."

Celestaine said nothing, keeping a weather eye on the darkness of the forest but the rest of her mind listening.

"We lost wars, back in those days. We lost lands. We lost our history, too. Where were our ancestral homes before we ended up in the pits of the earth? We don't even know. But that meant that *anywhere* could be ours, when we came back. Find a place you like the look of, during the invasion? Well, then, that's your ancient home from before time. We could tell ourselves it was *all* ours, once."

"You don't believe that."

"Of course not, but plenty fooled themselves into thinking it, because it was better than knowing *nowhere* was. And the Kinslayer made us strong, if only because he made sure the weak all died. He honed us, sharpened us by paring away the bluntness. He gave us monsters as allies. He taught us that, so long as we feared him, the rest of the world would fear us. And he made us proud to be ourselves. Maybe not the Grennish—I mean, who would be proud to be a Grennishman? But we were the Yorughan, the war-makers. He didn't mean to, but he made us feel worth something, for the first time in a long time. He took monsters and horrors and made-things and us, and he made us part of something. It was good."

He looked at her, searching for condemnation, but she was nodding slowly. "And you turned on him."

"And I don't regret it, because the thing we were part of was a lie. He'd have destroyed us, when we'd destroyed you. He killed any of us who got ideas, who asked questions. I'm lucky I worked that out before opening my mouth once too often. But..."

"You miss it."

"Even knowing it was a lie, I miss the lie. It was a good lie. And now it's gone. All the monsters and prodigies will die off, or else they'll become... less. Make accommodations, fit into your world, because we'll never have one of our own. Your people should be ready for those who would rather fight to the death, because there's still some pride in that, rather than ending up pulling some human farmer's haycart or carrying a hod to build your fine houses."

She wanted to say that it wouldn't be like that, but how could she? She didn't know, and she reckoned Heno had a better grasp of these things than she did.

"What I can do, I'll do," was all she could vow.

"Waste of your talents, really," and that was more the Heno she knew. He didn't speak of it again, but she saw the shadow of those thoughts behind his eyes more than once as they travelled.

That morning, there was another at their fire. What shape he had crept up in, Celestaine couldn't guess, but there was the wretched form of the Undefeated making a fist of making breakfast before Ralas's incredulous stare. Celestaine awoke to his plaintive voice as he tried to outline some grand saga, some great list of lies and omissions that would turn his sojourn as a badger for the war's duration into some grand struggle between good and evil.

"Everyone knows the Kinslayer came out of the earth," the Undefeated argued. "Who knows the earth better than a badger?" He didn't argue with any force, just whined away with an implacable endurance.

She sat up, startling him into silence. "Enough from you,

Deffo," she said. "You had your chance. You could have actually fought an actual sort-of-Kinslayer alongside us. That would have been a true brave thing they might have sung in every tavern taproom. And where were you?"

"You don't understand—"

"I do. You heard the name Kinslayer. You were worried you might be the next kin to get slain. And so you bottled it and ran and left us—us *mortals*—to deal with it. Think of that word, Deffo. We're mortals, Ralas possibly excepted. We die. Doesn't mean we don't stand up and do things that might get us killed."

"It's not the same," he whimpered, but his own voice showed just how little he believed it. "Please, give me another chance, Celestaine. I don't want to be just—"

"Just another person?" she asked him. "Not a great Guardian, champion of the gods, beloved of the people, but just one of us? Tough. Go back to being a badger."

After he'd slunk away from the fire, the five of them pressed on into the dry lands, following the directions Amkulyah had gleaned from the captive Aethani. Little clans of Grennishmen watched them from cracks in the rock; great vulture-like birds rode the arid winds above. In the distance, something like a huge harvestman stalked the horizon on great arching legs that must have been thirty feet long. Nothing approached them, though, for good or ill, and by dusk they were nearing their goal. They found a canyon just as promised, snaking into the earth, its sides leaning towards each other precipitously. Caves riddled the sides, mostly small round holes bored by various of the worm-like creatures the Kinslayer had favoured once, but at the canyon's end was the lair they had been told of, a tall cave mouth that had been carved into an archway, and beyond it the abortive workings of some outpost that the Kinslayer had decreed and then abandoned in the early years of the war, his gains against his enemies mounting faster than even he had anticipated.

There was a fire there, gleaming out at them in the growing dark, and Kul claimed he could see a single figure sitting at it, as though waiting for them. Nobody suggested going over and asking for hospitality, but they made their own camp within sight of it and waited until morning.

"You sure you don't just want to go warm yourself by their fire?" Doctor Fisher suggested sourly. Catt had decreed that they camp within easy sight of Celestaine's party, save of course for their shrouding magic. "If that Yogg mage casts his senses over this way, he'll sniff us out for sure."

"Only if you've not done your work properly," Catt said. They were in the hut again, watching Celestaine's campfire from one window, while another gave onto the lone fire built by their unknown quarry. Catt was just setting up a complex framework of lenses on a tripod, the better to spy on their opponent. "I was actually going to just go over and get the crown once it's full dark. I mean, why bother waiting? We could be gone by dawn. Of course, that remains an efficacious stratagem only if it's available to be abstracted, so let's see…"

Fisher looked from him to the currently bare table. "So we're going to eat soon, or…?"

"Oh, have it give us a cold spread or something." Catt bent down and peered through some of the lenses, slotting others in and out. "Big fellow, certainly. And still wearing a Templar's livery. I thought we'd established he *wasn't* a Temple regular?"

"Not established anything," Fisher grunted. "Unless he's got the crown out on a rock for polishing, what're you going to accomplish, exactly?"

"This individual has put us all to a great deal of trouble," Catt remarked, still fiddling with lenses. "I speak not just for the two of us, but for poor Celestaine, who has been forced from fire to frying pan and back in tracking down this collectable for us, and whose indignities I feel fiercely." At Fisher's snort he lifted his head. "What, you think that, just because I am similarly taking advantage, I can have no sympathies for the woman?"

Fisher's reply was occluded by a huge mouthful of bread, which was possibly just as well.

"There we are." Catt was at last satisfied with the orientation of the lenses. "I see a man, I see... a chest. He's sitting on it, unfortunately, but there is a distinct dweomer arising from it. Or from his backside, but let us hope it is the chest which is enchanted. The alternative is grim and bizarre."

"Could be any old magic tat," Fisher suggested, "or a false enchantment, you know, like they had in Ellas."

Catt tutted. "Unless I am misreading these devices like a mere novice thaumaturge, there is *something* of an appropriate level of magnitude out there, and though I cannot be absolutely certain of its presence within the chest, where else is the thing going to be?"

"Let me see it." Fisher waited for him to step aside and then put his own eye to the device, smearing the lenses with butter. "Hrm," he said, after a while.

"May I take it you concur?" Catt asked him.

Fisher straightened up from the lenses. "You don't want to go gadding about near him at night, Catty."

"Fishy, I don't *gad*..."

"Catt, hear me," Fisher said, seriously enough that even Catt couldn't just prattle through it. "You've looked, but you've not *seen*. You don't want to go pulling the nose of this one."

Doctor Catt paused, mouth still open, another torrent of words poised on his tongue. At last he shut it, eyebrows raised.

"Just *look*, Catty," Fisher insisted. "Not at the chest, at the man. Use Avandrel's Blue Eye and the Lens of Grand Sight together, like you should've been doing."

"Don't presume to tell me my craft," Catt said, wounded, and then did as he was told.

After a while he straightened up, looking a good deal more sober. "Oh, I see. One of them."

"Not just 'one of them,' Catty," Fisher said. "Him. The one of them you don't want to meet."

Catt grimaced and looked out of the other window, out at Celestaine's fire. "I suppose we need to let the poor woman break the ice, then, for all my conscience pricks at me."

"Just be ready to take to your heels when you've got the thing," Fisher said darkly. "He's not going to leave much around here standing, when he knows he's been had."

"HE'S NOT LEFT in the night," Amkulyah reported. "Just sitting there. He must have seen us."

"He's got friends around, then?" Nedlam squinted up at the canyon walls. Plenty of opportunity for hidden reinforcements in the pitted holes and caves. "Horde of Grennish come to bite our knees, maybe."

"A dozen Grennish with bows would make this an unhealthy place to be," Heno observed. "Celest?"

She looked from him to the others: big Ned, skinny Kul and timeworn Ralas. "He's not left because he's expecting us."

"Surely," Ralas agreed. "He's been leaving the damnedest trail all over this part of the world, trying to get us killed."

"And now there he is, waiting to see who's made it," Celestaine finished for him. "Someone who has a use for people who can survive all of that. Someone who needs heroes."

"Is that right?" Ralas didn't look convinced. "He must feel a bit flat, then, seeing us. Saving yourself, we're not traditional hero material: two Yoggs, a lame duck and these old bones."

"What are you thinking?" Heno asked her.

"I think it might be an old friend," Celestaine said hesitantly. "After all, he left, didn't he? He was in those last battles, everyone says so, but when I came to camp with news that the

Kinslayer was dead, where was he? Gone. Where? Where he was needed. And now *he* needs help. That's what I think."

"Wait, wait." Ralas held his hands up, glancing down the canyon at the archway, the burnt-out fire, the hulking figure. "You're saying you think that's *Wanderer* up there?"

"Yes."

"Because all this trying to get us killed doesn't seem like him," the bard went on.

"He never did anything the simple way. He did it so you'd learn, and need him less. He didn't kill Vermarod; he gave me the means to kill it. So now he wants us, with all we've learned."

"By 'us' you mean you," Ralas went on. "Look, Celest, I remember you and Wanderer. I remember him turning up with the sword and some sage advice. And, right, he was always there. And then I got killed a few times and missed the rest of the war, but I'll take your word that he was in it right to the end, the only Guardian who properly pitched in and didn't get killed for their trouble. And, well, you treated him like he was your magic uncle."

"My... what?"

"Magic uncle gives you a sword. Magic uncle always says the right things, always has the best advice. When the war started, Celest, you were a girl trying to avoid leading the Fiddlehead after your folks died. Magic uncle always had much more fun things to do than knuckle down and mind the farm. Who even *is* minding the farm, anyway?"

"I have cousins, plenty of cousins. Let them have it. That isn't even important." Celestaine could feel herself getting angry with him, mostly because bards could tell you the truth in such a way that it got through any kind of armour. "I'm going now. I'm going to speak to him, to ask him what this is all about. He'll have a good reason, I know it. He *knew* we'd sort out Thukrah, and Silvermort, and the Ilkand Temple."

"General Thuk had it all sorted out already," Nedlam muttered, but Celestaine ignored her.

"Celest," Ralas snapped. "Whoever this is, he left me to rot in the pits beneath Bleakmairn. You're going to tell me the Wanderer had a good reason for that?"

She stared at him, trying to force out the *Yes*, but not able to quite get it past her teeth. She had no answers, but she knew she was right, that this was all part of some solid plan of her erstwhile mentor, who *hadn't* abandoned her after the war. Who was waiting, just there, to throw off his helm and Templar tabard and...

"I'm going," she told them. "To the pits with you, stay here if you want. I'm going." She turned on her heel and stormed off up the canyon. Soon enough, she heard the rest of them following in her wake.

I'll show them. What, precisely, she didn't know, but she was in a showing mood.

The figure got to his feet as she approached. He was big, very big, but then plenty of Guardians could change their shape—look at Deffo's badger fixation. He wore solid, heavy armour plate, the shield sigil black on white, proud on his surcoat—not quite the current insignia of the Templars, but a more elaborate, archaic version. In one hand he held a huge hammer, something that Nedlam would have had to use two hands with.

"So." The deep voice echoed from behind the visor of his helm. "I knew someone would come eventually, no matter what trials I left behind me."

Her heart leapt. *I'm right!* "And here I am!" She flung her arms out, in that moment quite alone despite the others at her back. "I passed. I'm here." She felt a worm of doubt when no welcome was immediately forthcoming. "You... know me?"

"I do," the figure said heavily. "I see before me Celestaine of Fernreame, of that band known as the Slayers."

"Yes…" This wasn't going how she'd thought. "Take off the helm, will you? Just… be yourself, like you used to. You're sounding as though you didn't… expect me."

"I did not," he confirmed. "And I confess that, of all who might have come for the Kinslayer's crown, your presence here disappoints me greatly."

She stared at him.

"I knew the lure of its power would draw the greedy and the foolish," his leaden voice went on. "And I was prepared to meet with any not deterred or destroyed by what I had left behind. I expected something like *them*." And a gauntleted hand waved towards the Yorughan behind her. "Not you, not one who had done so much good, now turned to darkness."

"What…" She blinked, feeling as though she'd opened her eyes to find the world a wholly different place. "You're not Wanderer, are you?"

A derisive laugh issued from the helm. "I am what he always aspired to, the true defender of the right." And at last he lifted his visor, showing her a square, blocky face, as stern as a hanging judge, grey eyes pitiless as frost. "Know me, child. In your last moments, know me."

And she didn't, not quite. She'd seen the face before, or something close to it, but the memory hid itself away and she was about to awkwardly ask for a clue when Ralas called out, "I know you. I got a good enough look at your ugly stone face when we were locked up in Ilkand."

"Justice is a beauty all to itself," said the armoured man, and in that moment Celestaine cornered the errant memory.

"Lord Wall," she got out. Wall, the Ilkand Temple's greatest patron, the Kinslayer's greatest foe—save that he hadn't quite got to the battle when she and the other Slayers had sorted the enemy out for good. Wall, the warrior Guardian.

"I… don't understand," she said weakly. "Why did you want the Kinslayer's crown?"

"I? *I* wanted nothing with it," Wall told her flatly. "But I knew you mortals wouldn't leave well alone. I knew that, within a generation, one of you would use it to make yourself a new Kinslayer. And I knew I could use it to draw those with such fatal ambitions, and put an end to them. I am bitterly disappointed in you, Celestaine of Fernreame, but I shall go about my duty nonetheless."

"We wanted the crown to *help* people," Celestaine said, feeling as though the world was falling apart around her.

"There is no compromise with evil," Wall pronounced. "Evil is evil, and it must be destroyed wherever it is found. That you have come here in the company of the enemy's creatures shows how far you have fallen. And you will never have the crown; not you, nor any other greedy mortals. I have destroyed it, and now I will destroy you."

CHAPTER TWENTY-EIGHT

"You..." Celestaine blinked. "...did what?"

"I have ensured that this tool of the enemy's will never fall into hands that might use it," Lord Wall told her, in a smug tone. "And now—"

"Yes, yes." She waved away her impending demise irritatedly. "You *destroyed* the Kinslayer's crown."

Wall frowned, as if unsure why she was having difficulty with this. "A toy of the enemy's, a thing of dark power—"

"Of power," she corrected. "It wasn't a thing of the enemy. It was gems stolen *by* the enemy. From us, from his victims. Gems that could heal, rebuild. Good things, things we need, now we're all trying to work out what's still standing and where the next harvest's coming from. Things of *hope*. And you destroyed them."

Wall struck the butt of his hammer on the ground for emphasis. "Once touched by the Kinslayer, everything is tainted. Every last trace of his corruption must be driven from this world, seared from the land until not even the memory of him remains. And that includes those who would covet—"

"You *imbecile!*" she bellowed at him.

"How dare—?"

"What, you're going to rid the world of all memory of the

Kinslayer? He brought a war to *everyone*. His armies marched on every damn city there is, from Ilkand to Athaln, from Tzarkona Gate to the Seven Quays. Thousands of people were killed. Thousands more lost their homes, and many will never get them back. Relics were stolen, landmarks razed, Guardians killed, the damn *land* itself got all twisted up—just look outside your cave, Your Lordship!—and even the *gods*, nobody even *knows* what happened to the *gods*. And we're going to *forget* that, are we? We're going to wake up one morning and—what?—just wonder where Aunt Irelli went and why the Kishanti Clock is just this pile of stones?"

"You are already corrupted by his touch, Celestaine of Fernreame," Wall rumbled. "Perhaps it was when you faced him. Did he tempt you with power? Was that your fall from grace?"

"He didn't get much of a chance, on account of how I was cutting his hand off at the time. Which you'd have known, if you'd been... oh. *Oh*. That's it, is it?"

Wall was very still, watching her. It was the sudden lack of bombast that told her she was right.

"There's a lot of it going around, isn't there?" She risked another step towards him, because if things did go to crap then that hammer had far more reach than her sword. "I had Deffo—the Undefeated—sniffing about right after the Kinslayer's corpse hit the ground, wanting to salvage his reputation. Probably he's lurking in earshot even now. You two could get together, tell each other how simply marvellous you were during the war."

"I will have nothing to do with that worm," Wall sneered.

"Badger," Celestaine corrected absently. "And I think you'd have lots to talk about. You both spent the war doing precisely nothing to help."

This time he struck the head of his hammer on the ground in rage, sending her skittering back a few feet and bringing a curtain of dust down from above. "I gathered my followers. The Kinslayer would have fallen to us—"

"When?" Celestaine was done with listening patiently. "You got a bunch of people who told you how great you were, and you holed up in some castle so far north that the Yorughan'd have frozen their balls off trying to reach you. You thought we'd *lose*, the rest of us. You gave up on us and decided you'd start over somewhere cold and hope the Kinslayer wouldn't wonder where you'd got to. Or perhaps—!" And she was right back in his incredulous face, throwing her hand up to silence his protests. "Perhaps I'll give you the benefit of the doubt. Perhaps you'd have come south with your band of fanatics, when you felt like it, when it was too late for everyone else. You'd have been the sole voice of righteousness, because everyone else would be dead or enslaved. Just like you're trying to be the sole voice now."

"I am—"

"You weren't there!" she yelled at him. "Your damn Templars in Ilkand fought the Kinslayer three times and you weren't there for them. Your fellow Guardians died, and *you weren't there*."

"I am Lord Wall!" he roared back. "I was first amongst my brothers to cast the Kinslayer in the earth. You cannot speak to me like that!"

"I can, because you didn't finish the job," she shot back. "And you didn't help, and now you've decided you're the great judge of the whole world because it makes you feel better about doing *piss all* during the war."

Truth hurts, and she found confirmation of her words in his hammer, abruptly sweeping down towards her.

She barely got out of the way, sword leaping clear of its ravaged scabbard and grazing the hammer's shaft as it thundered past her. She had a sense of the others starting to move and shouted, "No, he's mine!" because she had the magic sword and they did not, and a blow from Lord Wall would kill even Nedlam stone dead.

*　　*　　*

"CROWN'S GONE, THEN," Fisher said. "I'll get the wagon."

Doctor Catt watched Celestaine leap back from a ground-shaking stroke from Lord Wall. Her sword flashed out, but he was far faster than his size suggested, turning aside her blade with the haft of his hammer without giving it a chance to bite. Her fellows were spreading out, the big Yorughan warrior to one side, the Heart Taker to the other. Their Aethani had an arrow to the string, waiting for his moment. Probably Ralas was about to rush in too, though Catt didn't see that going well for him.

"Come on, Catty," Fisher said. "If we hurry, we can maybe find a tavern before nightfall."

"Oh, don't be so pessimistic, Fishy."

"We can *definitely* find a tavern, then."

"Fishy, dear friend, I took a good look at His Lordship here last night, through all the lenses we had. You know what I saw? Power."

"Catt, he's Lord Wall. Whatever else is true of him, power he's got."

"Not that sort of power. The Guardians vary, it's true. Some are decidedly more vital than others, and Wall always used to be a superlative exemplar of the breed. But I saw power, Fishy." He winced as a hammer-blow came close enough to skin the tip of Celestaine's nose. "I saw the sort of power one might just get if one combined a number of magical gems into some sort of decorative headgear using the Kinslayer's particular flavour of dweomer. In short, I think our lordly demigod is dissembling. I think the crown's sitting nicely in that chest."

"You think Wall's lying?"

"I think the crown exerts a powerful fascination on the lowly and the mighty alike. I think that when the moment came for the hammer to fall, he had second thoughts. And you know what that means, Fishy?"

"Catt..."

"It means we have a distraction, and we have shrouding magic, and we have a chest that will doubtless yield to a little persuasion." He grinned fiercely at Doctor Fisher. "Out from under the very nose of a Guardian. The prospect rather makes one feel alive, does it not?"

CELESTAINE WAS DOING her best to drive Wall back, less to keep him off balance than to keep her friends from getting in the way. Between his hammer and her sword there wasn't much safe ground anywhere near the fight.

She couldn't match him for strength. When he swung, she had to give way. He obviously knew exactly what she wielded, though. She could move him just as he moved her, because he didn't want to risk ending up holding a stump.

She couldn't quite steer him, though. She had tried to back him into the cave, in the hope that he wouldn't have room to swing, but instead he retreated to the left, which put Heno at his back and Nedlam at hers. She saw the Yorughan mage begin to work up his white fire.

Will that even work on him? Perhaps it would be extra-effective against Guardians. Perhaps, as it had been powerless against the Kinslayer, so it would be powerless against Heno's old master's kin.

Don't want to find out just yet. She lunged straight down the middle, cutting at Wall's visor and hacking a chip from it as he fell back slightly too slowly. For a moment she was angling her blade at his neck, between helm and pauldron, but he had her measure and thrust the hammer at her—not how the weapon was meant to be used, but the solid head slammed into her abdomen, putting another dent in her breastplate and knocking her over.

That was the signal, as far as everyone else was concerned, for a free-for-all.

Wall had his hammer up to well and truly smite her, and Celestaine was rolling aside, trying to bring her sword up between his legs. Then an arrow spanged from the edge of his eyeslit, enough to send him stumbling and put him off his attack. It was followed, as though shot from the very same bow, by Nedlam.

The big Yorughan came in swinging, her ironbound club crashing into Wall's shoulder and buckling the armour, sending him staggering. Ned tried to stave in his helm with the follow-through, but Wall ducked into the swing, arm up to hook about the club, and deflect it. His mailed elbow smashed Nedlam in the face, and he wrapped a hand about her jaw and just shoved her away. Ned wasn't used to running into someone stronger than she was and ended up teetering off-balance as he wound up his hammer again. Then Heno's white fire wreathed him and, though it didn't seem to actually *hurt*, it infuriated Wall beyond all reason. He rounded on the Heart Taker, and Celestaine saw him practically frothing with rage through the slots of his visor. If there was an Enemy, capital E, then it was the Kinslayer, but in the Kinslayer's absence, the Heart Takers had always been the symbols of his power, and Heno even still wore the uniform.

Oh, death, went through Celestaine's mind, because Heno had clearly got Wall's attention.

Wall had been deft on his feet, but had kept his movements small, letting himself go inches aside from her strokes and conserving his strength, Now he *moved*, kicking away from her and whirling his hammer at Heno at full extension. The Heart Taker threw himself on his back on the ground, the only way to get out with his head still on his shoulders, and Wall already had his hammer up, about to turn him into a stain on the rock.

Another arrow landed, this time over the rim of Wall's breastplate and into his armpit. There was fine mail there, though, and Celestaine saw the shaft just sag in the armour without penetrating. She was scrabbling to her feet, tripping forwards, sword first, hoping to close the distance faster than the hammer could come down.

She heard Ralas swear as inventively as any bard could as he just leapt in the way, waving his arms like a madman and spitting out obscenities right into Wall's visored face. The hammer came down, but Heno had lunged aside in that moment's hesitation, and Ralas was well within its arc. The haft slammed into his shoulder but then he was hanging onto it like an arthritic monkey, so that when Wall swung the weapon back up, Ralas went with it, kicking at the Guardian's head.

Celestaine knew her moment when she saw it. She caught her balance and turned her stumble into a lunge, hacking into Wall's armour. She'd been aiming at the tassets that fell in sections about his hips, because she'd call it a win if she could get his metal trousers to end up around his ankles. She rushed the blow, though, slicing into the thick metal of the breastplate itself, peeling the metal back and pulling the blade out with a little blood along its edge.

THERE HAD BEEN a thriving magical collector's trade before the war, of course, and Doctor Catt had been an enthusiastic amateur. The Kinslayer had changed everything, though. Catt wasn't a Silvermort, to give thanks to the enemy for the opportunities he had brought, but it was true that the selection of powerful desiderata up for grabs had multiplied impressively after the Kinslayer began his campaign. Plenty of relics were displaced from age-old hiding places, either spoils of war or carried out ahead of the tide by their secret guardians. Plenty more were created by the Kinslayer himself—who, for all his many faults, had a ceaselessly inventive nature. Others, like the crown, were a combination of the two, and they were frequently the most potent.

Most collectors, faced with the chaos of war and its attendant risks, had quietly closed up their collections and gotten out of the trade for the duration. Doctor Catt was not among them. In the silver years of his life, with the world on fire around him, he had discovered a hitherto unsuspected love of taking risks.

Celestaine would never know, which he felt was a shame. She had fought battles and killed the actual Kinslayer, and no doubt thought of him as a meddling tradesman with too much money and too many toys. He hadn't been idle during the war, though; he had been in and out of occupied Cinquetann hunting for choice specimens, and some he had kept, but some he had put into the hands of the resistance. He had stood in the private chambers of enemy commanders and abstracted their battle plans or forged their signatures, he had walked unseen through the night-time camps of Yorughan whose morning battle plans would have to be redrawn without their enchanted battle standards or horns of wall-breaking. And he had profited mightily from it, in money and in acquisitions for his collection, but then he didn't know a single spy who hadn't been lining his own pockets while helping the cause of just.

And now he was creeping past a truly spectacular melee between the woman who slew the Kinslayer and the greatest of the Guardians, the gods' agents in the mortal world. Whoever won, someone was going to be down a crown by the end of the day.

There, within the archway, was the chest that Wall had been sitting on all night, waiting for this nonsensical challenge. For what it was worth, Catt agreed wholeheartedly with Celestaine about the Guardian's motives. Pure sour grapes at not being in for the kill; and whose fault was that exactly? Nobody but Wall's own self.

The fight took a sudden turn his way. Catt froze, one hand to his protective amulet, watching the Yorughan Heart Taker almost get turned into a decorative smear. Then everyone was piling on Wall, and Catt re-evaluated his greatest risk right then as 'being struck by a flying bard' as Ralas clung on gamely to the great maul.

Come on, old man, get your legs moving. Once he was sure the fight wasn't about to roll over him, Catt moved on, cutting a curved path over the rocky terrain, to avoid all the unpleasantness going on below. He heard Wall bellow in pain and had time to glance back and send an approving thought Celestaine's way. *She really is rather good at this. If she survives, I think she and I are likely to come to blows.* He would need to stack the deck heavily in his own favour to come out of that one ahead, but he was good at that.

And here he was, and there was the chest. He had his headband of lenses on, that he used for reading fine print as much as anything magical, but he flipped down two of the more unusual and examined the metal-bound container. *Yes, hard to tell against the radiance of the power within, but definitely something about the lock itself.* A rasher man might have just set to with lockpicks, but he had a piece of rune-etched chalk for just this occasion and marked the relevant warding sigils about the lockplate to disarm whatever nastiness had been lurking in wait for a less perceptive thief. After that it was out with the picks: while there were magics that could trip locks, they were clumsy and tended to ruin the mechanisms one time out of three, and Catt liked keeping all his skills properly honed.

It wasn't a good lock. It looked nice, and it was big and clunky. Probably it was what Lord Wall looked for in a lock, but Catt was able to throw the tumblers one after another with the aid of a spell that let him look inside at all the pieces. He understood that some people broke into other people's houses and containers without magical aid, which seemed like trying to win a fight with your laces tied together. *Even so, it's taken me rather longer than I'd like: unlike this lock, I am rather rusty. I should just buy a load of locks and keep my hand in.*

Things had degenerated into talking behind him, which wasn't ideal, but everyone was still obviously engrossed with each other, which suited him fine, He cast a look back at Fisher, who he knew could see him. *Wringing his hands with worry, the old fool.* Catt made sure to flash a big grin at the man before lifting the lid of the chest.

His face fell.

Nothing more than the bare floor of the chest, notably crown-free.

A false enchantment, Fisher had said.

Oh, bother.

SHE HAD BLOODIED Wall, but it was just a graze—and hurt, he was angrier and faster without becoming careless. Heno had scrabbled back out of reach, but Nedlam's next swing ended up with her club being swiped from her hands, flying ten feet to leave a crater in the canyon wall. Ralas went off at the same sort of trajectory, signifying the end of his active contribution to the fight. Then Wall turned back to her with murder obviously in mind, to find her closer than he'd thought and already hacking at his helm.

Her blade cut, shearing into the metal, but if she was hoping to bisect him down the middle she was disappointed. There was an awkward moment when her blade actually got stuck and she ended up getting a foot against his thigh and yanking furiously to free it. Wall struck her in the shoulder with the butt of his hammer, which sent her tumbling back, thankfully still in possession of her sword. In the brief moment's respite that won him, another of Kul's arrows rammed into his visor, not piercing but wedged into one of the slits. Wall batted at it, snapping the shaft but leaving the head in place as a wedge-shaped shadow in his view.

She was on her feet, at least, bunching up for another rush at him, but Nedlam got there just ahead of her. Possibly Wall had discounted her when she was disarmed, but an eight-foot-tall Yorughan was a weapon in her own right. She jumped him and got an arm past his hammer, crooking her hand around the shaft to put it out of the way. Her other hand ended up about his neck, trying to pry his battered helm off, levering at his visor. She was trying to give Amkulyah a shot at the face underneath, confident he would make it.

Wall bellowed and shoved. For a moment Nedlam was matching him strength for strength, and the two of them swayed back and forth, grunting and straining, as Celestaine ran in and circled round, fully intending to stab the Guardian right between the shoulderblades. Then Wall slipped down to one knee, apparently vulnerable, save that it had been a feint and Nedlam fell for it. She lurched forwards and over Wall's shoulders, and then he flipped her heels over head, to come down hard on her back.

He almost fumbled his hammer trying to bring it down on her before she recovered, contenting himself with ramming the butt down into her shoulder. The sound of breaking bone echoed down the canyon like thunder.

Nedlam screamed, a shrill, appalling sound from so huge a woman. Celestaine was already bringing her sword down at Wall's back but he was turning as she did so, hammer on the move so that it met the edge of her blade full speed, head on. She fully expected that weighty head to go whickering off into the sky like a startled bird.

Something gave. She felt that familiar contact and then lack of resistance that told her the sword was doing its job, ending up stumbling past Wall with the force of her own stroke. Recovering, she brought her sword back into guard ready for her next blow.

Dumbly she stared at the hilt in her hands, utterly denuded of the blade, which had buried itself twenty feet into solid rock somewhere.

Wall seemed equally surprised, but he recovered with more aplomb, ramming the head of his hammer into her chest to knock her down again, then putting a huge foot in its place to make sure she stayed there.

"So," he said ponderously, and she could just about hear him breathing, heaving within the helm. At least they'd made him work up a sweat. "So perish all those who would taint themselves with the power of evil." He lowered the hammer's head until it was touching her brow, pressing the back of her head into the hard ground. "You should have stayed on the path of righteousness, Celestaine, but it is those who were once good and who fell that must be destroyed most utterly, like the Kinslayer himself."

"Like you'd know about that," she got out. It was supposed to be defiance, but it sounded more like a whimper in her ears.

"I knew only the greatest seekers of evil would find me here," Wall went on, obviously happy to hear his own story of how right he was, now she wasn't in a position to argue. "I set trials to catch those weaker than you. Those corrupted heroes of less worth than you would have been killed by the monsters at Bleakmairn or in the Unredeemed Lands. Those lesser servants of evil would have been executed in Ilkand or Dorhambri."

"In—? You're casting Jocien Silvermort as an *enemy* of evil?" she gasped.

"He is the Liberator," Wall said simply, and then another arrow slanted off his visor and his head snapped up. "Enough! Your time will come, archer!"

Mustn't have anything spoil your moment of self-indulgence, Celestaine thought. "Silvermort was making a new Kinslayer, you goddamned idiot!" And then she cried out as he leant ever so slightly on the hammer.

"He is the Liberator," Wall repeated. "A good man."

"Oh, he—took you in—you gullible bastard," she got out through gritted teeth.

"Enough." And she had the sense he was genuinely hurt that she wasn't telling him how right he'd been all along and begging for mercy.

Wall's head whipped round—so fast that she thought another arrow had struck him. A moment later his foot was off her chest and he was whirling, hammer swinging, leaping back towards the archway and the cave.

"How dare you!" she heard him bellowing. "You think I don't see you, you little thief?"

Something shimmered there, and she had a brief glimpse of none other than Doctor Catt clutching at his brooch before the hammer swung sidelong into him.

There was a brief flare of purple as his magical shield sprang up around him, but the hammer shattered it to pieces and sent him flying out of the cave, tumbling end over end before fetching up in a heap along the canyon wall.

"So perish all who seek the crown!" Wall bellowed, apparently to the very sky itself. "And for what? Did you find it, little thief? You found nothing. You found only my trap for you. You die for an empty chest."

Catt didn't seem to have actually died quite yet, but his amulet was in pieces and possibly so was he, with blood on his lips and splashed bright across his torn robe. For once, he had no wit to bring to bear against the world.

"Now." And Wall stalked over, hammer raised, obviously even more angry that a single blow hadn't been sufficient. "Any more tricks, any more pitiful defences for me to destroy, evildoer?"

Something growled. The sound turned Celestaine's legs to water. It was all the wolves in the world, all the bears and tigers, every beast that had ever seen a human as prey.

Hammer still poised over Doctor Catt, Lord Wall turned slowly.

CHAPTER TWENTY-NINE

SHE THOUGHT IT was a wolf at first, big enough to swallow the sun. It stood on four legs at first, but then ran in on two, its long taloned arms ready to rake. For a bowel-loosening moment she thought it was coming for her, but then it was past her, tumbling her aside, howling its savagery at Lord Wall.

The Guardian stared and said, in a remarkably small voice, "*Fury?*"

Celestaine's stomach lurched with sudden vertigo as she re-evaluated what she was looking at. Only moments before, she had been made to think of the statues and carvings of the Ilkand Temple. Lord Wall had been their chief model in all his superhuman martial glory, but the Temple had boasted five Guardians at its height. The Custodian had been slain by the Kinslayer, the first ever of their kind to die. Vigilant had died defending the Temple when the Kinslayer came back. By then, the other Templar mainstays had faded away. Wall had gone north in search of new and more fanatical converts, and the other two had simply dropped out of sight after the Kinslayer's first defeat and before his resurgence. Celestaine knew all too well what the Undefeated had been doing, but nobody had ever discovered the fate of Fury.

She remembered the statues: a dog-headed man, jaws wide

in a snarl, bestial where the others—even the shape-changing Undefeated—were depicted as entirely human. But a dog, nonetheless; a defender of the hearth, the friend of mankind.

This was no dog, it was not even a wolf; it was every savage beast of the wilds. Fury might have guarded the Temple once, but he had been off the leash for a very long time.

Stretched about his barrel chest and shaggy shoulders was the ruin of a robe in the Cheriveni style, Celestaine could not help but notice, of the same drab colour formerly worn by one Doctor Fisher.

"Fury…?" Wall repeated, and then he had possession of himself again and all his self-justifications fell visibly over his face like a portcullis. "Even you? Even you are corrupted by this—?"

Fury was plainly as unimpressed by the rhetoric as Celestaine had been as he leapt at Wall mid-speech and slammed into the armoured Guardian's chest, knocking him flat. Celestaine thought it was over right then as the wolf-monster went for his throat, but a moment later Wall had thrust the haft of his hammer up, knocking the huge creature off him, then catching it a blow about the shoulders with the head as both of them leapt to their feet.

"Then die!" Wall was howling. "You were never as faithful as I! You abandoned the cause of right! Die for that alone!"

The two of them thundered together, both of them brimming with a strength far more than natural. Fury seemed by far the more dangerous, each talon like a knife, each fang like a dagger, but Wall had redoubled his speed and strength, laying into his brother with a thunderous might more like a storm than a man.

Facing that, Celestaine seriously considered just running far enough away that neither of them would ever find her. She had baggage, though, too much to just pick up and carry. Nedlam was groaning, plainly not about to to have it away on her toes. Heno had tried to haul her further from the scrum, but she had cursed and slapped at him with her good arm. Her skin was pale grey, like ashes.

Still, she was alive and obviously not about to drop dead unless Wall gave her another nudge. Yorughan constitutions were more than human, after all. The same could not be said of Doctor Catt, who was probably breathing his last.

And deserves to be, Celestaine thought fiercely. *The weaselly, treacherous little toerag.* And yet, and yet...

"Well, it looks like we're royally out of luck," she told them: Heno, Amkulyah, the reanimated Ralas.

"The chest's empty," Kul told her flatly. "The one Catt was after."

"We have bigger problems," Celestaine said. She could feel her next words coming on her like a tidal wave, something she was unlikely to survive. "Heno," she spat, hating herself. "Go sort Catt out."

"Kill him?"

"No, keep him alive!"

"What?" he demanded. "Piss on him."

"Heno, as you love me, just do it. Your fire wasn't even singeing Wall."

"I'm not a physician."

She gave him a level look. "We both know what you *were*, for the Kinslayer. You were about to do it to me, before you had that change of heart I thank the gods for every morning. Heno, a torturer-magician knows more than any physician about keeping the wounded *alive*."

The Heart Taker was abruptly very sober. "He won't... enjoy that."

"I don't care if he's comfortable, but keep him alive."

"And you?"

She yanked Nedlam's dagger from its sheath: long enough to be a shortsword. "I will fight."

"Celest—"

"I will fight," she repeated, more for her own sake than his. "Ralas, stick with Ned here. Do what you can. Kul? Watch for your shot."

The Aethani nodded.

Celestaine turned to where the two Guardians were tearing at each other. She saw Fury rip one of Wall's pauldrons off, sending the heavy metal spinning off to ring against the rocks. In return, Wall belted him across the muzzle, shattering a fang and bloodying his snout.

She was only human. Either of them could have crushed her and barely noticed. Her magic sword was broken, her friends were in disarray.

I don't know if stabbing up the Kinslayer in a frenzied ambush counts as a heroic deed. They keep telling me I'm a hero, though. About time I did something to properly earn it.

The Forinthi taught five different ways of killing with a short blade. Wall counted as an armoured target if anything on earth did, so she gripped Ned's dagger point-down like a theatrical murderer and ran in, dodging the hammer's backswing and then leaping up, scaling Wall like a mountain in the hope of burying that blade in the back of his neck.

RALAS HURT. NOT only the pain he had been living with for years, the memory of old injuries stamped into every muscle and bone, honed by the very magic that would always mend him just so far and no further. Now he hurt because Lord Wall had shattered him again, one more death for the tally. He knew he should be taking up a knife or a stone or something and charging back in to help Celestaine. After all, what was the worst that could happen?

The Forinthi said that wounds made you stronger, but Ralas was forced to admit that the country of his birth was an almost wilfully ignorant one. The worst that could happen was pain, and pain was something he was never allowed to get used to. Every knock and bruise brought with it a unique savour of hurt. The old and constant injuries didn't deaden the new, just added extra levels of pain. Watching Wall swing that hammer about, all Ralas could think of was how it would feel when it staved in his ribs or shattered his spine.

He couldn't; he couldn't follow where Celestaine was leading. He cursed himself for a coward, but the realist in him knew that he would achieve nothing and suffer greatly, and he didn't have it in him.

I have only my voice, and Wall isn't going to stop fighting if I sing a rondel at him.

Nedlam was trying to prop herself on one elbow to see what was going on. She looked in pain too, but more than that, she looked frustrated that she was missing the fight. Ralas saw Wall shake Celestaine off, and then she was hurling herself aside to escape the hammer. Fury smacked Wall across the helm then, claws leaving bright scars in the metal, and the armoured Guardian returned his murderous attention to his brother.

We have no part in this fight, Ralas thought, awed and horrified by the sheer force of the blows being dealt out, the two strongest Guardians laying into each other without quarter. He glanced at Heno doing something eldritch to Doctor Catt, who writhed and cried out under his ministrations. At Ralas's shoulder, Amkulyah had his bow half-drawn, his body still as stones, waiting for some opening.

So it's just me, then. Ralas stood, trying to get a knife from his belt and fumbling it, hands trembling like an old man's. *Gods, what can I do? This is no fight for mortals, still less for a used-up thing like me.*

The thought had a sequel though. Ralas was a gambling man, a habit that had been the original prompt for him taking up a travelling life where inconvenient debts might be left behind on the road. Right now he was willing to bet he wasn't the only immortal watching this fight play out.

"Hey!" he shouted, looking around at the burrow-riddled canyon walls. "I know you're there. You've been dogging Celestaine since before she found me. You won't have given up now." And he hoped to hell he was right, and that this would accomplish anything. "Now's your moment!" he shouted. "You come and pitch in, you cowardly bastard. You make good on all your promises, and I will sing the best goddamned song of valour and glory the world ever heard. This is your chance, for the whole of the pot. You can be the hero this time, but you have to act *now!*"

The echoes of his voice rang back at him, interspersed with the roars and snarls of Fury and the metal thunder of Wall's hammer striking stone. Ralas stood and waited.

CELESTAINE HACKED AT Wall's calf, but couldn't even pierce the fine mail there. Then his steel-capped boot lashed out at her and she caught the edge of it on her hip, a sharp flare of pain that would slow her as soon as her body forced her to acknowledge it. She tried to get her dagger up into his groin but only bent the blade against his armour. For a moment she had his attention, though—*a knife in the 'nads will do that*—but before he could crush her, Fury was wrenching at his helm again, jaws locking about his visor and twisting it out of shape.

Wall bellowed and smashed Fury in the jaw with a mailed fist, over and over. Celestaine saw at least one more tooth shatter under the pounding, but the metal visor was twisting still further, and Fury had a huge clawed hand about Wall's neck. The hammer whirled back, wild and uncontrolled in a single-handed grip, crashing in under Fury's ribs. The bestial monster yelped, just like a whipped dog, and tried to wrestle Wall for the weapon. Celestaine chose her moment and ran in again.

This time she waited for the hammer to reach the end of its backswing and just jumped on Wall's arm, riding him until he had brought her close enough to stab.

She went for his face, and that nearly turned out very badly, since Fury had the same idea and almost ended up using her as a toothpick. He shied away at the last moment, the air about her hot and reeking with his animal breath, and then she had Ned's dagger wedged behind the twisted visor, trying to get it into the flesh beneath.

She must have jabbed something soft; Wall roared and tried to swat her off with his free hand. She saw the gauntlet reaching for her head, about to crush her skull like an egg, but Fury snapped at it, grinding two metal-shod fingers between his horrifying teeth and giving her a moment's grace.

She rammed down on the blade, then nearly fell as the visor suddenly gave, hinging away on its one remaining pin to reveal Wall's rage-twisted face beneath. His eyes rolled, foam forming at the corner of his mouth. "Unworthy!" he was bellowing. "Unworthy!" and she wondered if he had just been chanting that single word all through the fight, muffled beneath his helm.

He dropped back a step to bring the hammer up, striking Fury beneath the jaw and sending the wolf-Guardian reeling backwards. Wall seemed barely winded by it all, feeding off his own anger. She knew he was supposed to be the strongest of the Guardians, but even Fury didn't seem to be making a dent in his reserves of power.

Too late for that kind of revelation, though. She tried to stab him in the face, given it was right there in front of her, but barely scratched his cheek and half-severed his chinstrap before he slapped her to the ground with bone-jarring force. He had her in the shadow of his hammer instantly, even as she was pulling her wits together, but Amkulyah shot him right in the eye, the cleanest and most perfect piece of archery she had ever seen

She heard Kul's yell of triumph: the shaft had gone deep. Wall threw his head back and howled, as bestial as ever Fury was, but he didn't fall. Blood coursed down the jutting shaft, and surely the eye was a ruin, but he was still on his feet, practically burning with divine strength.

"I judge you all!" he bellowed at them. "The world will know that you fell to evil!" And he was running towards Amkulyah, feet shaking the earth and bringing rocks down from the canyon walls.

The Aethani's round eyes went as wide as they had ever been and he fumbled the next arrow, letting it fall from the string. Fury came up suddenly from Wall's left to crash into him, but Wall took his charge and threw the wolf-Guardian past him, sending him rolling in the dust. Celestaine was already running, knowing that she'd never get there in time. The one thing between Kul and annihilation was Ralas, a flimsy barricade at the best of times, and now long past his best.

Then Wall was down, something erupting from the very earth to tear into his legs. Celestaine could see nothing but dust and teeth at first, and then Wall had lurched back to his feet, one shin bloody and torn, the mail peeled back like paper. There was a creature still trying to get its jaws about him, a hunched shape as big as a man, its blunt, vicious head striped black and white, dappled red with Wall's blood.

A badger. She was looking at a badger.

Deffo?

He looked rabid, and for a moment Wall backed off, trying to keep his legs out of reach of the badger's jaws like a squeamish Cheriveni confronted by a mouse.

Amkulyah had put more distance between himself and Wall. He must have been rattled, though, because his next shaft struck Wall's helm, wedging in the crack Celestaine had already cut into it and skewing the entire helmet sideways. Celestaine stepped in and lashed at Wall's throat, hoping to catch him while his head was canted up, and instead severed the chinstrap entirely, the helm spinning away.

Even in the heat of the fight, she had time to stare and shout, "Oh you *turd!*"

Across Wall's brow, driven into the flesh of his forehead where the helm's confines had pressed on it, was a creation of gold and iron, set with mismatched, garish gems.

"All that talk, and you're *wearing* the damned thing?" she shrieked.

"Lies!" Wall boomed. "I am the strength of the Temple! I am the righteous, the only true voice. I am the only one to be trusted with power! I! You cannot judge! You…" He sputtered over the words, foam spraying her, and then he had kicked the Undefeated aside and drawn his hammer back for the killing blow.

The huge badger was not to be brushed away, though, clinging to his leg, gnawing through his mail in a frenzy of desperation, and Fury had come up behind Wall to wrestle for the hammer again. Even then, he shook them back and forth, strong beyond mountains, strong as the bones of the earth.

The crown… She saw the gems blazing, all that stolen power feeding Wall's battle rage.

She lunged for him, trying to leap up and cut his unprotected throat, but he twisted so that she ran into his elbow and shoulder and sat back down hard, feeling at least one tooth loosen. Another arrow drove into his jaw, but Wall barely seemed to notice. He shook Fury off him at last, then picked up the squalling, snarling badger like a disobedient dog and threw it aside.

"Right," he told the world, and then Nedlam hit him.

She was holding her ironbound club one-handed, awkward and fumbling, but she had come in with all her weight, all the speed she could muster, stopping to let the head of the club whip forwards with the force of a battering ram. Any real wall would have had cause to feel the impact, and Wall took it straight to the forehead.

Nedlam let out a whoop, the old Yorughan battle cry, and it eclipsed Celestaine's cry of loss because her club struck the crown, cracking the gold across, sending a bright blue gem spinning loose from its mountings, ripping the whole band from Wall's head. There was a flare of spoiled power, magic twisting and writhing in the air.

Wall took Nedlam by the throat, his ravaged face purple. If he had any more bombast, it was strangled by his own rage.

Amkulyah shot him. The shaft went up under his chin, all the way to the fletchings. Celestaine, already on her way in herself, skittered back as Wall led Nedlam go and swayed, one gauntleted hand reaching up to the wound. He made a sound, then. A sound of utter grief and betrayal, and of pain, because the crown was gone from his head, and he must have been leaning on its power to overcome all those wounds. Blood abruptly gouted from his eye-socket and his jaw, a single convulsive pulse.

He fell to one knee, leaning on the haft of his hammer, mouth working but nothing coming forth but blood. In that moment only, he looked truly penitent.

CHAPTER THIRTY

"YOU'VE THOUGHT OF the possibilities, of course?" Doctor Catt was sitting up in bed, a tray on his knees as he tinkered with the pieces of the Kinslayer's crown.

Ralas raised an eyebrow but said nothing.

"In respect of your own individual predicament," Catt added; clearly Lord Wall had not quite beaten the long words out of him. "Assuming I can get any semblance of this contrivance into functioning order."

The crown itself had seen better days, but then Nedlam had not been gentle, and just being an artefact of making and unmaking did not apparently confer any unusual durability. Ralas would have expected the Kinslayer to have wrought it better, and perhaps had it encased in iron spikes and mounted on a huge skull helm or something similarly tasteful. As it was, it had been a delicate piece of work, not intended to be used for target practice by a big, angry Yorughan woman.

"You want to give me wings, too?" Ralas asked, watching with interest as Catt's clever fingers—the ones not still splinted—worked the blue gem back into its socket. Little wisps of magic danced about his hands, worming their way around his repairs and holding everything in place.

Catt would walk again, so said the camp surgeons at Kait

Hegumen's outpost. He would need a stick, but Ralas had never seen him without a stick as it was, so that would likely pose no great inconvenience to him. Tenet's Warding Amulet had not survived its encounter with Wall's hammer, but it had just about kept body and soul together for its wearer. After that, Catt's ongoing survival had come down to Heno's craft, which had never really been intended for long-term healing. It had sufficed to get him out of the Unredeemed Lands and into the Templar outpost, where there were a number of surgeons and healing magicians to take up the slack.

"I was given to understand by Celestaine that you were in rather a lot of pain," Catt observed. "Pain which, moreover, was beyond the reach of healing magic, because the spell that maintains your unnaturally robust existence returns you constantly to the recently beaten state in which you originally expired? Or was I misinformed?"

"Sounds as though you've got it down," Ralas agreed. "You're saying that trinket will patch me up, then?" He asked the question as a formality, already guessing at the answer.

"Ah, well, unfortunately I don't think the crown, even in its perfect state, would have been able to so amend the enchantment woven through you. But it could simply undo it, cut through its strands. Whereupon you'd…"

"Die."

"Peacefully," Catt protested, setting down the twisted crown so that he could gesticulate. "Only, I was thinking, there are certain other items I have access to, back in Cinquetann. There's the Branch of Ygstermandt, which could take your spirit and—I think, anyway—send you out into the world, make you one with all things. It's how I intend to go, when the woeful day finally arrives."

"But you'd test it on me, just to make sure there are no side effects?" Ralas suggested.

"You wrong me," Doctor Catt told him. "The offer is genuine, from one invalid to another, as a token of my thanks in, well, not actively killing me, and in recovering me to here so that I might convalesce."

Ralas gave him the side-eye for a while, but then shrugged. "Maybe I do wrong you. It's a kind offer, and that whole one-with-all-things business is a nice thought. And I do hurt, doctor. And when you're back on your feet and hobbling about doing mischief to the world, I'll still hurt. Everything's an effort, you know. Even just sitting here talking to you. I want to be like Wall, sometimes, so big and strong I can just break anything I don't like. But I'm not. I'm beaten and half-starved forever, and all I can do is use my voice for what little it can achieve. But it's a 'no,' nonetheless."

Catt raised his eyebrows. "You surprise me. If they told me it would hurt like this forever, I don't think I'd want to live."

Ralas shrugged. "There were times I didn't. This isn't one of them. It's life, Catt, it's my life. It hurts, but at least I'm not locked in a dark hole forever. Not much of a motto, but don't knock it 'til you've tried it."

Someone coughed awkwardly at the doorway, and Ralas looked up to see Doctor Fisher standing there.

He had been back in his familiar shape by the time they set off for the outpost, wearing one of Heno's spare tunics, which hung on him like a tent. He had driven them all in a sheep-drawn cart, Catt and Nedlam jolting on the bed. Nobody had dared speak much to him. The thunderous expression on his human face had been as daunting as the snarling beast's muzzle he had worn.

Catt had been out cold for most of that, and since he had awoken—and been put to work by an extremely sharp-tongued Celestaine—Fisher had stayed away. Now here he was, courage plucked up. Catt, who had been reaching for the crown again, paused.

"Ah," he said. "Hello."

"Hello, Catty," Fisher said quietly.

"Top marks on the keeping-secrets front," Catt said faintly. "So, what now?"

Fisher approached his bedside, hands gripped together before him. "I... want it to go back to how it was, Catt."

Catt raised an eyebrow.

"You can't understand," said Fisher, said the Guardian Fury, pillar of the Ilkand Temple, savager of the unrighteous. "I was sick of it. After the first time round with the Kinslayer, I couldn't do that again. I was sick of the faithful, sick of the gods, sick of all the others, so much babble, so little purpose left to us. And you mortals, you had *lives* and not just duty. I wanted a life. Catt, Catty..." Fisher got to the bedside as though the intervening space had been a great desert. "You're greedy, frivolous, flighty, you don't care about other people, you're... *fun*, Catty. You're just fun to be around, to be part of all your schemes, to watch you waste expensive words on people who can't give you change for them. I just... want that again."

Catt looked at him for a long time. "That may be quite difficult, given what I now apprehend of your true nature, Fishy."

Fisher nodded mournfully. "But I was thinking, back home there's Perinable's Bauble of Obfuscation..."

"To delete the memories, yes," Catt finished for him. "That would seem to be the most reasonable solution to this impasse."

Fisher paused. "You'd... do that, to yourself, then?"

Catt shrugged, then plainly regretted doing so. "My dear Fishy, I admit scooping out parts of my own brain isn't exactly my first recourse when faced with a quandary, but I honestly don't see another way around it. Just keep the redaction to a minimum, when you perform the procedure. Because I rather want things back the way they were, too, and it's not too great a price." Ralas saw a new thought strike him. "This is... the first time, isn't it? We've not been baubling my brain every couple of years since we met, have we?"

"Of course," Fisher assured him. "The first, and let's make it the last. Too much like hard work."

But Ralas wondered.

CELESTAINE HAD A new sword. Kait Hegumen had provided it, one of the Templars' stock. It felt clumsy to her, for all that it was a solid, functional weapon, as good as any soldier might require. *But I'm a hero.* The plaintive thought made her sick at herself. *What, precisely, did you do, that might be called heroic?*

"Prefer mine." Nedlam had been watching her try out the new blade on the fort's muster ground. She had her arm bound up, and it would be a while before she could play with her toy, but Wall's huge hammer was slung over her good shoulder. Celestaine wasn't sure that the world was ready for that combination, but Ned's were probably safer hands than those of the original owner.

"Smile, won't you?" Nedlam suggested. "We won."

Celestaine nodded glumly. "It doesn't feel like it."

"You want someone to give you a medal?" Ned asked.

"I want... to feel like the world's better for what we did. Lord Wall is dead. That's... it won't mean much to you, but he was one of the great Guardians."

"Great *tucku zaran*," Nedlam said with emphasis, which Celestaine knew meant a *pain in the arse*. "Anyway, we got your man Silvermort. Won't be liberating anyone any time soon."

"Hrm."

"What? He was a great thingummy too?"

"No, he was a bastard. The world's better off." Celestaine shook herself. "I'm sorry, Ned. I wish I could just... enjoy life, like you do."

The Yorughan made a rude noise, audible across the breadth of the fort. "No trick to it." She pulled a face at the handful of Arvennir and Kelicerati, midway through some deal, who had stopped their talk to stare. Olastoc, the Oerni Wayfarer, drew them back to their negotiations. He had come back from his shrine able to communicate with the spider-people a little, and there was talk of getting some Sheliac to teach them hand-sign. All good news, Celestaine thought, except...

"When we killed the Kinslayer," she told Nedlam, "most of the rest were happy. Garenand had all the free beer and women he could ask for. There were crowds, cheering, songs. But some of us aren't built like that. Roherich couldn't take joy in it, because he was already drifting away from us, from humanity. And me... I just remember the bad, Ned. I remember the battles we lost. I remember the people I had to leave behind. You know why I wanted to save the Aethani? Because I thought that might be the thing to make me feel *content*, for a moment, with what I'd achieved. And now I can't have that, and I'm just sat here thinking, what was even the point?"

"Ask the others," Nedlam suggested. "Me, I had fun. Made new friends. He did all right, too." She nodded to where, across the muster ground, the Undefeated was talking with some of the Templars. He had taken a great heroic-looking form, with a huge beard and golden, flowing hair. He had been talking about going back to the Temple in Ilkand, setting up as their resident Guardian. No doubt he would ride the wave of Ralas's promised ballad and the news of the gods' last message to their creation and do very well out of it. *More sour taste for the tongue*, Celestaine thought. *I preferred him as a badger.*

He'd helped, though, she had to admit. He'd gone against Wall, risked the balance of his immortal life. Perhaps a second chance would make something worthwhile out of him, restore him to the paragon he had once been.

But the world moves on, and most of the Guardians don't. They tarnish, they retire, they die. And where will we be without them? A little-child-thought, wanting the unreasoning security of a world with protective parents.

She sheathed her sword. It would never be right, she knew. She could try out a hundred mundane blades and never be satisfied.

Nedlam whistled piercingly, waving with her good arm. Amkulyah was picking his way around the muster ground's outskirts.

"Doctor Catt's done," he told them when he arrived. "As best as he can, he says."

She followed him into the infirmary, returning Ralas's nod as she entered. Catt had something in his lap that was not particularly crown-like any more, or not for any head that Celestaine was familiar with. She had assumed that remaking the crown would involve reforging, hammering it out on the edge of a lake of lava, something like that. Catt had mostly used wire, as far as she could see. He grimaced apologetically as he proffered it.

"A lot of the potency has leaked out, I'm afraid. It was rather a delicate thing, all told."

Celestaine's heart barely sank. She had been expecting some new impediment. "So it won't work. It can't do what we want any more. Fine."

Catt hesitated, and she saw quite clearly the thought *Maybe I can talk her into letting me keep it* creep into his mind and be embarrassedly shooed out again. He glanced up at Fisher, who was standing at the head of his bed looking reassuringly surly. "Well, it will, probably, a little. Its reach isn't changed, but you won't get much out of it before it's just scrap gold with a few nice stones. At which point the stones can still do some of their old tricks, I'd suspect, but it won't be an artefact of making and unmaking any more, and that, I'm afraid, is what you'd need to help out your Aethani."

"How much," Amkulyah interrupted him. "How many?"

"Four, perhaps. Six?" Catt shrugged carefully. "Keeping doing it until it falls apart, as the doctor said to the gigolo. Not quite what you were expecting. I really am very sorry."

"Six," Celestaine echoed, waiting for Amkulyah's reaction.

"Perhaps," Doctor Catt repeated. "And there's some other bad news."

"Of course there is."

"While I'm not endorsing anything Lord Wall said about the crown, it is true that some of the essential nature of the Kinslayer is bound to it. *His* essential nature, in this case, meaning his selfishness. He was not a creature that could ever have countenanced doing something for someone else while his own needs remained unfulfilled. Ergo, you cannot use his crown for another's benefit unless you yourself have no wish for it yourself. I must, therefore, recuse myself from further assisting you, because, well, I'm only human. However, you of course are a hero, my dear, and so I would assume..."

"No," said Celestaine.

"Hm?"

"I can't use it selflessly. This whole venture was a sop to my conscience. I want this godsdamned thing to make *me* feel better about myself, doctor. So, no, not me."

"Ah, well," Catt said, not in the least disheartened. "Then, while I had assumed you'd want the honour, I can think of a very acceptable substitute candidate in the person of the bard sitting by the door there."

Ralas eyed him suspiciously. "Was that what all the death-talk was about? Seeing if I wanted something from the Kinslayer's magic hat?"

"Mere serendipity," Catt assured him. "But am I wrong? Take the magic hat, why don't you? Do you feel the need to work a change in yourself, or perhaps conquer the world?"

Ralas snagged the misshapen crown and stared down at it balefully. "It's nothing to me," he said. "Ugly-looking thing anyway."

CHAPTER THIRTY-ONE

FROM THERE, IT was back to Forinth, just off the border with Cherivell, near enough that another day would have seen them at Bladno. This was where the Aethani colony was, that Amkulyah had left to seek her help. That was where the Kinslayer's crown would work its last broken miracle.

Entertainment on the journey was mostly provided by Nedlam complaining that she didn't need the cart and could have walked the whole way. She made sure not to make too much fuss, though, in case anyone made her do it, and she slept a lot. Yorughan mended fast. By the time they arrived she would be up and about and pushing the boundaries of what her injured arm could do.

Although their roads led in the same direction, they bade goodbye to Catt and Fisher soon after. Fisher took Celestaine aside and suggested to her that she should avoid Cinquetann hereafter.

"I understand," she said. Ralas had explained how things were left between the two doctors. It was hard to look on Fisher, knowing what beast lurked beneath his skin. She remembered the pair's home town, still recovering from its occupation. If she asked, would she hear tales of a monster that had torn up the Kinslayer's soldiers and never been caught? Quite possibly. Or would she just hear of an old antiques dealer? Either way, she didn't think Fury had been idle during the war.

They passed Bleakmairn, of course. Thukrah had already moved on from it, and Celestaine could only hope that Kait Hegumen's messengers had reached him, and that some measure of peace might result. She found herself looking at Heno and wondering how travelling with him in a year's time might be. Would Yorughan faces meet with acceptance; would the wounds of the war heal over enough? Or would there be those, like Silvermort or Wall, whose livelihood was in stirring up hatred and profiting from misery?

Or will the Yorughan bring the war, because it's what they were trained for, and it's easier than dealing with us? Equally possible. There were plenty of the Kinslayer's minions left alive, after all, above and below ground. And perhaps the Yorughan would make better generals than a mad, vengeance-driven demigod. *We might not win that war.*

The place Kul guided them to was called Grovesendry, part of the fiefdom of the Stipe clan, who had never got on with the Fiddleheads of Fernreame. Celestaine, turning up with her clan cloak hung about her, almost got them thrown out on the spot by a very belligerent patrol of young Stipe bravos. In retrospect, she'd got into Bleakmairn, Ilkand and even the Unredeemed Lands with less trouble. The two Yorughan got less harassment than she did.

Grovesendry was your standard Forinthi town, dug into a valley with a fort on the high ground to keep watch for raiders, now partially rebuilt. The Aethani quarter was... *a reminder of all they've lost*, was all Celestaine could think. The locals hadn't exactly extended a broad welcome to the refugees, and the shacks and shanties the Aethani had managed to raise looked as though the next rains would wash them away. They were busy, though. They had been in the mines, almost all of them; a sullen strength had been beaten into them. She watched them scratch away at the worst farmland the valley had to offer, work away at wood, cut stone, haul in loads of charcoal or peat. Aside from the woodworkers, whose craft the locals would at least appreciate, they were doing the jobs the Forinthi hated, repaying their reluctant hosts as best they could. Plenty of young Forinthi warriors had never come home, after all. An influx of strong backs wasn't to be turned away. For their part, perhaps the Aethani saw no option but to work, just as the Kinslayer had made them work. *Be useful or be thrown out?* Celestaine hoped her kin wouldn't do any such thing, and likewise hoped that the value Forinthi would normally place on hard labour was being extended to these guests. Times were hard for everyone after the war, though. Hospitality might still be a rationed commodity.

She remembered the glories of Aethan before the war: its high houses, the decorated beauty and pride of its people. Now all that was left were ghettos like these. The Kinslayer had taken more than their wings. Their land was gone, unreclaimed still, and even if they got it back, everything they ever built or made had burned.

What we bring them is pitiful, she knew.

Then Amkulyah had jumped down from the cart, his arms spread wide. They knew him, but there was little excitement, even when he started going among them, touching foreheads, telling them what he'd brought.

Celestaine glanced at Heno, beside her on the driver's board. He had been very quiet ever since the fight with Wall, hardly a word to share all journey. Now he all but glared at the Aethani, as though he'd only now understood what all this was in aid of, and didn't approve.

"What is it?" she asked him, not for the first time.

Heno just shook his head.

"You'll have to tell me some time."

"Probably. Let the prince have his moment," he growled, which at least was progress.

It look Amkulyah some time to gather a crowd of his people, and the scepticism in the air was palpable. Perhaps elsewhere there were energetic, bustling communities of displaced Aethani, but Amkulyah's kin here seemed still weighed down by all they had gone through.

Ralas had the crown, his arm thrust through it for safekeeping. He had found proper Forinthi attire along the way, a bard's white cloak signifying he was of no clan and held no blood or oath debts. He still looked rake-thin, his face covered with bruises, but the clothes lent a touch of the man she remembered to him. She wondered if he had kin and a home somewhere, a past he had never spoken of that he could yet return to. The life of a travelling bard was a hard one.

"We are ready." Amkulyah broke in on her thoughts, and Ralas hopped down from the cart with a wince. There were four Aethani lined up ahead of the others, all of them older than Kul, but not so old as to be parents, by Celestaine's guess.

"I dearly hope this works," Ralas breathed. "We're going to get stoned to death if it doesn't."

"I have said not to hope," Kul told him.

"Good luck with that one," the bard said, shuffling towards the line. "Stoned to death," he said again. "You first, then?"

Amkulyah took a hurried step back as though Ralas had offered him a snake. "No."

"But... you're the prince, surely you get...?" Ralas waved the crown at him vaguely and Kul backed off still further.

Celestaine went over to him, hand out but finding him beyond reach. "Surely..."

"How old do you think I am, Celest?" he asked her flatly.

"You're... young. Nineteen? Eighteen? Is this an Aethani thing, giving way to elders...?" She didn't think the prospective candidates looked like elders, though—plenty in the crowd had decades on them.

"Aethan fell at the start of the war," Amkulyah reminded her. "How long ago was that, tell me?"

"Ten years, of course, but I... Oh."

He nodded jerkily. "I never flew. My wings were barely grown when they were taken from me. Give them back to me now, what would I even do with them? And who could teach me to take back the air?"

"But you did all this..." Celestaine's voice tailed off. "I thought you missed it so much..."

His face was unreadable. "I missed seeing my people as they were. I remembered that." He flinched away from Ralas once again, as the bard offered the crown to him.

"Take it. You don't want it, so you should have it." Ralas cracked a bitter smile. "Best lesson of life, that. Only give power to those who don't want it. Would solve a lot of problems in the world. So take it, take the power in it, remake a few of your people. You don't need some human doing the honours. Give them a bit of pride back."

"You killed Wall, after all," Celestaine pointed out. "Not Fury, not me."

Gingerly, Amkulyah accepted the battered crown from Ralas, turning it over in his long-fingered hands. His eyes strayed to where his people waited.

LATER ON, AS dusk fell, she found Heno sitting above the Aethani village, looking up into the darkening sky. Night came on swiftly in the Forinthi valleys, the sun clipping the edge of the hills and then vanishing like a drowning man, leaving only the stars. The last streaks of gold were just dying as she walked up the slope to him, a dark shape on a dark hillside enlivened only by the silvery flash of his hair and beard.

"It's something, isn't it?" she asked him, but he just kept on looking. The last rays of the sun touched the handful of shadows wheeling and dancing over the village like huge bats, clumsy in the air after so long without practice, but remembering fast. Celestaine counted them, because it moved her heart at least from *a failure to all the world* to *better than nothing*. Eight. They had restored eight of the Aethani before the power of the crown had dwindled to nothing. Doctor Catt had done well.

"Tell me," she said, and when he didn't reply she prodded him under the ribs, where she knew he couldn't abide it. He rounded on her, and for a moment she was still, staring into what could have been a stranger's face, all tusks and flinty eyes. Then his reserve cracked and he pressed his fingers to his forehead as though trying to drive out evil thoughts.

"You don't want to hear it," was all he said.

"Tell me," she repeated firmly. "Look, it's me. If you can't tell me, then who?"

"What makes you think I'd tell anyone?" he snapped, but she kept looking him pointedly until his shoulders sagged and he let out a long, harsh breath.

"When we came out from the earth, you can't know what it was like," he said at last. "We'd been told of this land above that was full of our enemies. We'd been told that everyone there had conspired to lock us beneath the earth, to deny us the sky and the sun—not that most of us even knew what those things were. They were just things we couldn't have."

She nodded carefully, knowing that he would say it in his own time or not at all, now. Further prodding would yield no more.

"The Kinslayer never told us how beautiful the world was," Heno told her. "He didn't know how much we would love the sunlight and the trees. And of course, wherever he laid his hand the sun dimmed and the trees died. We came to this land, this... everywhere, that you took for granted. And it was everything we could desire, and we knew we'd never have it, and we hated you, because you had it all and wouldn't even fight for it. You just died or ran away. We hated ourselves for what we were made to do, but we couldn't live with that hate, so we made it a hate of you for being too weak to defend all that beauty."

He was silent for a long while and she put her arm around his shoulders, hugging him close.

"And we enjoyed it, of course. Like the Kinslayer knew we would, like he'd primed us to. Because if you hate yourself enough, and hate others enough, then doing terrible things to them becomes your only pastime, your only pleasure. Because in the moment when you rack them with fire, or slip your blade behind their eyeball, you have control, and that means something. It means something when the Kinslayer's your master and that's the only control you'll ever have."

Another long, strained pause.

"And then we came to Aethan, which was most beautiful of all, where the people were so free and graceful that even the sky was theirs. And we looked on them, Celest, and we wondered. We stared, open mouthed, at how they rode the air, the whole world spread beneath them." He clenched his fists before him suddenly, magic flaring from between his fingers and lighting up his tormented face. "And we *hated* them so much, for what they had. We, who had lived in the dirt all our lives, we couldn't stand it that they had all that freedom, that the world was theirs. But we had our armies, that had never lost a battle, and they didn't want to fight, didn't want to lose all that beauty they had, and so they gave themselves into our hands. And we knew we didn't have to stand it. If we couldn't bear to be in a world with the flying men, we didn't have to be."

"Heno…"

"It wasn't the Kinslayer, Celest," he told her hollowly. "*We* destroyed Aethan. We clipped the wings of its people, every damn one of them. Generals and Heart Takers and soldiers, all of us, we made that choice. We just couldn't stand them having all that, and us having lived with nothing for so long. It was too hard, and we were too strong, and there was too little to stop us."

The next silence was hers, as she thought through the implications, thinking back for any clue he might have dropped back when she proposed the plan to restore them. He had been like stone, though. He had given nothing away.

"But Ned and Kul, they... they're friends."

"Oh, Ned probably wasn't there. Probably she doesn't even know," Heno said, his arch superiority back just for a moment. "But I was. I cheered it on. It felt *good*, Celest. It felt good to make a whole people more wretched than we were."

"And now?"

He met her gaze at last. "If I were surrounded by Yorughan officers, perhaps? If we'd won the war? If I hadn't met you and done this. It would feel good still, Celest. We'd be clapping each other on the back and saying, *Remember the Aethani?*"

"And now?" she asked again.

"And now I've met you, and I understand that I'm a monster. Not because I'm Yorughan, but because I made those choices. I chose to be cruel. Just because I turned on the Kinslayer, don't think I'm like you. Don't think I'm *good*." He stood suddenly. "I'll go, Celest. I'll go find Thukrah, maybe. I'll... do something to help, somehow."

She grabbed his wrist and yanked him back down, hard enough to knock the breath out of him.

"Heno, I know you're no holy man. I know you turned on your master for your own reasons. You were a *torturer*, for death's sake! You think I was sitting here blissfully believing that you spent the war rescuing puppies and smuggling children back to their parents?"

He stared at her, but he didn't take his hand back.

"Look up there," she demanded, watching a winged Aethani pass before the yellow face of the rising moon. "You've done a little to put things right, just a little. And it's because of you the Kinslayer's dead; that's another little. We've all made wrong choices, and yes, you've made a hell of a lot more than most, but you've changed and you can keep changing. The Kinslayer isn't there to order you, and you don't have to live in a cave any more. So be *better*, that's all. Better tomorrow than yesterday, like Thukrah, like Kait. Not worse, like Wall and Silvermort. And stay with me."

He said nothing for a long time, but after a while he leant into her, and she rested her head on his shoulder, drawing her cloak about her as the night chill stole in.

THEY STAYED ON at Grovesendry for a few days, in which time the handful of winged Aethani had already started to make a difference. Their wingless kin walked differently and the locals looked on them with new eyes. An echo of what they had once been had re-entered the world. There was hope in the air, like the first fragrance of spring.

Nedlam didn't want to leave, and in the end she was quite tearful to part from Amkulyah. She was a good friend, Celestaine knew, and she didn't discriminate between her own kind and any other: fight alongside her—or on her shoulders—and you were her comrade, and she'd die for you if she had to.

What came next was that Celestaine went home and introduced her kin to her new friends, and that was a whole new barrel of trouble brought up from the cellar. Only her bringing a renowned bard along, and her insistence that she had no intention of staying on to run the place, went even halfway to smoothing that over. Still, she had been travelling a long time, and Fernreame was just coming into its true spring beauty. "A month," she told her cousins of the Fiddlehead clan, knowing that she'd be long gone by then, driven out not by angry relatives but by discontent and boredom.

But for now, she told herself, *try to be content, just for a few days. Is that so much to ask?*

And try to be discreet about Heno. Because there were limits to her clan's hospitality, and taking a Yorughan lover was probably beyond those limits by some several miles.

Ralas said he'd leave before then, but somehow never did, relaxing into the role of a bard, telling the old stories and singing new songs, fingers darting about the strings of a borrowed harp. Only Celestaine saw the pain crease his eyes when he sat down.

And then, days later, when the Fiddlehead had even grown used to big Nedlam shambling about the place, or sparring with their new crop of young warriors, there was a visitor.

They sent for Celestaine at dawn and she came yawning and scratching and dragging her cloak into place, clutching at her waist for a sword she would never hold again, and for which she would never truly find a substitute.

She saw the Temple livery first and woke up quickly, expecting trouble. At first she didn't know the man—tall and stern-looking, looking down at her with the dawn at his back. His hair was dark with silver streaks, though, and that gave him away: not a true son of the Temple any more than Wall had been; say instead an uncle or grandfather, some older relative who had seen the first stones of the Temple laid down.

"Deffo," she said. "I'd thought I'd had enough of you showing up like a counterfeit coin. Aren't you grand high wonder of Temple Ilkand these days?"

He smiled uncertainly, not quite sure how things lay between them. "I've found something out. Something you need to know."

She scowled. "I'm not going to like this, am I?"

"I don't know." He glanced over his shoulder as though worried about being overhead. "I have news of my brother, Celestaine."

"Your family," she observed, "is larger and more troublesome even than mine. Which brother?"

"My favourite brother." He leant in conspiratorially to say it, and she wanted to hit him. "Come on, Celestaine, which do you think?"

It was the lack of a sword at her waist that informed her, at last. "*Wanderer?*"

"I know where he went," the Undefeated whispered.

"And? What's that to you?" she demanded.

He looked hurt, and perhaps he had a right to. "It gets to you, this hero business," he told her. "But it wears off quick. They all like me, in the Temple, but the more I sit around, the less I like myself. The more I remember all those times I *wasn't* the hero. You know what I mean?"

"Oh, I do, believe me," she admitted. "What are you saying, Deffo?"

"I want to go find him. Surely you do, too. So you can come help *me* for once."

"Where did he go?" She felt a lump in her throat, the memory of that unlooked-for abandonment. *What was so important that you just left us?*

"Where else?" the Undefeated asked simply. "He went to find the gods and bring them back."

She stared at him.

"So...?" he prompted. "Gather your allies, come save the world."

"You're not doing the old-man-in-a-tavern act now."

"Come *on*, Celestaine, please."

She reflected for a moment that her cousins were starting to get on her nerves, and Nedlam's arm had healed very well, and, and...

"All right, then." And she was darting back inside, calling for Nedlam, for Ralas and Heno.